SECRETS

Rocky Mountain Legacy

Honor's Pledge
Honor's Price
Honor's Quest
Honor's Disguise
Honor's Reward

Diamond of the Rockies

The Rose Legacy
Sweet Boundless
The Tender Vine

Twilight
A Rush of Wings
The Still of Night
Halos
Secrets

www.kristenheitzmann.com

SECRETS

A Novel

KRISTEN
HEITZMANN

BETHANY HOUSE PUBLISHERS

Minneapolis, Minnesota

Published by Bethany House Publishers
11400 Hampshire Avenue South
Bloomington, Minnesota 55438
www.bethanyhouse.com

Bethany House Publishers is a division of
Baker Publishing Group, Grand Rapids, Michigan.

Printed in the United States of America

Library of Congress Cataloging-in-Publication Data

Heitzmann, Kristen.
    Secrets / by Kristen Heitzmann.
       p. cm.
    ISBN 0-7642-2827-7 (pbk.)
      1. Secrecy—Fiction. 2. Older women—Fiction. 3. Grandmothers—Fiction. 4. Home
ownership—Fiction. 5. Sonoma (Calif.)—Fiction. 6. Grandparent and adult child—Fiction.
I. Title.
    PS3558.E468S43   2004
    813'.54—dc22
                                          2004011996

To Barb Lilland
For the pleasure of once again blending words with you

May the Lord make you increase,
both you and your children.
May you be blessed by the Lord,
the maker of heaven and earth.

Psalm 115:14,15

My deep and heartfelt thanks to Kelly McMullen
for hours of brainstorming, reading and feedback,
for legal information and lots of other tidbits.

To Theresa, for sharing my tears

Liz, Theresa, and Kelly, for feeding my family

Judy, for your prayers

A ntonia gripped her grandfather's hand and tugged him into the darkness. "Come, Nonno. Don't resist me." His limp was more pronounced than ever, but haste was necessary. His shock of white hair glowed in the candlelight. There was no gas or electricity in the cellar, and no light in the passageway but the brass lantern that swung from her hand.

"Come—" Her words froze at the noise overhead. Through the wood and stone and earth it sounded like marbles spilled on a tile floor. But it wasn't. She had prayed Papa was wrong, that they had nothing to fear. But he was right. *Signore!*

A desperate urge to rush back, to fly up the stairs, seized her. They had found Papa! What else could it be? But Nonno's grip tightened on her hand. He said nothing, but the look of pain in his eyes galvanized her will. Nonno needed her. Gently she led him deeper into the silent stone throat that swallowed their presence as dread seeped behind.

Her heart cried, *Papa.* But her tears were silent. They must make no sound that might carry up and out. Suddenly the clasp of her grandfather's hand became a claw, and he stumbled to his knees.

"Nonno?" She dropped beside him as he crumpled, a shriek building inside her as he gripped her hand to his chest. *Nonno!* She must run for help! She must—

He clung to her and rasped, "No, Antonia. You must not be found."

Not be found? What did her safety matter if she lost the ones she loved most in the world? Tears dripped from her chin. Frantic thoughts scurried like mice in the tunnel even as great wells of grief drained from her eyes. She could not leave his side. She could only cling to his hand and echo each of his ragged breaths until they ceased. She closed her eyes in silent keening. *Nonno* . . .

CHAPTER ONE

Sunshine.
Dew upon the grapes.
A blue heron in the sky, legs trailing like ribbon.
Nonno's hand in mine. He stoops, plucks a grape,
the globe gorged on black earth and prayer.
Small, in his long knobby fingers.
A thick, tannic skin, but inside, the glut of
fog-swept mornings and lazy sun-drenched hours.
"Is it time?"
He curls it into my palm, closes my fingers over it. "Soon."
And he smiles.

The nurses at St. Barnabas hospital had given up trying to chase them out. As long as the family left a path for the medical professionals, they could keep vigil around the bed, and prayers filled the air like the oxygen tubed into Nonna Antonia's nostrils. Lance breathed in the faith of his family and exhaled his own.

Though bent and crinkled, Nonna had been the heart of their home his whole life, and they were not letting her go without a fight. He leaned close and squeezed the bony hand in his. Others might have taken that spot, like Nonna's own son—his pop—or Momma or his sisters, but in truth it was his place. Lance wouldn't say that out loud, but he didn't have to.

Nonna knew he was there. Even sedated, she knew, and his grip told her he'd be there as long as she needed. These last couple years he'd wandered, trying to find reasons for questions without answers. But he was there now, and they both needed the connection of that handclasp. *I'm here, Nonna.* If he could pass her his strength he would. Comfort and courage and a little of what he'd learned on the streets. *Fight back. Don't let them take you down.*

But he didn't have to tell her that; he'd learned it from her. His throat squeezed tight, recalling the compresses she'd held to one bruise or another. *"Don't tell Pop, Nonna."*

"The man's got eyes, ragazzo picolo. *He might notice."*

But when it came to it, she had always backed him up. *"Don't be hard on him. He's doing the best he can."*

Best was relative though, and that's where he came up short, unlike Tony whose best was the stuff of comic-book heroes. Another pang. Don't pile on, he told his mind, but when had he ever taken his own advice? He looked around the room. Momma's lips moved in prayer; Pop just held his head in his hands. He'd be exhausted after working his usual hours, then coming here when he got the call.

His sister Monica was trying to quiet Nicky, but the cramped space and choking worry must be driving the kid nuts. Monica sent him a glance, then slipped out around Lucy, whose toddler Nina was sleeping on her shoulder. His third sister, Sofie, should be studying. She was immersed in her doctorate program and couldn't afford this distraction. Not that she'd prioritize it that way, but that was the reality.

This was going to take its toll on all of them. He was in the best position to keep watch, since his responsibilities were their usual nil. There was something to be said for that; it made you available in a crisis.

But Lance didn't want to think of this as a crisis. They were still reeling from the last, from Tony. He glanced at Gina, small and dark, standing near the door, and knew the emotions churning inside her. His sister-in-law should definitely be home. He could handle things here. Nonna Antonia was a fighter. She'd swing back, and she didn't miss. She'd swung for his backside enough times when she wasn't too busy defending him.

They should go home and get some sleep. Pop hadn't had supper. Lance caught Momma's eye as she paused her praying. He nodded toward Pop, and she caught the gist. His family had a remarkable ability to communicate without words, though it didn't stop them heaping on the words as well.

They'd probably worn the hospital staff's patience a little thin, and he wanted Nonna to himself. Momma was the one to get that done. She stood up and started herding. He could almost hear the collective sigh from the nurses' station. Gripping Nonna's hand, he smiled, dipped his head, and dozed.

Lance woke with a sense of urgency as acute as his need to use the men's room. Nonna was awake. Her hand had pinched his with a death grip, and she was making noises like none he'd heard from her before. He made no sign that they horrified him, just leaned closer.

"What is it, Nonna?" He could make no sense of the sounds, and her agitation rose. He couldn't risk another vessel bursting with her straining, so he furtively pressed the button for the nurse. "It's all right. Give it some time and you'll be able to say what you want."

"Baa . . . baa . . ."

Her eyes showed a terror he'd seen there only once, and he didn't want her suffering like that ever again. He brought her hand to his lips. "It's okay, Nonna." What was keeping the nurse?

But then she was there, a willowy angel of efficiency, taking over where he fell short. She must have doctored the IV, because Nonna stilled and then slept, but there'd been something she wanted him to know or do. "How long before her speech comes back?"

The nurse raised her thin blond brows. "That's impossible to say. It's different with every case."

Nonna was not a case, and it would drive her crazy not to speak her mind. "What's the soonest?"

"It depends on the extent of the damage and the area of the brain and too many other factors. It could be days or years." She added gently, "Or never."

"She's trying to tell me something."

The nurse nodded. "It's very frustrating, but she needs to remain calm and allow the healing to proceed."

"Can you watch her a minute while I make a pit stop?"

The nurse smiled. "She'll be okay."

Lance looked at her sleeping and guessed Nonna wouldn't mind if he hit the bathroom, but her need was in his nostrils, lodged in his nerves and the bones of his hand. He had to learn what it was she had tried to tell him, but how? Maybe in the morning she'd be able to say more. He used the bathroom, then took up his place beside her, hooking his knee over the arm of the chair. "Good night, Nonna. Peaceful dreams."

Lance woke to a hand on his shoulder and the steam of a *macchiato* in his nose. He hooked fingers with Chaz in greeting and whispered his thanks. "How'd you get in?"

"They assumed I was family."

Lance grinned up at the tall Jamaican. They must have really worn down the staff.

Chaz nodded toward the bed. "How is she?"

Lance shrugged. "She's trying to tell me something, but I can't get it."

Chaz squatted down, his limbs hinged like grasshopper legs. He didn't ask anything more, accepting better than Lance the limitations of medical clairvoyance. It was anyone's guess how things would progress. And maybe Nonna would forget all about whatever had seemed so urgent.

But she didn't. While his family arrived to fuss and worry over her, she remained passive, but as soon as they were alone again, she tried to express it. He absorbed her frustration, but could not interpret her message. "You're going to be just fine, Nonna."

But that wasn't what she wanted from him. The doctor had explained things to her, to them. She had suffered a cerebral hemorrhage on the left side of the brain. While there were new treatments for a clot-caused stroke, which could sometimes prevent or reverse damage quickly, bleeding in the brain still required time to heal.

She was exhibiting aphasia, a disconnect in the brain affecting her ability to talk, listen, read or write; and dysarthria, weakening the muscles of her face, tongue, and lips. There was some paralysis on her right side, and the doctor warned they may see emotional lability—sudden mood swings resulting in tears. As though her condition wouldn't be enough, Lance thought.

He was having mood swings of his own, mostly resulting from his inability to understand what she needed. The message had lost none of its urgency, though Nonna still only forced it when they were alone. It was something for him and not the rest of the family. That formed an overwhelming need like a hole inside him, growing with every day.

He started bringing things from the house that she might be wanting. Her prayer book, her recipe cards—of nearly the same importance—her jewelry box that held the gold locket from Nonno, his wedding ring, and the other pieces of jewelry he'd given her over the years. The items were nothing of tremendous value, and they didn't prove to be the thing she wanted anyway.

Lance felt strange searching Nonna's bedroom. He'd hardly ever been in there, since she herself spent scant time inside its walls. She was early to rise and late to bed and in the thick of it for the hours in between. But there must be something she needed, and that was where she kept her things—that or the restaurant kitchen, but he'd tried her recipes already, and he couldn't imagine she wanted pots or utensils.

He had started with the things on the table beside her bed, then moved to the dresser top. Now he opened the top drawer feeling like a voyeur. These were his grandmother's dresser drawers, and he had no business in them, except that he didn't know what else to do. She had grown more agitated with each thing he brought, but there was encouragement to keep trying. He thought so, anyway.

So Lance fingered through her lingerie, feeling foolish until he found a packet of letters and pulled them out. Now this was promising. Love letters from Nonno? That might be something to offer comfort. He checked the drawer, but there was nothing else. He'd try the letters, and if she glared, he'd just have to keep trying.

But when he brought the letters, her excitement was evident. He set them on the table unit beside her bed, but she immediately started making noise. He snatched them up again. "You want me to read them?"

She squawked, a hard angry sound that he knew she didn't mean. It was frustration and panic and, sure, some annoyance with his density. But what else was new? "Nonna, I don't know what you want." He tried to put the letters into her hand, but she pushed them back at him.

Maybe it was one particular letter she wanted. He untied the string and took them out one by one for her to see. They weren't all the same writing. Some were definitely Nonno's script, but others were in there as well, and when he got to one of those, she groaned.

"Do you want me to read this to you?"

She groaned again with a hand motion that seemed to indicate she wanted to hold it. He handed it over.

"You want me to open it?"

A sharp sound showed her irritation. If she didn't want the letter out, was it the envelope? It was addressed to her, but that wasn't what she wanted him to know. He pressed her finger to the return address.

Suora Anna Conchessa
Santuaria di Nostra Signora del Monte
Liguria, Italy

"You want me to write this person?" Only the look in her eyes showed him her answer. "Call her? You want her to come?"

Her sound of frustration matched his own. "What, Nonna? I'm not a mind reader." She'd have slapped his hand for that tone if she could. "I'm sorry." Lance tried again, staring at the address and trying to guess what she wanted from him. Her nail paled where it pressed the address. "You want me to go there?"

Nonna sank back to the pillow with a sigh.

"You're sending me off to a convent."

A flicker on one side of Nonna's lips.

"Great. Well, maybe when you're stronger . . ."

She opened her eyes and glared. He wished he didn't know her so well that every glance communicated something.

"If I leave, who's gonna make you behave?"

She growled low in her throat.

"All right. I'll go." He'd go to the ends of the earth for her, but what was up with some Italian nunnery? Whatever it was, Nonna's adamancy was unmistakable, and beneath it, a fear that had taken up residence on her chest.

"You're what?" Rico's face showed what Lance felt.

"I don't know any more than that, but it's what she's been trying to say." Lance stuffed another shirt into his pack.

Rico had perfected the Puerto Rican stare. "So you're just out of here."

Lance jammed a pair of jeans down inside the pack. He didn't want to get into it with Rico. They'd already established irreconcilable differences, in spite of their history. It didn't matter if he was in Italy or Ecuador or the next bedroom.

"It's another excuse to run away, man."

Lance let that go, adding socks and boxers. "Talk to her yourself, Rico. Nonna needs something, and I'm the one to find out what." He looked around the apartment he shared with Chaz and Rico. He'd be traveling light, but he needed to cover the essentials.

"How long?"

Lance hooked his thumbs in his belt loops. "I don't know. But even if I stayed, the gig is over. Find someone else."

Rico tipped back his head with a growl. "There is no one else."

Lance cinched the pack and shouldered into it. He had a flight to catch. He clasped forearms with Rico. "Keep an eye on Nonna for me."

"You know it." Rico's grip was wiry, firm with years of friendship stronger than blood. They'd be okay. That friendship was based on more than one thing, and Rico would see that eventually.

The flight was long and made longer by the harried woman and toddler who shared the bank of seats. Three quarters of the way across the Atlantic,

Lance fell asleep with the child on his chest as the woman murmured heartfelt gratitude.

————

Putting and gasping along the spectacular road to the convent perched at the top of the mount overlooking the Gulf of Genoa, the European scooter was a sad excuse for his Harley. Forests of pine and lemon trees, almonds and herbs scented the breeze as the road burrowed through dark tunnels and burst again into the warm sunlight along the Tyrrhenian Sea.

As he climbed, the aquamarine water spread out below, and the city of Genoa clung between it and the rugged Ligurian Apennines. The resort-filled crescent of the Riviera di Ponente and the Riviera di Levante was a coastal playground, but Lance wasn't there to indulge. His road climbed ever steeper to the fortress-like convent that sprung from the stone and scrub of the mountain.

It was difficult to distinguish where the walls of the main entrance began and the mountain left off. He had booked a *cumbessia* in the convent and got pretty much what he expected: a cell. One barred window looking in toward the central courtyard, a door into the same. Running water—cold—and a bed.

The whole convent seemed to be slumping back into the ground. The flat, rectangular stones of the buildings looked as if they had been stacked without mortar, but they had stood for centuries. A permeating peace engulfed him. Compared to the Bronx, it was downright otherworldly. No phone, no TV. It didn't matter. They could have lodged him in a stable for all he cared. He just needed answers, and that meant finding his second cousin twice removed, Conchessa DiGratia, known as Sister Anna Conchessa.

Lance's request to speak with her upon arrival had been denied with no explanation. Not a promising start, but Nonna had been adamant when he verified her intentions before he left. She wanted him to talk to this cousin he'd never heard of for reasons locked in Nonna's brain. The sweet-faced nun who welcomed him, along with a handful of other pilgrims, invited him to explore the grounds but was unable to tell him when he might see his cousin.

So Lance walked the gardens and released the urgency that had dogged him all the way there. His New York pushiness would get him nowhere, and it was impossible not to experience the timelessness of eternity within the ancient stone walls. It was not forgetfulness, just a realization that even time spun by God's word alone.

Dinner was simple, but the nun who served them was not old enough to be Nonna's cousin. He broke the focaccia and savored the herbs that flavored it, plants he had recognized in the gardens surrounding the buildings. Content with the simple meal, he slept deeply on the plain, narrow bed and woke with a fresh expectation of accomplishing his goal.

After finishing breakfast, Lance asked again for his cousin. He waited at the table as the other pilgrims left for their daily activities. The nun who came to him was again too young. "I am sorry. But Sister Anna Conchessa suggests there is no grandson to her cousin Antonia."

He spread his hands. "She doesn't know me. I flew in from America. Here." He handed her the letter from Conchessa to his Nonna dated years back. "Show her that."

Elbows resting on the long table, Lance held his face in his hands, waiting. He hadn't supposed Conchessa would refuse to see him. Why would she doubt his word? Why was it impossible for her to believe Antonia had married and borne future generations? At least she could hear him out.

The woman came back and returned the letter. "I'm sorry. She is baking the bread for the Festival of the Annunciation. Bread is given to the faithful who climb the sanctuary path."

Lance seized the chance. "Maybe I can help."

The nun's brows raised, making wrinkles against the edge of her habit. She was obviously unused to pilgrims offering to join in the work.

"Tell her Nonna Antonia taught me to cook. I can bake bread." He didn't know if it was a language barrier or pure incredulity that caused her expression as she went once again to be his mouthpiece.

She came back a few minutes later. "If you will follow me."

He wasn't sure which of them was more surprised. He felt a little like a sideshow in her eyes. She had probably joined the order at eighteen, and her innocence arose as they walked, like the faint scent of soft candles, dispelling darkness. He followed her to the kitchen, where a woman stood who was easily as old as Nonna. Though the years had not bent her, she was no taller than his shoulder, barrel-shaped and hawk-nosed. He immediately knew his place, and when she motioned to the sink without speaking, he washed well with soap and water, then threw himself into the mixing and kneading of dough.

CHAPTER TWO

The whir of the saw and the beat of the hammer had been a constant melody over the past months; the scent of wood stain and paint wafting up on the Sonoma Valley breezes to the window where Evvy watched. Her new neighbor was industrious; the worn tool belt a fixture on her narrow hips as she worked sometimes into the night, strong and competent for one so young. But she seemed to go about it all as though she had to keep a step ahead of something or someone, even though she worked entirely alone. There was that element of attack, of driving herself, in each action.

Evvy knew the feeling. Every breath she drew through her sodden lungs was a challenge. If they knew how bad it really was, they'd force her into the hospital and she'd miss the resuscitation of Ralph's house. It didn't matter, of course. It wasn't Ralph's anymore. But she felt responsible anyway. Watchful. There were so many memories. And not just hers. Ralph's were muddled now, but he had told stories. . . .

———

The whine grew to a pained wail that set her teeth on edge in a way it never had before. It passed with a breathy whiff of new maple, mingling brazenly with musty damp and age. Rese breathed the scent that had filled her lungs more comfortably than the purest air. She let go the trigger on the miter saw and examined the fresh cut on the section of molding, then approved it with her fingertips.

Maple, oak, and cherry had been her companions as long as she could remember. The plane had molded her palm; the chisel had developed her eye and fingers. She knew her way around any power tool on the market, had shot nails, routered trim, sanded and carved and finished every wood worth using. She'd also laid pipe and run wires, though it didn't compare to working the wood. Nothing did.

Rese knew how to bid a job, how to recognize one she didn't want to tackle, how to see past the damage to a true gem like the one she'd found here in Sonoma. The property's value was elevated by the community alone—a rural, self-protecting city that recognized the potential for explosive growth and development around the vineyard industry, and chose instead to maintain its identity, unlike its Napa twin.

The place practically shouted, "Keep your glitz and glamour and big money. We're the old guard, and we like things the way they are." Only the decrepit condition of the villa, too historical to pull down and too unsafe to live in, had given her a wedge. Even so she'd used every argument she had to break through the no-growth moratorium on lodging—not that different from battles she had waged over permits and regulations. She wasn't building new lodging here, just resurrecting an existing property and making it earn its keep. She hoped.

The structure had been built to last, and once she finished the facelift, it would be as stately as at its birth. Not gaudy or ornamental, the villa had a simple grace that reflected an understanding of line and form, and she stayed true to those elements now, in her renovation. A master had to know the heart of a place to do it justice. That's what she'd been taught, but she'd always had the eye, and since this was the very last time, she had chosen carefully.

Rese swallowed at tightness in her throat as she climbed the frame of the scaffolding and fitted the cornice piece against the wall along the ceiling. The fit was good, the cut sharply aligning with the last section. A wave of satisfaction buoyed her as she stepped out onto the boards and tapped in a few anchoring nails to hold the molding in place. Such a little thing to matter so much. She caressed the wood, admiring its grain, absorbing the beauty.

Each board had its own fingerprint in the pattern of the grain formed by years growing in the sun and rain. She did not take for granted what had gone into each piece of wood she used, what made it strong, what made it supple, all the elements that made it beautiful, useful, and enduring. A California girl, she'd heard all the anti-tree-cutting arguments, but nothing compared to wood when it came down to it.

She did keep all the scraps, however, and many became the corner-piece carvings that were her trademark. Not many people were known by the work of their hands anymore, but she had determined from the start to be more than a nameless nail driver like the rest of the crew.

Years back, she had gathered the ends and spare pieces and practiced with the different chisels until the rounded handles felt more at home in her palm than a pen or a book or a jump rope. She could draw well enough to pencil her designs, but it was when she dug into the wood that the magic happened.

Rese climbed back down, slid the next board into place in the miter box and found her pencil mark. She aligned the blade with the edge of the wood, checked the degree of its angle and reached for the trigger. Before she could squeeze, the image struck her mind. Thick, callused fingers with blunt, chipped nails, the silver blur of the blade.

She pressed her eyes shut and drew long breaths through her nostrils, then seized the trigger and put the saw in motion, edging it into the wood. Another clean cut. She eased the molding out from the miter table, climbed the scaffolding and tacked it to the adjoining wall and ceiling. Focus and perform; don't think, don't remember, don't imagine what-ifs. Just find the rhythm in the wood.

The moment Lance stepped inside the neglected yard of the Sonoma villa, the very ground reached up and embraced him. Grapevines along the squat, iron fence beckoned like gnarled hands. Ancient blood stirred in his veins. It must be the place, or the ground would not cry out to him. The breeze ruffled his hair with spring-scented fingers. New sprouts and blooms awakened in the yard, but the house seemed still.

Its creamy stucco was flawless; no gutter sagged; no shutter listed. The porch posts were freshly painted white, though the narrow porch that framed the door drew no more attention than the long paned windows of the first floor or the arch-covered windows of the second. There was a pleasing symmetry that blended it all together, and yet . . . that feeling of pause, as though a great sleep had settled over its walls, and now it waited . . . and watched.

The construction pickup in the driveway read Barrett Renovation and explained the pristine condition of a structure more than a hundred years old. But none of that work had penetrated the silence. As his gaze traveled the plastered face before him, Lance realized how deeply the need had settled inside . . . the right—yes, the right.

The slate walk was somber as he covered its length to the worn, solid stairs beneath the arched portico and climbed. Before he rapped the door,

Lance laid his hand to the wood. *What will you show me, old house?* He closed his eyes and pressed his other hand to the inner pocket of his jacket; a second letter entrusted to him by the old woman he had come to love after three weeks in her convent kitchen, a letter with a return address matching the property he now inspected. *"Use it wisely, Lance,"* she had instructed.

I will, cogino mio.

But would he? He always started out with good intentions, even when they got him into trouble—as they had more often than he liked to think. He began with brilliance. It was seeing it through to the end that somehow eluded him.

This would be different. This wasn't about him. It was for Nonna. A vise squeezed his chest, releasing only when he drew a slow breath and knocked. The whine of a saw blade came from inside, and his second knock went unnoticed. He would have called ahead, but he'd only just seen his opportunity for introduction in the front window.

Lance tried the knob and opened the front door. The sense of purpose crept through his hand and up his arm as he peered inside at the broad staircase rising up before him. He almost pictured a young, graceful Antonia descending to welcome him with open arms and a kiss to each cheek. He'd never seen her that way, only softly wrinkled, like crepe, but she was beautiful still.

His gaze slid over the spacious front room; walls patched and awaiting paint, but seemingly sound and promising elegance. Muted gray and beige stone in the entry floor, wood for the rest. Tall ceilings and long narrow windows. The place was old, though not the hoary age of the Italian structures he'd seen in Italy. Age without infirmity; wisdom, not senility. Watchful, expectant maturity. He swallowed. He hadn't expected to react so powerfully to the house.

Drawing himself up, Lance called, "Hello." Or maybe he thought it only. "I'm home," he breathed, though he'd never set foot in the place. He shook his head. Way too quixotic. He stepped inside and sought the sound of industry.

―――――――――

A noise from behind brought Rese sharply around to the figure standing in the doorway with a look of belonging on his face, as though *she* had walked in on *him*. For a moment, under his dark-eyed scrutiny, she felt herself the trespasser. No way. She had spent too many years as the odd man out to accept it in her own dining room. "Did you want something?"

He hung his hands in his jeans pockets. "I'm looking for Rese Barrett."

"Yes?"

"You're Rese?"

"No doubt you expected a burly man with a crew." He didn't deny it, nor did he appear chagrinned at falling into the stereotypical mindset. He was probably another neighbor concerned about an inn, eager to instruct her on his personal expectations, as if she didn't know to provide enough off-street parking for guests and curtail late-night noise. On this fringe-of-town street only one house was close enough to be affected by what happened on her property, and that closest neighbor had yet to appear. Until now?

But the guy looked up to the cornice she held and said, "You need help."

"No, I don't." She sent a last nail nearly through the cornice and let go. Help and need were not in her vocabulary. Even now.

"You said so."

"Said so?"

He motioned through the wide doorway to the sign in the front-parlor window. The sun-backed, reversed letters did form a Help Wanted sign, and along with her name and phone number she had written in bold black the position available: maid/cook.

He came forward and reached up. "I'm Lance. Lance Michelli."

Sighing, Rese climbed down the scaffolding, hung the hammer in her belt and gave his hand a decisive grip. "You're a maid?" *She* did not make assumptions according to gender.

He said, "Cook," and before she could set him straight, added, "I've trained with two of the best chefs in Italy and New York." He glanced at the freshly hung cornice. "I can also do some carpentry."

She took in his spare frame, the stylish cut of his dark hair, and especially the diamond in his ear and tried not to snort. "I do the carpentry. And if your other claim is true, you're overqualified for my opening. Why don't you apply at the fancy restaurants on the plaza?"

He looked around the dining room's long, multi-paned windows and his tone deepened. Again she sensed his belonging as he said, "This place is just what I'm looking for."

She clamped down on her concern. "This place is a bed-and-breakfast—muffins, fruit. I don't need a chef."

"Why not espresso and pastries? Frittatas and crepes, almond focaccia and tarts?"

The idea sprang up with a life of its own. She tried to slap it down, but it slid into her mind as though it belonged there, much the same way he'd slid into her dining room. She frowned. She had not intended anything that fancy. Good breakfasts, yes, but . . .

"Or a nightly special," he went on. "*Saltimbocca* or *pollo marengo* or lasagna. What other bed-and-breakfast offers that?"

Her stomach growled. How long since she had stopped to eat? She didn't know half of what he was saying, but lasagna—she imagined the aroma seeping from the kitchen. She had not planned to serve full meals, though the kitchen was certainly sufficient for it. The family who built the villa must have considered that room the social hub of their lives. Personally, the less time she spent in any kitchen the better.

She looked him over again. She hadn't expected a response to the sign so soon after putting it in the window, had only just called in the ad. It was crazy to choose the first person through the door just because he talked a good line and appealed to her hollow stomach. But his idea did intrigue her.

Sonoma had its share of bed-and-breakfast establishments, and her competition was stiff. Most were within walking distance of the historic plaza; hers was nearer the outskirts of town. It wasn't a long drive in, but people would need incentive to choose hers over a closer inn. She hadn't opened yet, but she had put enough work into the place to form a protective attitude. Even when she renovated other people's property, she felt as though it was a little bit hers when she'd finished.

This time it was all hers, and she wanted it to work—needed it to. Again she felt the vise at her throat; again she forced it away. She wouldn't want a hoity-toity chef, but what about one who would produce irresistible food? Was this man capable of irresistible?

Maybe, but he was sidetracking her from the real issue. "Look, I'm sorry, but it won't work."

"Why not?"

"It's a dual position, maid *and* cook. I can only afford one person."

He considered that a moment, then shrugged. "Okay."

"Not okay."

"You can be a carpenter, but I can't be a maid?"

"That's not what I meant." And she flushed that he would think it. She was more fair-minded than any person on the planet. "The job is minimum wage plus room and board. I'm sure you can do better than that . . . and frankly, I'm looking for a woman." Let him sue her. It wasn't job discrimination; it was practical. She was not sharing her quarters with a guy. She had worked with men exclusively for too many years to choose that situation again.

His eyes flashed. "You won't be having male guests?"

"Male guests will use the upper-level guest rooms. And they leave."

"What about the building out back?"

"What?" Rese turned and followed his gaze through the tall, arched windows to the stone tumble almost completely surrounded by old grapevines. "It's not habitable."

"I'll make you a deal. You provide the materials and tools, and I'll do the work."

He'd make *her* a deal? She stared out the window as yet another thought wormed in to curl up with the last. She hated to lose the old structure but would not have time to restore it before opening if she wanted to have any track record before the main season began.

She glanced again at the diamond in his ear, his chic jeans and leather jacket—not the sort she would ever hire on to her crew. Besides, the building wouldn't pass code. "It would have to be wired for power and—"

He hung his thumbs in his belt loops. "I can run an electrical line."

And juggle burning torches and play a harmonica with his toes, no doubt. "You'd have to come off the box in the kitchen, and there's a problem in the wiring. The appliances work, but the other breaker's messed up. I haven't gotten to it, and I'm not sure when I will."

"I'll look at it."

She didn't hide her skepticism. "You've done that sort of work?"

"I've done a bit of everything."

Rese snorted. "Jack-of-all-trades and master of none?"

He jerked his chin and blazed her with his eyes. Talk about intense. He would be trouble, she could tell. Trouble she didn't need. She wasn't judging, but his hands were too expressive for manual labor, not a callus in sight. It was obvious.

But he said, "If I can rebuild the carriage house, I get the job?"

She perceived a keen desire that didn't quite make sense. It wasn't that great a job. He'd make more money at any restaurant in town, though he couldn't live in town on that. Room and board was a substantial perk, and one she had hoped would get her an appreciative employee.

She hadn't expected the woman she hired to build her own room, but if he wanted the job enough to tackle the carriage house, it would free the second room of her suite for an office. That thought of her own fit snugly with his implants. No doubt he would have suggested it himself if she'd voiced the need for computer space.

Rese expelled her breath. No point scrutinizing him further; she wouldn't tell anything more by appearance. It was productivity that mattered. "*If* you can do that, we'll make it a trial period, to see that you can also cook. And clean."

"Deal." His grip was firm and confident. "When do I start?"

"I'm opening the first of May." Just over three weeks to finish the renovation, a Web site, and other advertising and promotion. If he hadn't rendered the carriage house habitable by then, he'd be on his own for lodging. "Your compensated hours will depend on reservations."

"Okay." He glanced about. "Mind if I take a look around?"

"Go ahead." She slid a fresh board onto the worktable. "You might change your mind. It's a lot of house to take care of." And she was not compromising on the maid part.

Rese aligned the pencil mark while he wandered off. Three more sections and she'd have the cornice up. This room and the front parlor had been the most work, requiring both structural and surface repairs over the last few months, but the bulk of it was done and she was down to the finish work.

The six bedrooms upstairs had not been as damaged by time and vandals as the lower level. Her guests would sleep in mostly original architecture, not counting the bathrooms that had been added before her. Rese had determined that earlier remodel adequate, since there was only so much she could accomplish alone. With a jolt, she realized that had just changed.

*

Jack-of-all-trades and master of none? Did she know how condescending she sounded, her scornful gaze, that mocking snort? Rese Barrett had scoped him out and judged. In those few minutes, she'd seen . . . more than he intended? Lance frowned. Maybe it wasn't personal; maybe she thought the worst of everyone.

Walking through the rooms of the old villa confirmed his first impressions. Not an architectural marvel compared to its European forebears, but a stately structure nonetheless. His pulse quickened as he roamed the rooms, freshly papered and painted, though not yet furnished.

He'd learned from the people at his hotel that the address he asked about was being renovated as a bed-and-breakfast. Then he'd seen the truck outside and expected a construction crew, not a one-woman operation—formidable as she was. Rese Barrett's work was competent and interesting, but she could have no idea what secrets the old place held, what memories she'd papered over. She could not know the house had a story, or that the story was his.

He hadn't even known it until recently. Three weeks in Liguria had

brought him here, unsure of what, if anything, he'd find. He hadn't anticipated employment right on the property, but he should have. From the time
he'd left Nonna's side, every step seemed to be orchestrated. For once he
might just be doing exactly what he was meant to do.

Lance went down to the kitchen. No other room welcomed him as this
one, and he guessed it was more than the scant amount of attention it
seemed to have received. The tile floor might even be original. The gas stove
and oversized sink basin were dated, but that suited him just fine. He closed
his eyes and imagined the life this room had held, a young Antonia with her
mother, her grandmother? Sisters, cousins? He could almost hear the laughter, the scolding.

He laid his palms on the stone counter and breathed deeply. The cook
position was clearly a godsend. The maid portion—divine comedy. Rese Barrett? Penance. He could picture Nonna agreeing. But he'd live with that; he'd
live with anything in order to do what he'd come for. Nonna Antonia was
depending on him, and her need sharpened the razor edge of his own and
kept him from feeling guilty. He'd have the chance to find whatever Nonna
needed, and then Rese could hire the woman she wanted.

He went out the back door and fought through the tangled vines and
other brush to the carriage house, imagining the scents of leather and polish,
horsehair and manure, the squeak of harness and a creaking wheel. Instead,
he ducked beneath the sagging roof only to have weeds and mildewed wood
assault his nose, and there was no sound but the buzzing of a fly.

The walls would probably not cave in, though in places the mortar had
chunked out completely between the stones. The remnant of roof, however,
might very well come down on him. That was the place to start. Though he
hadn't planned on it, he had done this sort of labor before, among other
things. His experience was broad, and that would benefit him now, whatever
his new employer thought.

He could work on the carriage house as long as he was there, even if she
wasn't paying for his time. That way they'd both get something out of this.
The thought eased his conscience. She had put a lot of work into the villa,
and he was not averse to adding his own sweat. The place deserved it. How
much of its history did she know? It seemed she had recently acquired the
property. He might kick himself for bad timing, but it wouldn't have mattered if he had found it for sale. He could never have afforded it.

So for better or worse, Rese Barrett was his immediate future—which
might explain the premonition he'd had the moment he saw her, the sense

that she was part of his quest. Of course, that was before she opened her mouth.

———————

Through the window, Rese glimpsed Lance heading for the stone structure with the crowbar and ladder he'd requested. He would have his hands full making that place a dwelling. She was skeptical of the outcome, but it was worth a try. "Doing a bit of carpentry" could not compare to the years she had put into the craft—nothing personal. Excellence required a sustained attention and a diligence not many were willing to devote. But if he had construction experience and could make it safe, it might not need to be beautiful.

She could hardly believe she was thinking that, when quality workmanship meant everything to her. She tacked up the last section of ceiling trim and walked around the scaffolding, sinking finishing nails and plugging them with putty so they were all but invisible. The details of her own work were never unimportant.

She disassembled the scaffolding and turned her attention to the baseboards. Measure, cut, and fit. Not everyone would expect perfection in baseboards, but a misaligned fit would grate on her like a paper cut. Her hypercritical attention to detail might not be healthy, as some people had insinuated, but it was as much her nature as brown hair and brown eyes, and she could change those two more easily than the first.

Rese worked through the afternoon and packed up her tools as the last of the daylight faded. She would have turned on a light, except the chandelier for the central fixture had not arrived and only a pair of stiff wires extended from the ceiling. She had work lights, but could not bring herself to use them. *Yet,* she told herself. Yet.

Casting her gaze once more around the room, she heard activity in the kitchen. Her cook?

He was unloading a paper sack of groceries and glanced over as she entered. "Have you eaten?"

She shook her head, then jutted her chin toward the can he'd set on the counter. "I don't really like artichokes."

"You will." He drizzled olive oil into the old copper pan she had hung above the stove for decoration, apparently finding it usable. His fingers were deft as he minced a single clove of garlic and scattered it over the olive oil, then laid two flattened chicken breasts in the pan. The pungent aroma wafted up and tantalized. Maybe he did know how to cook.

Rese went back to her business and left him to his. The more she thought about it, the more delighted she was to relinquish control of the kitchen. She let that role peel away like the flaky skin of his garlic. If she never cooked again, she would not miss it one bit.

————————

Lance bathed the chicken in Chardonnay, then when it had mostly cooked off, he topped the golden meat with sautéed artichoke hearts and sprinkled it all with a finely minced basil leaf and fresh grated *parmigiano*. The crisp green beans cooked with olive oil and lemon were a perfect complement, and he garnished each plate with a slice of lemon on a trio of basil leaves.

He was hungry, but this meal was also to show Rese what he could do. He wasn't concerned about her disdain for artichokes. A lot of people thought they didn't like something because it hadn't been prepared well. He would be very surprised if she complained.

Earlier that afternoon he had torn off the carriage house roof, then ridden his Harley into town to wash up at his hotel room. The welcome he'd received there was far more genial than Rese Barrett's. Baxter had been cooped up too long and all but shoved him out the door with his shaggy head. After giving the dog time to run it off, they had shopped for ingredients, then headed back to the bed-and-breakfast together. He was hoping to keep the animal there even before the carriage house was habitable. He would ask Rese after he fed her. Things usually worked better that way.

He poured two glasses of water and went in search of her. The second floor was empty, but he found her just outside the only lower-level bedroom, which must be her own quarters, now that he thought of it. By the state of her hair, she was fresh out of the shower. Since it formed a dark cap around her features and was even shorter than his, he guessed she didn't fuss much with it. "Dinner's ready."

"We need to establish some rules. You're not allowed past that door." She indicated the door into the narrow hall that separated her suite from the kitchen.

"Okay." He started back through it. If she wanted cold food, she could have it cold.

But she followed him out and took a seat in one of the two rickety wooden chairs in the kitchen. Where she had picked them up he could hardly guess, but he hoped she intended to do better for her guests. He sat down, breathing a silent prayer over the food, then watched intently as she took her first bite.

She cut another bite and ate it. No comment, no change of expression. He cut into his succulent chicken, breathed the aroma of blended oil and herbs, cheese and wine, then took the bite. Perfect. What was her deal?

She rubbed the napkin over her mouth. "I'll need you to fill out an I–9 and a W–2 and produce two types of identification and references."

"Would you like that before you try your beans?"

She frowned down at her plate. "No, we can eat first." She stabbed a bean and bit it in half. He could tell by the way her teeth broke through that it was perfectly *al dente*. She chewed and finished the other half, then went back to her chicken.

He sipped his water. What was her game, to intimidate by disinterest? Annoy by lack of expression? How many women had a savory meal cooked just for them and ate it in stoic silence? It wasn't as if the sheer tantalizing pleasure on her tongue kept her mute. He might have served up a boiled hot dog on a bun.

Baxter barked outside the back door, and she raised her head. Lance laid down his fork. "It's only Baxter."

"You have a dog?"

"I was just going to mention that." If Baxter hadn't forced the issue he would have worked into it gradually. *Do you like animals? How do you feel about one on the property?*

"What does he want?"

"To make sure I haven't forgotten him. Normally he's not insecure. But this is all new. We've only been in town a couple days."

She got up and went to the door, peering through the glass to where he had left the cocker-retriever mix under the nut or fruit tree. "Is he hungry?"

"You want to give him your chicken?"

She glanced over her shoulder. "I'd rather finish it."

Well, what do you know. "I fed him before we came back. He's just lonely."

She opened the door and went out. He huffed a short laugh. At this rate the dog held the best chance for wowing her.

Baxter's plaintive whine ceased as it always did with a good ear scratch. *Guess the dog won't be a problem.* Lance cut another bite of the fragrant chicken. Maybe he just had to find the right meal. Everyone had some food they couldn't resist. Rese came back in and washed her hands, then sat.

He said, "Tell me what you like to eat."

She shrugged. "Anything I don't have to cook."

"There must be something you prefer."

Again that direct gaze. "Food doesn't excite me."

Did she have any idea how disagreeable she was? She wouldn't last a week in the hospitality business with that attitude and personality. "Well, then what does?"

She looked up and studied the walls and ceiling with mute captivation. "This place," she whispered finally, with a wash of emotion that caught him off guard.

Lance's chest tightened. He did not want to hear that tone in her voice, the same emotion he felt for the villa—a house that might not be hers at all. He stabbed a bean and bit it in half. The meal had lost its appeal.

CHAPTER THREE

Through the gray mist that had settled on the valley over the past two days, Rese supervised the delivery of the beds and dressers. She had ordered the pieces from an estate selling through eBay, and this first batch had arrived in the Ryder truck three hours earlier.

She'd spent the morning hours with the movers, checking each piece for damage, directing placement, then overseeing the setup. As soon as the mattresses were in place, she made up each bed with that room's linens. Home décor wasn't her passion, but she had enough of an eye to create themed rooms that her Web site could display by name.

She entered the Jasmine Garden and stretched out across a slender-framed, king-size canopy bed twined with white gauzy veils. The brand new, top-quality mattress felt deep and welcoming, the down comforters and duvets extravagant. Maybe she'd gone overboard. She didn't really know what was expected.

But it was her nature to use the best base elements to create the finest finish. Working on that assumption, she could hardly choose cheap bedding for a bed-and-breakfast. Wasn't that the point? "Bed" and "breakfast." Her part was satisfactory, and if the food she'd sampled the other night was any indication, Lance would hold up his end.

He was volatile, though. The way he'd glowered through that meal—did he hate to cook? Then why take the position? Serious second thoughts flooded in. Her initial impression had been mixed, but he'd talked his way through her doubts—not necessarily a good thing. She had called his references, and though he hadn't stayed anywhere very long, people liked him. Popularity didn't count for much; it was effectiveness that mattered.

She sat up and looked out the bedroom window. Baxter came out the carriage house door, tail wagging, head high, assessing the situation, then went back inside where Lance was working. Definitely a bonus, there. He should have said he had a dog first thing.

She went back to work, unpacking the boxes of photographs and lamps, decorative items and books to match each room's motif. She had not yet purchased TVs or the units to hold them. That was another sort of shopping altogether.

Her stomach growled. Lance had not demonstrated any of the breakfasts he'd mentioned. After arriving both days, he'd gone straight to work on his project. It shouldn't matter. She'd gone a long time without eating much of anything. Now suddenly food was important?

Rese went down and made a piece of toast—hardly a tantalizing breakfast. She would not have noticed its bland ordinariness before Lance had arrived. Chewing the crisp but mostly tasteless offering, she wandered into the dining room and surveyed the work still to be done. The furniture's arrival had interrupted her progress, but she studied the room with a critical eye.

The wood floor needed sanding and a fresh treatment of polyurethane, though most of it would be covered by an area rug in muted ecru beige, and greens that would complement the soft butter-colored walls. She had stained the woodwork a natural maple, and the carved pieces to ornament the doorways would get a rubbed finish when they were ready.

Elegance without stuffiness. It was certainly spacious, unlike modern dining rooms scarcely sufficient for a family meal. Well, families were larger and closer in the days this house was built. She'd be knocking around in it without guests.

Turning slowly around, she wondered about the people who had eaten together in this room, cooked in the vacuous kitchen, planted the overgrown garden. Who had slept in the rooms above? This house had a story so thick she could feel it. Some structures were like old sachets with no scent left; this one emoted something powerful yet just beyond her grasp. That was why she chose it—that and the deplorable condition she had found it in.

She wished she knew more about it. Maybe the clutter in the attic where she'd found the kitchen chairs would offer some history. With it right above the freshly finished bedrooms, she should clean it out and make certain there were no rodents and as few spiders as possible. As the day was already interrupted, she would just have a look and see what she was up against. At the walk-through, she'd been told it held junk, but there had been no access to see for herself. She doubted anyone had been up there in years, maybe decades. No doubt anything valuable had been plundered long ago.

She stopped at the base of the attic stairs, glancing through the doors to the now-furnished bedrooms. A whisper of excitement stirred in her. It was coming together—almost too quickly. Soon the work would be done. But she didn't want to think about that.

Rese climbed the dark flight and stepped into the attic. Two small windows allowed weak daylight, and a single bulb dangled from the center beam. There were stacks of newspapers, several broken chairs that matched the two she had salvaged for the kitchen, some thoroughly disgusting drapes, and an electric fan plugged into the outlet that held the overhead bulb.

The air was stuffy, which was probably the purpose of the fan. She reached down and pushed the On button. It buzzed loudly to life and stirred the dust and items near it. Everything she spied from the near end was newer than the villa by decades, at least, yet was still trash. It should all be hauled out, but her stomach clenched at that thought. What if she grabbed the drapes and something wiggled? She squeezed her fists. She had not been born with a fear of mice, spiders, and things that jumped out; it had been spitefully developed. But . . .

She sensed movement behind her and shrieked, spinning around, fists clenched. Lance stepped back, hands raised in surrender as adrenaline transformed her fear to anger.

"What are you doing! Why did you sneak up like that?"

He reached over and turned off the fan. "I didn't sneak."

Her chest heaved with indignation and passing fear. "What do you want?"

He searched the cluttered expanse behind her. "Will this be inspected for health and safety?"

There were probably ways around that. Only public areas had to be customer friendly. She could keep it locked, but now that she'd taken a closer look, she'd rather take care of it. "I don't know. But it ought to be cleaned out." She patted an upholstered chair back and sneezed.

He waved the dust away. "I'll do it."

"You will?"

He shrugged. "I'm the maid, right?"

When they opened for business, yes. "What about getting your room done?"

"I have it all torn down. Need to wait for the lumber and drywall to be delivered."

Over the past two days, he had removed the dangerous roof and cleared most of the brush and vines to get at the place. She'd seen him plugging holes in the stones with hand-mixed mortar. All of his time and effort had cost her nothing so far. But she'd have to pay him to do the attic, something she could certainly clean out herself.

She lifted the corner of the drape with the toe of her shoe. "It could be nasty."

"Nasty doesn't bother me."

It shouldn't bother her. But her stomach turned at moldering, vermin-infested refuse. She liked old, not foul, things. She could make herself do it. But if Lance was willing, why not turn it over? Delegation was acceptable.

"Okay. I want to see anything interesting or important. Anything that might work in the rooms, and especially things about the house, records and stuff. I'd like to know more about this old place." She rested her hands on her hips and gave it a final once over. Some of the details of this attic she'd rather not know.

"Where do you want the garbage?"

"Timbuktu?"

One side of his mouth quirked.

"Haul it to the driveway for now." She had expected him to balk at the maid's portion of the job. This wasn't cleaning toilets yet, but he certainly seemed amenable. And that would leave her to the work she did best.

———

Lance exulted. It was exactly what he'd hoped for. The door had been locked when he had his first look-through, and he couldn't exactly ask to inspect the attic. But then here she was, needing him to clear it out. If that wasn't God, what was?

Grazie, Signore. The quest burned inside. So it wasn't the Holy Grail he sought. Nor even necessarily treasure. What he hoped to find went much deeper. But she was right about one thing. There was a lot of refuse to plow through. He gathered the mildewed drapes, dragged them down the stairs, and dropped them in a heap outside.

Next he brought out all the broken chairs and piles of *Index Tribunes* that dated from the eighties and were therefore of no use to him. Stained lampshades and cracked vinyl blinds he added to the pile. An assortment of stiff, warped shoes. Even an old push lawn mower, though why anyone would have hauled it to the attic was beyond him.

A shower fixture he inspected, then set in the discard pile. A vase he found tucked into the eaves warranted more attention. He wiped it off with an old cloth and put it aside for Rese to consider. He wasn't even sure what he hoped to find. But the sooner he cleared out the disorder, the simpler his task would be.

Rese came up after a couple hours, smelling of wood stain. An oversized man's shirt hung halfway down her thighs and was rolled above her wrists. She glanced over the area he'd cleared, but asked, "Were you going to make lunch?"

He looked at his watch. Almost two. He hadn't realized it was that late in the day. But he didn't want to stop, and he was in no mood to cook for her again. "No."

She stood arms akimbo. "You are on the clock."

"For cleaning the attic. Even in a dual position, I can only do one job at a time." Though the fact that she would ask was curious. He had noticed sandwich ingredients and packaged soup. She could make something for herself.

She wiped her forehead with the back of her wrist. "You'll have to fluctuate between them as the situation requires."

She must have worked up an appetite, but he was skeptical of its effectiveness. "Are you asking me to fix you something?"

"You should show me what else you can do."

He sat back on his haunches. "So you're asking?"

She raised her chin. "Forget it. I'll make a sandwich."

Stubborn woman. Obviously preferred issuing orders to making requests. But he did need to stay on her good side. This was one job he couldn't lose. "I'll put something together."

"There's not much to work with."

He turned off the fan he had employed in spite of its obnoxious noise. "I can run in and get stuff."

"I'll give you money."

He cocked his head. "Why don't you make a list?"

She raised her hands, warding off that thought. "I have no idea what you'll need."

He grinned. "Just tell me what you like."

"I don't really care."

"What do you buy?"

Her hands clamped her hips again. "Macaroni and cheese, ramen noodles . . ."

He held up a hand. "I get the idea. But you have to do something for me."

She shot him a skeptical look. "What?"

"Sit with Baxter when I start my bike." He headed for the stairs. "Or he'll want to ride along."

"How does he do that?" She followed him down.

"I have a sort of saddle across the front of my seat."

"You're kidding."

"No."

"I can't believe you take your dog on a motorcycle."

"Well, he wouldn't ride anything but a Harley." Lance turned at the base of the stairs.

"It's still dangerous."

"No more than for me."

Hands clamped to her hips again. "He doesn't have a choice."

Lance paused. "Sure he does."

She swung down around the newel post. "Not if you've trained him to do it. It's like making him jump through fire or something. He does it to please you, not because he wants to."

Why was she making this an issue? "Then you shouldn't have any trouble holding on to him."

She frowned. "How badly will he try?"

"You'd better hold his collar. And remind him he doesn't want to go."

She glared as he went out. Given the food items she had mentioned, he decided to give pasta a try. Maybe fettuccini tossed with shrimp and broccoli, a lemon butter sauce with capers and shallots. He started the Harley and heard Baxter bark. *Not this time, buddy. You don't really want to. You just think you do.*

Lance swung the bike out of the driveway and down the lane. Interesting that she ascribed the dog's pleasure to obedience. Sure, he'd tucked the pup into his jacket on their earliest trips, then created the sling saddle that supported Baxter's legs. But the truth was the dog hated to be left behind, and when that was the transportation, he took to it as easily as the back of a truck or the seat of a car. Between his arms, Baxter rode in comfort and safety.

Lance reached the Sonoma Market and parked, wishing he'd just taken the dog along, but he was hoping Baxter would cement his position with

Rese. He went inside and chose organic vegetables and the other items he would need. When he got serious, he'd make his own pasta, but for now the packaged variety would do. He paid, realizing Rese hadn't sent money after all, but that was okay. He'd just hand over the receipt. He loaded the items into his travel bags and drove back to the villa. It was quiet inside as he passed through to the kitchen, and he was surprised to see Rese still sitting with Baxter in the backyard.

The animal had his head in her lap. She had obviously taken his directions seriously, and Baxter had conned her into feeling truly sorry for him. They must have heard the bike when he drove in, but neither cared too much by the looks of it. Just as well—he had lunch to prepare.

———

Rese sat with the dog wagging at her side. She had not intended to waste the day, but hunger and the thought of Lance's food had interrupted her staining. Even then she would have worked while he was gone, but as soon as she cuddled his dog it was all over.

Hiring Lance had diminished her productivity. Just having him around broke her focus. It had never been that way before. She could have a whole crew around her and hardly know it, unless she came across something that needed attention—like a dog. She smiled down, and Baxter nuzzled her with his wet nose.

She petted his ears as she surveyed the tangled garden. Sunlight crept between the fronds and leaves. Buckled flagstone paths ran among overgrown planters of hydrangea and azaleas, beds choked with callas and peonies just starting to bloom, profuse lilacs clogged with spider's webs and bird's nests.

The trees had not been pruned in years, nor the hedge trimmed. A cascade of honeysuckle scented the air with a sweet peppery smell, and to her right, honeybees droned in a patch of sweetly cloying white alyssum, then rose up, reeling in drunken pleasure. Left to the temperate sun and morning fog, the garden itself had overindulged.

With care it could be lovely, but Rese knew almost nothing about gardening—flowers, shrubs, or trees, until the latter had been sawn into lumber. Wood she knew, not green, growing, blooming things. She sighed. Every time she thought she was getting close, she found more work, and that was both a relief and a frustration.

She got up and crossed to the carriage house. The roof was off, the old wood stacked neatly outside one wall, and Lance had begun clearing the ground—for a cement slab, no doubt. He appeared methodical and orderly, two things she appreciated but would not have instinctively ascribed to him.

She had little reason to doubt his ability or thoroughness, judging only by his appearance. He was proving himself as good a cook as he'd claimed. Why shouldn't his other claims be true as well? His varied experience might not mean he wasn't proficient. She was reading that in because her own ambition had been so specific.

She glanced up at the window of the house across the hedge. A face peering out? She couldn't be sure with the light as it was. And she didn't want to stare. She turned back toward her own house. Had Lance finished making lunch? She recalled his thunderous brow the last time he cooked.

Trouble. She had thought it in those first moments. Well, she had said a trial period, and that gave her an out if he proved unreasonable. She started for the house and stubbed her foot on an uneven stone all but hidden by trailing ivy. "Ouch." Baxter nosed her sympathetically, and she sat down again beside him. The garden would have to be tended. Maybe Lance could handle that as well. She certainly didn't want to be sued for personal injury.

Rese stroked the dog. She could sit for days petting him. He was so gentle and responsive. And yes, he had cried when Lance drove away without him. But her attention had eased his distress. She had comforted him even as he had filled a void she'd carried too long. *"Why can't we have a dog, Dad?"*

Because it was too much work. Their hours were too long. Their business took them both away for extended periods, and one did not have an animal underfoot when concentration was needed. She drew a sobering breath. Rese knew only too well what happened with distractions.

Lance had softened the saffron threads with wine and crushed the fennel seeds, sautéed the garlic and shrimp with a touch of cognac, then prepared the pasta and broccoli. It wasn't complicated. As Conchessa had taught, the quality of the outcome lay in timing and seasoning and prayer. *"You don't have to be fancy to be striking. Do it simply. Do it well. Do it with love and adoration. That makes it an offering."*

He loved having her words in his head. Though she had no chef's credentials and imparted none, in three short weeks she had tempered the epicurean excesses he'd learned from Nonna Antonia. Conchessa didn't use any ingredient not readily available or grown in the convent's garden. He appreciated her simplicity, but also Nonna's New York extravagance. He could incorporate both. If he were staying, he'd start an herb garden of his own and create masterpieces both simple and fancy.

For now, he dished the meal onto two plates, gave each dish a fork and napkin, and carried them outside. Rese looked up, a bemused expression on her face. Baxter wore the same. Good grief, they'd fallen for each other. Lance lowered one of the plates to Rese with the napkin caught underneath.

She took it, surprised. "I didn't expect delivery."

He settled onto the ground and gave Baxter a nudge with his knee, getting a reciprocal tail wag. "I didn't expect nursing care for the con dog."

Rese laughed, and Lance couldn't help watching her. If someone had told him the first day she was capable of that sound he would not have wagered money on it. Maybe it had been a really bad day, and that accounted for her lack of culinary enthusiasm. Even he had a slump now and then. But he'd put extra care into this effort.

She took a bite, chewed and swallowed, then proceeded with the next. He waited, but she didn't say anything, bite after bite. What was her problem? She'd even requested this meal!

Well, he was certainly not going to ask how she liked it. He ate his, satisfied that it was both balanced and delicious. Maybe she'd killed her taste buds eating all that packaged junk. Maybe she didn't know food was supposed to taste good. She finished it without a single comment. He couldn't help sending her a puzzled gaze.

"What?"

"Did you like it?" He ought to bite his tongue out.

She said, "Both meals could work for specials—if I decide to do that."

Lance swallowed the desire to shake her, took her plate with his, and strode into the kitchen. He washed them at the sink, then toweled his hands dry.

As he climbed the stairs, his phone rang. The jolt of anxiety made his fingers clumsy as he dug it from his pocket and saw his parents' number. Bad news? He'd just gotten started. Surely God would give him time . . .

"Lance here."

"Hey, *mon*?" The greeting rolled off with the musical intonation of Chaz's Jamaican accent. "You went to Rome and they didn't make you pope?"

He could hear laughter in the background. Anxiety drained like sand from a sieve. "Not Rome, Genoa." Chaz hadn't been there when he'd flown back home, gathered his bike and his dog, and headed for Sonoma. Lance had been purposely vague with those who were there, and they'd probably put Chaz up to this call. He didn't like keeping things from them, but

Nonna's wish was clear. This was for him and no one else.

"What are you doing on the wrong side of the country?"

"I'm working." Lance reached the attic and surveyed the challenge before him.

"There's no work in all the Islands of New York?" It comforted Chaz to think of the burroughs as islands.

Lance smiled. "Not like this." Mostly without pay and for undisclosed reasons.

"You're crazy, mon. You should come home."

"You sound like Momma. She standing behind you?"

Chaz laughed his slow, rolling laugh. "Giving me the evil eye. You know—the one that means no food until I find out what you are up to." There was a commotion, and he heard Momma in the background, then Chaz laughing again.

Lance had a pang of homesickness. He'd been pretty scattered the last few years, and it would have been nice to stay put for a while. But he was doing something important, more important than Momma or anyone else knew. "How's Nonna?"

"Not good."

His heart lurched.

"She tried to slap a nurse."

He tipped his head back with a grin. Desperation and fury, no doubt. But if she was strong enough to have a temper . . . *Thank you, Lord.* "Keep an eye on her for me, Chaz."

"Two eyes, I see better that way, mon."

Lance laughed. "Yeah. Me too." He'd need both eyes and all his wits to handle this situation. But the call had reaffirmed his intentions. No irritations would weaken his resolve. Not with Nonna still so debilitated. Her words from the letter written to Conchessa years ago came back to mind. *I cannot give you names or details but I feel it in my heart, a storm worse than nature. I fear we will lose everything.*

CHAPTER FOUR

Watching the young people next door made her feel strangely insubstantial, as though seeing the world she would leave, a play progressing without the players from the previous scene. It was an unusual thought. The pneumonia in her lungs had eroded her strength and left her bored and reflective—vaporish. Not her accustomed mode at all.

But to have Ralph's house occupied by strangers—young people making it something different, something new—gave her pause. Even if hours in bed hadn't driven her nearly batty, her condition certainly provided an excuse to take an interest in the goings-on next door. A nosy old busybody? No, a sick old woman with a view. Evvy chuckled, coughed, then hacked.

Oh, for a good deep breath without coughing, and a doctor who didn't look at her as though she might wither up and sail off on the next breeze. X-rays, antibiotics, this and that top-notch treatment. Her adverse reactions to all the drugs so far brought it down to her own constitution and whether it cared to carry on.

Just now the little drama next door gave her something to ponder, and that was good. Once she lost interest in life, she would take the chariot ride and welcome it. She might just nudge the driver over and take the reins herself. *Here comes Evvy Potter, Lord, ready or not.*

She was not morose. Her friends called regularly, and the more mobile of them came to visit, but risk of contagion, since she couldn't tolerate the antibiotics, had put a damper on her social life. No, she was glad for the distraction of the dark-haired woman working like a hired man with her tools in her belt and brogans on her feet. Evvy was itching to see what had been done inside, but . . . if it was too different, would it be painful?

Stuff and nonsense. Change was a fact of life; to let it cause pain was a weakness she didn't possess. A momentary, mellow pining after better days couldn't be helped. Beyond that? No Pitiful Pearl, she. Each day had something, some small moment to gather in like a bubble on her wet palm.

And the little vignette played out in the next door garden had given her that moment. She chuckled, stepping back from the window. It didn't drain her to stand there as it had before. She was improving, despite dire warnings from the doctor when she refused another antibiotic that would inflate her like a blowfish or spread a rash over parts better left unmentioned. She almost felt well enough for some fresh air. But she'd promised to rest a few more days, and she could ponder the tension that had been almost palpable in the scene she'd just witnessed.

She laughed softly, thinking of Ralph and his frequent exasperation, though he was too courtly to give full vent. It was bittersweet to recall. She hadn't seen him in so long, being too ill to risk a visit. Soon, perhaps, God willing. She sighed. All things in their time.

Just as Rese settled in to finish staining the trim, the chandelier arrived. This was not going to be a personally productive day. But she had enough experience to roll with it. She maneuvered the ladder beneath the socket, then went and called Lance down from the attic. She could install it, of course. But this was a chance to test his boast before she turned him loose on the kitchen fuse box and the wiring of the carriage house. She'd see whether he was just blowing electrical smoke.

When he joined her, she handed him the tool that stripped and cut wires. Maybe it was unfair to keep doubting him, but in spite of the positive references, she couldn't help it. Something niggled inside, and Rese knew better than to ignore it. When a situation seemed too good to be true, it usually was. Lance showing up with the skills he claimed was just not quite believable.

He took the tool. "Did you shut the breaker off?"

She sent him a scathing look.

He climbed up and trimmed the wires, stripping the ends free of old plastic.

So he knew what the tool was for. "Make sure you get off any corrosion."

"Uh-huh." He stuck the tool in his back pocket. "Okay, come on up."

"Up?"

"Bring the fixture."

Two of them on the ladder? She shifted the chandelier's weight. "I'm not sure that's safe."

He looked down. "My intentions are strictly electrical."

She glared. "I mean for the stability of the ladder."

"Well, neither one of us can hold and attach that monster alone."

Valid point. She climbed up with the heavy bronze chandelier until her feet filled the left half of the rung he occupied. Thankfully he was not a big man like her father. Their combined weight was probably not much more than Dad's alone. But there were still two of them, and she was trapped between Lance and the ladder, holding the chandelier up as he connected the wires and twisted the wing nuts.

She would have preferred to let him hold, but she hadn't set it up that way. Rethink her strategy? No, she still wanted proof. Trapped like that, she smelled the attic in his shirt. How many times had she smelled like old musty rooms? Maybe she did right now. That, or sweat and wood stain. She'd take that scent over—

"Screwdriver." He said it like a surgeon, and she had never liked to play nurse.

But she pulled the tool from her belt and handed it over. As he attached and tightened the anchoring bolts, she held the chandelier steady until he lowered his arms slowly with a hint of amusement. "Bulbs?"

She looked down. "I'll have to get them."

He held her elbow as she stepped down a rung. She pulled it away. Couldn't he tell she'd been on ladders all her life? She just didn't care to share them. It was tempting fate to use equipment as it wasn't intended. She reached the floor and called up, "I can do the bulbs myself."

"Fine." He came down and handed over the screwdriver. "I need to know about some items in the attic."

She slid the tool into its slot in her belt and said, "Show me." Curious to see what he'd found and how much progress he'd made, she followed him up.

He led her to the wall and pointed to a half dozen rolled woolen rugs. One was spread out across the others. "They're in decent condition if you want to clean them up. They were wrapped in mothballs."

She could smell that, an odor she adored in spite of its toxicity. The floral colors would work for several of the rooms. "Great."

"Where would you like them?"

"The second-floor landing." She looked around. "What else have you found?"

"Not much. A vase." He handed it to her. "Most of the stuff is garbage. Makes you wonder why folks don't throw it away in the first place."

"Maybe it was still good when they stashed it here. Or had sentimental value." She looked at the vase, painted with wild flowers, tipped it up and studied the bottom. There was faint writing there, and she angled it to the light bulb. A signature. Probably the artist. "I wonder who Flavio was?"

Lance snatched it. "Who?"

"It says Flavio on the bottom. The artist, I guess. It looks hand painted." Rese glanced around the attic again. "I'm surprised it's survived up here. I would have thought everything of value had been looted."

Lance's fingers tightened on the vase, a frown creasing his forehead.

"What's the matter?"

His smile looked forced. "Nothing."

She searched his face, not nearly gullible enough to believe that. "You're upset about something."

He handed the vase back. "I hate the thought of vandals and thieves. Things of value lost to greed and stupidity."

"I doubt there's anything in here that's seriously valuable." She turned the vase in her hands. It looked and felt old, dimmed by a black film, though Lance must have wiped it off. There were no doubt years of dust inside. "Where was this?"

"Tucked in between the eaves behind the newspapers. Probably full of spiders."

She shot him a glare, then turned the vase upside down and shook it.

He laughed. "I already did that much. No spider with any decent web would dislodge so easily."

She felt the narrow channel of the neck, considered the wide bowl beneath and imagined too clearly exactly what he described. When he reached for the vase, she handed it over.

"I'll clean it out for you."

Rese took a few steps deeper into the attic, rested her hands on her hips. A case of canning jars and an old bike might bring something at the antique store. A chewed-up vinyl chair probably housed mice. Lance might be teasing about the spiders, but she was glad he'd tackled this job. "Anything else?"

"Not yet."

She turned at his tone, but he smiled blandly. She did not have time for his games. "Well, call me if you find anything."

"Would that include wildlife?"

She frowned. "Anything living you may consider yours."

He'd consider more than that his. Lance turned over the vase and read the signature there for himself. How many Flavios could there be? Only one that he'd heard of when Conchessa told him Antonia's lineage and what she'd learned through years of letters.

Flavio came into the story much earlier than Lance had intended to look. Was there a date on the vase? He pulled a box of magazines underneath the light bulb, climbed on it, and held up the vase. '89. If he was right, that was 1889—and Flavio had once courted his great-great-grandmother Carina.

Curbing his excitement, Lance worked until it grew too dim in the attic to continue. If he were simply clearing it out, he would make much quicker progress, but he had to search carefully, or he might miss something important, as he'd missed the signature on that vase.

He carried it downstairs with him to the kitchen, carefully soaked and washed the grime, then dried it as the heirloom it was. He'd have to make sure Rese kept it in a safe place. For now he set it in a corner of the kitchen where she'd be unlikely to notice.

A twinge stirred inside. He wasn't keeping it from her. He was just getting answers. He'd decide what to do with them when the time was right. He stroked the globe of the vase, then he went and found Rese working in the dining room.

He squinted up at the flame-shaped bulbs in the chandelier, then noted her progress. She was creating an ambient space, perfectly suited to his culinary ideas. "Are we serving dinner to the guests?"

She turned from the trim she stained with smooth even strokes, then followed his gaze back over the room. "I haven't decided."

He didn't miss her switch from plural to singular. But then he was only the lackey. Whatever sense of ownership he'd gained in both the kitchen and the attic were in his own mind. "I'm leaving now. It's too dark in the attic." He dug in his jeans pocket for his keys. "I'll finish tomorrow."

"You're not cooking?"

He fought to keep the resentment from his face. "I signed out." He'd already logged more hours onto the pad in the kitchen than a normal workday, and she didn't merit another personal effort. "There are ramen noodles in the cabinet."

She nodded. "Good night."

He walked out, and a sharp whistle brought Baxter running. Lance climbed onto the Harley, and Baxter leaped into his lap and sat. Yeah, no wanting in that dog. Lance secured the hind legs into the leather pockets and started the bike. He picked up burgers at Murphy's for both of them and drove to the Sonoma Valley Inn.

In his room with Baxter, Lance took up his guitar and pondered Rese Barrett's Wayfaring Inn. The name didn't fit. It sounded weak and transient for a place that had stood so long and known hard work and suffering. And loss. He clenched his jaw.

What had Nonna been trying to say? He pictured her tortured efforts to give him the message, something she wanted him to do for her, something it might be too late to do. *No.* He slapped his hand on the guitar, giving Baxter a start.

Nonna Antonia would recover. She was a fighter. And as she fought to regain her faculties, he would pursue a cause he didn't yet understand. He might be tilting at windmills, but the faded envelope she'd pressed into his hand had sent him to Conchessa, and what he'd learned there had brought him to Sonoma.

Without speaking, Nonna Antonia had sent him on this errand as she had so many others through his boyhood years. She couldn't explain it with half her face hanging and half her brain uncooperative. But she'd sent him off to do something important, and he meant to do it. The brightness in her eyes when he'd kissed her papery cheek had told him she knew he would do whatever it took.

Rese lay in the dark. Why did nighttime have to be a battle? Sleep her enemy? She had spent most of her life in old houses, and she knew the sounds they made. She knew the dark held no monsters, the shadows no ghosts. Why couldn't she fend off the emptiness as thoroughly as the real-life taunts and teases?

The engineer's report had been thorough, and she'd addressed the structural issues, fortifying the villa with sound construction and new seals on the old windows. It should be tight as a drum and strong as an ox and . . . all that kind of thing. But lying there now as wind bullied the house, shouldering the walls with monstrous heaves, she heard another moan. It sounded like a person in pain, a pain that spoke of sorrow and anger and wrongdoing.

Nonsense. Nothing but wind. Unless . . .

Had Lance stirred up something in the attic? Even as she thought it, a howl tightened the tendons of her neck. What terrible thing had happened in the house? She didn't want to know! She pulled the comforter up with a jerk. *Don't be stupid.* What if someone saw her like this?

Oh, wouldn't the guys just love to learn she was spooked. Scared to be alone? Scared of a little noise? No way. But what was it? She jammed a fist into her eye and rubbed. It didn't matter. She needed to sleep.

Her shoulder ached; her arm didn't seem to have a place to go, and she'd have a stiff neck before it was over. She forced her muscles to relax. It was quiet for long enough that she almost succumbed, then a sharp thump jolted her, and she listened hard. All the bad movies of deranged people locked in attics and all Mom's ghost stories converged in her mind.

She should never have told Lance to clean it. That caught her up short, and anger stirred. What was she thinking? She was not afraid. She just wanted to sleep, and the noise distracted her, made her wonder. Had she missed something—but what? She'd been methodical, thorough. Except for the attic.

She'd done no work up there, marshaling her resources and energy into the areas requiring it. Once Lance had it cleaned out she would inspect and correct whatever weakness the wind had found. There was a logical explanation for the moans. No ghosts or . . . people in pain.

But what if *he* had come? A frisson of real fear climbed her spine. If Walter . . . *Stop it!* She had not thought of him for years. He wasn't real. Had never been real. She knew that. But . . . *Stop.* She had enough trouble sleeping without adding irrational thoughts. Irrational? She'd spent more nights than she wanted to recall watching for Walter in the shadows.

That didn't make him real, and she refused to waste another minute on it. She rolled to her side and punched the pillow into shape. Temperature, moisture, age, some flaw the wind exposed. Those were the things that made houses noisy in the night. Sound carried when everything was still.

A low howl sounded above her. She gritted her teeth. If there were critters in the attic, Lance would find them. Anything else, she would correct. As soon as he had it cleaned out she would do a thorough inspection. She pressed her eyes closed and made them stay that way. She would not tolerate irrational fears. If she could face down the unruly men in her father's work crew, she could face an empty old house.

And sleep in it. She would sleep. She would.

CHAPTER FIVE

Knees crusted with dirt.
Sharp snick of the knife.
The warm weight of the fruit in my palms.
How easy my feet, how light. My basket overflows.
Other hands. Many hands. Hands joined together.
We laugh. We sing. We dance between the vines.
It is the best time there is, when the land
gives back what we have poured out.

When Lance arrived the next morning, he let himself in with the key to the kitchen door that Rese had given him. He saw no sign of her, but the cadence of the morning news came through the wall from her suite. Since he didn't want to get caught where she might expect him to cook, he logged his starting time on the pad in the kitchen and went upstairs. Payment was secondary motivation. Money had never been enough to keep him somewhere, and it meant even less this time. But since cleaning the attic was the only thing he was being paid for at the moment, he'd keep track of the time.

The air was damp and chilly under the eaves this morning, and he realized he'd left the small window open all night. He bent and lifted a portable movie screen that must have blown over, then climbed across the piles and closed the window. He turned back and surveyed the situation with an almost tangible anticipation.

There might be nothing else in the attic remotely connected to him, but in his dreams he'd crept through the debris, finding pieces of the story buried in corners. And Nonna Antonia had watched over him as he fit them together like a broken mirror, then peered inside. It wasn't only his reflection in the glass, but Nonna's and others with her.

With that in mind, he set about removing rolls of linoleum and old paint cans. It was amazing the place hadn't combusted, and after an hour or so, reality was dispelling his dream. As Rese said, the chances of finding something of value up there was less than likely.

Too soon she came up, her assertive posture hammering home the truth of the situation. He was a minion. "Sounds like war up here." She looked around as though expecting something besides him, an army he might have smuggled in?

"The hammock." He motioned toward an old steel frame with a crispy canvas sling he had dragged into the cleared section of the floor. The thing weighed a ton and had rubber grips on the bottom that slid like a washboard when he pulled. "Want it?" His mouth twitched with laughter, but she had to look twice before she caught the joke, then dismissed it with a shrug.

"With a new sling, it wouldn't be bad."

Given her penchant for resurrecting old things, he shouldn't be surprised. But he gave it a dubious inspection.

She tipped her head. "We could spray-paint it."

Had she actually said we? "Where do you want it?"

"Out back for now. I'll help." She grabbed one side of the frame and lifted, realized its mass and adjusted her grip. "Ready?"

He caught the other side and followed.

"Watch the stairs, here. They're steep."

"Thank you." He couldn't help grinning behind her back. He'd safely navigated those stairs quite a few times now. But if she felt better instructing him, more power to her.

She tipped the hammock sideways to pass through the door, and he noted the flex and shape of her in T-shirt and painter's pants. A loose T-shirt no more hid a shapely form than an unshapely one, though he guessed she meant it to.

Why she didn't make more of what she had he couldn't guess, but it was just as well, considering he had a job to do. He could only attribute his errant thoughts to that seriously misplaced sense of connection. They lodged the hammock near the garden shed. "Until I decide what to do with it," she said.

Ah. So the work was "we" but the decisions were "I." This girl wanted control.

"Fine." He went back up. So far there had been nothing resembling records or personal papers of any sort in the attic. He would probably do all the work for nothing. But he hauled out another stack of newspapers, these from the late sixties, and left them in the driveway with the others.

There was a button jar and a box of handkerchiefs that a woman might find interesting. He put them in the "things for Rese" spot and removed a web-infested pile of rags to find a mouse nest complete with scurrying creatures that escaped into the eaves. They'd have to put out traps.

Lance hauled the rags down to the driveway and informed her. Did he imagine her shudder? She walked like a man, worked like a man, acted like a man, but was that a girlish gesture?

He said, "We'll need traps."

"Get whatever you need and give me the receipts."

"You want the kind where they stick inside and wiggle around until they die, or the ones that snap their necks?"

She shot him a dark look. "Did you need to ask that?"

"You like to make the decisions."

"I gave you charge of the wildlife."

Like God with Adam.

She drew herself up. "Use the ones that do it quick. I don't want them to suffer."

"Okay. I found a couple things you might like. You wanna see?"

She was studiously indifferent. "Bring them down later."

He hadn't imagined it. She didn't want to go near the mice. Huh. He wouldn't have guessed her a chair climber. Anything but. Though he could imagine what she'd say if he voiced it aloud. He fought a smile, then laughed silently. She was the sort of woman who just begged teasing—not that he'd ever dream of doing it.

Rese took a few minutes to regain her composure, wishing she had not pictured what he described so clearly, and definitely glad Lance had tackled the attic. She didn't have to feel guilty. It was a simple division of labor.

She stepped out into another gray morning that did not mean rain. In the valley, nearly every morning began with a dull sky that yielded later to thirsty sunshine that drank up the morning moisture and returned warmth. It was why the grapes thrived, a giving and taking, a rhythm she sensed even if she had no patience for it. At this hour, the dew had dissipated, but the sun had not yet broken through, and it was not as dry as she'd have liked.

But she had wasted time yesterday and was getting a late start today. Fewer distractions would be a good thing. Crossing to the garden shed, she gauged the moisture still dampening the surfaces. It would be better if it was dry, but she'd given it as long as she could. She hauled the ladder out and stretched it to the roof, then went back to the shed for the brush.

This was one job she did not relish, but with the chimney coughing soot at every bump, she had to sweep it before the gas conversion could be done. She climbed up with the long-handled brush and extenders, then pulled herself onto the roof. It was high and steep, and the tiles were slick as she'd expected.

She walked carefully, though she'd been traversing roofs and scaffolding as long as she could remember. There was no excuse for carelessness no matter what your experience. The tiles had withstood the ravages of time better than she would have expected, and that had been a major selling point for this particular property.

From the corner of her eye she saw Lance hauling a load out to the driveway, but she kept her attention on the slippery surface. She reached the chimney and circled it with the strap attached to her waist belt, then prepared to lower the brush. Strident screeches and flapping wings erupted at her face. She jerked backward, fending off the birds with the brush. In spite of the strap and belt, her foot slipped and one knee hit the edge of a tile. She bit back her cry, but a moment later Lance climbed the roof to her.

"Are you all right?"

She gritted her teeth and rubbed the knee. "Why wouldn't I be?"

He noted the turkey buzzards still circling. "Looked like a scene from *The Birds*." The corners of his mouth quirked. "They must be roosting in there." He steadied himself by the strap attached to her belt.

Rese pulled herself up. "They'll have to roost elsewhere. I need to clean the chimney so the gas conversion pipes can go through."

"Let the installers deal with it."

"Yeah, well, I'm the installer." She positioned the brush again.

"You're doing the conversion?"

"I don't trust anyone else with gas." Lance gave her a curious look, but she didn't analyze her quirks or explain them. She thrust the brush into the chimney and sent him a sideways glance. "I don't need help."

He looked up. "Sure?"

"Yes, I'm sure." Rese jammed the brush down and attached another segment to the handle. Cranky from lack of sleep, her knee throbbing, she smarted worse from his seeing her panic. The birds' initial aggression had been startled fear, and she should have realized that and backed away. Instead she'd shown fear and weakness. He made no further comment, though, as he stood watch.

Ash-scented dust arose as she scrubbed a century's crud from the walls. It would have been worse dry, so there was some benefit to the damp, even if it had made her look stupid. She swiped her arm over her eyes and nose. Lance kept his gaze on the sky, but the birds circled lazily, too stupid to realize the destruction to their domicile.

She added the last extender and scrubbed the lowest portion. Maybe not a professional job, but adequate for her purposes. She drew the brush out, detached the extenders and said, "That's it. You can go down now."

He slid his gaze from the sky to the ground. "Ever notice how up is easier?"

She detached her strap and slid it from his hand. "Don't think about it. Just go." She read the hesitation in his face and noticed today he wore a small gold hoop in his ear. A man who changed his earrings. "Don't tell me you're acrophobic."

"Hadn't really thought about it before." He clung with one hand to the chimney.

She slacked a hip. "Oh, that's great. You come to the rescue, and now I have to carry you down?"

He jutted his chin. "Did I say that?"

"I don't see you going."

"I'm going." He leaned a little.

"Impressive." She arched her eyebrows.

Mumbling, he let go of the chimney and started down the roof—as she'd expected. Goad a man's pride and he's capable of anything. He reached the ladder and pulled himself over the edge without looking up.

She snatched up the brush and started for the ladder herself, then swung over the side too confidently. The brush caught the gutter, and she gouged her side on the edge of the ladder. Clenching her teeth, she hung immobile until the pain lessened, then slowly started down. Stupid birds. Stupid man. Stupid . . . Rese. She'd been careless.

The flash of a blood-spattered wall seized her mind. She pressed her eyes shut and paused her descent, fighting the images until the pain radiating from her side penetrated her mental paralysis. The injury couldn't be that bad, even though the safety plastic had long since broken off the aluminum edge that gouged her. It just hurt. She reached the ground and tossed the brush and attachments, then turned to find Lance still there. She had expected him to huff off and be long gone, but he must have seen it all.

"How bad is it?"

"Not." She pressed her hand to her side.

With a firm motion, he pulled her hand away and lifted the edge of her shirt. The soft flesh above her hip was fairly mangled, blood filling the ridges. The air made it sting even worse.

"First aid kit?"

She sighed. "In my tool box. I'll take care of it." She tugged her shirt out of his hand. "It's no big deal." Except the embarrassment. Accidents happened when you lost your focus. If he hadn't come up on the roof, she wouldn't have lost it, but she wasn't passing the blame.

She was answerable to herself and took full responsibility. She had learned early on to be neither a hindrance nor a liability. But between her side and her aching knee, she hadn't done too well with this one.

Inside the garden shed, she yanked open the lid of the first aid kit, took out three medicated bandages and attached them to her side, stinging more with indignation than pain. Next time he lifted her shirt, she'd take his head off with a shovel.

Oh, heavens, they were amusing. She could almost imagine the Lord had provided them for her entertainment. She had worked the window open an inch or so to let in the spring air and seen the two of them on the roof like scarecrows, arms flailing as the buzzards flapped about them.

They were no longer in sight, but she stood at the window drawing the inch of fresh air in with small, pathetic breaths. She still imagined herself a robust, mite-sized dynamo, in spite of the cane, the aches, the time it took to do any small thing. Young at heart was a cliché, and Lord knew, her heart was as old as the rest of her. Youth, however, was a matter of perspective.

It might truly be wasted on the young, as the saying went, who had too little experience to see clearly. Take the angst-ridden pair next door. Without perspective, it was easy to squabble over little things. All that energy, and so little temperance. Evvy chuckled. That was what made them so much fun.

A small brown wren landed on the side of the roof beneath her. It hopped about in troubled bursts, finding a seed or a bit of fluff for a nest. She hadn't filled her feeder in over a month. No wonder the bird tipped its head so scornfully her way.

"Have you not heard? 'Look at the birds of the air; they do not sow or reap or store away in barns, and yet your heavenly Father feeds them.' You'll have to look to Him for now, as I do . . . as I do."

Evvy turned from the window and surveyed her room. It looked a little weary these days. Too long since it had received a thorough cleaning. Rainbow dust motes fluttered in the sunbeams breaking through the morning clouds, but the surfaces showed little settled there. That much she could do and did.

With her hand gripping the footboard, she made the sliding motion that was her gait now that arthritis had settled in her knees, then let go and reached for her dresser. Over the years she had emptied the place of things people found valuable, leaving her room and most of the house quite Spartan. When she and her mother had moved in next to Ralph, things were still affordable. She wouldn't be living in the house now if she hadn't inherited it. But the antiques still housed there would keep her solvent until the end. More than one dated back almost to the Bear Revolution when California declared itself its own country. Her mother had collected; she dispensed.

There were only a few things atop the rectangular doily on her dresser. No jewelry box, just an eyeglass case, hairbrush and comb, and two silver-framed photographs. She gazed at them fondly, her beaus. One in a soldier's uniform at the train station, the other in his garden, the one that grew just over the hedge from her own. She lifted the photograph of the soldier, studied the strong lines of his young face. Duty written there. She nodded and set him down.

The other face showed humor and a *joie de vivre* in the many lines around his eyes and mouth. Oh, he could charm a rat to dance. But she hadn't given him the advantage. They could battle it out when they all three gathered in heaven. She chuckled and started the trek to her bathroom.

Lance stalked to the carriage house. Yes, Rese had looked as though she needed help. But next time, unless she was frothing at the mouth, he would not repeat that mistake. In fact, frothing might not be enough. Talk about an attitude. He should have let the buzzards have her.

He grabbed the shovel he had left leaning in the corner, and the blisters on his palms smarted. He hadn't done this sort of work lately. But if Rese could handle her end, he could handle his. *Acrophobic? Carry me down?* A bee flew in and buzzed his head, and he batted it into the wall where it droned dizzily along until it took flight through the open roof.

Lance thrust the shovel into the sandy ground. Gulls and pigeons winged overhead, and the buzzards still circled. Restoring the carriage house was on his own time, thanks to his impulsive offer. He could have gone back to the attic, but right now he needed to forget he worked for Rese Barrett. That was a sham anyway, a means to an end.

He started digging where he'd left off. He had to clear the vegetation and make a smooth bed for the cement slab. But as he thrust, the shovel scraped. He cleared the sand and found a paving stone. Huh?

He cleared some more. Not just one stone, but several. He moved to another area, and another. A floor—one that great-great-grandfather Quillan might have laid himself, with stones cut from the nearby quarry.

Lance bent and stroked the stones, feeling the labor that had laid them, the care and pride that put such a floor in a carriage house. He pressed his palm there, eyes closed, purpose and connection surging once again. *Lord.* In spite of Rese and her attitude, in spite of his own shortcomings, there was something here that mattered, and it was all part of a plan. He carefully cleared stone after stone, cut so precisely and set so tightly he might not need grout at all. He'd rather keep it in its original condition.

It was a gift unsought. The property offering itself, saving him time and effort by the work of hands that came before. An inheritance. Lance swallowed the swelling in his throat, humbled and grateful. He was making too much of a simple thing, but he couldn't help it. Life was fragile, and the shadows left behind touched those who came after.

Hooves and feet had trodden this floor, but Lance knelt on it now and blessed those feet, those hands that laid the stones to make his floor. He had no right to think of it as his, but Conchessa had told him to trust the urgings within and sense his way. He pressed his forehead to the stone wall. *Show me.*

After several heartbeats, he opened his eyes. Enough dreaming. Back to work. He pulled himself up by the shovel. Strange so much sand had accumulated. He almost suspected it had been intentional, though even if the place had been used as a garage or stable or animal pen later on, it would have been better to keep the stone floor.

He continued to clear it, filling another wheelbarrow. He emptied it into the shallow gully behind the structure, then took up the shovel again. He didn't mind the work now. It was a labor of love. *Do it simply; do it well.* And appreciate what came of it because nothing was sure. Nothing in this life.

He cleared the rest of the floor in a few wheelbarrow loads, then set about sweeping. The large flat stones were well laid, level and tightly fitted, and he cleaned them off now with due care. Whisking the broom, he glimpsed something metallic wedged into the corner.

Like an archeologist on a dig, he squatted down and dug it out of the crusted dirt with his fingers. Breath catching, he turned the skeleton shape over in his hands, then tapped the dirt from the filigreed base blackened with age. A key! How symbolic was that? But a key to what?

He glanced around him. The lost carriage house doors or a carriage itself? Maybe a trunk or something in the house—in the attic? Lance rubbed it with his fingers, heart rushing with heightened hope. He didn't know yet, but he *would* put the pieces together and learn what he'd come for. He closed the key into his palm. A key to unlock secrets . . .

Baxter ran in, frisking, then ran back out. A moment later, Rese appeared in the doorway. "Your lumber's here."

He slipped the key into his pocket and turned. "Okay." He pushed past her to accept the delivery. Rese, of course, would pay.

No surprise that she oversaw the lumber unloaded beside the carriage house, but she did surprise him with, "You estimated that well."

He stared. A word of praise? *I have found favor in your eyes, O great one?*

She paid the drivers and sent them on their way. "You'll want a tarp on the drywall overnight. I have some in the truck." She motioned toward her vehicle. "Help yourself."

He started to thank her, but she was already heading back to the house. "How's your side?"

"It's fine." She kept walking.

And he had to agree, at least the glimpse he'd gotten of it earlier. He looked away. What was he thinking? She'd have a royal fit if she read his thoughts. Heaven forbid he think of her as a girl, much less a woman. Better he remember she was his means to an end.

He covered the drywall, then whistled for Baxter. Lunch time. He'd been petty yesterday, ignoring Rese's obvious request for an evening meal. But the same reluctance nagged him now. She wasn't insulting or critical of his cooking, just so irritatingly blank.

With the dog before him, he drove into town and ate lunch at the Cucina Viansa on the plaza. The focaccia sandwich wasn't anything to rave about. No one made focaccia bread like Nonna, not even Conchessa, though even hers would put this one to shame. But Baxter wouldn't know the difference. Lance carried the remainder outside where the retriever had attracted a crowd. "Entertaining again, Baxter?"

The three women turned. "Is he yours? He's adorable. What a great dog."

A freckled blonde said, "Aren't you worried he'll run off?"

Lance shrugged. "He knows I'm inside. He'd be insulted if I tied him."

They laughed. "He's so friendly."

"And gentle." That from the taller brunette.

"Hear that, Baxter?" Lance handed over the sandwich that Baxter accepted in a gulp. "They've got your number."

Baxter wagged, eating up the praise as readily as he'd taken the food. Lance mounted the motorcycle parked at the curb and the dog jumped aboard. Not one person scolded. They laughed and exclaimed and waved as he secured Baxter and drove away.

Rese was nowhere in sight when he parked and went back to the carriage house, but she had set up a workspace along the outer wall with the tools he'd need to begin framing. He glanced at the house with a guilty twinge. She'd prepared it while he had lunch in town? He sighed. Her meals were not his responsibility.

She had probably set up the workstation to make sure it was done right, though she could have expected him back in the attic. His excitement now was for the old structure, but she wouldn't have known that, would she? He looked toward the house. Maybe she wasn't as oblivious as he'd thought.

He pulled the tape measure from his belt and got to work. As afternoon drew on to evening, he cut and built the struts and beams for the roof, framing out skylights to supplement the one small window in the back wall. French doors in the front where the old carriage doors had hung would also keep the feel open. He framed out standard sizes there, thankful for the two summers he'd worked with Habitat for Humanity. Building the kingdom of God—literally.

This was not unlike the basic places he'd built for people needing decent housing, except for the existing stone walls and the incredible floor. Tomorrow he would frame out the bedroom and bath, and after that he'd trench for plumbing, gas, and electrical. He laid down Rese's hammer and looked at the walls lying flat across the stone floor. What would Quillan Shepard think of the changes made here? Thinking of his ancestor made him want to do it well, to make him proud. Lance clenched his hands and closed his eyes. *Lord, help*—

"You've made progress."

He spun.

Rese stood in the opening, but squatted suddenly. "Oh wow. I didn't know there was a stone floor." She touched it with near reverence. "I thought you'd have to pour a slab."

"I have no idea why it was buried in sand."

"It's great. Look how well the stones fit together."

She looked so utterly likable he had to bite back the announcement that his great-great-grandfather might have laid it. He didn't know that for sure. Quillan could have hired a team of Italian stoneworkers. Sonoma had plenty of them working the quarry, since those stones had also paved the streets of San Francisco. The floor might even have been added later, by another relative, or not.

Her gaze went over the framework lying across the stone. "You're glassing the front? I thought you might." She was good.

He asked, "Where did you learn construction?"

She stood up. "My dad. Where did you?"

"Habitat."

She pressed her hands to her hips. "You built homes for the poor?"

She didn't have to look so incredulous. "What part has you stunned— that I would, or that I could?"

"Both frankly. You don't look the type."

And there he'd been thinking positive thoughts about her. "What's the type?"

She shrugged. "Bigger, stronger, less . . . stylish."

Good thing he wasn't violent.

She noticed his scribbled plan lying among the two-by-fours. "You're partitioning?"

With a sigh, he picked it up and showed her. "Bed and bath." He'd done plenty of plumbing work in Pop's building, where much of his family still lived.

She looked up. "I didn't budget a bathroom."

I didn't budget a bathroom, he mocked. "What did you think I'd use?"

She frowned. "It's an expense I didn't plan on."

"You're getting a heck of a deal here." She knew it too. Labor far outweighed materials.

She stood a long moment, then nodded. "Okay."

"Gee, thanks."

She slanted him a glance. "It's not like any of this was in my original plans."

He swung his arm. "Say the word, I'll go away." Where had that come from? He wasn't going anywhere. But she irritated him more than anyone he'd known.

She faced him full on. "No need to get emotional."

Now his hands were on his hips. "Emotional? You know that word?"

She raised her hands. "Cool it. I'll budget the fixtures." She turned to leave.

"You didn't answer my question."

She looked back over her shoulder. "What question?"

"Got a concept of emotion?"

She met and held his eyes, but didn't answer, just turned and stalked toward the house. Lance ran a hand over his mouth and jaw. Stone. Obsidian. Marble. He could plant her in the garden for a fountain. A tune started in his head, and words joined to the notes. *In the garden cold as stone a woman, skin of bronze. Heartbeat still and silent, and scorn is in her gaze.* He shook his head. In spite of her lean curves, she was totally devoid of feminine softness. He frowned as she disappeared into the inn. No man in his right mind would take her on. Good thing she had a business to run.

His heart skipped stride. No, wait a minute. She did not need this house more than he. Nothing personal. It was ancestral.

CHAPTER SIX

Rese did not appreciate his insinuation. Just because she didn't laugh her head off or cry her eyes out didn't mean she was without emotion. She'd worked hard for her self-control, too hard. And these last months, harder still.

He had no idea what a strain this whole project had been, a daunting exercise in determination and fortitude after . . . Her throat clenched. Capable of emotion? He should climb inside her skin for a day, see how hard she worked just to go on. She hadn't expected sympathy from the guys, and when it came it was harder to take than their taunting. But she hadn't shown that either. She wouldn't. Rese raised her chin, thinking how surprised they had been when she sold the company and walked away.

Her stomach growled. She had hoped Lance might make dinner. He hadn't cooked since yesterday's lunch, and wasn't that what she'd hired him for? She jerked open the cabinet and studied the scant assortment of canned vegetables and packaged soup. She closed it and went to the refrigerator. She'd had a sandwich for lunch and didn't relish repeating it.

She huffed. When did that begin to matter? Food was food. It kept a body working. She had wanted more of Lance's cooking, but there was no way she'd go out and ask him now. He wasn't on the clock while he built his own place. Materials and tools. That was their deal.

She supposed materials did include bathroom fixtures, and the stove to heat the place as she'd seen on his drawing. She should have thought of that, and would have under ordinary circumstances. If she had planned the carriage house remodel, she would have considered all the details and their cost.

She'd been scrupulously on budget until Lance came. But it was true she was getting a deal—labor for materials, and the carriage house finished. She closed the refrigerator and stalked to her suite to shower. The water stung the gouge on her side and reminded her of her carelessness. That would not happen again. If she kept her mind on her work, there would be no room for accidents.

When she came back out, she found Lance washing at the kitchen sink. She searched his face quickly for signs of irritation, but he seemed to be over it. "Are you going to make dinner?"

He shook his hands dry. "No."

"I'll buy the ingredients."

He grabbed a towel and rubbed his forearms. "I'm tired."

She knew how that was. How many times had she dragged into the kitchen, wanting nothing more than to have the meal materialize like magic? As she had wanted just now? Lance's magic.

Rese shoved down the disappointment. She'd grab something to eat, spend the evening trying to get tired enough to sleep . . . She drew herself up. "I was thinking. You don't have to keep your hotel room. You could stay upstairs until your place is done." She caught hold of her upper arms. "That way Baxter wouldn't have to be cooped up."

"He's fine."

She glanced out the kitchen window to where the dog lay, head on his paws, under the almond tree. "Why pay for a room when mine are furnished and ready? You could choose—"

"I thought you didn't want me in the house."

Rese dropped her gaze to the floor. She had made that point, but last night had been eerie and more sleepless than usual. She didn't want to go through that again. If Lance heard noises, she'd know she wasn't imagining it. "If you are all the way upstairs—"

"I'm not likely to molest you?"

She turned, surprised.

"You don't have a high opinion of men, do you?"

Where did he get that idea? "Look, it was just a thought. Don't get—"

"Emotional?"

"Can I ever finish my own sentences?"

He crossed his arms. "All right. Don't get what?"

"Upset."

He rolled his eyes to the side.

"I was going to say if you were upstairs and I was down here, we'd each have our own space. By the time you're finished out back, I'll be taking guests, so I won't be alone . . ." She hadn't meant to say that.

He cocked his head. "Are you scared?"

She huffed out a breath. "No."

One side of his mouth pulled. "Tell the truth."

"I'm not scared, it's . . ." For once she wished he'd furnish the last word. She ran her fingers over her hair. "I haven't slept well. The house is . . ."

"Haunted?" The smile spread.

"Don't be ridiculous."

He laughed, then gruffed his voice. "You want I should protect you?"

She glared. "I'm not sure what a man with an earring could do."

Face hardening, he reached up to his gold ring. "This makes me less of a man?"

"I didn't mean that."

"Yes, you did." The fire was back in his eyes.

"I'm just not used to it, that's all. The men on my crew—"

"Your crew?"

She swallowed. "Yes, my crew. Is that hard to accept? That I bossed a construction crew?"

"No, I can see it perfectly."

Somehow that wasn't a compliment. She threw up her hands. "Forget it, okay?"

He drew his upper lip in between his teeth. "You think I'm a wimp."

She shot her gaze to the ceiling.

"An emotional weakling."

She drew breath to argue, but he stepped close and glowered. "Just because I don't walk around scratching and belching, because I happen to like the look of an earring, that doesn't mean I'm—"

"I didn't think you were." She squirmed under his gaze.

He swallowed. "You don't exactly bring out the best in a man."

That hit her low. "Why not?"

"You walk and talk and act tough."

"So?"

"So you are not a man, even if you have a man's name."

"My name is Theresa."

He stopped and studied her for too long.

She looked away. "Don't call me that; I hate it."

"Because it's pretty?"

She didn't answer. Dad had called her Rese since she was little. It was Mom who called her Theresa, and mostly when "he" had come.

"I bet you'd just hate it if I said you were pretty."

A flush crawled up her neck. She didn't have to listen to this.

"Well, I have news for you. You are pretty. Short hair, baggy T-shirts, and all."

She fumed. "Are you finished?"

"No. I'd like to take you out for dinner tonight."

"What?" She jammed her hands to her hips.

He leaned against the counter. "That's right. I'm asking for a date."

The man had lost his mind.

He cocked his head. "Unless you'd rather have a sandwich or a can of beans."

Her stomach protested, but she brought up her chin. "I don't date my employees."

"Consider me a partner."

"I don't need a partner." She uncrossed and recrossed her arms.

He said gently, "Consider me a friend."

Rese had no ready answer to that. She'd spent most of her life with men. But her energy even as a girl had been spent besting them. "I don't know how to do that." Not that she excelled with women either. Her best friend, Star, should have been a butterfly. She flitted in to suck the nectar of acceptance and carried away particles of stability, which she nevertheless lost along the way.

He pushed off the counter. "Well, first you agree to spend time together. Like an evening over dinner."

She shook her head.

"Why not? You'd have eaten with me if I cooked it."

"That's different."

"Because I'm working for you?" He made it sound ugly.

Had she meant that? She understood that relationship. Knew how to handle it.

He narrowed his eyes and shook his head. "You are really something." He crossed in front of her, went out the back door and whistled shrilly for his dog. A minute later she heard his motorcycle roar to life, then fade. She stared across the kitchen to the cabinets that held her dismal choices. It didn't matter. Her appetite was gone.

Lance parked on the square and let Baxter down. He stretched the kinks from his back and decided to walk a bit in the park that made up the center of the square. Massive eucalyptus trees dangled flimsy leaves, the bark of their trunks peeling in shreds. It was a beautiful evening. It would have been nice to spend it with someone.

He hadn't meant to ask Rese out, but at least she could have considered it. It wasn't as though he'd come on to her. Sure he'd teased a little, but she needed lightening up. Serious lightening up. Even so, he wouldn't have asked if her voice hadn't ached with loneliness. The statue was hollow. He'd heard the echo.

He stopped and watched a spindle-legged bird with a body like a loon walk toward the small pond and fountain. Lots of green-necked, brown-flecked and white ducks paddled in the water and perused the lawn. It was a pretty scene, but made him think of the buzzards. *Was it only this morning?*

"Hey there, Baxter."

Lance turned to the freckled blonde he'd seen at lunchtime. "Hi."

She stooped and petted the dog's ears. "Hi." She wore a blue knit top that didn't quite meet her drawstring pants. Her waist was tanned and freckled like her arms.

"I'm Lance." He held out his hand.

She stood up and took it. "Sybil Jackson." The name fit her, a combination of exotic and girl next door.

"You live here?"

"All my life." She slid the strands of hair back behind her shoulder. "You, though, are either new or visiting."

He put on the Bronx. "Whatchu talkin' about?"

She laughed, a sultry, throaty laugh that made him think of hot afternoons out on the pavement singing harmony with his pals for the quarters people tossed. He gazed across the plaza to the historical buildings that formed the square. "Any place good to eat?"

She smiled. "Lots of places."

"What do you like?"

"The Swiss Hotel's good." She pointed to a building nearby on the plaza.

"Care to join me?"

She rested one hand on the small of her back and looked him over. "Sure."

Well, what do you know. He hadn't contracted leprosy. Lance made Baxter stay outside the door, then motioned Sybil ahead of him as they passed under the balcony into the front lobby. The historical placard outside said it had been General Vallejo's home in 1850. A glassed-in display cabinet behind the desk showed the original adobe bricks that made up what would have been the back wall.

The dining room behind the lobby was of newer construction, but Sybil informed him the same family had run the place for four generations. It was nice to converse with a woman who understood normal interaction. No big come-on, but she was obviously interested in what he might have to say. Not only that, she waxed rhapsodic when she learned he could cook.

"I fantasize about men in the kitchen."

Okay, so it was a big come-on. But after Rese, was that so bad?

She took a bite of steak between her teeth. If Rese was all back off, Sybil was the opposite. She closed her eyes and softly moaned. "Gourmet breakfasts?"

"I might be cooking dinner specials as well."

Her lids rose to half mast. "Dinner before and breakfast after. Perfect."

What had they put in her drink?

She said, "Tell me how you learned to cook."

Good safe family lore. "My grandmother taught me."

"Your grandmother?" Sybil obviously hadn't expected that.

He described the hours spent in the restaurant with Nonna, the herbs and spices that had developed his nose, the aromas wafting from the kitchen out to the street. His heart swelled and squeezed with the memories.

Knowing how frustrated and alone she must feel, he prayed Nonna would be home soon from the rehab facility. Visits from the family were not the same as being the heart of it, as she'd always been. But he didn't want to go into that with Sybil.

"I started helping in her kitchen when I was seven, was pulling down a wage by thirteen. I learned to do it all by taste and touch."

Sybil's lips parted as she made more of that than he'd meant. Given the shape and scent of her, it could easily go to his head. He knew the signals, and they were all green lights. But that was not his intention.

He paid for their meal and picked up the scraps he had bagged for Baxter. Then he walked Sybil out and squelched any further thoughts she might have. "I better get Baxter home. Thanks for joining me."

With Baxter between his arms, he drove to the hotel that cost him a hundred eighty-five bucks a night plus a fee for Baxter. Rese's offer was looking better and better. He sprawled across the bed and dialed his parents' number on his cell. There was no answer, so he called his own apartment and got Chaz.

"No change, mon. All things in God's time."

"You only say that because you're not from New York. We natives have a custom. It's called storming the gates."

"I saw something like that last night. Not pretty."

"Did Rico survive?"

Chaz laughed. "He wasn't in it, mon."

"Well, don't tell him what he missed. I'm not there to get him out."

"He wants to talk about that."

"I'm sure." Lance squeezed his forehead. "Don't tell him I called."

"The Lord detests lying lips."

"I'm not asking you to lie, Chaz. Just don't offer him the bait. Is he playing tonight?"

"Somewhere. He'll come home whining."

"No doubt." Lance stretched and yawned, then signed off and lay there, tired enough to sleep just like that, his body feeling the physical labor more than it should. Maybe he was a wimp. Scrawny, weak, and *stylish,* as Rese said. She was probably solid rebar.

But as he dozed, he wondered if she was afraid in the big, old, creaky house. He shouldn't have said *haunted.* But then, she deserved it.

CHAPTER SEVEN

Rese sat on the edge of her bed, elbows to her knees, chin in her palms. It was ridiculous to imagine ghostly specters traversing the halls upstairs, congregating in the attic. She didn't believe in ghosts or Mom's banshees, even if it had sounded like it.

"What's a banshee, Mommy?"

"A wailing spirit that cries almost as loudly as you."

"Why does it cry?"

"Because someone's going to die."

Mom and her banshees. But Rese glanced around the room, got up and closed her door, then made sure the window was locked. Stupid. Mom's fanciful notions only superseded Dad's practicality at night—when she was vulnerable. Rese jerked a glance over her shoulder, then scolded herself.

Dad would say she was being ridiculous, and he should know. It had been Dad and her since she was nine years old. He had come to the school every day to pick her up in his big truck. She'd done her homework at whatever million-dollar renovation he was on. And once her lessons were done she'd started her real learning. Dad said she noticed things no one else would. And she had pointed them out to his crew—anything cut wrong or nailed carelessly, especially the finish carpentry. She was a stickler for perfection. If something didn't match up, do it over.

By the time she was fourteen she was handling the tools herself. At twenty-one, she took charge of Dad's second crew. She made sure nothing they did was substandard to his. And she didn't care at all what they thought about that, or the snide remarks they made. She pretended not to mind the pranks either, but they were harder to ignore, especially when they got cruel.

Rese curled up on the bed. Her stomach growled. She should have eaten. She could go out now to the kitchen just on the other side of the hall. But then she'd be out in the big, dark space. There were no noises like the night before, no howling in the attic, but the silence was almost worse. It had a gobbling intensity she could almost put fangs to. Good grief. She should make herself do it. But she lifted the covers and hunkered in.

Every time she started to doze, she thought she heard something. Had Lance been serious? Did he see something in the attic he hadn't wanted her to know about? Mom had told her tales that would never have been admitted into children's literature. But that wasn't what she really feared. It was him. The "friend." She hadn't thought about him in a long time. Why was he surfacing now?

Because Dad was no longer snoring in their home? He had always provided a barrier. Mom's "friend" left when Dad came home—or at least she and Mom didn't talk to him when Dad was there. The pain of missing her father clenched her insides. She had never been alone until now; at twenty-four, had never lived without him. They were partners. She had skipped college to work with him, developing the knowledge of wood and stain and paint and pipes. They had a thriving business, until . . .

Now the other images pressed in. Rese gave up. She turned on the lamp and clicked the remote on her bedside table, getting something brainless on the small TV across the room. Some people read books to help them sleep. She wasn't big on that. Dad either. She could not remember him ever once reading a book. The newspaper every day, but never once a story for enjoyment. *"Life has enough lies; why should I read someone else's?"*

It had been Mom who loved stories. And Dad had a point. Rese sighed. Those were mixed memories. She leaned her head back and flipped through the channels, not interested in the reruns or late-night shows that flashed across the screen. With how hard she worked during the day, she should be able to sleep at night. Fighting with Lance hadn't helped. Why did he take everything so personally?

Rese punched the pillow and shoved it back behind her, trying to focus on the Subaru commercial and forget that she was alone in a house that fairly breathed on its own. Last night's moans had become a brooding silence.

She should walk through the place, every room, even the attic, and prove to herself there was nothing there. Of course, nothing was there. She didn't have to prove it. She knew all about old houses. She'd torn them apart and viewed them from the guts out.

Guts. She closed her eyes and shuddered. This was ridiculous. Take control! She tossed the remote down and threw off the covers. Just to the kitchen for food. No. She couldn't stand in the cavernous kitchen without knowing the rest of the place was empty. She pressed a hand to her breastbone and opened her bedroom door.

The narrow hall was silent. She opened the door to the kitchen. Darkness engulfed her, and she fumbled for the wall switch. Her palm rubbed the wall until she found it, but no light came on. Right. That light had yet to be rewired. Only the gas stove and refrigerator were operational. But the stove's overhead light would work.

She crossed the hard tile floor. A warm glow burst around her when her finger found the switch. With several breaths to calm herself, she made her way from the kitchen to the dining room. She turned the dimmer only enough to illumine the space. No ghosts. She passed into the front parlor. It had originally been two small parlors that she had opened into one because of the damage to the dividing wall. Empty now, it seemed overly large, but furnished with conversational sitting groups, it would be a nice place to serve the afternoon hors d'oeuvres.

The staircase rose up from the far side. Maybe she'd convinced herself already. She didn't have to go up. *"Chicken. You're nothing but a chicken girl."* Bobby Frank was a jerk. She didn't have to prove anything to him. But she had. She'd climbed all the way up the tree to the wasps' nest and earned the stings to prove it.

Rese swallowed. "All right, Bobby. Watch this." She started up the staircase. The wood stayed quiet beneath her feet. She reached the wide, oval-shaped landing and walked into the first bedroom. Empty. She moved from room to room, leaving the lights on and the doors open.

Now for the attic. She was not giving up without finishing the job. Besides, she hadn't seen how much Lance had cleared out since he notified her of the mice. The thought of something warm and living—even a rodent—seemed almost comforting at the moment. Too bad they'd gotten traps. Well, at least she could see whether the traps had done any good.

Rese took a deep breath, pulled open the attic door, and started up the creaking stairs, groping as the light from the hall diminished the higher she went. A light over the stairs would be a good idea. Maybe Lance could wire it. But then, after this she would have no need to go into the attic after dark. Her toe caught on the edge of a step and she stumbled, gripping the single wooden rail and listening for murmurs overhead.

Had the spirits huddled together in some dark corner, waiting for her head to appear over the edge of the floor? She swallowed hard, then climbed into the attic, breathing the smell of dust and mice and old vinyl. Lance had cleared the whole front area. The empty floor lay pale under the moonlight.

Okay, she'd gotten a look. No, she had to walk in and turn on the light, let the banshees know that no one was dying tonight. No leprechauns, no fairies, no howling ghosts. She reached for the chain and stopped. What if she pulled it and mice scurried across her feet?

Rese let her hand drop. She'd proved enough. No bogeymen, nothing to go bump in the night. She left the light off, backed down the stairs and closed the door behind her, then turned off the hall and bedroom lights. She was alone, not a spook in sight. And especially no "friend."

She went down the main stairs and turned off the entry light, the parlor lights, dining room, then kitchen. She opened the door to her hall and shrieked, then punched the shadowy figure as hard as she could.

"Ow." He caught her hands.

Lance? She couldn't see him well in the dark hall, but she knew his voice. Breath burst from her lungs, and she dropped her head to the wrists confined at his chest, feeling so weak she wanted to punch him again.

"Calm down before you hurt someone."

"You deserved it." Her chest heaved. If he thought this was funny . . .

"You're shaking like a wet dog."

"What do you expect?" She tried to break loose. "Let me go."

"Not until you're through throwing punches."

She jerked one hand free. "I'm through." But he'd better have a good reason for haunting her hall when she'd told him not to pass the door. "What are you doing in here?"

"I came to tell you I was moving in my stuff. I didn't want to worry you." Still gripping her other wrist, he walked her into the kitchen and turned on the stove light. "I called to you through the door."

"I was in the attic."

He half turned, and the light reflected in his obsidian eyes. "What were you doing up there?"

"Checking the traps."

He rubbed a thumb along the edge of his mouth, clearly skeptical.

"I was inspecting your work."

"With the light off?"

She tugged her wrist free. "How do you know it was off?"

"I looked up the stairs first. The attic was dark, but everything else was lit up like Christmas."

She could well imagine what he was thinking. She ran both hands through her hair. "Well, stay out of my suite from now on. It's private."

He nudged her into a kitchen chair. "You're still shaking."

"I was fine until you jumped me."

"I was only coming out."

She pressed her palms to the table. "From where you weren't supposed to be."

He sat down across from her. "What were you doing in the attic?"

She clenched her fists. "I was checking out the house."

He raised his brows. "For spooks?"

She glared.

"You are tough. I'm not sure I'd go into that attic in the dark. But then I know what's up there."

"Don't start."

He laughed. "I meant of a natural kind."

She rubbed her eyes.

"Tired?"

She nodded. It was after midnight. Not that it meant anything to her brain. She had this duel all too often. But what was he doing moving in at that hour?

"I'd make you a steamer if we had our latté machine."

She peeked through her fingers. "Steamer?"

"Steamed milk with, hmm, amaretto syrup."

"Sounds good." She dropped her hands to the table.

He leaned on his forearms. "Order our machine."

She could feel the heat from his hands inches from hers, like static leaping from one source to another. *Our* machine. She was too tired to argue semantics. He'd be the one using it anyway. "I'll think about it."

"Raspberry truffle latté. Peppermint mocha."

She swallowed. "Why did you come back?"

"So you could pummel me in the dark." He sat back and studied her.

She sighed. "I need to go to bed."

"I'll be quiet."

She pushed up from the table and went into her room, comforted in spite of the scare he'd given her. It hadn't been an intruder she had feared when the figure moved in the dark. Or even a ghost. She had thought she was seeing Walter at last.

Though he hadn't meant to scare her, there resided near his solar plexus a wicked satisfaction. That was twice she'd attacked him in fear—no doubt about her place on the fight or flight spectrum, which begged the question why he had worried about her being alone in the big house. But it had nagged him until he acted on it, even though he'd already paid for the hotel. Some excessive urge to protect, or an overblown attempt to feel necessary.

Lance went out and brought his backpack and guitar in. She'd said he could pick any room, so he headed up the stairs with his gear. He chose the room nearest the stairs and the entrance to the attic. A nautical theme of the ancient mariner sort. It was done simply in navy and beige with a walnut highboy, a black iron bed and a strapped trunk at its foot. A ship in a bottle, naturally, on the mantle over the small brazier. An old watercolor of a boat in tempestuous waters over the bed, a net and harpoon on the side wall, and a captain's chair in the corner.

He sat on the bed and bounced lightly. She'd bought quality. He glanced through the bookshelf that held a copy of Robert Louis Stevenson's *Treasure Island*, Melville's *Moby Dick*—as though anyone would stay long enough to read that—a collection of seafaring poems and a history of whaling.

Was Rese sleeping yet? He had worried about her being scared, then done the very thing he was trying to avoid. It wasn't his fault, though. He had called out to her, then headed down the hall when he got no answer. A tool-wielding woman was not the sort to surprise in the dark, though she'd seemed anything but formidable.

He sat down on the bed. The way Rese had shaken in his grip, her fear must have built longer than the jolt he'd given her. Checking out the house? How many people would face the place alone at night when her mind must have already been churning?

This house didn't scare him. If there were ghosts, they would know him. Maybe help him. But Rese was a stranger, there by happenstance. She had no history, no blood to connect her. Strange how that sent a sense of responsibility coursing through him. Rese Barrett was not his responsibility, but he would tread carefully for her sake. Not that she would return the favor, were the roles reversed. But that didn't matter.

Lord, help me do this without hurting her in the process. He dropped to his knees and rested his forehead on his clasped knuckles, seeking direction and wisdom, two things that always seemed just out of reach. He knew it was there for those who sought. *"Seek and you will find."* But sometimes he felt like the last kid in a game of sardines, searching and searching for the others all crammed together in the hiding space while he kept walking by in the dark. He climbed into the bed and opened the small, gilt-paged Bible. The ribbon was in Matthew where he'd left off.

Red ink caught his eye, setting off the Lord's words. *"Then Jesus said to his disciples, 'If anyone would come after me, he must deny himself and take up his cross and follow me.'"*

Lance pondered that. It wasn't new, or even difficult. He was ready and willing. He'd taken up many crosses, some not even his own, standing as a kid with the weak, the rejected, the picked-on. Momma had treated his bruises, saying, *"Your heart gets you in trouble, Lance, but never stop hearing it."* Dad usually added, *"You might listen to your brain sometimes."*

He read on: *"'For whoever wants to save his life will lose it, but whoever loses his life for me will find it.'"* An ache filled his chest. He knew how fragile life was. Strong, vital men evaporated. Lives charged with purpose. . . . Tony's life filled with purpose, then just . . . gone. Lance swallowed the pain. *"'What good will it be for a man if he gains the whole world, yet forfeits his soul? For what can one give in exchange for his soul?'"*

Tony's soul was with the Lord. But his life should not have ended. They'd all been reeling since. *What were you thinking, God?* He clenched his hands. *You got the wrong one.* Like he could tell God his business. But why leave a screw-up and take the one they all looked up to?

"'For the Son of Man is going to come with his angels in his Father's glory, and then he will repay everyone according to his conduct.'" That part worried him. It didn't account for intentions. If he meant well, but still screwed up, and conduct was what mattered. . . . Lance rubbed his face. He set the Bible on the table. Somewhere in there it said God judged the heart. He'd count on that.

CHAPTER EIGHT

Fresh basil gathered warm.
Pungent cheese.
Dough soft as baby skin.
Pressing, turning, folding, rolling.
Rhythm.
Pulse.
Laughter.
Life inhabits our kitchen.
Sorrows are lightened, burdens shared. Joy seasons
the moments passed between us on a tasting spoon.

Rese woke to the muffled sounds of activity in the kitchen and an aroma of something spicy and wonderful. *Lance.* She rose and pulled on a light sweatshirt over her knit shirt and lounge pants, since the mornings still held a chill. She washed her face in the small bathroom between her bedroom and the extra room she had set up as an office. She brushed her teeth and went out to the kitchen.

Lance looked over from the stove. "Morning."

"Good morning."

"Sleep well?" He spooned some meat mixture into the center of a thin sort of pancake.

"Surprisingly." She had slept better than any night she'd been there, waking only once to remember Lance was upstairs.

"Good." He rolled the pancake and placed it into a baking dish.

She yawned. "Did you?"

"I slept great—once the ghosts quit chattering."

She half smiled. Let him have his joke; she had set herself up. "Chai?"

She accepted the cup of tea he handed her. She could get used to this.

"It'll be better when I can froth the milk. With the latté machine." He poured something over the rolls in the pan then set them into the massive oven. "What's the plan today?"

He was obviously a morning person. She pressed her hands to her temples. "Gas fireplace conversion. And I need to work on the Web site."

"Web site?"

"You know, pictures of the rooms, rates, reservations. . . . What?"

He rested his hands on his hips. "Rese with a chainsaw; Rese with a sledge hammer. But Rese with a Web site? Boggles the mind."

Now she knew how he felt when she doubted his abilities. "I took a class on it when Dad's business needed a Web site." By his look of incredulity, he was intentionally turning the tables. She ignored the bait. "I thought you could make up a few things as sample breakfasts. Food pictures are always a good sell."

"Only if the food looks good."

She noted a subtle stiffening in his face. "Won't your food look good?"

"You tell me."

"It ought to. That's what I'm paying you for." She noticed the vase they'd found in the attic. That would be a perfect accent with a sprig or two of fresh blooms from the garden. "I need to get the brochures printed and the Web site up soon."

His expression was inscrutable. "You want the dishes photographed together or individually?"

"You're the food man."

He took the copper skillet from the stove top. "The kitchen isn't exactly set up. I need to order some equipment."

She chewed her lower lip. "I don't know. I haven't bought the TVs yet, and that's a major expense."

"TVs?"

"For the bedrooms."

He set the skillet in the sink. "Why do you want to do that?" He swabbed the pan with the washcloth, then rinsed it with steaming water. "You should make this a connecting place, a get-away-from-it-all experience."

His thought resonated in her mind as they all seemed to, but she could not picture it. "What will people do?"

He sent a look over his shoulder. "Beyond the obvious, they might talk, play games, read to each other. After touring the vineyards, people want to relax with a good merlot and a wedge of brie and let go the busyness of life."

Like a fish surfacing for a look at the airy world above, she gave him slow-blinking curiosity. Was he serious?

He turned and met her gaze. "You want this to be special, don't you?"

She tried not to look as though his ideas were foreign to her. But she blurted, "Read to each other?"

"Why not? And by the way, you've got a bocce pit out back. Framed in anyway, just needing sand."

"A what?"

"Bocce. Italian sand bowling. You play it with a set of colored balls, like bowling and croquet and horseshoes all in one." He toweled the pan and hung it on the wall. "But as to the kitchen . . . I have a catalogue that carries most of what I need."

Rese frowned. He was intentionally distracting and confusing her. Trying to slip his ideas in again. "I hadn't budgeted much in kitchen stuff."

"No kidding?" He hung the towel on the rod, and then turned. "You can't expect my best results without proper equipment."

"Your results have been fine."

"Really." He crossed his arms over his chest, a skeptical and combative expression on his face.

"What's the matter?"

He leaned his hip to the counter and studied her.

She did not appreciate the scrutiny. "If there's something on your mind, say it."

He turned and drained the water from the sink. "There's nothing on my mind."

Because he didn't communicate with his mind, but with his heart or soul, his emotions. What was she supposed to do with that? She had never worried about her employees' feelings. She'd been too busy protecting her own.

Rese nodded to the pan over the stove. "I bought that at an antique shop. For decoration."

He pinged it with a flick of his fingers. "Copper's the best heat conductor. It's the most useful pan here."

She sighed. "I guess you'd better show me the catalogue."

He went upstairs and came down a moment later with a glossy gourmet kitchen supply catalogue. Even wholesale, things wouldn't be cheap. She was frugal by nature and training, careful never to let a job go over budget if she could help it. Already he'd added the expense of the carriage house remodel.

Now it seemed he wanted a dream kitchen.

But if she didn't purchase the electronics for the bedrooms . . . She tried to imagine people reading to each other and playing games, lounging around with merlot and . . . Okay, fine. No electronics.

She listened to the items he requested. There weren't that many, and the most expensive by far was the latté machine. He made it all sound so good, but he'd better be there for the long haul or it would be wasted. Near the end of their search through the catalogue, he stood and removed the pan from the oven.

A warm savory wave rolled through the kitchen, and when he set a plate before her, the steaming sausage aroma made her mouth water. She couldn't recall experiencing that phenomenon before, her mouth actually wanting what she hadn't even tasted yet. It was ridiculous.

He sat down with his plate and spoke a blessing. His prayer surprised her less than her own impatience to take the first bite. When she did, it was worth the wait. She chewed carefully, enjoying the spiciness of the meat inside its delicate roll. Nothing like that came out of a box. Her guests would have the best breakfasts in town.

She cut and ate bite after bite, feeling the warmth spread into her stomach. She never had eaten last night. The fright Lance gave her had driven the hunger away, and she had forgotten that was her original intention for getting out of bed. Now she was glad to have come to breakfast hungry.

She wiped her mouth and looked up at Lance. "Do you think you'll get to the wiring in here soon?" She didn't want to repeat their scramble in the dark.

His jaw clenched as he stood, and he carried their plates to the sink without answering.

"Lance?"

"When do you want it done?"

She stood up. "As soon as possible."

"Fine." He bit the word.

What was he upset about? They'd had less than thirty minutes of conversation, and she was sure she had said nothing insulting. She had even agreed to buy his toys. Asking him to express his grievance had gone nowhere, so she shook her head and walked out. She had work to do. Lance Michelli could stew in his own juices—a phrase especially appropriate for her moody chef.

Lance refused to let her bizarre silence ruin his day. Whatever her problem, it was hers. He had the position, and that was all that mattered. Not the fact that he'd prepared something fabulous to make up for scaring her, or that they'd conversed as equals regarding plans and possibilities and purchases. No, the moment food was set before Rese Barrett she went mute. Even Nonna would throw up her hands.

After cleaning up, he went to work on the kitchen wiring. Rese had provided tools and supplies, displaying her knowledge. Interesting that she didn't insist on doing it herself. Had she an electrifying experience in her past? Maybe it had created the dead zone in her epicurean center.

Lance fumed as he traced the wires, looking for the problem. So, it bothered him. Maybe if Rese was off with a jackhammer somewhere, he'd forget it. But she had joined him in the kitchen, pulled the stove unit from the wall and was preparing the gas feed for the fireplace on the other side.

Essentially they were working in the same space, and he had no choice but to notice. She was confident and efficient. She was also strong. He had almost asked if she wanted help with the stove, but she managed to move it without him. In fact, his offer would no doubt have been insulting, and then she would have brought up his earring. *Not sure a man with an earring could help. Must make you weak and emotional.*

Lance found the problem in the switch itself and set about repairing it. No fixing the short in Rese, however. No rheostat in her brain to create a gentle glow, only full flood or blackout.

"You're mumbling."

He glanced over his shoulder and frowned. "Sorry." He focused on the wires, then catching a flash of color from the corner of his eye, he turned.

A woman had joined them, her rosy tangerine hair clipped up and spiraling down like fireworks around her face. Her lips were shiny pink, her blue eyes rimmed in iridescent green. The tail feathers of a peacock tattoo showed just above the neckline of a white spaghetti-strap shirt that barely concealed anything.

"Wow," she said. "Feel the charge in here."

"Star!" Rese stood up and drew in the rainbow.

Not at all the reaction he'd expected. They couldn't know each other. She had appraised him with cool disdain when he walked in on her, but there they were, arms entangled, this Star giggling and fluffing Rese's hair. "You're all short again."

"You're red again."

"Do you like it? I like it. It makes me impulsive."

Rese crossed her arms. "I have news for you, Star. It's not the hair."

Star laughed. "I can't believe you bought this place, but I can tell you've fixed it." Her pirouette spread a flash of curls that settled on her shoulders as she faced Lance. "Who's the sexy pirate?"

He was too surprised to answer, but Rese said, "Lance Michelli, my cook."

Her cook. "Don't forget maid." He held out his hand to Star.

She slid her palm into his. "I pray you, sir, don't jest. For you are no maid."

"It's a job description. That's how I'm known around here."

Still holding his hand she looked over her shoulder at Rese. "I knew I felt sparks." She licked a finger and touched his wrist, making a sizzling sound. "Hot."

Then she let go and flew back to Rese. "You always steam the men working for you." She laughed. "Can I stay here awhile?"

Rese cocked her head. "I'm not really open yet."

"Good, 'cuz I can't pay."

"Now there's a surprise." Rese actually smiled. "Lance is in one of the rooms upstairs. You can choose another."

Thirty seconds to give Star a room. Three reluctant days for him. And his was temporary.

"Thanks." Star hugged her and rushed out.

Lance didn't care, as long as he could fulfill his purpose. But what if Star was the woman Rese had hoped for? If she decided she didn't need him, what then? He turned back to the wall and seized the wires.

Rese joined him. "That was Star."

"So I gathered."

"She's a little . . ."

"Impulsive."

"Blunt." She leaned her shoulder on the wall. "Sorry about the pirate thing."

"I've been called worse." By Rese, actually. He'd take pirate over weak and emotional.

Rese went back behind the stove. "She won't stay long. She never does."

Lance twisted the wire. "You could give her a job." The dual position he currently held, for instance.

"Oh no. I want to stay friends."

Ah yes. No smudging the line. No relationships with mere employees. At least there was no threat to his position as bondservant. He finished the connection, walked over, and threw the fuse, then went back and tried the switch. Let there be light. No more scaring Rese in the dark. Good thing. He'd almost cared.

"You did it." Only moderate shock on her face before she squatted back down behind the stove.

He touched a hand to his forehead with a bow of obeisance, but she didn't notice. "Guess I'll finish the attic now." He started toward the stairs as Star came through the front door with three brightly colored cloth bags that he guessed held clothes.

"Need a hand?"

"Sure." She flopped them into his arms. "I have to choose a room." She took the stairs on tiptoe, her short, filmy skirt flaring out.

Lance averted his eyes to the steps as he climbed, then stood in the hall as she danced from one room to another. She stepped inside one, and he started that way.

"Pink. Breathing pink light is good medicine. I read that in a book."

Breathing pink light. "Do you want the pink room?" It was a blend of soft pink and cream with a rose trellis over the headboard. A little feminine, but nice.

She stepped a few feet in and turned around slowly. "How do I look?"

How did she look? He thought this was about where he could set her bags down. "You look fine."

She pressed her hands to her head. "Fine? I need to radiate." Star flitted past him to the room across the hall, plantation bed with a green spread and rain-forest watercolors on the walls. She extruded her arms and hung her head back, her neck making a graceful arch and her chin a delicate peak. "Now?"

Lance swallowed. "Radiant."

She flew over, grabbed his overburdened arms and pulled him into the room.

He clutched the bags. "Leave them here?"

"Yes, anywhere."

He dropped them.

She leaned in and kissed his neck, leaving a pink smear he could feel. "'How beauteous mankind is! O brave new world that has such people in't!'" She stepped back and spun around.

"Okay then." Lance went out rubbing his neck. His palm came away glittery. He headed up the attic stairs, wondering how he'd landed between a stone and a manic fairy.

CHAPTER NINE

Rese needed to convert the fireplace, the last big job before finishing the dining room floor and moving on to the front parlor. Alone, she had accomplished the things she'd planned each day. Then came Lance. He was shouldering a couple big projects, but since he'd come, her concentration had stunk. Now Star . . .

Rese sighed. She loved Star. But maintaining any sort of focus would be impossible, evidenced the moment Star came back down.

"This place is a museum!"

Rese sat back on her heels. "Not your style?"

"I love it. I truly do." Star circled the kitchen like a firefly caught in a jar. "It's just so old."

Rese smiled. "That's the idea."

"My room is perfect."

"The Rain Forest?"

Star giggled. "You peeked."

"I didn't have to. It's the most colorful."

"Your cook is adorable. You shouldn't torture him."

Torture? Rese got up, still mystified by his snit. "Lance takes things personally."

Star's laugh rang. "What wit resides in your fair head. You've no idea how you sting, but cry 'fie!' when they buck."

Rese put her hands to her hips, but Star circled her neck and hugged. "Now I shall go and find me gainful employment."

"Really?" Not that she wished to discourage her, but the thought of Star with a real job . . .

"Doubt not." Star blew a kiss and left the kitchen vacant and dull, Lance's light shining feebly.

Rese turned off the switch. Had she stung him? She frowned at the thought. His mumbling and short-tempered responses showed she might have. But how? She'd given him a room, agreed to buy his equipment. She replayed the morning's conversation, certain again she had not insulted him. He was the one shooting barbs about the Web site.

She shook her head. Not her problem. He had his job; she had hers. As long as they didn't share the same space they'd be fine. In Star's absence she intended to complete her project. Lance could buck all he wanted.

———

The things at the back of the attic were much older and nastier than the rest. The vermin had congregated there. Every one of the traps had sprung, though one had failed to catch the beggar that stole the cheese. Lance emptied the traps and hauled out rotted blankets and old leather boots. He swept out mounds of fluff and filth. A basket of fabric strips all but disintegrated in his arms and mouse droppings littered the floor as he lifted it.

He puffed the dust away, then held his breath, waving a hand to clear the cloud. Something caught his eye, and he stooped. A flat metal box with an Alpine scene on the cover. His heart raced. Exactly the sort of thing he'd hoped to find. He dropped the fabric and picked up the box.

It looked like a woman's stationary set. He tried to open the latch, but it was locked. He shook it. Papers by the sound and weight. It could be nothing more than writing paper, but his excitement surged.

He jerked his head around at the sound of someone on the stairs. Quickly shoving the box under the moldy fabric, he stood up and faced Rese. "Hey." He rubbed his hands on the seat of his jeans. "Got the conversion done?"

"Yes." She searched the space with her gaze. "And you're almost finished here."

"You do not want to mess with what's left, believe me."

She cast a disparaging glance at the pile. "I've handled worse. But I'm glad you volunteered." Her hands went to her hips. "Maybe after lunch—"

"Go ahead and eat. I'm not hungry." True enough. The smell and condition of the things he'd hauled, the incredible frustration of cooking for her, but most of all the desire to see inside that box sent any notion of food from his mind.

"Oh. All right." She lingered another moment, then went back down.

So he hadn't been totally forthcoming. Technically, he supposed everything in the attic belonged to her. Morally, he could make an argument otherwise—if Nonna had lost something . . . or everything? He stooped and retrieved the box, accidentally kicking over the button jar, the contents spilling out as it rolled across the floor.

He set down the box and stopped the jar's rolling, then did a quick search. Nothing but buttons. He scooped them back into the jar and closed the lid tightly. He would bring it down to Rese. If she was in the kitchen getting food, he could reach his room undetected on the way. But where was Star?

Lance reached the landing and saw her door standing open and the bags exactly where he'd left them. The room was empty. He ducked into his own, slid the metal box into his drawer, then brought Rese the box of handkerchiefs and the jar of buttons. She was warming canned ravioli, which she certainly deserved.

"Where's Star?"

"She went to find a job."

So Rese really wasn't hiring her. "I won't get close since I'm filthy, but I thought you might like these." He set them on the counter. "Hankies and buttons."

"Oh." Not quite the awe she'd expressed over the stone floor, but certainly more interest than she'd shown any of his meals.

He said, "Could work nicely in that white room." Why did he feel as though he were presenting her a peace offering? It was her own stuff even.

Rese nodded. "I could put the handkerchiefs behind glass. But people might steal the buttons."

"You mean take one as a keepsake?"

"Or more. Old buttons are quite valuable. I'd hate to lose them."

Lance swallowed. If she felt that way about buttons . . . "Glue the lid shut."

She raised her eyebrows. "Practical suggestion from a man with an earring."

"Will you get off that?" He'd gone to the plain hoop, hoping it would draw less attention.

She laughed. "Want some ravioli?"

"That's not ravioli. It's cat food wrapped in soggy cardboard."

She looked into the pot. "Oh."

He headed for the door. "I should have the rest of the junk out in a trip or two. I'll get it swept up, then I'll need a serious shower." And a look into the tin box.

Cat food in soggy cardboard. She had never thought of it in those terms, but it fit. Unfortunately. She scraped the limp squares off the bottom of the pan into her dish. She couldn't really expect him to cook all their meals. Especially when they weren't even open for business yet.

It didn't matter. Eat and get back to work. Soggy cat food or not.

As soon as she'd finished eating, Rese got her digital camera from the office and went upstairs. She should have photographed the rooms before Lance and Star moved in. But then she hadn't expected Lance to arrive in the middle of the night, or Star at all. She had learned long ago to expect nothing from her friend. There was less disappointment that way. Star was who she was.

Rese hid a smile. Lance had certainly seen it up close and personal. Not that there was anything else with dramatic, emotive Star. Like Lance? Rese sighed. Maybe she was the odd one.

"Got a concept of emotion?" Lance's words had stung. It wasn't that she didn't feel. She just wouldn't let it show. It made her vulnerable, weak— something she'd learned never to be.

Rese didn't know what wind had tossed Star her way this time, or how long it would last. She appeared and disappeared like a magician's assistant, though Rese rarely glimpsed the magician. The real question was how she'd known about the inn. *"I can't believe you bought this place."*

Who had told her? Rese frowned. Who even knew? She'd sold everything, left Sausalito, then found a place to fix up as her own after . . . The pang came so sharply it almost doubled her. She drew a hard breath and forced her attention onto the task before her.

She raised the camera and took shots of the four empty rooms, then tugged Star's bags into the hall and photographed that one. As she'd said, Rese was not surprised at the room choice. Star might have been a brightly plumed jungle bird or an iridescent dragonfly. There was no other room she'd want.

Lance had chosen the one she decorated for Dad, with his appreciation for anything nautical. In another time he'd have been a shipwright. The door was closed, and she heard the shower running. She'd have to get those photos later. Lance had not made up any special dishes, so she may as well leave the Web site until tomorrow and do the carpentry in the front room today.

She had good maple and her lathe and router for building shelves into one wall. Her heart soared with the prospect. She didn't mind the other aspects of construction, but carpentry was her passion, especially hand carving the decorative pieces.

Nothing pleased her more than shaping the wood into leaves and curls, notches and grooves, a lost art maybe, with cheap prefabricated pieces replacing the painstaking work of artisans, but not in her homes. There was at least one hand-carved piece in every place she'd renovated; mantels, decorative panels, even a newel post of lions on the spiral staircase in one San Francisco mansion. Her signature.

———————

Lance toweled dry and dressed in his other pair of jeans and a clean T-shirt. He was going to have to do laundry, but just now there was only one thing on his mind. He made sure the door was locked, then took the metal box from his drawer. Besides the Alpine scene, it had a brass fitting at each corner and the lock was brass.

It might be nothing more than a souvenir left by someone who had lived in the house. But the Alps could be significant, given the family's origin in the Piemonte region of Italy bordered by the Alps and Liguria, where he'd found Conchessa. The box looked European, and it was definitely old.

He took his pocketknife from the dresser and pulled out the toothpick. He didn't want to force the clasp if he could help it. Working the toothpick into the keyhole, he moved it around while putting easy pressure on the lid.

Accumulated grit came out of the hole. Maybe it was just clogged. He worked the pointed piece all over inside the hole, then tried again to open the lid. This time it shifted but still held. Most likely locked then.

As he tipped the box, the papers shifted inside. *Lord, this has to be something. Help me open it. Let me see inside.* He opened the screwdriver attachment and tried it in the hole. It just fit, and he worked the flat edge around until it caught, then carefully turned. Holding his breath, he tried the lid, felt it give, then grate open. He looked in, excitement building like suds in a sink.

Folded newspaper clippings, yellow and brittle, but intact. He lifted them carefully out and read the top headline: *A Hero for Today.* His gaze flew over the story. An attempted train robbery on the Union Pacific, and Quillan Shepard had thwarted the attempt. Lance exulted. His great-great-grandfather. Nonna had written of him to Conchessa in the letters he'd poured over with his aged cousin in the Ligurian courtyard. Nonna's words betrayed a girl's exuberant fondness close to what he felt for her.

This was the place, his family home, and Quillan, it seemed, larger-than-life. Even reading past the journalist's exuberant style, the story was dramatic. Mustering a party of passengers, armed with their sporting rifles and hand-guns, Quillan had faced down the robbers and talked them into leaving.

Lance raised his brows at the next information. Quillan knew the leader of the gang, Shane Dennison? The article claimed Quillan had been involved in a robbery with Dennison years before, but was cleared of the charges.

> *It's the old story of a boy enamored with a man, only to be shown the stark truth of that man's nature. But Quillan Shepard redeemed himself and took action on the side of right against the very one who had shamed him. This stalwart man of doughty countenance is the stuff of today's hero.*

Lance rubbed the back of his neck. Stalwart man of doughty counte-nance. He doubted anyone questioned Quillan's manhood. Of course, until Rese, no one had questioned his own. The article ended with a charge for people to stand for what was right, even in the face of personal risk. A smile tugged his lips. He must have a dose of Quillan after all.

Lance set that article gently aside. The next seemed to be a follow-up to the same story, though it came from a Cheyenne, Wyoming, newspaper. Headline: *Robber Cut Down by Clerk's Foresight*. Lance read on.

> *Notorious bank and train robber, Shane Dennison, was shot dead Wednesday at the Fort Laramie bank. Bank clerk, Simon Blessing, claims he saw the notorious outlaw in a poker game at the saloon. "I recognized the mole under his lip from the new posters." Certain there could be trou-ble he alerted bank owner, Thaddeus Marsh. Law officers were ready when Dennison made his move on the bank. Dennison was shot trying to exit the window. Two partners were captured and await trial.*

It read like an old western dime novel. But the next were even more impressive. They were articles about Quillan from the *Harper's Monthly Mag-azine* that included pieces of his poetry. Conchessa had let him take a book of Quillan's poetry, which he had read on the plane ride home, finding a connection with his own song lyrics. Had he inherited his poetic nature from this man of long ago?

Lance was fitting the pieces together as in his dream. Maybe it was a prophetic dream, the Lord promising resolution. It nagged a little that even when he'd assembled the shards, the mirror was still broken. But right now he was finding pieces.

He picked up a packet of letters and untied the string. The first smelled of musty age, and he was glad it had been protected by the metal box. The thick paper unfolded with difficulty. It had been hand ornamented with roses at the bottom, but they were faded almost unrecognizably.

March 13, 1883
My dearest Carina,
    Felicitations on the birth of your son, Vittorio DiGratia Shepard. And congratulations to your husband. I accept with gratitude your request to be godfather to the child. He will benefit from my tutelage in ways your Quillan falls short, pride in the old country, and the history of our people. In this and all, I will fulfill the holy task as though he were my own.
                    Fondly,
                    Flavio

Lance raised his eyebrows at the man's swagger. That guy had courted Carina and seemed to think of Quillan as an afterthought. Interesting they had chosen him for such an important role in Vittorio's life. Quillan must have been confident of his relationship with his wife. He carefully folded the letter and slid it into the envelope.

The next was on thin vellum with no ornamentation at all. It had the same smell of age, but felt brittle rather than stiff. With careful fingers, Lance unfolded it.

October 12, 1925
Darling Antonia,
    How pleased I am to celebrate your fifteenth birthday. Today the house will be filled with good cheer and well wishers, but there will be none who look upon you with more joy, not even the young rascals whose heads you have turned, than your own papa. You are still my ragazza picola.
                With love and tenderness,
                Papa

His grandmother's fifteenth birthday. And the Vittorio born to Quillan and Carina was her father. Ragazza picola: her papa's little girl. He'd obviously doted on her. Why had she hardly mentioned him?

Something stirred inside, deeper than family pride. This was his past, his ancestry, and he knew so little about the lives that went before him, the lives that made him. He closed his eyes and imagined his grandmother Antonia as a fifteen-year-old beauty. But there came instead to his mind a brown-haired, brown-eyed woman.

Lance opened his eyes with a jolt. He did not want to picture Rese just now. Not while he was keeping this secret. How would she react if he showed her the box and its contents? If he told her who these people were, who he was. . . .

The next letter was definitely in a woman's hand. He stared a moment at the form and shape of the words, not even caring what sentences they formed, just appreciating the beauty of the strokes. Then he began to read. *Dear Mr. Michelli.* Lance jerked, an almost electrical thrill passing through him.

> *My nonno is the least of your concerns. He is very forward thinking and accepting. It is my papa you will have to convince, and since he is no less discerning than I, your chances remain bleak.*
> > *Most sincerely,*
> > *Antonia DiGratia Shepard*

His grandmother had a sense of humor—and a healthy self-image. He turned the paper over.

> *Bella Antonia,*
> > *I am up to the task, I assure you. I will call tonight at eight.*
> > *Your ardent admirer,*
> > *Marco Michelli*

Nonno Marco. He'd used her own letter to reply. Self-assured. Passionate. Lance had always felt an affinity. He smiled. His grandfather had come to America with nothing but "my mandolin across my back and my good looks"—in his own words. Apparently, he didn't even have money for paper or postage. But in spite of Nonna's dismissive tone, he had made enough of an impression for her to keep this scrap of correspondence.

Lance closed the letter and put it with the others. The only things left in the box were two photos. A sepia picture of a blond woman with *Helena* penciled on the back and another of an older man with a shock of white hair, sitting at a desk with a pen in hand. Lance's throat tightened. It had to be Quillan Shepard, though there was no name inscribed.

He took out the packet from Conchessa that he had also stashed in his drawer. From it he drew the small book of poetry with pages worn as soft and pliable as cloth. He opened the book and gently turned the first leaves to an etched illustration of his great-great-grandfather. The hair was the same length and thickness, and the expression equally compelling. Lance studied the photographs again, then carefully put everything into the box.

The contents had proved his family's connection to the house and matched the things Conchessa had told him. Though there was nothing in the box that answered his questions or solved the problem he'd come to solve, it was a start. Anticipation rose up. The Lord had brought him there for a reason. *Show me. Let me do your will.*

Lance put the papers back into the box and slid it once again into the drawer. He flipped open his cell phone, pressed the number for Nonna's room and waited. She wouldn't answer herself, but there was usually someone with her. If she was up to it, they'd hold the phone for her and he could tell her what he'd found.

But the phone rang with no answer. Maybe she was in therapy, raising and lowering her arms in the pool, whatever little steps she was taking back to health. Now that he thought about it, he wasn't sure what he should tell her.

The last time he had spoken with her directly, she had tried to talk, and the effort had frustrated and weakened her. It was better in that respect to talk to the others, but this information was for Nonna alone. He wasn't sure how he knew that, just a sense they'd had between them from the start, his knowing what she needed without her asking, and vice versa.

He would wait until he had something more, something solid to tell her. He only hoped whatever it was would bring her peace.

CHAPTER TEN

The crushing of the grapes.
Juice and remains divided;
one to its lauded use, the other humble.
Stems and skin returned to the land, renewing its vigor.
But the juice, ah, the juice. Cana's treasure.
Always we strive for the miracle.

Rese was vaguely aware of Lance going out the kitchen door, probably to work on the carriage house, but she was preoccupied. Carpentry had become a bittersweet love, the sounds and smells rife with memories that came no matter how hard she tried to block them.

The first months of renovation had been a welcome blur of activity, but every day now the numbness wore off. The pangs grew sharper, the images more debilitating. Wasn't time supposed to lessen pain?

She heard a car outside and looked through the front window from her perch on the scaffolding. A loose-hipped blonde climbed out. What was she selling? The woman didn't come to the door, but started around the side of the villa. Rese tightened her brow. She must have seen Lance and assumed he was in charge. Typical.

He would no doubt redirect her, but when the woman still didn't appear at the door, Rese climbed down and passed through to the kitchen. The woman was there with Lance, all right, one hand on the small of her back in a feminine posture intended to show it all without appearing to. *The name's Blonde, Dumb Blonde.*

The woman laughed with Lance as Baxter nosed into her other hand. *Traitor.* Lance was animated as he turned and gestured toward the carriage house, obviously describing the work in progress. The woman nodded and smiled as though they knew each other already. Something tightened inside Rese's ribs.

Lance motioned toward the villa, and Rese ducked out of sight, mortified that he might have caught her watching. She climbed back onto the scaffolding and measured the space at three different heights. The old walls were more plumb than newer construction.

She loved the quality that had gone into things in times past. Maybe that was her problem; she'd been born in the wrong century. Of course, she would have been banned from carpentry altogether a hundred years ago by virtue of her gender. So, she was simply a misfit, and when it came down to it, she didn't care.

Voices sounded in the kitchen, then Lance called, "Rese?"

She swallowed the tightening in her throat. What was wrong with her? "In here."

They came in together. Lance said, "This is Sybil Jackson. Do you care if I show her around?"

Yes, she cared.

Sybil flipped her hair back with that lithe gesture Rese despised. "I freelance for the *Index Tribune*. Lance said this house has history. Maybe I could do a story on it."

Rese looked from her to Lance. "What history?"

He shrugged. "Any house this old has history. You ought to look into having it registered."

"It would cost me too much to renovate. I couldn't use any materials except those specified authentic and appropriate." Rese dropped the heavy-duty measuring tape with a loud clatter, pleased when Sybil jumped.

Lance handed it back, then walked Sybil to the stairs. "The guest rooms are finished. They'll give you a better idea."

I just bet. Rese traversed the scaffolding as Lance and Sybil went upstairs. Sybil's slinky glide had brought up a dark memory. Alanna. Mom had taken the role of Alanna too far, pretending sometimes even after Dad came home. He had not enjoyed it, either, the way Mom slid herself around him, talking in that husky voice not her own. Sometimes he had put her forcefully away from him, ordering her to stop acting that way. Then Mom would laugh, Alanna's hateful laugh.

Rese forced herself to concentrate on the task at hand. *Do not lose your focus.* But that thought only brought worse images to mind. A wave of dizziness spun her head. She gripped the metal framing, her legs weak with the sheer suffocating helplessness.

She pressed her hand to her face, trying not to recall the blood pumping into her lap, the coppery tang of life escaping. She staggered, went down on her sore knee, her breath coming sharp and shallow. Tears welled up behind her eyelids, a sensation as foreign as it was unwelcome. She resisted the pain as she would a hammer blow to her thumb, but she couldn't shake the sight and smell of blood seeping through her fingers.

"Rese?"

She couldn't respond. The scaffolding shook.

"Rese?" Lance climbed onto the plank and took her arm. "Are you hurt?"

She forced her eyes to open. "No." She glanced down at Sybil, then pushed up to standing. "Just lost my balance."

He studied her, but didn't press the issue. "We're going to grab some dinner. You want to come?"

"No." She knew well enough three was a crowd, and she had work to do.

"Sure?"

She nodded. The sooner they were gone the better. She didn't need an audience.

Lance left on his motorcycle with Sybil Jackson holding on around his waist and Baxter barking forlornly in the circular drive. Rese climbed down the scaffolding and called the dog into the parlor. Once the furniture was in place and the inn open for business, Baxter could not be allowed inside. But at the moment, in the empty room, she and the dog would commiserate.

The talk this time centered around Sybil and her work as a free-lance columnist. She sipped the Chateau St. Jean Fume Blanc, a local wine she had ordered by vintage. "I've always known exactly what to say and how to say it."

Or as Rese might put it, *I know exactly what to do and how to do it.* Were all the women in the area alpha females? He studied Sybil, the hair falling to her shoulders like the straight drop of a waterfall, fine and soft—he knew just by looking. When she stood to visit the ladies' room, the space between her shirt and skirt was enough to show her navel ornament. She might be good with words, but she excelled in the subliminal. He curbed his reaction with an effort.

She had taken him by surprise, showing up at the villa, but her manner had been friendly and professional. Now she was slipping back into her previous mode. Or was she simply sensuous by nature? Unlike Rese who . . . *Rese.* Was she okay? Concern stirred.

Lance seriously doubted she'd lost her balance, but he had no idea what caused the agony he'd seen in her face. Something was wrong, but maybe Star was with her. He frowned. Not much relief in that thought.

Then Sybil was back, gliding into her chair like moonlight on a river. Oh, she had the moves. But what really interested him was her knowledge of the area. What part might she play in his search? Or was she a distraction he didn't need? She picked up the discussion where she'd left it, the challenge of writing for a small paper with a long and continuous history in a community that rightly, in her opinion, resisted growth and development in disdain for its greedy twin, Napa. Her opinions were crisply stated, well thought out, and obviously intelligent, if one-sided. She cared about her community.

"So you've lived here your whole life?"

"I got my degrees at Stanford."

"Then home to Sonoma."

Her hair draped her shoulder. "I'm spoiled. My family's been in banking here for four generations. I couldn't really imagine living anywhere else."

"Your family's got roots."

"My great-grandfather Arthur Jackson opened the bank in 1921 and had his finger in most every pot in town. We're in a lot of local history."

A thrill of possibility warmed his neck. Or was it the hand of God directing his quest? "Do you write about it?"

She rolled her eyes. "I focus on current issues, what matters to people now. Especially politically and civically. Like the moratorium on growth. I don't know how Rese got her lodging petition through the council, except that men like my father are more interested in revenues than protecting the climate of this city."

"Rese can be pretty convincing. And since she's reclaiming an existing property, I suppose that would benefit all except her direct competition."

Sybil slid her finger down the goblet stem. "Her direct competition are people like the Sebastiani-Cuneos at the Stone Cottage."

"Prominent families."

"People who protect what we have here from strangers butting in."

"Do you fall into that camp?"

Sybil brushed her hair back with one hand. "I want Sonoma to stay the way it is and not sell out to big money like Napa."

"Rese is hardly big money." Though how she'd swung a piece of Sonoma real estate he didn't know.

"A crack in the dam."

Lance quirked his mouth. "Sounds a little snobbish, but I suppose that's understandable given your family's status."

"I only told you since you seemed interested in history."

"I am." At least since Nonna had sent him to Conchessa, and through her to this opposite end of the country. Surprisingly, Sonoma reflected their Italian roots much better than the furor of the Bronx. He had always thought Nonna out of step with the fast-paced, straight-talking New York scene. But this wine country was her birthplace.

"Banking here through Prohibition and the Depression must have been a challenge."

She shrugged. "Not every banker jumped out the window."

"So your great-grandfather came through it okay."

She arched an eyebrow. "He diversified."

"Rum running?" He'd read how prominent wineries had marketed grape concentrate and yeast with the caution that adding water might result in fermentation—as legal a product as their sacramental wines, but not exactly in the spirit of Prohibition.

With a wry smile, she rested her elbow on the table and bent the wrist like a gooseneck. "My fine upstanding family? Really. Don't you know my father's up for mayor?"

"No, I didn't." How would he?

"Not that it matters to me. I stand on my own feet." She rubbed her calf against his shin. "How about you?"

"I haven't stood on anyone else's lately."

She laughed. "I mean *Michelli*. Any Mafia skeletons?"

"You mean the guy in cement shoes in my closet?"

She laughed again. "You didn't show me your closet."

He took the check from the waitress and gave her his credit card. No, he hadn't shown Sybil his closet—had not, in fact, shown her his room, particularly because he hadn't made the bed or picked up his clothes. "If you do a story on the inn, how would you research its past?"

She shrugged. "Property titles, tax records, anything that might have been published somewhere about the owners."

He'd already done that.

She drained her wine. "It isn't the greatest property. There used to be a better villa near it that was torn down."

"Why?"

"Age, quake damage." She shrugged. "I don't know." And clearly didn't care.

"This one is well built. It's stood the test of time."

She dabbed her mouth with the napkin. "That doesn't make for a thrilling article."

He signed the charge slip and tucked his copy into his shirt pocket. "What about the fact that Rese is renovating it herself? Women's interest and all that?"

Sybil fixed her gray-blue eyes on him. "I was sort of joking when I told her I might do a piece. This area has enough people who all think their inns are original and fascinating." She flicked her hair back over her shoulder. "Now if there was a scandal there or something criminal, she might get some free advertising that way."

A protective surge gripped him. "She wasn't asking. You brought it up."

"I just wanted you to show me around." She stood up. "Ready?"

He took the keys from his pocket, wishing he'd made her take her own car. The way she pressed into him on the Harley as he drove back left nothing to the imagination. He came to a stop beside her car and cut the engine.

She straightened a little, but didn't let go of his waist. Instead she rested her chin on his shoulder and spoke into his ear. "You could show me your room."

"Too many skeletons in the closet." He slid out of her grasp and got off the bike.

She climbed off slowly, letting the skirt slide up her thigh.

Lance looked away. The lights were on in the front parlor. He could see Rese at work, still up on the scaffolding, no sign of dizziness. He'd seen her on the roof, the ladders. She was like a cat. She didn't lose her balance.

Sybil slid a hand across his waist and gripped his shirt. "If you show me your room, I'll show you mine."

He looked back at her. "Sybil, I'm not looking for a relationship." Relationships got him in trouble. Big time.

"In the morning I'll pretend I don't know you." She caught her thumbs in the waist of his jeans.

The physical attraction was tempered by a vague repulsion. He stepped back, breaking her hold. "I'd have to confess it."

She crossed her arms, pressing her chest up and out. "What does it take to absolve you?"

He gave her a smile. "Divine decree?"

She cocked her head and eyed him. "This *is* a challenge. A saint who's sexy as sin."

"I'm not saying that. I just don't want complications."

"Well then . . ." She took her keys from her purse and turned to her car. "I'll see you around."

He nodded, but hoped it would not be too often. Intelligent and beautiful as she was, predatory women did not attract him. Not even one from the ruling class of Sonoma, California. Releasing a long slow breath, he went into the house.

Baxter scrambled up and slid on the wood floor to meet him. Lance had wondered why the dog didn't come bounding the moment he heard his bike on the drive. "Hey you, con dog. Got her to let you in?" He glanced up.

Rese leaned on the railing. "He was upset you left without him."

"Thanks for easing his distress." He eyed the wall of shelves she was building. She was meticulous—no slapping it together for Rese Barrett. And no simple utility. The shelf was a lovely piece of work; nicely grained wood, trim pieces decoratively routed.

"He's good company." She climbed down to her worktable.

"Hear that, Baxter?" He squatted down and rubbed the dog's head. "The lady likes you."

She measured a piece of trim. "Dogs are easier than people."

Interesting thought. He stood up. "Let's take him for a walk." Where did that come from?

She pulled her safety goggles over her eyes. "I want to finish."

Fine. He'd go upstairs and ponder his close call. But when she finished routing the piece, he was still there, watching. Her hands were sure and strong and reminded him of the street artists in Italy. She remounted the scaffolding with ease, not even looking where she stepped. She might have gotten dizzy earlier, but he doubted it. Something had upset her.

Rese checked the fit of the piece, then, satisfied, climbed back down. He met her at the bottom, took the goggles from her head and tossed them lightly to her worktable. "Baxter needs a walk."

She looked down at the dog.

"Tell her, Baxter."

The dog barked.

She laughed, then shot him a scornful look. "It's just a trick."

Undaunted, he nodded toward the door, and she capitulated. Outside, Baxter frisked like a pup, but Rese grew stiff and silent as they started down the lane, her hands shifting around until they hung like wooden posts at her sides. Her unease amused him, in light of her usual bullheaded confidence. It was a little like seeing a bouncer sweat, or a lifeguard snubbed.

He eyed her. "What's the matter?"

"Nothing." She rubbed the back of her neck, let the hand drop.

Lance caught it in his, more to constrain it than anything else.

She pulled away. "I'm not blind."

"Just as stiff and salty as Lot's wife." He grinned.

"Because I'm not mashing myself against you?"

Whoa. No soft-pedaling there. An instant recollection of Sybil on his bike. Was that what had Rese so uptight?

"Your shelf is coming nicely."

She looked over her shoulder to the villa. "I should be working on it."

"Need a break sometime."

"Why?" She looked at him. "If you're doing what you're meant to, why should you stop?"

Good point. If you knew what you were meant to do. But he wasn't going there with her. "Too much of a good thing?"

She proceeded in silence. He would obviously carry the load of this conversation—if they had one. "So why renovation?"

"My dad." Her arms tightened around her.

A chilly breeze caught them, and she shivered. With anyone else he would slip off his jacket and put it over her shoulders. With Rese, he might get his head taken off. "He taught you well."

She brushed aside the branches of a mimosa leaning into the sidewalk. "He was an incredible craftsman."

Lance caught the past tense and the stitch it gave her voice. "I can see that by your work."

"We did some very famous homes, a lot of jobs on Nob Hill. His love was taking something really old and making it new without changing the heart of it."

"As you're doing with the inn."

Rese nodded. "He was trained by his father and he trained me."

"No brothers?"

She shot him a glare. "Are you saying if there were boys, he wouldn't have trained me?"

"Something like that." Let her think him sexist; he'd faced his pop's and brother's ribbing, spending so many hours with Nonna in the kitchen. He knew how it worked.

She shook her head. "No brothers. My mother died when I was nine."

At least that grief wasn't raw, like the other. "Who took care of you?"

"My dad. I spent all my free hours on his work sites. I learned more by watching and questioning there than everything they taught in school."

"Not a great student, huh?"

She stopped. "What makes you think that?"

He whistled Baxter out of someone's yard. "Well, if sawing and hammering were your best subjects . . ."

"You forget the mathematics and engineering and physics and symmetry and calculating and designing that go into construction."

"True." He picked up a stick and tossed it for the dog. "You don't read, though."

"How would you know?"

He grinned. "Only a nonreader would put something the length of *Moby Dick* in a weekend room. You can't know the angst of leaving a story midstream."

She took the stick Baxter brought to her, instead of him, and tossed it. "It matched the theme."

"And the parlor bookshelf?"

"I'll fill it for people who like to read."

Lance ducked under the branches of a bottlebrush tree and studied the yard planted with lilies and snowball bushes. "We ought to clean up the garden."

She nodded. "I was going to ask you to. I don't do well with plants."

"Really?" He picked a windblown umbrella seed out of her hair. "You're sprouting."

She half smiled.

"Hey, that's better."

"What?"

"You almost look like you're enjoying this."

She tucked her hands into her pockets. "I like to walk."

"Some girls might add 'with you'."

Rese slanted him a glance. "You mean Sybil?"

"Oh, man." He must have looked funny because she laughed, that great laugh that rarely happened. He was tempted to tell her he had hoped Sybil would help him dig into the past, but that might reveal too much. Then again . . . "How much do you know about the inn?"

She shrugged. "It's structurally sound, much better constructed than any house along this street. Whoever built it made it to last, earthquakes and all."

Only Rese would address that aspect. "So who did build it?"

"I don't know." She squeezed Baxter's head and thanked him for the stick he once again brought to her. "I don't have any original papers." She heaved the stick. "I got it for a steal at the bank auction since it had been empty long enough for the lower level to be vandalized."

"The bedrooms weren't?"

"The stairs were out." She clapped when Baxter caught the stick in the air. "Some idiot started a fire there. The first thing I did was rebuild them."

He stopped and looked at her. "You rebuilt the stairs? That's new construction?"

She smiled. "That's renovation."

"You're very good." He expected her to blush the way she had when he told her she was pretty.

Instead her face pinched a little and she said, "I learned from the best."

They walked in silence again, Lance sensing her grief. He knew the smell of it, the way it tinged the air with the odor of sick souls. And he thought of Tony, lost in an instant, and the way his family had reeled. Two Michelli sons, and the one who had his life figured out was gone.

Rese rubbed the goose bumps on her arms. This time he took off his jacket and offered it to her.

She shook her head. "Why should I be warm and you be chilly?"

"I've got long sleeves." His chambray shirt let the air through, but it was better than her T-shirt. "I wore it one way, you wear it back. Equal opportunity warmth."

She just said, "No thanks. I'm okay."

He wasn't going to force it on her, even though something tugged inside as he watched her shiver. That strange connection wavered between them, but she must not realize it.

"So if you don't take walks with guys, what do you do on dates? Go to the movies? Dinner? Dancing?"

She snorted and kept walking.

He narrowed one eye. "Arm wrestle?"

She stopped and put her hands to her hips. "None of the above."

He reached for her hand again, her palm cool and callused in his.

"Lance."

He swung their joined hands lightly between them as they walked. "Want to know my idea of a great date?"

"No."

"A nice walk hand in hand, a happy dog frisking along. A pretty woman with a great laugh. A chilly evening that requires I surrender my jacket—"

"You didn't have to surrender it."

"I tried." He tucked both their hands into the jacket pocket, a position she tolerated for less time than the first.

She pulled away and separated their hands. "I told you I don't date my employees."

"Why not?"

She looked up at the sky, exasperated. "It's bad policy."

"I think your previous employees were thickheaded thugs."

She actually smiled and dropped her gaze. "I don't even know if it'll work out having you cook. What if I don't have enough guests to pay you?"

He winced. "You'd make breakfast yourself?"

She punched his arm.

He caught her hand and tucked it into his elbow. At her glare, he said, "Pretend I'm blind."

"Deaf would be easier. If I knew you'd be this much trouble, I never would have hired you."

"Haven't seen much competition." He covered her hand in the crook of his arm and strolled.

"I cancelled the ad and took down the sign." She cocked her chin at him. "You're close enough to the woman I hoped for."

"Ouch."

She looked away. "Sorry."

He was not inclined to let that one go. But she looked back with her umber eyes more sincere than he'd seen them yet and repeated her apology.

"Is it the earring?"

She shook her head. "I didn't mean it."

Baxter took off into the inn's yard as they turned into the drive. She took her hand out of his arm and hurried toward the house. "I need to finish the bookshelf."

Jaw cocked, he watched her go inside. Rese Barrett was one interesting egg. Befriending her might be as formidable as finding Nonna's secrets, but he sort of liked the challenge. He went up to his room and took up his guitar.

CHAPTER ELEVEN

A strain of melody.
The song I can't recall.
Drifts through my mind like a shadow searching,
Leaving the notes behind.

Rese couldn't resist. She had hoped Star would be back by now, but there was still no sign of her. And the playful, energetic music coming down the stairs had to be Lance. If he was playing a CD, there would be other instrumentation besides the single guitar, and as she neared the door, she could tell there was nothing more. She tapped.

"It's open." The music didn't stop.

She opened the door and saw him sprawled carelessly on the bed, picking the lively tune. He ended it and straightened. "Did I bother you?"

"No. I just didn't know you could play."

He leaned back into the pillows and strummed softly. "Jack of all trades."

She wished she hadn't said that. He was obviously accomplished in many areas.

"Want to hear something?" He drew one knee up and his bare foot nestled into the coverlet, his toes curled slightly and the tendons raised beneath the skin. Strange how vulnerable a bare foot could look.

This was not a situation she'd planned on when she specified separate spaces, but she pulled the captain's chair out a little from the corner and sat down. "Okay."

"What do you like? Rock, classical, bluegrass?"

Even his music was scattered. "Anything."

He started a melancholy pick, then sang a ballad about a boy finding his way. His plaintive tone rolled over the words with feeling until he launched into the chorus with a stronger voice and complicated strum.

It was something she had never heard, and as she listened, she wondered why not. She sank into the chair as his fingers worked the strings and his voice ebbed and flowed. He looked at her while he sang, one with his art, as she was when the wood took shape in her hands. The story of a boy's search for meaning unfolded, then Lance's voice trailed away, and his fingers slowed and stilled.

She let the tones evaporate, then said, "I don't know that one."

"I wrote it."

She leaned forward. "Really? Are you the boy?"

"He's an 'everyman' type, but I wrote it at a tough time."

She settled back in the chair. "Tough how?"

He hung both arms over the waist of the instrument. "First big trouble I got into."

Rese braced herself. "What kind of trouble?"

"Helping a friend escape her stepdad."

"Escape?"

"He was . . . messing with her." Lance rubbed the top of one forearm. "So, I took her mom's car and got her out of there." He glanced up at a place on the wall as though sinking back in time.

Rese leaned forward. "Where did you take her?"

"As far as we could get before Gil roared up behind us in his truck."

Rese stared. "Were you arrested?" Felony car theft and kidnapping?

"The officers turned me over to Tony . . ." He gave a half smile. "Which was not better. My brother wore the NYPD blues like second skin, and having his kid brother dragged in with an underage girl, a stolen car, and his partners yucking it up—well, it wasn't pretty."

"How old were you?"

"Sixteen."

Rese folded her arms. "What happened?"

"Tony let me sweat it out on a seat at the station, where I saw firsthand the sort of people he dealt with. Finally he found time to question me. My story didn't match Cici's since she was spouting whatever Gil demanded."

"I bet that made you mad."

Lance shrugged. "I knew why she did it. And Tony knew me. He said 'Lance, next time you try to help someone, use your head, not just your heart.'" Lance dropped his gaze to the bed. "I don't know what he said to Gil, but the charges were dropped, and like everything else, it became a story Tony told to razz me." His smile seemed sad.

Rese sensed something deeper than embarrassment, but Lance brought his hands back to the guitar. "Here's a little flamenco." He launched into a Spanish-style song where the fingers of both hands flew on individual strings, strumming and picking with a strong rhythm.

When he stopped she couldn't help but stare. Now the earring fit, as did his hypersensitivity and high-strung nature. Emotions poured out on the notes.

"You want to do entertainment?"

He raised his brows. "For our guests?"

There was that 'our' again. "You could play in the evenings. Take requests."

He slapped the strings with a back-of-the-finger strum and sang, "When the moon's in the sky like a big pizza pie, it's *amoré*."

She laughed. "I'm serious."

He set the guitar aside and wrapped his arms loosely around his knees. With his jeans pulled up, she could see the dark hair of his legs running down his bony shin to the instep of his feet. "I don't know, Rese, you might find me indispensable."

"You could have a tip jar."

"Is that your way of saying you won't pay me?"

She smiled. "It's just a thought."

He cocked his head. "You really want this to work, don't you."

"Of course." She laced her fingers. "Why go to all this work if—"

"That's what I don't get. I can see you fixing up the place; that's what you do. But running it? Won't you miss the sawing and hammering?"

Her chest tightened. She had told herself this was it, the last project, done in Dad's honor. She could not go on as they'd been, not without him. "No."

He studied her a moment. "Well, don't get me wrong, but . . . you'll have to work on your presentation."

"Presentation?" What was he talking about?

"Interaction."

Was he saying she was unfriendly? Doubts and fears crowded in, the things she knew would be a struggle. "I can show people to their rooms."

He stood up, took hold of her hand and walked her downstairs to the front door. She stood, confused, when he went out into the dark and closed the door behind him. He knocked and she opened it, only slightly more puzzled than annoyed.

"Hi." He smiled. "Sorry I'm late. I know check-in was at three, but I had some trouble with my bike. Were you in bed?"

"That's none of your business."

Lance leaned his hand on the doorjamb and grinned. "That's what I mean."

"If some turkey asks me a personal question . . . "

"Rese, it is personal. Hospitality is about connecting. You make people feel at home."

"If they want to feel at home they can stay home."

He put his shoulder to the jamb. "Then where would you be?"

She studied his earnest face. "All right. Yes, I was asleep, but it's no trouble. May I show you your room?"

His smile spread slowly. "I'd rather see yours."

She scowled. "You have the wrong place, jerk."

He tossed back his head and laughed. "Good. I see you know where to draw the line."

She huffed. "Would you come in already? It's cold outside." The night mist had spread over the yard.

Lance stepped into the entry between her and the wall, and she closed the door just past his shoulder. He placed a hand on her waist. "What will you do with unruly guests?" His hand burned warm as he glanced down at her mouth.

She should have grabbed something hard to wield. "I can take care of myself." She stepped back, furious that her pulse had decided to rush.

"So have you had this place long?" He motioned toward the stairs and she started up.

"We just opened in June."

"We?"

A Freudian slip for sure. "My lunatic cook and I. His food is marvelous, but—"

"What?" Lance stopped on the stair beneath her.

She half turned. "I said his food is marvelous, but he—"

"Say it again."

Standing just slightly above him, she stared into his face. "Say what?"

"That my food is marvelous." He joined her on the same stair without breaking eye contact.

She moistened her lips. What was he getting at? Why did he have that molten look in his eyes? She was making a joke about the lunatic, but that didn't seem to be the issue. "Your food is marvelous."

"Do you mean it?"

She spread her hands. "You're the chef. Don't you know what you can do?"

He caught her waist in both hands. "Repeat after me: Lance, that was delicious."

He *was* a lunatic. "I just—"

"Say it, Rese."

The hold he had was sending warmth up her ribs, and she couldn't recall his words. "What am I supposed to say?"

"That was delicious."

She repeated it.

A triumphant smile found his mouth. "Thank you. I'm glad you enjoyed it."

Something clicked in her mind. She *had* offended him. But how was she supposed to know? Dad had never once commented on her meals, a pattern instilled in both of them while her mother was alive. They didn't criticize the stuff served up as supper; they bore it. After it was just the two of them, Dad had eaten in exhausted silence, then lumbered off to watch TV. That was how it was done.

But weren't there times when she had put special effort into their dinner, that she hoped he might say something? She had reveled in his quiet praise of her carpentry, and yes, wished he would notice her other efforts.

It was uncomfortable to recall. She stared at Lance. "Are you finished now?"

He let go of her waist. "You haven't shown me my room."

"It's at the top of the stairs."

He motioned, and she reluctantly led him to the top and stopped in the open doorway. "This is your room. I hope you'll be comfortable."

"I'm sure I will." He stepped into the doorway with her. "I hear you have music after dinner."

Her heart jumped. Was he saying he would do it? "Yes, a guitar soloist."

"Is he any good?"

He was certainly fishing tonight. She looked into his face less than a foot from hers. "What I heard was very good. Just don't request *It's Amoré.*"

Lance laughed, then slowly sobered. His gaze dropped to her mouth.

A rush of panic made squid tentacles of her legs. "Don't look at me like that."

"Like what?" His voice was latté smooth.

"Like you want to kiss me."

"I do." His hand found her side again, warm and firm.

Her lungs were sucking something thicker than air. "Well, don't."

He met her eyes. "Don't you wonder what it'd be like?"

"Kissing a man with an earring?"

"Kissing me."

She did not wonder and she wouldn't. This had gotten out of hand. "I don't kiss the cook."

He cocked his head with a half smile. "Okay."

"So . . . I hope you like your accommodations. The chef will have something . . . delicious for breakfast."

He drew a breath and released it. "Good night, Rese."

"Good night."

He closed the door behind her. She should not have gone up there. He was obviously the sort to stake his flag on any ground she surrendered. He had caught her off guard from that first glance—the look that made her feel like a stranger in her own home. A shiver crawled her spine, and she glanced quickly behind her at the empty hall. But it was just that. Empty.

CHAPTER TWELVE

Nonna Carina
Cherished, a little spoiled, even with her hair more white
than black and her skin no longer blooming petal soft.
A jut of her chin, a swish of the skirts.
Nonno Quillan's eyes dance. Unperturbed.
Her foot stomps.
Deep laughter.
Indignation.
He catches her into his arms. They have always been so.
Such is life. Such is love.

Lance spent most of the night trying to forget he had almost kissed Rese. And worse, that he'd shared something personal and painful as well. Memories of Tony were hard enough. Memories of Tony cleaning up his messes, harder still.

Tony was the guy every kid wanted to be. When he went into the schools wearing his NYPD uniform, he drew people like iron to a magnet. While cops were not always popular, Tony's mystique made him larger than life. As his kid brother, Lance had basked in the afterglow—until he got old enough to make decisions that cost him even that.

A pang of regret. Why had he chosen that song? And told her that story? Guilt? Maybe he wanted her to doubt him, to guess he was misleading her. He wouldn't, if there was any other way. Until he found what he came for, he had to keep his business to himself. And nearly kissing her? Well, that fell into his innate weakness. Momma said he had an Achilles' heel where his heart ought to be.

Lance couldn't even pretend she needed him. Without that excuse, what was it? Because standing on the stairs, when she had looked into his face and said his food was marvelous, he had exulted. Now, with the morning sun spilling into the kitchen, he began to cook for the toughest critic he'd ever faced. As quietly as possible, he whipped up a crepe batter, then the ricotta filling and the berry sauce.

Rese came out of her hallway looking sleepy and disheveled and adorable. She yawned and stretched like a gangly kitten, then plunked herself down at the table.

He said, "Come here."

She looked at him as though he'd ordered her down for twenty push-ups. He had already been to church and purchased and prepared the breakfast ingredients, but she dragged herself up and padded over, barefooted and cranky. He poured a dab of batter into the too-large copper skillet. Then he closed her hand around the handle and helped her rotate it to spread the batter into a thin layer over the bottom.

"It'll be more uniform when we get the crepe pan. But you get the idea." He caught a hint of interest in her face, which was more than he'd expected. He handed her the spatula. "It only takes a moment for a crepe this thin. You don't want to crisp it or it won't roll nicely." He motioned for her to flip it. "Loosen the edges, then just slide under it gently."

She flipped it and glanced up.

He smiled. "Good. Now grab a plate."

She took two from the cabinet and set them next to the stove. He slid her crepe onto the plate, then quickly spooned a strip of ricotta filling and rolled it. He ladled the berry sauce atop and handed it to her. "Enjoy." And he meant it.

He whipped up his own in moments and sat down with her.

She looked up. "Lance, this is delicious."

His mouth pulled sideways. She had repeated it like a child reciting math facts. "You like the texture of the filling, the sweet but tangy sauce, and the light, buttery crepe?"

"Sure." She put her face down and finished the crepe. "Let's make another. I'm starved."

"You shouldn't skip meals." He walked her back to the stove.

"I wouldn't have if you'd been cooking."

That was the truest compliment yet. He poured the batter and again closed her hand inside his on the handle. The motion of the pan was almost sensual, and with her arm along his, her hand warm, and the back of her neck so accessible, he had to force himself to concentrate on the task. They set the pan down, but he didn't let go. She glanced up, and her sleepy face was so tempting.

"Should I flip it now?"

He glanced at the crepe. "Let it go a tad longer."

"A tad?"

He jabbed her ribs lightly, but she jumped. "Ah. Ticklish."

She warded him off with the spatula and a look that would have stopped Attila the Hun.

He nodded at the pan. "It's ready."

She went all around the crepe with the spatula, then tried to slide it under.

"Careful. Loosen it there." He guided her hand.

The front door opened and Star's voice sang out, "Ah, glorious perfume that taunts the palate."

Rese stepped away as the zany dame interrupted them. "It's Lance's crepes."

"What peril must I face, what deadly deed commit to win that rare prize?"

Lance looked at Rese who said, "Sit down. You can have this one."

He slid it from the pan onto a fresh plate, filled and rolled it and spooned on the sauce, then set it before Star who had taken his seat. "Rese made this one."

"All I did was fry it. You made the batter and filling and all."

"Next time I'll wake you up, and you can start from scratch."

She glared. "Don't even think about it."

"You might enjoy it."

She shook her head. "I've been cooking since I was nine. I will not enjoy it."

Star sighed over her first bite with drama even Lance found excessive. How on earth were these two women friends?

He said, "No offense, Rese, but you haven't been cooking." She opened her mouth to object, but he pointed his finger. "If I handed you particle board and said make me a cedar chest, could you?"

"Of course not."

"It's the same with food. You might have prepared meals, even 'cooked' them. But that's not the art of it."

"This"—Star dangled a bite of crepe from her fork—"is art." She wore the same outfit as yesterday, and her hair was even crazier. "But then art requires the eye of the beholder, as manna begs a discerning palate."

Surprisingly astute, and his point precisely. But he wasn't sure he wanted to be on the same page with her.

"Did you know the Benziger vineyard commissions artwork for their labels? The only stipulation is to incorporate the Parthenon." Star took the bite. "I spent the night there."

"In the Parthenon?" Lance and Rese said together.

"The little one on the Benziger estate where the old doctor smoked weed."

Lance was getting the picture now. Only a chemically modified brain could function like Star's.

"I thought you were looking for a job," Rese said.

"I was. But I met someone and he offered me a private tour and one thing led to another and . . ." She waved her hand. " . . . here I am for crepes."

Lance turned to the stove and poured a crepe for Rese, assuming she still wanted another. Star had certainly broken the mood.

But as soon as she finished eating, Star stood up. "I have to change. A certain young vintner is waiting for me."

"For an interview, I suppose," Rese said.

"Of course." Star flitted out.

Too many questions he could ask about that one. How did they meet; what did they talk about? He held Rese's chair, then set down the fresh steaming crepe and said, "Art."

She looked down at her plate. "Maybe if I'd done something like this, Dad would have noticed."

Ah. "He didn't appreciate you?"

She picked up her fork. "He appreciated my carpentry." She cut into the crepe.

Lance took his seat. "So that's where you excelled."

"I excelled, so he complimented."

"You don't think it works the other way around?"

She looked puzzled. "Excellence is praised."

"Praise inspires excellence."

She shook her head. "No. If you praise substandard work you encourage mediocrity."

"Even mediocrity is a step toward excellence."

She leaned back in her chair. "But if you receive the reward before you accomplish the goal, why push on?"

"Because the goal is worth it." He slid Star's plate aside, turned his hand on its edge. "If I want to get from here, to here." He slid it sideways across to hers. "I can't always make it in one plunge. First I might get to here." He set his hand a third of the distance. "Did I accomplish something?"

She nodded. "I guess."

"So smile."

She gave him a dim version.

He moved another third. "Have I come closer to the goal?"

She smiled without prompting, but not overly enthusiastic.

He slid his hand over and took hers. "Now where would I be if you had frowned at my first attempts?"

"You'd be appropriately respectful of our differing positions."

That implacable hierarchy. He sat back. "You need a partner more than a cook."

"No, I don't." She stood up and carried her plate to the sink, then turned to leave.

He said, "Wash it."

She looked over her shoulder. "What?"

"I'm not on the clock. You can wash your own plate."

She huffed, but did it.

"The point is, people perform according to expectations, but gratification is born of appreciation."

She raised her brows and sighed. "Okay." Then she added, "Thank you for the crepes. They were marvelous." She even sounded sincere.

He quirked his mouth. "Not bad for a lunatic cook?"

"Right."

"Thank you."

"You're welcome."

He stood up and washed his plate. "We might need a dishwasher if we have a full house most of the time."

"Lance." She put her hands on her hips.

"Just a thought." He wiped his plate dry.

"Your thoughts are expensive. Every time you open your mouth I'm deeper in debt."

He started for the kitchen door. "I'll just feed Baxter and get to work on my quarters." With mad Star in the house, finishing had become expedient.

"Good. I'll be in the parlor."

"Eating bread and honey?" He ducked out the door as the sponge sailed toward his head. She might be a tough nut, but oh, he enjoyed provoking her.

Hard as she tried, Rese could not get out of her head the things Lance had said about appreciation. It seemed disrespectful to her dad's memory to consider the argument's validity. Encouragement for the steps along the way? She thought she had worked to master what mattered to her. Had she, in fact, needed the reward of her father's praise? Did she work harder in the only area she stood a chance of earning his respect?

She sighed. It had not been easy for Dad after Mom's death. He did the best he could. And she tried to be what he needed. They had carried on in the only way they knew how. If Lance wanted appreciation, she could show it. That didn't mean she needed it herself. Good grief.

She climbed onto the scaffolding to sand the bookshelf. This was not the most ornate house she had worked on, but it lent itself to her talent with grace. She had never renovated a place she intended to keep, not a place of her own.

A knock came on the door, but she was high on the scaffolding, so she called, "Come in."

The front door opened and a miniature woman crept inside. She wasn't as small as her stoop made her, but even so, her hands were bird claws, one clasped over the perch of a cane. Her hair was a peculiar shade of blue. Rese assumed it was supposed to be gray.

The woman raised her cane. "So you're the one who took over Ralph's place."

Rese wasn't sure how to answer that.

"I'd have come sooner but the pneumonia had me down flat." She worked her way in closer. "I've watched you through the window, though."

The face she'd seen from the garden? A wash of relief. Just a little old lady, curious about a new neighbor. Rese set down the sandpaper and climbed off the scaffolding. "I'm Rese Barrett."

"Honey, can't your nice man to do that for you?" She waved her claw toward the bookshelf.

No doubt she meant Lance, if she'd been observing them from next door. "No. I do it myself."

The woman did a slow turn. "Ralph wanted to fix this place up, but never got to it. He was my sweetheart."

Rese raised her brows.

"We were very discreet. Didn't want the others to know."

"The others?"

"The gang." She fixed both hands over the cane head. "We all met Wednesdays for euchre, right here in this room. Though . . ." She screwed up her face. "It's bigger now."

"I took down a wall." Eyeing the expanse, Rese imagined a "gang" of oldsters cackling over their cards.

"Just love euchre. I almost always win." The woman's laugh became a cough nasty enough to send a shock of concern through Rese.

Her own breath quickened. "Are you all right, Ms. . . ."

The woman waved her off. "Good heavens, don't do any of that Ms. stuff. I am Miss Potter. Miss Evvy Potter. That's two *v*'s so people don't say Ee-vy. It's for Evelyn. But Evelyn was my mother's name so I became Evvy."

Well, now that was cleared up. . . .

"My first beau was killed in the second great war. Served under Patton. Most of the men from around here came back, but not James." She sniffed and shook her head. "I met Ralph when I was seventy-three. I live next door there." She pointed out the side window to the house Rese had guessed, then leaned in conspiratorially. "He was a younger man. Sixty-nine. Scandalous."

She laughed. "But oh, we did get on. Sixteen years we were neighbors— and sweethearts—and no one guessed." Her eyes sparked with humor. "We made it a game to be particularly testy with each other."

Evvy Potter shook her head sadly. "He had to go to the home. He just wasn't strong. And he was slipping a little." She tapped her temple. "Not that I would tell him."

Rese said, "It must be hard."

Evvy shrugged. "When you live to be ninety, you get used to losing friends. We'll all be storming the pearly gates soon enough."

Heaven. A comfort, Rese supposed, for those who believed it.

"What did you say your name was?" Evvy's gaze was sharp again.

"Rese Barrett."

"What sort of name is Rese?"

"Short for Theresa." That was two people she'd told within days.

Evvy nodded. "And that young man I've seen?"

"He's my cook. He'll help me run the place."

"I thought you might be taking guests. This is too much house for one. Ralph said so constantly." She formed an impish grin. "Mostly when he was proposing. *'Evvy, this house is too big for me. It needs a wife inside.'*"

"You said no?"

"I lived fifty-two years with my mother, and thirty-eight alone. Ralph was a wonderful diversion. But I had no mind to move in with the man."

Rese had to smile at that. "You can still come over if you want. I don't know what guests I'll have, but there may be some who know euchre."

Evvy's face crinkled like crepe. "That's nice." She started for the door, then mentioned over her shoulder, "And don't mind the noises at night."

Rese froze, hearing again the moans and howls of that one particular night.

"I'm certain it's not haunted. Even though someone was murdered here."

The hairs stood up on Rese's arms. "In the attic?"

Evvy raised her brows. "I'm not sure what room. Ralph might know. But I don't think I ever asked."

Rese scrutinized the parlor after Evvy closed the door. Murder. Old houses always had history, as Lance said, but not many had the dubious honor of murder. She should have asked who and why instead of where. But she was not sure she wanted to know. She could imagine too well once the lights were out. If she had a name and a face to put to the creaks . . . It hadn't been as bad since she confronted the ghosts the night Lance scared the breath from her.

"Re—"

She spun with a cry.

Lance stopped, hands splayed before him. "What?"

She closed her eyes at what a fool she'd just made of herself. All because some old woman spooked her. She jammed her hands to her hips. "Did you need something?"

He matched her position. "Roofing nails."

"Oh. I'm out. You'll have to go get them."

He eyed her quizzically. "Need anything else?"

Tranquilizers. That was three times he'd sent her heart to her throat. Not counting last night in the doorway of his room. That was a different jolt altogether. "No."

"Everything all right?"

"Of course." Rese turned her back and gathered the scraps of maple from the floor, laying them across her worktable. Why hadn't she explained about her neighbor's visit, shared the wonderful news that blood had been spilled inside these walls? Blood never went away. You could paint over it and with the right equipment, it would still show up.

Her lungs compressed. She heard the roar of pain, saw the blood flung onto the wall. *Dad!* Herself in slow motion, running toward him as he fell.

Warm, ruby-colored fluid, coursing through her fingers. Rese clenched her fists against her face and tried to breathe. Then she started to cry, the tears she had fought filling her palms as his blood had.

She jerked as Lance took her shoulders and turned her. What was he doing there? Hadn't he gone out the door?

"What's the matter, Rese? What happened?"

She shook her head. "Nothing."

He tipped her face up.

"It's just . . ." She pulled away, putting distance between them. "Thinking about Dad. How—"she sucked in a breath—"he died." She forced herself to look at him.

His eyes were soft and deep. "How did he die?"

She swallowed. "We were working. Just the two of us. An old lodge near Muir Woods." Dad had loved those woods, the majestic redwoods reaching to the sky, a towering testimony to time and survival.

"We were so far from everything." If it had happened in the city, emergency services would have gotten there. Instead there'd been only her. "It had gotten dark, and I was turning on the work lights." A blaze of white flashed behind her eyes, an electrical jolt. Her cry cut short by—She pressed her hands to her face and shook her head. "I can't." Saying it out loud was worse than months of silence.

She lowered her face. "You can go. I'm fine."

"You're an unreliable judge of that."

She frowned. "I'm fine, Lance. Go get your nails."

"I don't want to leave you alone."

She half smiled. "With the murdered person?"

He shot her a queer glance. "Murdered person?"

"According to my neighbor, someone was killed in this house."

"Which neighbor?"

She jutted her chin toward the side window. "Miss Evvy Potter. I've reached an understanding with the ghost, though. I haven't heard any moans lately."

"What else did she tell you?"

"She was in love with a younger man. He was only sixty-nine."

Lance cocked his head.

"They kept it quiet though. So the gang wouldn't be jealous."

He half smiled. "She sounds like fun. I might have to get to know her."

"I don't think she'd go quite that young."

Lance stroked his chin. "You never know."

"You might believe yourself the hunk no woman can resist, but Evvy is too independent for you." She closed her arms around herself.

"I like independent women. I even like cranky, confused, unsociable women."

"I'm not unsociable."

His smile creased his eyes. "You thought I meant you?"

She scowled. "Would you go away? I have work to do."

"You won't faint on the scaffolding, will you?"

"I never faint." Though she'd been all but catatonic by the time the emergency vehicles reached the cabin. She would not think of that now. Certainly not before Lance left her in peace. She crossed over and climbed the scaffolding like a monkey. *Faint. Hah.* He would faint before she did.

Rese lifted the hand sander, but just before she continued on the spot where she'd left off, a sound like a muffled gunshot came through the wall.

Chapter Thirteen

Momma smells of verbena and summer roses.
A rustle of taffeta. Small white hands.
Skin like unskimmed milk, fresh and smooth,
but lacking sweetness.
Beautiful, but I find no comfort there,
for discontent clings to her like a hungry urchin.

L ance fondled Baxter's ears as the dog begged a ride. Mounting the bike, he glanced back toward the house. He'd have to take Rese at her word. Her wrenching tears had stopped the moment he touched her. She wanted to grieve alone. And he had enough to think about.

A murder in the villa had to be significant. Even though other people had lived in the house, Nonna's silence suggested a past tragedy, and her urgency now indicated a wrong she wanted to right. What greater wrong was there than a life cut short? A thrill of anticipation. What else did Rese's neighbor know? As old as she sounded, she might know quite a bit. Maybe all of it.

What had Rese said her name was? Potter. Eve Potter. He glanced at the smaller house next to the villa, its sloping roof ending in a trellis of verbena and a garden almost as untended as theirs. It must have been built after the DiGratia vineyards were gone, or perhaps it was an addition for an in-law or married offspring.

Lance hesitated. Should he talk to its occupant now? Too obvious. As he started the bike, Baxter jumped aboard, determined not to be left behind. They went into town and bought the supplies. The dog was glad for the drive, short as it was. It had been too long since they'd had some open road. *Soon, buddy. Soon.*

He couldn't ignore Nonna's charge, and his fresh concern for Rese added to it. But once he'd done what he came for, he and Baxter would hit the road. Wouldn't they?

Back on the property, Lance went to work on the carriage house roof, the sun heating the back of his neck and shoulders as he hammered the plywood. His muscles pulled and bunched, remembering and responding to the work. His hands had hardened.

From below, Baxter whined a soft welcome. Resting one knee on the rafter, Lance paused and looked down. Sybil. His first thought was to hide, but that was a little hard on the roof. Then he considered how Rese would handle it—up front and in your face. He'd just tell her he wasn't interested.

He set the hammer on a crosspiece and climbed down while she fondled the dog. Then she stood up, showing six inches between her low-slung shorts and the paisley shirt that matched her lavender naval ornament. He could not keep his eyes from going there, but thankfully Baxter demanded her attention again.

Laughing, she petted the dog's neck. "Been riding your Harley, Baxter?"

Lance answered for him. "He's mostly hung around here."

She looked up. "Why don't we take him somewhere?"

He leaned on the doorjamb. "I can only manage one passenger at a time." Though, technically, with Baxter in front, Sybil could have the back seat.

She straightened, pressing her palms to her lower back, the sun glinting on the beads and silver that accented her sun-tanned navel and sharp hip bones. "It's a great day for a ride. Seen the vineyards yet?"

He dragged his gaze back to her face. "No, but that'll have to wait. I've got a lot to do."

"She doesn't give you a break?" Sybil stepped inside and looked around.

He could blame it on Rese, but that wasn't true. He'd crafted the deal. "It's my time, but it's short."

"You're going to live in this?"

He looked around the space, three times the size of his cell at the Italian convent and, unlike his apartment at home, shared with no one. It felt more his than many places he'd stayed. Yeah, he could live there. "It's got character, maybe even history." Murder and mayhem.

She rolled her eyes. "There you go again."

He spread his hands. "A neighbor told Rese someone was murdered in the villa."

Sybil tipped her head to the side. "Still angling for that story?"

"Well . . ."

She rested her finger on her cheek. "Is this for Rese or you?"

Rese would want any information he got, but would he tell her? He shrugged. "I'm just 'satiably curious."

She smiled. "You know what happened to the Elephant's child."

He'd pegged her for an avid reader.

She eyed him now. "I tell you what. I'll apply my journalistic expertise." She smiled. "And you join me at the jazz fest tonight."

"Jazz fest?"

"A female jazz ensemble at the park. Six o'clock."

Lance rubbed the back of his hand across his chin, damp with sweat. He could handle jazz in the park, especially to get information he might not find himself. There had to be more than he'd come up with, especially if the neighbor's tale was true. Nonna's letter to Conchessa suggested a tragedy, and now this neighbor claimed murder, but he'd found nothing in his local search—not that he really knew how to go about it.

Maybe Sybil was the key. "Sure." He smiled. "Find me something good."

Sybil patted Baxter, then tossed her hair over her shoulder. "See you at the park."

Some of his best friends were women. Some of his worst nightmares too. He could always let Sybil know what a screw-up he was. In spite of her flagrance, she had class and pedigree. She'd dump him in a minute.

———

The moment Star walked in, Rese knew the escapade was finished and the aftermath imminent. She climbed down from the scaffolding and led her up the stairs to the Rain Forest room, guessing they had only moments before it hit.

"I know it was stupid. I don't even care." Star's eyes grew glassy fragile, then tears washed out. "I was only trying to forget."

Rese stroked her matted and tousled hair, the spirals twisted into knots. Star always trashed her hair. But they would brush it out, strand by strand. The rest wasn't so easy to untangle.

Star gulped. "It hurts, Rese."

"I know." Sometimes she wished she could let the hurt out the way Star did. But it didn't seem to help, and she already regretted her own quick bout of tears.

"He said I needed medication."

"Who did?"

"Maury."

Rese didn't suppose they were talking about the vintner of the past two days. That would have been backlash, not the cause of Star's sudden appearance and subsequent collapse. She should have assumed impending crisis. "Who's Maury?"

Star clenched her teeth. "We shared a studio."

And more, Rese guessed. Star had no barriers and no discrimination. But it was significant that she'd pursued her painting with the guy. Significant and risky.

Star grabbed her sides and wailed. "I could have broken through—done something more than play parts at . . . fairs and festivals—if he hadn't . . ." She squeezed a fist, then pressed it to her chest with a cry. "'And where th' offense is, let the great axe fall!'"

Figurative language, Rese hoped but was . . . not completely convinced. Star in a fury took on mythical proportion. She collapsed onto the bed sobbing. "I believed him."

Rese sat down beside her. "What did you believe?"

"He had the contacts. He said once they saw my work—" Star clenched her teeth. "He loved me until he realized . . ." She rolled to her side. "I challenged him at first. His style changed, improved. But he couldn't stand that." She raised upon one elbow. "'Company, villainous company, hath been the spoil of me.' I can never paint again."

Rese worked a red, knotted strand of hair free with her fingers. "Don't say that, Star."

"My muse is dead. He strangled her." Star's head collapsed to her shoulder.

Rese drew the tangled sections out and let them fall. "She'll come back. You'll see."

"Why can't I be like you?" Star sprang up and grabbed her shoulders. "You don't need anything."

Right. The only perfectly autonomous person on the planet.

"It's because your mother died, while mine . . ." Star blinked away the tears. "I wish mine had died."

"I know." This was old ground. Star found Mom's death miraculous, a freedom from hardship, while Star's had continued. No explaining would change that view.

"Can I stay here?" Star smeared her palm under her nose.

Rese stroked her shoulder. "I'm hardly going to kick you out."

"I'll clean or something." Star wiped her face with her shirt.

"You might find a different job."

"I can't look yet. I just can't."

"Okay."

Star moaned, rocking. "I wanted to be through with this. The Looney Toons."

Rese stiffened. She hadn't thought of that in a long time. Maybe Mom's death had freed her from some of it. "We're not Looney Toons." Rese made Star look at her and bored the truth in. "We're no crazier than anyone else. Everyone has junk."

Star hugged her fiercely. "I can't live without you."

"Yes, you can. You're stronger than you think."

Star tipped her head back. "I am strong as the earth, high as the sky, deep as the sea."

Rese smiled. "Yeah."

Star laughed. "Hoh—I needed that cry."

Rese sobered. She had needed to cry for too long, but until this morning with Lance . . . and even then she'd cut it short. Well, she and Star were different people.

"Let me brush your hair." Rese took the brush tines gently through Star's hair until the curls came free. They were the same age, but Star had always seemed the little sister. "Now rest. You'll feel better." Rese wished she had something better to offer, something that might wash away the years of self-destruction, or at the very least offer hope and peace. But what was there? As Star drifted off to sleep, Rese stood carefully from the bed and returned to her work.

———

The evening was warm and clear, the lawn sun dappled through the draping eucalyptus, oaks, and conifers. Nearly six, and already the park plaza was filled with families and couples and seniors clustered around tables or on blankets spread with picnic food and wine. Italian influence; Lance smiled.

He walked between Rese and Star, who was surprisingly still and cogent. Cogent mainly because she hadn't opened her mouth. From the look of her eyes she was either coming down from something or deeply upset. Rese acted as though nothing had changed, so maybe Tinkerbell had these fluctuations.

He glanced about for Sybil, but didn't see her yet. Technically, he shouldn't have asked Rese and Star along. He had expected Rese to refuse, but she said, "That's perfect for Star." And she had driven them all in her truck.

They reached the little amphitheater and Lance found a space for four. "Want something to eat or drink?" There were vendors on the other side of the city hall in the square. A farmers' market was set up there, though he couldn't tell specifically what the booths held. He did see a corn dog kiosk, but didn't mention it.

Rese turned to Star. "Do you want something?"

Star's hands rose and fell in her lap like injured birds, but she didn't answer.

"I'll see what there is." Lance left them there and strolled toward the booths. Bouquets of vibrant sweet peas caught his eye on one side while another booth held poppies, daisies, peonies, and buttercups. Fresh vegetables, peaches, strawberries, and honeycomb scented the evening. An ostrich farmer set out baskets of feathers, eggs, and packages of ostrich jerky.

He came to a booth with a long line for homemade gumbo. Where he came from that was always a good sign. Rico would not frequent any place where he didn't have to wait. Lance got two bowls of gumbo and two Italian sodas from a neighboring kiosk and carried them back in a shallow cardboard box.

Rese handed a bowl and a cup to Star, then took her own from the box. "What about you?"

He glanced around. "I'll wait awhile." No sign of Sybil yet. Maybe she was looking for him somewhere else. "I'll be back." He headed up the concrete steps and out around the pond. Ducks assessed him for food, but when his hand was not forthcoming, they turned to better prospects.

The sweet scent of kettle corn wafted on the air as he rounded the pond and saw Sybil. Her blue ankle-length skirt was slit all the way up one thigh, but she managed to look glamorous, not trashy. Her toe-strap sandals slapped the sidewalk lightly as she approached, and he caught a whiff of perfume. But what interested him most was the folder she carried.

"Sorry I'm late. I didn't really expect to find something."

"But you did?"

She flicked the silky hair back over her shoulder and opened the folder. "I'm not sure what to make of this." She took out a copy of an *Index Tribune* article and gave it to him.

He checked the date and his pulse quickened.

Local Man Shot Down

Late Monday night Vito Shepard was gunned down in his home.

Vito Shepard. Quillan's son Vittorio?

Neighbors were jolted from their sleep as shots rang out "like war" in the early hours. "I never heard a Tommy gun before, and hope to never hear it again," said neighbor Joseph Martino. "It's a tragedy."

Others feel the victim got no more than he deserved. "The Italian element has thumbed its nose at the law too long," said one prominent citizen who wished to remain unnamed.

Police found Mr. Shepard dead in his home, amidst rumors of ill-gained wealth. A search of the property revealed no such cache. No witness to the slaying has come forward. Authorities are looking for Mr. Shepard's daughter and request any information as to Antonia Shepard's whereabouts.

Vito killed; Antonia missing. Lance lowered the paper as sorrow and a sense of injustice seeped in. Disappointment as well, with the mention of ill-gained wealth and the "Italian element." Organized crime had grown out of Prohibition, and San Francisco had its own mob. It was possible members of his family had become involved, especially when the law seemed so unreasonable to people who had grown and created wine all their lives. It wasn't about getting a cheap drunk, it was celebrating the bounty, the essence of their lives and the fruitfulness of the land.

People understood that now, with the flourishing Napa and Sonoma Valley vineyards. But in the thirteen years when Prohibition had changed the genteel inclusion of wine into the get-drunk-fast mentality of the speakeasy, people were not so understanding. Power mongers on both sides used the issue to gain control. But the feds did not gun down operators in their homes. This was a private execution.

He had joked about the guy in cement, but it wasn't funny. That Italian stereotype lingered into the PC age, and now it seemed possible there was truth to it.

Lance looked up. "Well, that's interesting."

"If you like that, try this." She handed him another copied sheet.

He recognized it as an obituary.

Vittorio DiGratia Shepard died quietly in his home Sunday night. He is succeeded by esteemed poet Quillan Shepard, father, and a daughter, Antonia. Funeral Mass, family only.

Lance checked the date, but it matched the first one. He looked up. "Died quietly?"

"It seems that was the official version."

His chest squeezed.

Sybil flicked the first sheet. "This was never published. I found it in the archives, but it was not printed in the paper."

Lance frowned. "Why not?"

She shrugged. "Someone didn't want it there."

"So they ran the obituary and left it at that?"

"That's how it seems. I checked the police files."

He couldn't help a look of surprise and respect. "And?"

She shook her head. "No smoking Tommy gun."

Lance looked from one sheet to the other. "Could the first story be wrong? Some zealous reporter looking for a beat?"

Sybil caught her hair back and let it fall. "Possible, I guess. But I doubt it. Especially if it was archived. And your neighbor had heard it rumored. I've gone with less than that."

Lance considered the information. If he raised awareness of a past wrong, would it help his case? Nothing connected him directly—yet. Rese would still not . . . A serious twinge seized him. He didn't like keeping secrets. But how could he not? He needed answers, then he'd decide what to do with what he learned.

"So is there a story here?"

Sybil shook her head. "Old news." She smiled. "Now if Vito's ghost starts to roam . . ."

"How do you know it's not?"

She slipped her hand into his arm. "Is it?"

"Rese heard moans the other night."

By her expression, Sybil's mind had taken that statement and run. But she just smirked and said, "Well, when she sees the bullet-ridden body let me know." She tugged him forward. "The music's starting. We won't get a seat."

"I have places already."

"How?"

"Rese and her friend."

Sybil stopped and looked into his face. "You brought Rese?"

So it *had* been cheating. "She needed to get out."

"Are you two together?"

He could say yes and end her pursuit, but it was also one of the only areas he could be honest. "Strictly business." Though Rese's expression when he sat down with Sybil was interesting. Star was still in another world and hardly responded when he introduced her. Sybil's reaction to both women would have amused him if Rese wasn't suddenly looking brittle. He was not getting this right, and the aftermath might be more than he wanted to face.

Surprisingly, Sybil didn't press him for anything past the concert. Maybe because of Rese and Star. Maybe she was simply changing strategy. As soon as Lance got home, he went to his room and read over the articles again.

Nothing explained why Antonia's father was shot down, or by whom, or how that affected the property afterward. Why had the Shepards—or the Michellis, through Marco's marriage to Antonia—lost their land and this house where he now slept? Who was involved in the execution, and could they have driven the family away?

If the story was hushed up, changed even as far as the police files, someone in power was behind it. And if so, what chance was there that anything of value remained? Yet Nonna's urgency suggested that something remained to be done. It had been enough to send him there, and with God's help he'd find her secret.

CHAPTER FOURTEEN

I am wise for my years, seeing beyond the surface.
Angel sight, Nonna Carina calls it,
the knowing of others' pain, others' joy.
My heart pulses with a rhythm outside me
that I cannot ignore.
My spirit dances. My spirit grieves.
My spirit knows what my mind does not.

Even open to the air, the carriage house had a smell of age. Lance drew it in, wondering. It wouldn't come from the stone walls, and the rafters and framing he had built over the last three days were new. The floor? Just stones on dirt. He sniffed. When he tried to smell it, he couldn't. It only came when he first stepped inside the walls.

He sighed. Probably his imagination. He looked down at the floor. He had trenched and laid the pipes up to the outer wall. Now he had to raise the floor to bring them in; wedge the stones up, dig under the wall, and plumb the bath. Why was he so reluctant?

He took up the crowbar he had laid in readiness, fitted it under the first large stone and pried it loose. A pang twisted his insides. What on earth? It was only a floor, regardless of Rese's reverence and his own admiration.

He gripped the edge of the stone and raised it. He had numbered them with chalk to make sure he replaced them correctly when he was through. Now he set the stone aside, confident he could restore the floor when he was finished. The earth beneath it was packed hard as rock itself. He would have a time digging through that to bring in the pipes. He levered the next stone up and set it with the first.

He had positioned the bathroom at the front of the bedroom side so he would disturb as little of the floor as possible. But he should grout it there. The previous artisan would understand that much. He levered the next stone and found rock, not dirt under that one, a rougher chalk-colored block. Huh. He wouldn't be digging through that.

But there it came again, the feeling of regret. He frowned. Part of him wanted to lay the stones back down and forget having a bathroom. But that was ridiculous. He could hardly ask Rese to share hers, and the others upstairs went to the guest rooms. Whoever ended up living in the carriage house needed facilities, and he was the one to build it. At least he could give the whole process the care it deserved.

He ran a finger over the stone. It was as cool and rough as any stone not exposed to sunlight. He caught a whiff of age again and cocked his head, trying to place it and conjuring images of Italian chapels and grottos. He pictured Cousin Conchessa with her black veil and beads.

Lance shook his head. He was going off the deep end. He put the crow-bar under the next stone and raised it. Rock underneath again. They had built the carriage house over bedrock. He would not get pipes through that. But then he saw the seam. Throat tightening, Lance set the floor paver aside and studied the rocks underneath. They were mortared together. Definitely not natural.

An older floor from a previous building? Maybe this wasn't even the original carriage house, just a garage added later. He jammed the crowbar into the dirt beside the rock and worked it down. It ground up its side, but did not lift an edge. He thrust deeper into the same hole. Again it scraped the side without lifting it. The stones were obviously thicker than the pavers of his current floor.

Lance got the shovel and with difficulty cleared a foot deep at the side of the rock. Another shovelful revealed another seam of mortar. They were blocks about a foot wide and eight inches deep. This was a manmade struc-ture. A tomb? He shuddered. Was that what he'd sensed? Maybe they'd bur-ied Vito Shepard right there. A mass for family only. He rested the shovel blade on the stone.

He'd wanted to dig up the truth, but not literally. If this was the tomb of his great-grandfather, or anyone else for that matter . . .

He could reframe the bathroom elsewhere, but then he'd have to trench again and who knew what else he'd find under the floor. Besides, there was no proof it was a tomb. What else then? He eyed the ground with no ready answers, but maybe it was a mistake to cover it before he knew. If something was hidden on the estate, it just might be underground. Then why didn't his heart quicken as it had with the box? Why did he feel a dull sorrow as though . . . something had been lost?

Lance scanned the floor. The part he'd unearthed was a solid block anyway. He'd need a jackhammer to get through there. If it continued in either direction there might be an opening, and he'd keep that option available. He could bring the pipes in at a slightly different spot beside the mortared blocks without changing the placement of the fixtures too much. He walked out and eyed the trench. It would work. For now, he would leave it undisturbed and bring the pipes in beside it.

He dug out the section beside the rock, working hard to penetrate ground long undisturbed. He tunneled under the wall and connected his trench from the other side. Then he brought the pipe through, but the whole time he worked, he wondered about the blocks. How far under the floor did they go? How far toward the villa? Was there an opening? To what?

He wiped the sweat from his forehead with his arm and saw Rese approaching. He stood up quickly and met her just outside.

"The kitchen equipment came. I checked the shipping receipt and accepted delivery."

He rested on the shovel. "Great." He should be more excited. He really did want to do a good job of it for as long as he was there. But his thoughts were so steeped in the past it was hard to consider the present. And what was the future?

She said, "I'll let you organize it all."

"Good." He smiled. The less interference he had in the kitchen the better. If that even mattered.

"How's it coming?"

He looked down at the trench. "I'm ready to plumb." If she didn't go inside he would say nothing about the rock whatever-it-was.

But she walked through the opening. "I see you had to raise the pavers. I guessed you would."

He turned his eyes skyward, and a moment later she asked, "What's this rock in here?"

It was actually out there as well. He had found it with the shovel. It was certainly long enough so far to be a tomb. He walked inside. "I'm not sure. Maybe just bedrock."

She knelt and scrutinized it as he'd hoped she would not. "No. It has mortar."

"An old foundation maybe."

She glanced up. "The blocks are stacked. It's a wall or something."

He should have filled that revealing hole. "It might be a tomb."

Her eyes widened. "What?"

He told her what he'd learned from Sybil, both the unpublished article and the conflicting obituary.

She looked up from her squat. "You think it's this Vito Shepard's tomb?"

He shrugged. "Could be."

She stood up. "And you just kept digging?"

"Gotta get the pipe in somewhere."

She frowned. "Why bury someone here?"

"If it was all hushed up or scandalous, the family might have buried him here and made a good job of it."

She looked into the hole again, clearly skeptical, but not a hundred percent sure he wasn't right. "It could be something else, though. A root cellar, maybe."

His breath caught—or a wine cellar. It would do no good to get her thoughts going that direction. She'd want to excavate, and whatever element of secrecy he hoped for would be lost.

He notched his brows together. "Under the carriage house? That doesn't make sense. I had to raise the floor to find it. Quite a hassle if you need potatoes." And a wine cellar would have been in the house, maybe that immense pantry. *Sure, convince yourself.* He couldn't look at her. "You want me to dig it up?" There, he'd made an effort.

She shot him a glance. "Right."

"Might be perfectly harmless."

"Might be a whole mausoleum." She cocked her jaw and studied the hole. "Do you think people . . . go somewhere after death?"

"One way or the other."

She looked unconvinced. "Could some get lost?"

"You mean hang around as ghosts?"

"Don't answer that." She held her hands up. "You better cover it up. I don't want any more moaning in the attic."

He should tell her the open window had made the noise, but just now her superstition might gain him some privacy. In compromise, he offered a slim comfort. "I haven't heard anything. And I'm right beneath it."

She nodded. "Too many ghost tales. Mom loved them."

"You didn't?" He set the shovel against the wall.

"Not exactly." She enclosed herself in her arms and shivered.

He cocked his head. "The way you scoured the house that night for spooks, I thought you were immune."

"Better than waiting for them to get me."

He studied her face. "You could have left."

"I don't run away." Maybe to prove her nerve, she squatted down and rubbed the dirt from the mortar between the two blocks. "Aren't tombs marble or something?"

"Not if you live in Sonoma with a quarry and stonecutters. And you have a body that needs burial."

"But wouldn't it be deeper?"

"Not if it had an entrance."

She jumped up, hand to her throat, then turned with a glare.

He smiled. "I'll get it closed up by tonight."

"Make sure it's not . . . disturbed."

"Cross my heart." He made the motion. He'd taken a chance with the tomb theory, and it seemed to have warded her off. He wanted to explore this possibility alone, but he would not be disturbing whatever was there. He was part of it.

––––––––––

Rese had intended to ask him about the popping sound in the wall, but with all the talk of tombs and ghosts, she'd have sounded paranoid. It could have been air in a pipe or any number of structural shiftings. She only imagined it sounded like a gunshot because of Evvy's story. In fact, she had no idea what a gunshot sounded like, not through a wall or any other way.

Lance's recounting of the newspaper article had recalled the noise to her, but she would have been ridiculous saying, "Hey, I heard that gunshot in the wall." But had she? People said old walls had ears, old houses remembered. Had Vito been shot in the parlor? Had a bullet struck that wall and the sound waves gotten trapped and . . .

She clenched her hands into fists. Don't be stupid, her dad would say. Plaster and wood don't have memories. So, air in a pipe, then. Not worth mentioning to Lance. The real question was why he had articles about the villa. And why he hadn't told her before.

She sighed. Maybe this whole thing was crazy. Tombs underground, noises overhead, a business she knew nothing about running. It was Dad's dream to fix up a place of their own; her idea to make it an inn, make it profitable so she could walk away from construction. What had she been thinking? Dad would never have left the work they loved . . . the work that killed him.

Rese's stomach clenched. He had always said *someday*. And then he had no more somedays. That was why she had to make this work. That and her meltdown after his death. She pressed a hand to her temple. She could not go on with the crews as before. Even if they would cooperate, she couldn't do it. The sounds, the work itself was forever connected to that night. She had to get through this one last renovation in his memory, and then she hoped to never wield a saw again.

That talk of death and murder in the house had supercharged her memories. Or maybe they were there already, waiting for her resistance to break down. Star's tears had left her drained and listless and sleeping through the day; Rese could not afford to let down.

She sanded the bookshelves until there was no flaw her fingers could detect, then brushed on stain. She knew this work and if she could keep the thoughts and memories away, she could complete it in a way that would have made Dad proud. A final tribute to all he had taught her. And then what?

In spite of the pain, renovating was the easy part; redefining herself was another thing. As Lance so kindly pointed out, she did not have the hospitality personality. Was it something she could learn? Or did it take someone like Lance whose natural charisma drew people in and made them do and think and feel things they never would have without him?

She shut down that thought. This was her inn, and she would be and do whatever it took, regardless of Lance. He worked for her, and she couldn't expect him to carry it, not when his track record showed she'd be replacing him sooner rather than later. She knew better than to depend on anyone but herself.

Rese went into the office to work on the Web site. She still needed pictures of Lance's room. She'd ask him when he came in. Her stomach growled. They had worked all through lunch and evening drew on. Better yet, she'd ask him now.

She went back out and saw that he had connected the pipes for his bathroom fixtures, plumbed the sink and stool, and was installing the self-contained shower halfway over the floor where the blocks lay. So that was settled.

"Lance, I need to get some pictures of your room for the Web site."

He looked up from his knees. "Uh . . . the maid hasn't been in yet."

"I can straighten it up." She had cleaned up after Dad many times.

He sat back on his heels. "Can it wait until tomorrow?"

She shrugged. "I guess so." She had plenty of other things to do. "By the way, Star's offered to clean."

He wiped his hands on his jeans. "I thought you wouldn't—"

"She needs to stay awhile." Rese didn't want to tell him much, but added, "She's having a hard time and . . . if she cleans the rooms, you could landscape."

He studied her a moment, then said, "That's one less room to rent."

"If I need it, I'll move her in with me." They'd spent plenty of nights together. Some Dad didn't even know about, when Star climbed in through her window, shaking and ravenous and half wild with pain.

Lance bent back over his work. "Okay."

It was her decision, but his agreement felt good anyway. She should let him get back to work. She should do the same. But she said, "Can you think of something that might make a strange pop inside a wall?"

He looked up. "Pop?"

"Kind of a bang. Muffled." She huffed. "I was working in the parlor, and I heard something like a muffled gunshot."

He gave her just the look she expected. "Gunshot."

She was in deep now; may as well complete the thought. "Maybe that's where Vito was shot. What if people are playing games and reading there and . . . hear gunshots or see blood spots appear on the walls?"

He crouched back and laughed. "Quite a wild imagination, Theresa."

She scowled. "Do not call me that."

His whole face entered into his smile, even when he was mocking her.

She raised her chin. "So I should forget about it?"

He looked through the opening toward the house. "If the place is haunted, we'll know soon enough."

Why was that not comforting? Dad would tell her not to be silly. Death was the end of it. There were no spirits going to heaven or eternal flames below. Life ended. Bodies went back to the earth. *Was it true?* She certainly sensed nothing of her father. He was gone. She had watched the life leave him, then held him lifeless.

"Are you okay?"

She looked at Lance. He was altogether too perceptive.

She drew a long breath. "Yes."

"Sure?"

She was not going to fall apart on him again. "Well, I am hungry."

His smile was way too soothing. It crept inside and made him matter. That bothered her. It bothered her that she wanted his opinion, sought his advice. It had bothered her that Sybil hung on his arm last evening. It shouldn't matter, the attention Lance was bound to attract. But in the time he'd been there he had begun to matter.

Maybe she'd photograph *him* for the Web site. Chef Michelli's creations. Definitely a good idea. They'd reserve every room. And a poster for the entertainment, with Lance smiling over his guitar. That would bring them in droves. Her stomach twisted.

"Rese?"

"What?"

"I asked what you wanted to eat."

She shook herself. "Oh. Anything." She could accept the comfort of his food.

So they were back to that, were they? Fine—anything then. He pulled open the refrigerator, took out the bread and . . . boiled ham. Perfect. He flung together two sandwiches, added a handful of potato chips to each plate and set hers on the table. "Dinner is served," he called and sat down with his own. *Thanks for the food, Lord.* He'd had worse in his college starvation days.

Rese came back, surprised. "That was quick. I was asking Star if . . ." She glanced down at the plates with a studied expression that showed no disappointment. She had the stone look down well. ". . . she wanted to eat, but she's not hungry."

He hadn't even thought of Star. She'd been holed up since the jazz fest, barely showing her face. How Rese thought she'd get any work out of her was beyond him. But hey, he'd give up the bathrooms.

Rese sat down and crunched a chip, then moved on to the sandwich. Lance took a bite of his—as bland as it looked. A meal could go quickly with no conversation, and he was determined not to be the one making it happen. Halfway through the sandwich, he wished he had made a better effort. Smoked turkey on rosemary focaccia with roasted pine nuts. . . .

He set the remainder of his sandwich on the plate and stared at Rese. "What is it with you and food? I know you got thrown into making meals, but what's with the no conversation rule?"

"I talk."

"Not over food, you don't." He laid his palms on the table. "Rese, sharing a meal is a ritual found in every culture on earth. The breaking of bread signifies connection, acceptance, relationship."

She shot him a glance.

"I don't mean relationship that way. Just relating, interacting, sharing a moment of time on the journey."

She wiped the napkin over her lips. "Meals were stressful."

"Because you had to cook?"

"Before that." Her eyes were dark and mysterious when she looked up. Was she actually opening up? "It was unwise to comment on what Mom made, so we stayed quiet and got through it."

Lance studied her, trying to grasp the dynamic. Sure there were things Momma cooked that they didn't like as kids. Calamari for one, lamb's head for another. But nothing could have made his clan sit around the table in silence. "A meal is not something to get through. A meal is life."

She looked down at the sandwich.

He expelled his breath. "Not this particular meal. I should have done better."

"It's fine."

"It's not fine. That's the problem. You have no discrimination."

"Yes, I do."

He leaned forward. "You don't express it."

"What am I supposed to say? This is a plain, icky sandwich?"

"Yes!" He gripped the table edge and shook it. "You're supposed to show disappointment."

She searched his face, startled. "That would make you happy?"

"Yes, Rese. When I serve you something a shade above dog food, I'd like to see disappointment."

"I am disappointed."

Lance crowded the table. "Then when I ask what you'd like, don't say 'Anything.'"

"What should I say?"

"Say 'Something with chicken' or 'How about a salad' or, even, 'Surprise me.'"

She looked as though he'd just suggested stand-up comedy in a trucker bar. He collapsed back in his chair, growling.

She rolled her lip in, fighting a smile.

"You think it's funny?"

"No, I . . ." She dropped her face, biting hard on the grin.

He stood up and hauled their plates to the sink. *She* was laughing at *him*? Rese Barrett with all her peculiarities?

"Don't get mad."

He spun to face her. "Get mad? You're enough to . . ."

She raised her chin. "Go on. You've been wanting to say it."

He yanked the faucet on hot and squirted in the soap. "It wouldn't do any good."

"It would keep you from stewing."

"I don't stew." He wadded a washrag and tossed it into the water.

"And you mumble."

He swashed the soapy cloth over the plate and ran it under the steaming faucet. "You'd drive anyone to mumbling." He shoved the plate into the drainer.

"I'm not in the habit of stroking male egos."

Fury surged. He stormed over and leaned his wet arms on the table. "Stroking my ego? Is that what you think I want?"

"I don't know what you want."

"Well, you're just a peach to work for. I'll bet your crew—"

She looked up with stark pain that froze him. Energy surged between them through two long breaths. Then he straightened. "I'm sorry. I shouldn't—"

"Have said what you thought?" She gripped her hands together. "You're right. It wasn't easy maintaining control of men who thought I had no business telling them their work was not good enough, that the fit wasn't tight, the edge wasn't smooth. How dare I dock them for coming late, for not finishing on time, for showing up with beer on their breath."

She pressed her chair away from the table and stood up. "I was only the boss's daughter with no right to take over the second crew—even though I could do every piece of work as well or better than any man there."

She started to shake, and Lance wished he hadn't provoked it.

"Rese . . ."

"I heard their comments. Endured their pranks. I learned to open my lunch box away from me, so the mice and snakes wouldn't jump into my lap. I kept quiet when—" Pain and fury washed her face.

"When what?"

"It doesn't matter."

He gripped her shoulder. "What?"

"Two of them got mad that I'd caught some shortcuts in their work." She looked aside.

"You were their boss. It was your job."

"I was fourteen. Dad was the boss."

He felt her tension and his instinct kicked in. "They hurt you?"

She shrugged. "They waited until Dad left for something. One groped while the other introduced me to the joys of French kissing."

Imagining her trapped that way, his anger flared. She'd only been a girl, annoying maybe, but that was no excuse. "You told your dad?"

Her eyes burned. "And give them the satisfaction?"

They'd known she wouldn't. Why else take the risk? His fury surged. "They got away with it?" It was Cici all over again, and he felt as helpless as he had then.

"They said they'd gotten into a fight. How else to explain a swollen tongue and black eye?"

So she'd handled it herself. And what about now? Would she deck him? Lance raised her chin, wanting to undo the ugly memories. "It's not supposed to be that way." She read his intent, he was sure, and he braced himself for a blow or a shove as he lowered his lips to hers. Her mouth was completely unschooled, yet the contact sent shock waves through him. What was he doing?

He drew away. "It's supposed to be nice."

She swallowed. "It's supposed to be business."

He grinned. "In the kitchen I make the rules."

She shook her head. "No. In here, you . . . cook."

He cocked his head. "So how was it, kissing a man with an earring?"

She glanced at the ring in his ear, but somehow it didn't seem to be her focus. "Different."

"From?"

"The other time." Her brow pinched.

"Good." But it wasn't good, because he wanted to repeat it.

She stepped back, a wary look suggesting she'd read that thought.

His mouth quirked. "You're safe with me."

She stared into his face a long moment, then said, "I know."

When she walked away, the force of her trust hit him like a boulder. She did trust him. His thumb tapped against his thigh. He didn't want to hurt her; he just . . . had a mission to accomplish, and then? She would not end up with less than she'd had before he came. Not less. Though how on earth he would accomplish that he couldn't say.

CHAPTER FIFTEEN

She had intended to work on the Web site, but not a single thought would penetrate her brain. Rese shut down the computer and stared at the kitchen door. Lance had wanted his kiss to be nice, but it was so much more than nice it scared her.

Granted, the only other kiss she'd experienced was the one she had ended decisively, leaving Charlie sounding like a deaf-mute for days. And that was ten years ago. Lance churned feelings she had no defense against. Why had he kissed her?

Maybe he collected kisses like trophies. But he hadn't kissed Sybil, even though they'd driven home on his bike plastered together. Yes, she had watched through the window. Sybil had been all hands, and Lance had pulled away. Maybe he liked a challenge. Did he think she was playing that game?

Rese touched her lips. There was nothing predatory in his kiss. It was sweet and gentle, as though he'd felt a duty to— She jolted. If he felt sorry for her, she'd scream! She was not some victim who needed pity, and the very thought brought back the vulnerability of the original incident. So she'd been assaulted. That would be the technical term, though hardly as damaging as it sounded. She hadn't let it hurt her.

And the thought that he might have kissed her out of pity made her angrier than a hammered finger. She scraped back her chair and stalked out. He was not in the kitchen anymore. He must be in his room. Not the best place for a confrontation, but if she recalled that it was *her* room he used by permission. . . .

Rese took the stairs with determination. A simple question, that was all. Then she could assure him she did not need his sympathy. Why had she brought up the stupid subject at all? She rapped on the door and waited.

A drawer closed inside, and she hoped she hadn't caught him undressed. "I can come back later if—"

The door opened. His eyes were warm and curious. Her question stuck in her throat. Whose stupid idea was this anyway?

Mirth found the corners of his mouth. "Yes?"

Rese swallowed. "I don't want you to have the idea that . . . that . . ."

He curled a hand around her waist. "That?"

"I need your sympathy or . . ."

He tucked a finger under her chin and kissed her before she could finish the idiotic sentence. His hand cupped the back of her head and the kiss deepened. This was not what she had intended. Or was it? Her heart tried to exit her rib cage as her lips melded with his. All thoughts of drawing away were mutinously denied by the passion she discovered inside.

He eased his mouth away and spoke through hoarse breaths. "That's not sympathy."

She leaned back into the doorjamb, equally hoarse. "What is it?"

"I guess the word would be attraction."

"Why?"

He searched her face. "Because in spite of everything, you're basically adorable."

Adorable? No one in his right mind would ever apply "adorable" to her. She should be insulted by the thought, but his words sent liquid fire through her. "You said I'm manly and . . ."

He forked a hand into his hair. "Don't ask me to explain it."

"This complicates things."

"Tell me about it."

It was exactly why she should have waited for a woman to take the job. She hated this weak-kneed vulnerability. She straightened her shoulders. "We can't get involved. In a personal way. If we're working together."

His eyes hooded. "The all-important professional hierarchy."

She backed into the hall. "That's right." But was it? She didn't know anymore. It had worked before, making the guys respect her, keeping them in their place.

"Fine." He raised his hand to the door. "Was that all?"

Now it was as though she'd put the nail gun to her chest. "Um, yes."

He closed the door. She walked woodenly across the hall. Maybe Star . . .

But she was tumbled in her covers, breathing with a whine through her nose. Rese went down the stairs. No way was sleep coming. And reading was hopeless. It was time for physical labor. Something like buffing the new polyurethane on the wood floors, though that would be noisy. She hauled the buffer to the parlor and started the machine. Yep, noisy.

Lance pulled the pillow over his head and held it there with both arms. He deserved it, he supposed, but how long could she keep it up? He guessed that his ears would stop noticing before she ceased and desisted. Star must be comatose. Fine. He could sleep through anything given the right mindset.

He hummed a tune he'd written in Liguria, and thought about the things in the box. He'd barely had time to hide it, thinking Rese might come right through the door by the sound of her feet on the steps. Then she'd stood there, looking so . . .

Sympathy? He was the one deserving sympathy. He plastered the pillow tighter to his ears. It was his own fault for crossing a line he hadn't intended. He should thank her for ending it. He rolled to his side and kept the pillow pressed to his ear. Would she keep it up all night?

Welcome to the insomniac inn. He rubbed a hand over his face and burrowed deeper, drowsiness coming in spite of the racket. As he drifted off, he wondered if there would be any finish left on the floor by morning. He dreamed Rese was sinking through the boards with the machine grinding them to sawdust. He gripped her hand, explaining it was nothing personal. It was ancestral; couldn't she see it was ancestral?

Lance shook the dream from his head in the dim morning light. He raised up on one elbow and noticed the silence. Good. She'd gone to sleep. He got up, washed and dressed, then went out into the crisp, rain-scented air, his morning routine too ingrained to ignore. After feeding Baxter and telling him to stay, he rolled his bike silently down the drive, then started the engine and drove into town.

The difference this morning was that after church, he went to the graveyard. The older section held lots of interesting graves, but he was there with a purpose. He needed to find someone—or not. Half an hour later, he did. *Vittorio DiGratia Shepard. March 13, 1883–1931.* So it wasn't a tomb he'd unearthed. Rese would be relieved, but then she'd get curious all over again. Better not to tell her. Not yet.

He studied the tombstone one more time, then looked to the one beside it. Helena Glorietta Shepard. The blond woman in the photo? Year of death

1918. There'd been a number of deaths in this graveyard that year. Some epidemic? He didn't know his history well enough to recall. The marker next to that read Carina Maria DiGratia Shepard, and she had died in 1929, two years before her son.

Helena's grave bore a verse from St. John: *I am the resurrection, and the life: he that believeth in me, though he were dead, yet shall he live.* But Carina's marker had a poem. *So a soul traversing life, alone until it finds, one to which it cleaves, and for eternity it binds.* And the name Quillan Shepard. A last tribute to his bride? Lance looked from that marker to the next, and the others beside them. Where was Quillan's grave? He searched the nearby stones, but Quillan was not among the family. Strange.

He'd expected to be missing a grave for Vito, not his great-great-grandfather. Maybe the marker had been there but was lost to age. But there was no gap between those stones and another family's markers. Maybe he was famous enough to have a place of honor. Lance walked the cemetery, but found no grave marker for Quillan Shepard. No doubt he lay in some other yard with moss on his stone and grass covering the mound. Shaking his head, he returned to his bike, drove back to the inn, and went inside.

Rese met him in the entry. "Where were you?"

"Church."

"On Thursday?"

He caught his thumbs in his jeans. "Yes."

Her brows crowded together. "You go every day?"

"Unless I have reason not to." What was with the third degree? He had no set hours, though all the other days he'd been in before she got up. Perusing the cemetery had held him up, but he'd have thought she'd sleep in today.

She jutted her chin. "Why?"

What did she care why he went to church? "I just do." A habit established from his birth, one he was compelled to continue. The first time he'd served on the altar he had felt personally called by God. Swelled by the desire to do something great, he'd gone home and given Sean McMahan his Mickey Mantle card. When his pop made Sean give it back, he'd realized it was not easy to find God's will. Try as he might, he'd been missing it ever since.

Rese was obviously not satisfied with his answer, so he added, "I'm better for it." God only knew how badly things might go otherwise.

She leaned against the banister. "Better how?"

How was he supposed to explain the need to start his day in the Lord's presence, the way he left feeling commissioned to make a difference and hoping one day he'd get it right? After last night any explanation would fall limp.

She straightened. "There's a mouse in the pantry."

"Really?" Was that what had her all worked up? He followed her down the hall. A rodent in there would have slim pickings because he had yet to stock the shelves with food. He had set up an account with a specialty foods purveyor for the imported items he would need if they served dinners, but had not ordered anything yet. Rese had her own delectable choices in the cabinets with his basic ingredients, but there was nothing to entice a mouse into the pantry, only the equipment he had stored there so far.

Rese pulled open the door. He looked inside, searching the floor, then along the shelves, stretching up on his toes to inspect the highest. He raised his brows at Rese.

"It was in there." She closed the door and crouched to examine the crack between the door and the floor. "No way it got out here." She opened it again, stepped in and searched the empty space. "There must be a hole somewhere."

None offered itself to view. "I can set a trap." Though he frankly didn't see where or how a mouse would get inside unless the door was opened. Maybe one of them had failed to click it shut.

Her hands pressed her hips. "How could it get out? I closed the door the minute I saw it."

He cocked his head. "I don't know, Rese. But it's hardly a national threat." Though it might be to her after what she'd shared about her lunch box. He drew her out of the pantry and shut the door. "I'll set a trap. If it's hiding in there, we'll get it."

"I just don't see how it got out."

She was fixating. He looked her over. "Did you get any sleep?"

"An hour and a half." She shoved her hands into the pockets of her jeans.

"That's not healthy."

"I'm used to it."

"That's even worse. Maybe you imagined the mouse. I'd be seeing things on that amount of sleep."

"I didn't imagine it. Do you want some oatmeal?" She motioned to a pot on the stove.

"You're cooking?"

She shrugged. "You weren't here."

He wasn't that much later than usual, and some mornings he hadn't cooked at all, but that hadn't inspired her before. Maybe it was the sleep deprivation.

He leaned on the counter. "Sure, I'll have some." He eyed the pot on the stove. At the level she had the heat, it would be interesting.

"Lance, about last night. . . ."

"I'm sure the floor is lovely."

She turned from the stove. "I guess it kept you awake."

"Only at first. Then it was kind of hypnotic."

She dropped her chin with a half smile. "Sorry."

"You worry too much. How's Star?" At her hesitation he added, "Mind my own business?"

She shook her head. "If she's going to stay here, you'll see it all for yourself."

"You mean there's more?" By her frown he guessed that sort of joke unacceptable. "What's her story?"

Rese chewed her thumbnail, then lowered her hand. "She's had lots of junk. All her life really. She was born addicted to amphetamines."

So he'd been right about the chemically altered brain. "Is she using?"

"No way. She won't even drink."

"You sure?"

Rese nodded. "Not with what she's lived with. Her mother checked into a country club clinic, dried up enough to keep Star, then went home to more booze and pills."

"Not pretty."

"It wasn't." Rese folded her arms. "But Star spent most of her time with me."

"I don't think you rubbed off."

She smiled.

"But she's lucky she had you. Friends are invaluable." Lance jutted his chin. "You're steaming."

"Huh?" Rese turned. "Oh." She lifted the pot off the burner. "I always scorch it." She pulled off the lid.

"I doubt it's too bad. We caught it in time."

"You caught it, you mean." She dragged the spoon through the wad. "You're right. It only burned a little."

The seared smell wafted from the pot, and he could see the brown film on the bottom of the pan as she plopped two servings into bowls. "Using a lower heat would help."

"I guess they teach that at chef school."

He took the bowl she handed him. "Something like that."

They sat down and he asked, "Were you going to get Star?"

Rese shook her head. "She needs to come out of it herself."

What exactly she was coming out of, he didn't ask. He took her hand, and before she could pull away he said grace, then added a blessing for Star and let go.

"You always say the same thing."

He lifted his spoon. "Well, it covers it all. Offer thanks, ask for His blessing, and give the glory to God."

Rese studied him pointedly again. "Why do you believe in something invisible?"

"You don't grow up Italian in New York without a healthy fear of the Lord."

"But you're talking to something that isn't there."

Lance hadn't expected a theological discussion, but the oatmeal would be no worse for the delay. "He's there. And my part is to honor and serve Him."

She tensed, like Baxter hearing something human ears could not detect. "You do whatever God wants?" Definite strain in her voice.

He dug out a chunk of oatmeal. "I try."

"So this . . . *being* says go here and do that, and you up and go?" Her eyes pierced him.

"It's not quite that clear, unfortunately."

"You don't actually hear or see him?"

He considered her a moment, trying to catch the thrust of her question. "You mean an apparition?"

She looked away. "I don't know what you call it. But Mom had a . . . friend too."

He paused with the spoon half way to his mouth. "Friend?"

"Walter. He usually came when Dad wasn't home, when it was just Mom and me." She stood her spoon in the oatmeal. "It took me a while to realize I was the only one who couldn't see him."

Lance took his bite, uncertain what to say. "What happened to her?"

Rese looked out the window. "Our furnace malfunctioned; she died of carbon monoxide poisoning." Her fist closed on the napkin. "Now if I could just get that through to the insurance company."

He frowned. "They thought it was suicide?"

She blinked and turned to him. "I mean Dad's life insurance. He forgot to change the beneficiary. His will gave me his other assets, but the insurance supposedly goes to my mother. They can't find a death certificate to transfer it to me—or so they claim."

Not good. "Do you have one?"

Rese shook her head. "Why would I have it? I was nine years old."

"In your Dad's papers?"

She huffed. "It's a stall tactic. I've been round and round with them. They just don't want to pay me the money." She scraped the last of her oatmeal onto her spoon. "I bought this place with what I got selling the business and our Sausalito property, but there's no cushion if things are slow or my cook spends more than I planned."

Lance smiled, then sobered. "It would have to be on file in the county where she died. Get a copy and send it."

She glanced up. "I tried."

"And?"

"They gave me the same runaround."

Lance did not want to state the obvious. If there was no death certificate . . . "Did you go to her funeral?"

Rese shook her head. "I stayed with Dad's sister for a while. A few weeks, I think."

"And then?"

"Then I went home."

"Do you remember the night she died?"

Rese stayed quiet so long he guessed he had pushed too far. Then she said, "I . . . don't know."

He wiped his mouth and set the napkin aside. "I'm hanging drywall today. Want to help?" He'd already rocked the bathroom with its water-resistant wallboard. But the ceilings would go better with two of them.

"Okay." She carried their bowls to the sink.

"Thanks for the oatmeal."

She looked into the scorched pot. "I guess it's better when you cook."

"I appreciate your effort."

Rese raised her eyes like a fawn having a first look at the world. Praise must have been scarce indeed. He did appreciate her effort, even if the result weighted his stomach like rubber cement. But what really weighed him down was concern for what she'd shared. And he'd thought his was the mystery.

CHAPTER SIXTEEN

The swing carries me high and back.
A pretend sister pushing from behind.
An older sister helping me swing.
A younger sister who waits her turn,
and another too little to swing.
Maybe more.
I pretend there is a momma still,
to call us in for cakes and tea.

Rese struggled against the images in her mind; her mother's arms embracing a vision, dancing and twirling until she staggered and dropped to the floor. Then the tears and the begging. *"Please don't go. Don't leave me alone."* Sobbing and dragging herself across the floor. *"I don't love them more than you. How? How can I prove it?"*

Rese pressed a hand to her face. As if she could ever forget that night.

"Why do I have to go to bed now? I can't sleep."

"You'll sleep or the banshees will get you."

"The banshees aren't real. And neither is Walter."

The slap. *"Go to bed, Theresa. In the morning everything will be different."*

Rese swallowed the pain in her throat. Why was she digging those memories up now? Because of Star's reappearance and all their history together? Or was it Lance, who drew words out of her like liquid through a sieve?

Rese stared into the sink, remembering. She had been so afraid to fall asleep. She didn't want everything to be different. She fought it, but the next thing she knew Dad was carrying her out of the house as paramedics strapped an oxygen mask to her face and the ambulance siren filled her ears. Why couldn't they save her mother too?

She pushed the thoughts away as she crossed the garden to the carriage house. Baxter bounded out and circled, herding her inside with playful leaps and licks. She returned the love with strokes to his head and ears, then joined Lance inside.

They worked together making a ceiling and the dividing wall that really changed the appearance of the old place from an outbuilding to a home, enhanced by the stone of the perimeter walls. If Lance wasn't going to live there, it would be an awesome unit to rent. But he was. And she'd rather have that than income—a thought that caused mild panic.

Her heart rolled over every time his hand brushed hers or his eyes turned her way, but that was gratitude. He'd accepted the things she told him without probing or mocking. And most of all he hadn't looked at her as though she might be crazy too.

They stopped to eat some fruit and crackers and Sonoma Jack cheese, then went back to work. When they'd finished the drywall, she eyed the seams between the boards. "Can you tape and texture?"

Lance wiped his hands on his jeans. "Probably not to your satisfaction."

"Then I'll do it." The moment it was out she knew how superior that had sounded.

But he smiled. "Knock yourself out. I need to run into town anyway."

Baxter jumped up and ran as soon as Lance approached the bike. Okay, maybe the dog did enjoy the ride. He leaped up between Lance's arms, and for a moment she wished herself there instead. Too bad Lance was brainless about safety. The wind ruffled both his and Baxter's fur as they pulled out, heads unprotected.

Rese started the tape with a jerk and applied it to the crack between the sheets of drywall, wishing she could seal up her thoughts as easily. So he was attractive. Amusing. Attentive. And those were only the A words. Bold, caring, and dashing. *Stop it!* He listened well. He knew when to let it go. He saw inside her.

She sliced the tape with a box cutter and moved to the next crack. He wasn't big and tall like Dad, commanding space and attention. All right, he did command attention, but that was his eyes. And he used them. And he knew it.

Her cook thought a lot of himself, right down to the ring in his ear, which she was actually starting to like. The tape ripped from the roll down the seam with a rude noise and the smell of adhesive. A motion caught the side of her eye. Star? But it was Sybil in the doorway, Sybil looking svelt and sunny in lemon and white, like a merengue pie someone forgot to sweeten.

"Is Baxter here?"

How quaint, asking for the dog. But then she remembered Baxter nosing Sybil's hand and felt doubly betrayed. Rese straightened from her squat. "He took a ride with Lance. I'm not sure when they'll be back."

"Lance put you to work, hmm?"

Rese scowled. "It's my property."

"Right." Sybil smiled. "Tell Lance I came by. He'll want to know." The tip of her tongue touched the edge of her top teeth as she turned and sauntered away.

Rese went back to taping. That was exactly why she would not think of Lance in any terms but her own. The work gave her a focus outside of past memories and current emotions. Work gave her purpose, something Sybil obviously disdained, as though taping and pressing mud into the cracks was something to smirk about, something beneath her, something that might break a nail.

Rese knew the type and it irked her that she'd let it get under her skin. She was proud of her knowledge, her expertise. She was not inferior to some . . . whatever the doll was with the beach tan and bikini and a plastic male version in the next box over. Rese frowned. So why was she wasting her energy thinking about it? As she set up the applicator to blow texture, she heard Lance's bike in the driveway.

A moment later he joined her with a bag of groceries in his arms. "How's it coming?"

Baxter bounded in and Rese was glad she hadn't begun to apply the sticky white substance. "You'll have to keep him out of here."

Lance called the dog out and made him stay. Then he stepped in and observed her work. "Very good."

Tape and mud were hardly challenging. She rested her hands on her hips. "I'm going to texture it now."

He nodded. "I picked up some things for dinner."

"Then go do what you do and let me finish." Way sharper than she'd intended to sound.

He shot her a glance.

"Oh, Sybil was here. She said you'd want to know."

He cocked his head. "Thanks." Then he sauntered out in much the same way his slinky admirer had.

Interesting that Sybil's visit had annoyed Rese. With nothing but employment between them, what should she care who came visiting her cook? But maybe he wasn't the only one fighting the attraction.

He had not intended to care. She was his means to the truth, and it wasn't fair to engender feelings she obviously didn't want either. She was right not to mix personal and professional, but how could they spend time together and not grow close? That was the part he never could get. He was wired to connect, especially with women . . . especially women with issues.

Do you have to fall for every troubled chick you find? Tony's frown was only half mocking the second time Lance landed in the precinct. His throat tightened. What had he been trying to prove anyway?

He wouldn't consider Rese troubled. But issues? Oh yeah. He'd sensed it even before she dropped the clues. But that wasn't his problem. As Tony said, he didn't have to fall for anyone. Just how he kept it from happening, he'd have to figure out.

He strode toward the villa with Baxter at his side. Sybil was another story. He'd told her right out he didn't want to get involved. That was probably all the more intriguing to a woman of her sort. He'd known them too. But since he'd requested her assistance, and she had come through for him before, he'd have to find out if her call was more than social—whether he wanted to or not.

He told Baxter to lie down on the stoop, then carried the groceries inside and took out his phone. A quick call to set something up with Sybil and . . .

The phone rang in his hand and he answered it. "Ay, Lance. You ready for the best news of your life?"

"Hi, Rico." He didn't have to speculate very hard on what Rico would consider the best news of his life.

"I got Saul Samuels. *Saul Samuels.*"

"That's great, Rico. Hope it works out for you." Lance pulled the ricotta and fresh herbs from the bag.

"I'm not talking me, man. It's your lyrics that got him. I sent a CD, and he wants to hear more."

Lance removed garlic. "I'm not doing that anymore." How many times had they rehashed this conversation?

"He's talking recording, and he's sure there'd be some road jobs, like a tour, ya know? Tour, Lance?"

"Yeah, I know. How 'bout dem Yanks?"

"Are you hearing me, man?"

"I hear you, Rico. But I'm through with the band."

"So you took a break. Got your head straight."

Lance gave a half laugh. "Not a break, Rico. I'm not playing anymore."

"But this is it. I feel it."

"Then go for it." Lance folded the empty bag and tucked it into the cabinet.

"Not possible. The magic's in the mix, what you got, what I got; the way it's always been."

Maybe. But that didn't change his decision. "You and Chaz—"

"Chaz is great, man, but he ain't you. Whatever you had to prove, you've done it."

Lance shook his head. "I'm not proving anything, Rico. I just can't do it anymore."

"Can't write the songs going through your head all the time? Can't play the guitar until it weeps? Can't use the voice and talent God gave you?"

The trouble was he hadn't used it for God. It was all about Lance. Leaving the band and the lifestyle and the complications and temptations wasn't about proving anything. It was trying to find God's will, to be . . . different, better. He closed his eyes. "I'm sorry, Rico. Get another guitar."

He didn't need the distraction or the lure of Rico's dreams. Even before Nonna's stroke he had put that aside. What happened with Tony was a wake-up call that he better get his life right before it was too late. Lance rubbed his face and stuffed the phone back into his pocket, his connection to the people who mattered, the life he knew was there for him to pick up when he was ready. But there were just some things he was not going back to. Rico would have to find someone else.

With the ingredients laid out on the counter, Lance set to work. Anyone could follow package directions and make lasagna, but not his lasagna; a variation of the traditional Bolognese but including the spicy sausage he bought at home from the D'Auria brothers, though here in Sonoma he had found only a fair substitute. Cooking centered him, but still, his mind churned. Having found Vito in the cemetery, he pondered the blocks under his floor. With Rese working in the carriage house, he had worried that she might bring it up. He didn't want to lie to her, but he did intend to pursue it.

Lance mixed up the pasta dough, rolled it out, then stretched it gently by hand until he could see the pattern of the cloth beneath it. He cut it into broad strips, then hung them over the rack to dry. He'd have used a chair-back if Rese hadn't ordered the rack, but she'd been amenable to almost everything—in spite of her "expensive cook" comments. She wouldn't regret it.

He went to the pantry for the cheese grater, pulled open the door, and a mouse skittered across the floor and disappeared. Just as Rese had said. He got down on hands and knees and glimpsed the hole two fingers wide beneath the lowest shelf in the back. Aha. The trap he'd placed was sprung, and he tossed that mouse body into the trash. But as the second mouse had just demonstrated, there were more where it came from. The wall could be full of them.

While he didn't share Rese's fear, he did not want mice in his kitchen. He scooched under the shelf for a better estimation of the size and shape of the hole, then he went outside to find a wood chunk to plug it. That and some caulk. . . . He searched the ground, then crouched down to gather a couple chunks that might do.

"I'd like a word with you, young man."

He looked up from his crouch, but not very far. The woman was a wizened bird, not an inch taller than Conchessa, only Conchessa had the shape of a small barrel and this one had to work to hold up her clothes. "Ma'am?"

"Since when do you let that poor girl work so hard when you're as able-bodied as any I've seen?"

He glanced toward the carriage house just behind him. "I've found the best thing to do with Rese is stay out of her way."

The woman eyed him like a severe headmistress on a recalcitrant youth. He shrugged. "She's a better builder than I am. Ask her yourself."

Then she smiled. "I like a man who isn't threatened by a woman's abilities."

No, he wasn't threatened by Rese. Annoyed. Intrigued. Attracted. He picked up the wood chunks and stood. "You must be Eve."

The woman made a painful noise. "Not Eve. Evvy. Evvy Potter."

"Well, Miss Potter, I'm cooking lasagna. Would you like to join us for dinner?"

She gave him a slow-lidded blink. "This I have to see."

He wasn't sure exactly what she meant by that. "It won't be ready for a while."

"Lead on, my boy. I want to watch."

Watch him make it? He started toward the house, keeping his pace short so she could keep up. Baxter nosed her when she reached the door. When she pulled her skirt away, Lance called him off and gave the dog a head rub as Evvy Potter passed through the doorway.

"You will wash your hands, won't you?"

"Yes, ma'am."

He made a good show of it at the sink and decided not to plug the mousehole just yet. The less Evvy knew about that, the better. He left the wood chunks on the counter, then turned the drying noodles as Evvy chattered about her nephew who fixed every kind of moving vehicle, but couldn't operate the coffee maker. "He thinks it's beneath him."

Lance sautéed the sausage in butter in place of the usual ham and bacon, then added the ground veal. In their time he put in the diced vegetables and mushrooms, garlic and nutmeg. Tomato paste, wine and chicken stock—since he couldn't find veal—cream and parsley. That completed the Bolognese sauce, and he prepared to make the Béchamel sauce.

"How did you learn to cook?" Evvy asked, seemingly convinced, now, that he could.

"My grandmother and my cousin Conchessa." He was glad Rese hadn't asked specifically. She assumed his credentials to be a little more authentic. He melted more butter over low heat and built the Béchamel with milk, flour, salt, and nutmeg.

He wanted to ask Evvy what she knew about the villa, but she kept on other subjects, mainly her relatives, and he could only nod and reply as expected, while grating the Parmesan and layering the lasagna in the pan.

"Did you tell me your name, son?"

He glanced over his shoulder. "It's Lance. Lance Michelli."

"Lancelot?"

He laughed. "No, just Lance." He'd always been glad he didn't end up Guido or Dodi. He slid the lasagna into the oven and closed the door, and since he didn't want to veer into another long subject, he asked, "So, Evvy, have you lived next door for long?"

Her answer included what he already knew from Rese, the romance she'd had with Ralph and his subsequent decline that precipitated his move into the assisted-care facility. Lance sat across from her at the small table and listened. Then he said, "Your house doesn't look as old as this relic."

She chuckled. "No. Ralph was very proud of this old house. Said it had secrets."

Lance straightened. "Did he know the secrets?"

Her pale blue eyes sharpened on his face. "He told his tales, and every time they got better."

"What tales?"

She waved her bat-like hand. "I could never reproduce them. He is the raconteur."

Lance didn't care how she told the story, just what information it contained. "Miss Potter, you've shown yourself a fine storyteller."

"You are a flatterer, young man. Unless you are saying I talk too much."

Lance raised his hands. "I never meant that at all."

Evvy laughed then coughed, the latter shaking her whole frame. "Now see, I have talked too much." She wheezed in a thin breath, and started to rise.

He got quickly to his feet and helped her. "You're not leaving?"

She nodded.

"But you haven't tried the lasagna."

"It's too rich and spicy for me." She gripped her cane and hobbled toward the door. "But I dare say Theresa will love it."

Theresa? He couldn't stop the grin. "I could make you something else."

Evvy waved her free hand. "Don't trouble." She turned at the door he opened for her. "I did enjoy watching, though." She waved a finger. "You are an artist."

That took him by surprise. "Thank you. Think of what you'd like to eat sometime and let me know."

She nodded. "I'll do that."

Lance watched for a moment as she teetered through the garden. He hadn't gotten the information he wanted, but he'd made an impression and had an excuse for future visits. Besides, he liked her.

Star came in, vibrant in purple. The sundress draped her girlish curves and swirled around her thighs as she spun. "What do you think?"

A Marilyn Monroe effect with the dress, and her red spirals once again bounced to life. No sign that she'd been holed up inconsolable. "Radiant."

She laughed and caught his hands. "If I didn't love Rese, I'd take you away."

He didn't correct her misconception. Star was off even his scale of troubled.

She reached out and fingered his earring. "You need something iridescent."

"That would go over well with Rese."

Laughing, she put up her arms and twirled. There was something heart-breakingly fragile in the motion.

"Can I get you something, Star?"

"Color. I need color."

That seemed to be a theme with her. "There's color in the garden."

She clasped her hands beneath her chin. "Colors in the garden." Then she went out, flitting from flower bed to flower bed. *Lord, the broken people* . . .

Lance washed up his work area, then went to see how Rese was coming along. Star was perched in the branches of a sprawling oak like a mythical, plumed bird. He passed her without comment, then entered the carriage house.

Rese turned. "Was that Evvy I saw leaving?"

"My lady caller."

Rese snorted. "You're not her type."

He leaned in the doorway. "She was actually impressed."

"By what?" Rese coiled the cord around the sprayer.

Surely she didn't intend to be so insulting. He suspected it was a defensive posture. Torque him off, and he'd lose interest. It ought to work that way. It had at the start.

"By my culinary art." Lance took the tool from her. "The walls look good."

Rese bent and gathered the rest of her things. "It's turning out better than I thought it would."

Better than she'd thought *he* could do. "I'll do the windows and doors tomorrow, then trim it out."

"You'd better let me do the finish work."

Lance cocked his head. "I can use a miter box."

"I'll do it anyway."

"That wasn't our deal."

She started past him toward the shed. "If you leave, I'll be renting it."

He felt a twinge. "Why do you think I'm leaving?"

"I mean when."

Had she been convincing herself of that while she worked? Did she want him out after last night? He followed her to the shed and set the sprayer down outside the door. Amazing how much he'd come to consider the place his. He'd never had such a clear direction as this.

It was not just a job; it was a mission. His sense of purpose had not diminished. Yes, he wanted answers. But with growing intensity, he wanted his quest to not conflict with Rese's dream. And with equal intensity he wanted to take her in his arms and assure her of that. Not a good idea. He worked on Baxter's head as she hosed off her tools.

Star waved to them from the tree.

Lance said, "Is she okay up there?"

Rese shielded her eyes from the setting sun. "She's a great climber. Made it through my window in all kinds of weather."

There was plenty to that story, he was sure. He still could not see them friends. Even if they'd grown up together, the two girls could not have been similar in any way. What was the bond? But then, what was his bond with

Rese? They were almost as opposite as she and Star. "Dinner's going to be a while. Want to take a ride with me?"

She shook her head. "You don't use helmets."

"So?"

"So I'd rather not spend my life as a vegetable."

"I'm a safe driver."

Rese closed the shed door. "And all the other vehicles on the road?" Even as she spoke, a furniture delivery truck backed in and almost took out his Harley. Rese sent him a look, then went to direct the action.

With the parlor and dining room filled with an eclectic assortment of small tables, benches, and chairs, and the delivery crew on their way out the door, Lance tossed a salad of crisp romaine with red wine vinegar and olive oil. Plain enough to complement the rich flavor overload of his signature dish, along with warm, crusty bread and Chianti.

Rese walked into the kitchen and stopped. She looked at the pan atop the stove and let out a sigh. "You made lasagna?"

He raised his brows. That was more of a reaction than he'd hoped for. "Take a seat. I'll get Star." They had salvaged a third chair that he hoped Star was ready to use. As far as he knew she hadn't eaten in a day and a half. He filled her glass with Perrier, then went out to get her.

She swung her legs slowly as he approached the tree. "Coming up?"

He shook his head. "I have dinner ready."

"Oh, blessed man, free me from this snarc." She reached out her arms and dropped.

Small as she was, he still crashed his shoulder into the trunk as he took her weight against his chest. Her hair tangled across his face, but he got her to her feet without falling. *Mamma mia*, she was crazy. "Let me know you're coming next time."

She smiled. "I used to fly, but my wings are gone."

What could he even say? She started for the house, humming. Shaking his head, Lance followed. Inside, he put the salad plates and the bread basket on the table, then sat down, bowed his head and prayed the blessing.

When he finished, Rese had fixed him with the gaze of an owl on its prey. "What about the lasagna?"

He glanced at the pan. "It needs to set." But her anticipation was tangible, and he got up soon and cut it. He put the squares on plates and carried them over in a cloud of aromatic steam. The pungent flavors of sausage, garlic and tomato, wine and cream cheese brought the expression to Rese's face that he had wanted since he'd come. He had found her comfort food.

She swallowed her first bite, eyes closed, and said, "Don't expect me to speak."

"You don't have to." Lance leaned his head back and watched her. It had been worth the effort to finally elicit a reaction she couldn't control. Not even Star's scrutiny dulled his pleasure. He silently thanked Nonna Antonia for this particular dish, a marriage of Northern and Southern elements they had developed together.

Star said, "You could open a restaurant."

"That's sort of the idea." He turned to Rese. "Dinner specials?"

"You mean here?" Star clasped her hands. "Marvelous. I'll play the serving wench. I already have my costume."

Lance raised his eyebrows at Rese.

She glanced from one to the other. "What would it look like?"

Star spiked her fingertips to her head. "Brainstorm!"

Lance said, "I could make up a weekly menu. You post it in the rooms." He envisioned something similar to Nonna's own operation where many people had standing reservations and ate whatever she made for the day.

Star's fingers fluttered. "Lance cooks; I serve. What will you do, Rese?"

Rese sat back. "I guess if Lance plays music after dinner, I'll be doing dishes."

Lance shot her a smile. "Yeah. Too bad there's no dishwasher."

She glared.

"What music?" Star caught his arm.

"I play a little and sing."

"Then I'll dance!" Star swept up and spun around the table.

Lance joined gazes with Rese, who only raised her brows with a smile. Her acceptance of Star puzzled him. It didn't seem to fit her rigid nature. He said, "Wine list?"

"Limited, maybe. Local vineyards. A dozen choices?"

Lance considered that. He would have gone for the Italian labels he enjoyed, but this was, after all, Sonoma. "You get the license. I'll choose the wines. We'll need place settings."

Star came to a stop and draped her arms over Rese's neck. "Let me pick the dishes."

Rese laughed. "I can't spend a hundred dollars a plate for works of art."

Star hung her head down, and the rosy spirals encircled Rese like an exotic fern. Lance eyed the two women together. Something intangible connected them, some feminine mystique. And he realized that even though Rese functioned in a man's field, she was as different from him as Star. And that difference created the spark. *Grazie, Signore.* The world would be a dull place with nothing but men.

CHAPTER SEVENTEEN

Nonno stands taller than any man I know.
Papa keeps looking for two more inches.

The breakfast entrées Lance created the next morning looked great as Rese captured them for the Web site. Crepes, almond focaccia, and frittata di carciofi—artichoke omelets he served earlier—and, of course, the lasagna. She took the close-ups, then said, "Now stand there and hold the focaccia."

"What for?"

"I'm including a picture of the chef."

He folded his arms. "C'mon."

She looked up over the camera. "Bashful?"

"I'm not wearing my diamond."

She snorted. "Like that would matter." She held up the camera and snapped one, then another. "Could you smile?" She snapped again. The man looked good through a lens. Okay, he'd look good through anything. "Now one with your guitar for the promo poster, and then we will get your room."

"I cleaned it for the occasion."

"Good."

"Just don't open the closet."

"Skeletons?"

He scowled. "Sybil asked that too. Do I look like a don?"

"It's the pirate thing." She headed up the stairs and waited outside his door while he opened it. Why she felt so playful and energized she couldn't say. But this morning felt truly like a new day, not just another. And it had been so long since it felt that way.

She was riding the wave of their brainstorming last night. Lance had talked and then sung, and Star had sparkled. Rese smiled. She had absorbed

156

their excitement, caught the vision, then slept surprisingly well. No wonder it translated to this near euphoria.

Lance went into his room. He pulled a thin leather vest over his T-shirt, then opened a small box on top of the dresser. He removed the gold ring from his ear and replaced it with the diamond stud. "No more pirate, just pure Ritz."

Rese's heart jumped when he turned and washed her with a velvet gaze.

He knew it, too, by the amusement in the corners of his mouth. "Where do you want me?"

Her throat squeezed. "What?"

"For the picture." He grinned.

She couldn't say he'd done it on purpose, but her mind was misbehaving big time. "Well, not in here. They'll be breaking down your door."

He cocked his head. "They?"

As if he didn't know exactly what she meant. "Would you get out so I can shoot the room." She pushed him aside and searched her best angle on the Seaside room, still smelling of his shower and mellow aftershave.

Lance carried his guitar into the hall. He was complying with her working relationship terms but was well aware of the effect he had. He expected her to falter, to give in to his charm. Good thing she'd mastered self-control.

She photographed the room, then directed him downstairs. "Dining room. Where you'll be playing."

He took his place in the corner near the parlor. His was not razzle-dazzle, just natural appeal. Why was it so easy for some people? She hadn't mastered charm, hadn't considered it high on her list of necessities. If Lance worked at his, it sure didn't show, but somehow he had it and she didn't. She caught a great smile with the camera, then a couple "action shots" as he played. No one should be so multi-talented.

"Here you are." Star walked in wearing a turquoise scarf crisscrossing her bust and a pair of tiny Lycra shorts. Her skin was so fair, it almost glowed, but her nails were painted fuchsia and peacock feathers dangled from her ears. A waft of perfume followed her in as she announced, "I'm going shopping."

"Do not buy more than one plate for me to see."

"Oh, I'm not shopping for that." She wiggled the tiny beaded purse that hung from a chain around her waist. "I'm spending my inheritance. Want to come?"

Rese shook her head. "I have work to do."

"'Blessed are the horny hands of toil.'" Star blew Lance a kiss and drifted out the door.

Lance leaned his guitar in the corner. "I thought she didn't have any money."

"She gets a quarterly check from her mother, but she doesn't use the money to live on."

He cocked his eyebrows.

"It makes her feel dependent."

"How can using her own money make her more dependent than mooching off you?"

Rese frowned. "She's not mooching. She's . . . well, she's part of this, isn't she? Room and board, just like you." Except he was working hard to earn his keep.

Lance didn't press that aspect. "She just said she's spending the money."

Rese expelled a breath. He wouldn't understand, but she felt compelled to explain Star. "She does spend it, but not . . . responsibly." She thought of all the crazy ways Star had blown the check in the past. "It's like throwing it away."

Lance slacked a hip. She knew how it sounded. If she thought about it, she'd agree, but Rese understood why Star did it. "It's guilt money. Star calls it Judas's silver."

"Guilt for what?"

Rese straightened. "For all the meals her mother never made, the events she missed, and all the parties she threw where Star became the back-room attraction." She hadn't meant to tell him that. But he was Lance, sucking the truth from her.

He looked toward the door where Star had disappeared.

Rese didn't give him time to comment. "I want to work on the Web site now." She took the camera to the office, determined to finally bring that project to a close. The sooner the site was operational—she froze—the sooner they'd have guests. That was the point, right? The rest was all preparation for her new direction. Her heart hammered. Planning with Lance and Star was one thing, actually doing it another.

Guests were not ogres with knowing eyes. This was a fresh start. She wasn't labeled here; neither was Star. They were not the Looney Toons anymore.

She chose the final pictures, wrote the descriptions, completed the cost and reservation page. Work helped. It kept her mind busy. It was always good to have her mind too busy to wander. Unguarded moments were too hard to control.

She clenched her fists. What did that have to do with Web sites and inns? Nothing. *So stop thinking that way. It's going to be fine. It will all work out.*

She expelled a long breath, clicked the print command, then snatched the papers and hurried out to the carriage house. Star was gone, but even if she was there, Rese would have headed for Lance first. He was more involved with the business; the whole food plan was his idea. It was not affirmation she needed, just . . .

Baxter came and pranced at her side, his expression saying that he deserved whatever love she lavished on him with no performance on his part except to lap it up. She laughed and wrapped him in her arms as he licked her throat and chin, then stood up before his tail demolished the pages.

Lance had the front of the carriage house closed in with French doors and panel windows, but the doors stood open to dissipate the paint fumes as he worked. When she walked in, he said, "Pretty soon you'll have to knock."

She hadn't thought in those terms, but he was right. It was almost his space. She held the copied sheets out.

"What's this?" He set the roller down and took them.

"Web site up and operational." Her one college course on Web page design had taught her what she needed in order to create the site for Barretts, Inc. That site had been good, showing examples of the places they had renovated, before and after shots, and close-ups of banister detail, cabinet work, and her carvings. But this site was better. She refused to think it was because Lance was in it.

He glanced through the pages. "Good work. It captures the place well."

His words sank like well-placed nails, straight, tight, and effective. "There's even music on the home page. And look." She surprised him with Baxter's photo.

"Now there's a sell." He hadn't commented on his own pictures. He handed the pages back and smiled. "That's great, Rese."

A smooth hand rubbing in the finish. Okay, she'd wanted his approval. It felt good, even if she didn't need it. She turned and studied his progress from inside. With the white walls, the place felt open and bright in spite of the limited windows. "The skylights were a good idea. Even if you shade the front windows for privacy, you'll have daylight."

"Mmhmm." He rubbed a line of paint from his thumb onto a rag.

She peeked into the bathroom. He had grouted the floor, and there was no sign of the rock structure beneath. She turned back to him. "You don't mind living over a tomb?"

He tossed the rag. "No."

She couldn't help thinking how disappointed she'd be if someone built over Dad's grave without any thought of what lay beneath. But then, if Dad was right, and there was nothing after death but flesh returning to dust. . . . Her forehead squeezed. She shook her head. That was too . . . senseless.

Because of her encounter?

Her spine turned fuzzy. It always did when she thought of it. The night Mom died, when she had fought sleep with everything she had . . . there had been someone in her room, urging her to resist, to fight, not to give in. Someone she had trusted. A presence she couldn't ignore.

Dad had run into the house and carried her out, but he'd only been inside for those moments. So that left two possibilities. Someone supernatural, or the same delusions Mom had known. She shuddered.

"Rese?"

She startled out of her reverie. Lance was going to think her crazy if she kept drifting off. "Yes?"

He had come up beside her. "There's nothing to worry about. I don't believe the dead threaten the living." His words were only half as comforting as the warmth in his eyes.

She swallowed. "What do you believe? I mean about death."

"You die; you're judged; you spend eternity with Jesus or without."

He made it sound obvious, but it wasn't. Rese frowned. "Does it matter?"

He expelled a short breath. "It matters."

"Hellfire and all that?"

"I think the torment is forever missing the Lord's will, and knowing it."

She searched his face. "But . . . if you don't know . . ."

"He'll find an open heart."

Rese's throat tightened. "You mean He'd find someone who needed him, even if they didn't know it?" She had imagined maybe an angel in her room, not Jesus himself. That was too much to believe, too impossible—and way too awful. It made her feel a gaping loss and deep, unexplainable fear.

She pulled away, brought the papers up to her chest like a shield. His religion and Mom's behavior were too close, invisible voices telling you how to live, expecting obedience in hopes of some future peace. She might not like it, but Dad's way was simpler. She'd rather think of him in the ground than in eternal torment. And if that meant forgetting the one in her room . . . well, she wasn't even sure that was real.

Lance watched her go. He hadn't intended to be featured on her Web site, his part receiving such prominence. It made it seem permanent when all he wanted was to give her a good, solid start so they could both come out ahead. But something else nagged.

What had upset her? Probably grief. If he didn't know Tony was with the Lord, didn't believe there was something greater after death, how much harder would the loss be? Rese didn't seem to believe much of anything, and more than likely it had been the same with her dad. But death was obviously a germane subject. He should have told her it wasn't a tomb, set her mind at ease.

He had ascertained that there was no opening in the structure underneath his bathroom before he grouted the floor. It extended at least six feet outside the carriage house and probably farther since he hadn't yet found an end. Once he started on the garden he could explore that without notice. If he found anything dangerous out there, he would tell Rese.

Inside the carriage house was another story. That was his domain. Not technically maybe, but in his mind. With the house renovated and the attic cleaned out, he was running out of possibilities. The only one left to him, it seemed, was whatever lay under his dwelling.

Sybil's article mentioned hidden wealth that a search of the property had not revealed. Nonna had not specified losing wealth in her letter to Conchessa. She feared losing everything, and it appeared they had. But he sensed it was something specific Nonna needed, now that death had tapped her shoulder. The doctor had as much as said a stroke like hers was a harbinger of worse to come. She might have years still, or not. But the incident had awakened a need kept silent too long.

Lance frowned. In all the years he'd known her, all the hours they'd spent in the kitchen, she had never mentioned Sonoma. She had said a few things about her papa, mostly what he liked to eat and things of little consequence. She had told him he died young, but she had never mentioned murder or Nonno Quillan or hidden treasure.

So much he didn't know; he almost felt betrayed. He could have done this for her before she was incapacitated. He would have done anything to help her. Why had she kept it quiet until it was too late? The thought jolted him. Not too late. She would recover. Maybe what he found, what he did here, would help her. Maybe the stress of keeping the secret had caused the stroke. Now only he could undo it.

Lance swallowed. He wasn't the one for the job. Something this important, this momentous—Lance stopped. Tony wasn't there. He couldn't hide in his brother's shadow, couldn't default to the one who took naturally to heroic deeds and got things right.

Lance's throat squeezed. He loved Tony. He'd loved him with the same fierce devotion they all had shown. But it wasn't easy following after him. Tony had taken strides no kid brother could reach. But Nonna needed help, and he was all she had.

He finished with the caulk, then cleaned up in his bathroom. It was ready for the trim work Rese was going to do. He still didn't like that. He wanted the satisfaction of completing something. The habitat houses had been teamwork. This would have been his.

He glanced toward heaven. *Yeah. I get the message.* Maybe if he ever did accomplish something on his own it would spoil some deep, divine purpose, like his humility. He wiped his hands on his T-shirt and sighed.

───────

Evvy set aside the devotional and studied the blurred outlines of the far wall. Her eyes were unable or unwilling to transition from the close reading to making sense of the paintings and the tapestry bellpull that hung there. The bellpull looked like a figure standing straight and silent, and she wondered which guardian it might be.

"If you're death, let's be quick about it."

The tapestry remained.

"Not today, then? What have I left to do?"

She stroked the small book she had set aside. Oswald Chambers had scolded her again from the pages she'd read year after year. Maybe she hadn't always done her utmost, but she did seek God's highest glory. He'd been father, brother, friend, and lover, Lord and Savior through all the high and low points of her life. Now He was simply her destiny, and when He called she would be ready.

Until then, she'd prefer He deal from the straight deck He'd used so far. Even losing James had not been unexpected. She'd known, sending him off at the station, seeing the firm set of his jaw, the cold light in his eyes, that his life would play out in the war. She'd been devastated, but not surprised.

The Lord had not proclaimed His purpose, but neither had He practiced sleight of hand. There was no shell game meant to beguile her eye, to set up false expectations, then eliminate her chances. No, her course was simply laid out beforehand. It would be what it was. She slid into her late morning doze; not much difference between the wakeful and subconscious moments anymore, both a decoupage of memories and dreams. The secret to life was acceptance and trusting that the Lord knew His business.

CHAPTER EIGHTEEN

Rese slid the dogleg chisel into the wood, curling a sliver up before it. Her favorite part of every renovation was the carvings that made it hers. This one was the decorative piece to fit over the dining room doorway. The room was elegant enough to support the fancywork, and it might play a bigger role in the inn than she had expected. Two meals a day, plus music.

She positioned the tool again. She had penciled in the design, but it came to life when she started cutting. Since the grounds had once been a vineyard, she carved grapes and leaves and curling vines, drawing out the shapes from the heart of the wood, and pouring her own heart in.

Lance came in and looked over her shoulder. He blew lightly under his breath. "Nice."

She glowed without pausing the tool. Having entered the carving mode, she didn't want to pull out, even to accept his praise.

"Hungry?"

"I'm working." She pushed the tool deeper into the wood, making the groove around the leaf, chipping around a stem. Tiny pieces and slivers came away, leaving the design in their place. She had sharpened the leaf and rounded most of the bunch of grapes when Lance slipped a plate onto the table beside her. A round, flat bread with pungent herbs and pale nuts, melting cheese drooping from the sides with crisped edges of thin-sliced ham.

Hunger hit her like a hammer. Rese turned and met his eyes, laughter in the creases, and confidence. Once again he'd demonstrated the effect of his cooking—and his disregard for her schedule and focus. She picked up half the sandwich and bit in, then sank back in her chair as the flavors permeated her concentration. Nothing used to break through it. Now all he had to do was set a plate beside her and she was eating out of his hand. Not good.

"What can I get you to drink?"

"Water." She wanted nothing to compete with the herb-laden bread, smoky ham, and mellow cheese. "Lance, it's delicious," she said when he returned with her glass.

"Good."

She sensed his satisfaction, pleasure in pleasing her. No wonder it had rankled before when she said nothing. He didn't want praise. He wanted to know that he had accomplished his goal, carried out his mission of mercy to the stomachs in his charge.

He turned to leave when Star burst in, arms filled with boxes. What had she done this time? Lance was already moving to lend her a hand. He seemed surprised by the weight of the boxes compared to their size. "What's in here?"

"You'll see." Beaming, Star headed for the stairs. "Come up, Rese."

Her zone was now obliterated. She may as well see what Star had purchased. Taking the sandwich with her, she followed Lance and Star and the boxes upstairs. They put the load on the bed, and Star immediately opened the first. "Come out, little fella." She pulled a vibrant orange frog sculpture as large as her palm from the box. "This one's Tad. He's the baby."

It must be made of something heavy, but it looked ready to spring from her hand. Star set it on the dresser, and Rese couldn't help smiling at the expression on the creature's face. Lance had opened another box and removed a blackish green frog splayed full length.

Star said, "That's Leapfrog. They're the creations of a bronze sculpture artist called the Frogman."

Rese stared at the outstretched amphibian Lance had freed from its box. "Wonder why."

Star giggled

"They certainly fit the theme." Rese would give her that.

"This is Showoff." Star displayed a green frog in a handstand, then took out the next. "Blue Over the Edge." Made to dangle from a shelf. Next she lifted a bronze-colored one with gold circles and black feet. "What's Up."

Each one was incredible, but as a mob, a little overwhelming. Star didn't believe in restraint. A rainforest room filled with frogs was just her style. By the time the boxes were emptied, fifteen frogs and one toad perched around the room in every position imaginable.

Star clapped her hands. "Aren't they wondrous?"

Lance grinned. "They do have personality."

Star twirled. "I knew you'd love it." She turned to Rese. "You love them, right?"

Rese nodded and smiled. As long as Star occupied the room it was perfect, but for guests?

"I bought every one in the store." Star set the frog on a shelf and pointed to the plate Rese had carried into the room. "I want what Rese has."

Lance nodded. "Okay." He motioned Star out of the room before him.

Rese stared around the room after they went down, taking in the effect of the frogs. They really were incredible: brilliant, shiny hues in shapes that sprang to life. So Star, so very Star. She lifted Tad and saw the price on the bottom. That quarterly check was gone.

Rese went down, past Lance and Star laughing in the kitchen, back to her work, idly finishing the sandwich. It had seemed like a gift, something special from him to her. But as Star proved, it was simply lunch.

After a while, she heard Lance's bike revving. She got to the parlor window as he drove away with Star behind him, ruby spirals trailing like ribbons. Stiffly, she went back to work. The tool moved as she directed, freeing slivers of wood and forming the design, but she was wishing she hadn't shown him how much she liked the meal, hadn't told him anything about her and Star.

She had given him too much importance, listening and incorporating his ideas. Too much authority even in her own mind. No wonder he acted her equal. She sighed. Why couldn't it ever be easy?

The shadows were stretching when she heard the Harley return. She didn't go look. She had finally found peace in the wood. But her chisel stopped as Lance came in alone. "Where's Star?"

"In town." He nodded toward the door. "Let's go for a drive."

She shook her head. "I told you I don't—"

"C'mon."

"Lance, I—"

"Just come out and see."

Exasperated, she got up and went with him. Then she caught sight of his bike with a shiny black helmet on the seat.

"Star and I went all the way to Santa Rosa for it. Her head size should be close to yours."

"You didn't have to do that."

"You'd have ridden without one?"

"No . . ." But she hadn't intended to ride with one either.

He walked her down to the bike and unstrapped the helmet. She looked from it to the motorcycle. She'd never ridden in anything less rugged than a truck. The bike looked insignificant—Dad had called them road hazards. Lance positioned the helmet on her head, and it fit snugly but not uncomfortably. He pulled a leather jacket from a side pouch, a lady's version no less.

"Protects you from debris." He wore his own soft black one.

This was crazy. She put on the jacket, and then Lance was helping her onto the seat. What was she doing?

He climbed on in front and raised her feet to the pegs, bringing her knees against his hips, and said, "Hold on."

She put her hands on his shoulders as he started the bike with a roar of barely muffled machinery. A whiff of exhaust stung her nostrils as they went down the driveway and onto the street, Baxter barking his disappointment at being left behind. Lance drove sensibly through town out to the Petaluma highway. How far was he planning to take her?

She tapped his shoulder. "Where are we going?" She had to holler over the bike's engine.

"You'll see."

She did not like surprises, but he enjoyed his secrets. Hers, he coaxed out with ease until he knew everything there was to know. Even Mom. Even *Walter*. A seeping dread crept in that Lance could use that knowledge against her. And it was her fault.

They wound through grassy hills dotted with cattle and occasional vineyards, like quilts spread out to dry. It wasn't the main vineyard road with the gates that invited tourists to view and taste. These fields were mostly natural countryside, and she wished she could enjoy it.

The air smelled of yellow blooms and earth and Lance. A ground squirrel darted toward the edge of the road and back into the grass. The sky blushed with the sinking sun. Vines of a lone vineyard rushed up to meet the fence with dark gnarly trunks in a froth of green, then pale green-gold grass took over again.

Rese felt the road as she never had in the truck. She was vulnerable, even with a helmet. Lance was smooth and sure, but she was completely without control; not a position she accepted well. Peachy clouds stretched through the sky, and shadows sprang long and thin in the westerly light. But the beauty of the evening could not ease her agitation.

When Lance pulled off at the top of a hill, she didn't know whether to be relieved or more concerned than before. The answer came when he took her helmet, then removed a bottle of wine and a bag of something edible, she guessed, from the bike's compartment. He meant to share a meal outside the context of the inn.

Striding to the wire fence, he stepped on the bottom and held up the middle.

She looked at the gap. "I don't think we're supposed to go in there. It's private property." Not that rules or limits meant much to Lance Michelli.

"It's just to keep the cows in. I doubt they'll mind us having a picnic."

She ducked through the fence and took in the scatter of amber cows grazing far up a scrubby hill. Cattails and broad leafy reeds marked a moist depression. The grass whispered softly in the breeze.

Lance headed for the single twisted oak a short way inside the fence. "Are you cold?"

She shook her head. She was generating enough body heat to ignite the field.

"Then we should sit on the jackets. I don't have a blanket."

They should keep the jackets on and ride back to the house where she had a semblance of control. But he had taken the items from the bag; strawberries, pepper jack with a little cheese knife, a package of sesame flatbread, and plastic goblets for the wine.

She would have forgotten the knife and goblets. And the corkscrew. But he'd covered all the details. She sat down as he opened the wine and filled the goblets. She took the one he handed her, but when he raised his to toast, she said, "Lance."

He touched her glass with his. "To sharing the journey."

"This feels like a date, and I told you—"

"Can I say the grace now?"

She looked down at the food. "Yes, fine, and then—"

"Bless us, O Lord . . ."

His words washed over hers, words to a being no one could see, but who could find an open heart. Her heart felt anything but open. "We need to talk."

"Over food? Rese, you astound me." He broke a thin, crispy flatbread and laid a sliver of cheese on it. Handing it to her, he said, "Eat."

"Don't tell me what to do."

"All right, but the flavor escapes in the air."

She took the food, but didn't eat.

"You'll like it." He nudged her hand nearer her mouth.

"I don't like it. You're—"

"I meant the cheese."

"I told you I don't date my employees." Her voice sounded tight and hard.

"So it's not a date. You're hungry; I'm hungry. Let's eat." He bit into his cracker and cheese.

When she didn't join him, he frowned. "What is it with you? Is everything a contest? Fine, you win."

"This isn't about winning. If we don't maintain a professional distance—"

"What? What's the worst that could happen?"

"I could fire you."

"You can't fire me; I'm on your Web site." He sprawled out and sipped his wine.

"Did you ask if I wanted to be here with you? No. Do you listen to anything I say? No. Even the thickheaded thugs, as you put it, knew who was in charge."

"What about Star?"

Rese rested her flatbread on her knee. "What about her?"

"I don't see you ordering her around."

"I didn't hire her." And Star was unmanageable anyway.

"I thought she was the maid. Oh, and the waitress."

"It's not the same."

He hunched forward. "Of course not. She's not a man."

"That has nothing—"

"Oh, come on, Rese. It has everything to do with it. You're so threatened—"

"I am threatened?" She crushed the flatbread in her fist. "You're the one playing hot macho lover and backing me into doorjambs and dragging me off on your bike when—"

"Dragging you?" His face darkened dangerously. He tossed the wine from his goblet and hers, corked the bottle, and scooped the rest of the things into the bag. Rese snatched up her jacket as Lance went through the fence without stopping to hold it. She should have known he would take it personally, miss the message in a fit of temper.

She hadn't expected him to trigger hers. But *threatened*? The day she was threatened by Lance Michelli . . . She climbed through the fence and met him at the motorcycle, wishing with everything in her they didn't still have the drive back. But she pulled on her helmet with a stony glare and climbed on behind him.

She held gingerly to his shoulders as the bike roared beneath her, then gripped hard when acceleration tugged her backward. She clung to his leather jacket as he furiously claimed the road, the wind from his speed buffeting them, then gripped his waist hard as they leaned at an angle that felt parallel to the ground. "Stop it, Lance!" But he couldn't hear her, and he didn't care. He was one screaming emotion.

It was pure spite and defiance, and she clung, terrified. She would fire him the minute they got back, and the words filled her mind with comforting rage as they covered the miles to the villa, though she wasn't sure she could stand when he skidded to a stop in the yard. She let go with a jerk, ready to tell him—

Star came flying out the door. "We're in business!" She waved a paper over her head. "I took our first reservation."

Rese stared at her. A reservation already? The first day of the Web site?

Lance kicked down the stand, climbed off, and walked away. With Star standing there, gaping, Rese was not going to do any less. She stood up, legs shaking, removed the helmet, and went to see the paper Star waved like a flag.

She was right. He knew it. She had told him the rules, and he'd taken the job anyway. It didn't matter what she decided to do with Star, or how their relationship worked. Like the workers in the Lord's parable who came the last hour but got the same pay, Star's arrangement was none of his business. He'd gone into the job with eyes open, signed on because he wanted access to the property without telling her the whole truth. She had been upfront about her doubts from the start, but he'd pushed through her arguments to get what he wanted.

Lance went into the carriage house and examined the work still to do. In the failing light he couldn't see well. He needed light fixtures installed. He needed furniture. He . . . wasn't even sure he'd be there tomorrow. Rese was spitting mad. He'd heard her hollering, driving back, and ignored it.

He leaned against the wall. He had wanted to be with her, to cheer her up, take her mind off things a little. But she hadn't agreed to a picnic; she'd barely agreed to a drive. In typical Bronx fashion, he'd bulldozed her. That wasn't who he was, but Rese made everything difficult, brought out the ugliest parts of him. All he wanted . . . was to help Nonna? Could he truthfully say that? He'd better, because tonight might be all he had.

He went to the shed for a crowbar and flashlight, but Rese had locked up her tools. He turned back to the carriage house. She might come out any moment and can him, but until then he'd do what he came for if he had to use his bare hands. With the light even dimmer inside his room, he knelt at the edge of the floor just outside the bathroom. *Sorry, Quillan.* With his pocketknife, he pried the first stone loose, then used his fingers to lift it.

The blocks were there, continuing under the floor. He proceeded quietly to the center of his main room and beyond, lifting more flooring than he'd wanted. He kept the stones in perfect order beside their resting places so as to replace them rightly. Near the far wall he gripped a paver and paused.

A narrow strip of dull metal was visible at the edge. Lance rubbed it with his fingers. Recessed into the floor and caked with dirt, it had gone undetected when he swept. He worked the dirt out with the knife and pressed the piece toward the stone. He felt a click. That part of the floor shifted enough to get his fingers in. He pulled and jerked until, with a squeal of wood and rusty metal, he raised the trap formed by four square pavers on a wooden frame. He gaped into the blackness below, heart hammering. *Lord, is this it?*

The opening was clogged with timber. Lance sat back on his heels and considered that. There had been the layers of sand on the flooring, now this tangle. Someone didn't want this cellar explored. Nonna?

Lance stretched out on his stomach and leaned over the opening. The wood pieces appeared old and unfinished, wedged in tightly. He gripped the end of one and tugged, but it didn't budge. It was almost dark now, too dark to see what he was doing. With a crowbar and enough light, he could remove and dispose of the wood, but the shed was locked and Rese might fire him before he had another chance.

Why had he pushed her? He hung over the edge frustrated. He'd found something promising and wouldn't have the chance to figure it out. Should he make his peace? *Lord?* For his purpose, he could grovel. Or was it that he wanted to make it right anyway? Not that she'd listen. It was remarkable she hadn't come breathing fire already.

He got onto his knees. First things first. He swung the hatch shut and heard it click, the metal edge fitting back along the stone. He rubbed his hands on his jeans and surveyed the floor. Now that he had found it, the trap device jumped out at him. He scooped some dirt from beneath the other stones into the narrow slit. Better, if not perfect. What if Rese noticed it when she trimmed the wall along the floor?

There he was thinking as though they'd continue their efforts. Well, she might continue without him. In fact she'd said as much. She could rent the carriage house for two-fifty a night—with breakfast. And that was his shred of hope. She still needed his meals. She had put them on the Web site. And now they had a reservation. *She* had a reservation.

He had to stop thinking in terms of *they*. Rese had made that more than clear. He'd apologize if that's what it took. He supposed he owed her one after that ride back. What had he been thinking? He'd lost sight of his reason for being there and started believing the role. He'd imagined himself making a go of the place that might have been his if tragedy hadn't changed Nonna's course.

He expelled a breath and went inside. Star was in the front room unpacking books for the shelves Rese had built. He looked for Rese, but she wasn't there.

Star slid a book into place and said, "She went to bed."

Lance checked his watch. Just after nine. That was early for her, but she was probably planning his departure. She'd sleep well on that thought, or be up all night with a power tool. Either way, come morning, he'd face the music. He glanced toward the kitchen through which he'd find her if he wanted to. But he would have to pass the sacrosanct door, and that wouldn't be a good way to begin his abjection.

He was dying to get down into the cellar and check it out, but without tools that was out of his hands. He went upstairs and called home. Needing the grounding of family? Or a safe place to lick his wounds.

"Mom?"

"What kind of trouble are you in?"

He sat down on the bed. "What makes you think I'm in trouble?"

"You call at midnight, you're in trouble."

He looked at his watch. He'd forgotten the time difference. "I'm fine. I just wanted to know how things are going. How's Nonna?"

"Some days better than others."

"Is she talking yet?"

"Constantly. Only no one can understand her. She tries too hard."

"You and Pop okay?"

"Why don't you come home?"

"I have something important to do." If she wasn't half asleep she'd pursue that. Instead she murmured a prayer. Some of his important things hadn't turned out so well.

"Rico was here." Ricardo, the ever hopeful, recruiting the troops. "He has a new agent. He's going to call you."

"He already did. Bye, Mom. Get some sleep." The call had only rekindled old issues. Looking back wasn't going to help him out of this one. He took up his guitar and picked out a melody for lyrics he'd write if he'd added yet another screw-up to his name.

CHAPTER NINETEEN

Thunder crashing.
Silence rent.
A rage of nature unleashed.
And oh, the sad and sorry grapes crushed before their time.

Rese went to the kitchen in the morning. There were two plates on the table with puffy, bowl-shaped pastries filled with something creamy and topped with raspberries dusted with powdered sugar. No sign of Lance, but Star sat behind one pastry, breathing the aroma with a sigh. "You have to admit the man can cook."

Bribery, that's what it was. "Where is he?"

"He said if you wanted his head, he'd be in the garden. But you're supposed to eat first."

There he was giving orders again. She started for the door, then glanced once more at the pastry. No point wasting it. It wouldn't sway her. She sat down with Star. Neither of them said a blessing. She cut into the pastry. Lance wasn't there to notice her reaction, to expect anything from her. She could eat it in peace.

It was fabulous, of course. His best effort yet, except for the lasagna. She ate silently, disinclined to discuss the situation with Star. She wouldn't understand anyway. The pastry was so large, Rese couldn't finish it, but thinking it might be the last of its kind, she hated to waste it. "I doubt this will keep very well."

"I'll eat it."

Rese slid it over to Star. Shaped like a preteen, Star ate as though she might never eat again, except on her down days when she didn't eat at all. But that had nothing to do with the thoughts roiling in Rese's mind. There

173

was no putting it off. She drew a long breath and made for the door.

"Rese."

She turned. "Don't say it, Star. It's hard enough as it is." If she even began to harbor doubts, too many feelings would get in her way.

"He's really nice."

Nice didn't make up for reckless, spiteful, and defiant. If she let it go it would escalate; she knew that from experience. Show weakness once, and become a target for every kind of defiance. She had to be steel.

Closing her eyes, she turned the knob and went out. Lance stopped digging and leaned on the shovel as she approached. He expected what she had to say; she could see it in his face. He knew it was coming, and probably that he deserved it. But suddenly she didn't want to say it.

She clenched her hands. Feelings had no part in this. Let him think her without emotion. She tried to retrieve the fury of last night's drive, the way he'd terrorized her. Completely out of line. Way over the edge. Instead she heard the words of his song and saw the boy still looking for himself. *Stop it!*

His impulsiveness had gotten him arrested. His cop brother had told him to use his head, but he obviously hadn't learned. He still acted and reacted strictly from his gut. She could not trust him. He read the resolve in her face and tightened up. She had expected a preemptive argument. Unfortunately, this time he waited for her to speak. "Lance . . ." *Just say it. You're fired. Two words. Say them.*

He gripped the shovel handle. "It won't happen again."

She looked into his face. "What won't?"

"Any of it."

She expelled a short breath. "What specifically?"

He spread his hand. "Strictly business. You're in charge."

He finally got it? If he respected her authority, stopped making things personal. . . . His earnestness seemed forced, but he had said the right thing.

She looked from him to the carriage house. As she'd lain awake last night, she had made plans for it. Trim it out, furnish, photograph, add it to the page. She'd get a good rate. More than she'd pay a cook to bake muffins. She could still taste the pastry, custard, and berries. Steel. She had to be—

"I'm sorry for scaring you." His voice was low and controlled.

She turned back, flushed with fresh annoyance. "I wasn't scared. It was stupid, that's all. I don't allow stupid. Not where safety is concerned."

"I had it under control."

It hadn't felt that way to her. "I'm sure you think so. But your behavior showed otherwise."

He didn't argue, and that was remarkable in itself. Maybe they'd needed this incident to reestablish order. With their first reservation already, it might be better to keep him than start over. Or was she making excuses?

She knew how she should handle it. He wasn't the only cook in the world. She could advertise for another. But it wouldn't be Lance. And the entertainment? She could change the Web site, burn the flyers. This wasn't his place; it was hers. She could do it without him. *Don't give in.* If she let him win . . .

He didn't speak. He was going to make her say it. One way or the other. *You're fired, Lance.* She'd done it before. It had always been the right decision.

She pressed her fingertips between her eyebrows. "I guess if we understand each other, I'll keep you on."

He didn't respond, and it had sounded heavy-handed. His eyes showed anger and hurt. But he was controlling himself. That was an improvement. He must really want the job. That was good, wasn't it?

She felt a gap between them. As it should be? The sinking inside her was proof of that. "All right, then." She turned at the sound of someone in the driveway. A construction pickup, one she recognized. She stilled as the driver climbed out, then closed her eyes. One storm already, she did not need another.

But he caught sight of them and approached. Her throat filled with sand. He had new gray hairs in the brown curls at his temples, but he was in the prime of his strength. His jeans were worn and dusty, his boots as well. His tan T-shirt formed itself to his chest and a pack of cigarettes in the square faded into the pocket. His smile was tentative, but she didn't encourage it.

"What do you want, Brad?"

He stopped and spread his hands. "Do I look like I want something?"

Lance perched one foot on the shovel but made no other move.

She said, "You always want something."

Brad closed the distance and looked her over. "I just came to see how you are."

She expelled a hard breath. "How did you know where to find me?"

"Your Web site. I've been looking for it."

He'd been looking? She glanced at Lance, but of course she had squelched any sign of concern from him. If Brad was a threat, Lance would now stand back and watch.

Brad surveyed the villa. "So this is it, huh? Replace the roof?" Roof work being his specialty.

"No. It's in good shape."

He tucked his fingers into his pockets. "Want to show me through?"

"Not until you tell me how you knew about this."

He studied her more closely than she liked. "Still tough, aren't you?"

She drew herself up.

"Okay, then, Ms. Barrett. Rosita told me you bought this place."

Rese sighed. Letting Rosita go had been the hardest part of the whole transaction. She'd been the office manager for Dad since Rese was little, but the new owners had their own office staff. "Did she send you here?"

"She didn't send me, just told me what you were up to."

Rosita had been privy to the whole business, even helping with the paperwork. Rese hadn't thought to ask her not to tell, hadn't thought anyone would even want to know. Why was Brad here? He had what he wanted— her out of the way.

Brad and Lance shared a nod, and Lance went back to work. "So can I see what you've done or not?"

Rese brought him inside and walked him through the villa. Brad was one person who knew the quality of her work from long experience. He was suitably impressed by the staircase and banister, the bookshelves and wall patching, the tightly fitted moldings and floorboards. "Signature work, Rese."

It felt good to hear it.

"You were always good with detail."

She rested her hands on her hips. "It's done except for the carving."

He nodded slowly, knowing from experience that no project of hers would be finished without a carving. "Then what?" He ran his hand along the banister as they went back down.

"Then I hang up my saw."

He stopped at the bottom. "No way."

She nodded. "Why do you think I sold?"

He frowned. "Well, that's a good question. We might at least have discussed it."

She didn't respond. No way was she discussing anything with him in the dark days after Dad's death. Even now she couldn't imagine discussing ideas and considering possibilities with Brad as she had with . . . *Don't think about Lance.* That would only complicate things more.

Brad expelled a breath. "The new ownership isn't working out so well. They undercut bids, pad materials. Lots of shortcuts, but they're trading on your dad's reputation, pretending it's the same entity."

Rese's chest squeezed. Numb with shock and grief, she hadn't scrutinized the buyers as she should have. But it wasn't her problem anymore.

"Some of us are talking about breaking away. Starting our own gig."

"You're the top dog?"

He nodded. "As it looks right now."

"Congratulations." It was what he'd wanted all along.

"I'd like you on board, Rese."

Her heart thumped like a single hammer blow. "What?"

He looked around. "This is swell, but not really your thing. What do you think of Plocken and Barrett?"

She could not believe what he was saying. Not that he'd been the worst of them. His had never been overt, just a slow simmering resentment. They almost lost him when Dad made her the second crew foreman and kept Brad as site manager. She'd had grudging respect from him at best. "You want my name."

"I knew you'd think that." He took the pack from his pocket and shook out a cigarette.

"Not in here."

He tucked the cigarette behind his ear. "I want your skill, your eye." He looked around the room. "Your carving." He took the cigarette off his ear and said, "Can we go outside?"

She pointed to the door. "Outside, in your truck, down the street; I'm not interested." And she was starting to shake deep inside.

"Walk out with me."

It seemed the best way to get him to leave. She preceded him.

He stopped on the porch. "I was surprised as heck when you sold out. I would have stayed on."

"I didn't hear Barrett and Plocken."

He flicked his lighter and lit up. "We can discuss it."

She snorted. "Let me guess. There's a bet. Ten bucks says she falls for it."

He tightened his brows. "There's no bet, Rese. We just want you back at what you do best."

She turned away as tears stung. What she did best? That was before every sound, every action, brought panic and pain.

"I'm being up-front here." He blew the smoke from his lips. "We can take the market back."

"Who's going to finance it? I sold the assets."

He looked up at the villa. "You'd turn something here with the work you've done. You know it's good."

She swallowed the lump filling her throat. It would be her first solo effort, all the profits hers, all the satisfaction. She had increased the value immeasurably. But she'd shaken and almost passed out every time the memories. . . . She pushed past him. "Go home, Brad. I'm not selling."

"At least think about it. You've got my number." He went down the steps, but she was back inside before he reached the walk. She could not begin to guess his motives, or those of the rest of them. Too bad if they didn't like the new ownership. They hadn't wanted her either.

————————

Lance chopped the edge of the flower bed with the blade of the shovel, separating the overgrowth and tossing it aside. In the night he had determined his plan of action should Rese retain him. He couldn't remove the wood from the cellar without an inconspicuous place to put it. But the garden's condition was such that he could use the wood as borders for new beds and build up existing dividers.

Rese had asked him to take that task on, and he didn't get the impression she would interfere much. She seemed to leave the things outside her expertise to him—the sign of a decent manager. So he could prepare the grounds for the timbers, then work them in little by little while she focused elsewhere. That suited him fine. The more distance between them the better.

The morning was warm, the overcast burning off sooner than usual. The citrus scent of his sweat mixed with the rich, loamy ground. He hacked another cut through stems and roots and tossed aside the excess. It would take all summer to reclaim the gardens, but he only needed as long as it took to clear out the hole under his floor.

Luckily they'd "reached an understanding" and Rese would "keep him on." If she'd expected weepy thanks, he'd disappointed her. He had apologized for his recklessness, and now he knew his place—unless he established the real order of things. If Nonna had been driven from her property unlawfully . . . He wiped sweat from his temple with his shirt sleeve and saw the visitor coming his way. Lance paused.

"Brad Plocken." The man extended a palm as callused as his these days.

Lance shook it and gave his name, but Brad's business with Rese did not concern him. She was not his responsibility. She'd made that clear, and he was thankful for the clarification. He could focus on what mattered.

"You work for Rese?"

"That's right." By God's grace and more self-control than he had known he possessed. Interesting Brad hadn't assumed they were partners or in a relationship. He must know Rese well.

"How's she doin'?"

Lance looked toward the house. "Fine, I guess." Terrific now that she'd established control and put him in his place.

"She's a bear, isn't she?" Brad grinned. "But she's good. Too good. Drives guys nuts."

Lance assumed Brad meant her carpentry.

"She thinks I'm out to get her. I admit there's competitive juices, but mostly I wanted to know if . . . well, if she still has it. She was pretty messed up by the time I got to the site."

Lance leaned on the shovel. "Her dad's accident?"

Brad nodded. "Sawed right down his forearm—took off his hand."

Lance winced.

"Arterial blood bursting everywhere. She was covered in it." Brad drew on his cigarette with his brows pinched together. "Rese tried to tourniquet, but there was too much damage."

The scene was all too vivid. No wonder she hadn't been able to talk about it. A quiver of sympathy. He'd feel it for anyone in that position.

"The heck of it was, he'd always harped on safety."

A message Rese had taken to heart.

Brad shook his head. "There he was cutting with a saw that had lost its guard. Go figure."

The smallest decisions had consequences a person could never foresee.

"I've known Rese since she was twelve. Never seen her cry. And she'd had cause."

Yes, she had shared some of that cause.

Brad tapped the ash from the end of his cigarette. "When I saw her sitting there, tears in sheets through the blood, but not making any sound, no sound at all . . ."

Lance frowned. The one time he'd seen her cry, she'd stifled it immediately. Obviously not something she did easily.

"Her dad asked me to look out for her if something happened to him, but she wanted no part of that."

Lance shifted his grip on the shovel. "She likes to do things her way."

Brad laughed. "Don't I know." Then he sobered. "She's not as tough as she seems. For a while there I thought it might go another way."

What did he mean by that?

"You know about her mom?" Brad touched his head.

"Not much." He had sensed a trust level in that disclosure that he didn't want to betray.

"Schizophrenia."

"Rese told you that?"

Brad shook his head. "Vernon. Her dad." He hooked his thumb in his belt loop. "When Vern died, Rese went three weeks without making a sound. And that's weird, let me tell you."

Not weird if silence was already a coping mechanism.

"I thought she'd gone under. But she came out of it, all of a sudden, and sold the company. Just like that." He clicked his fingers and ashes fell from the cigarette.

That was her business. Why was Brad telling him? "I can see why she wouldn't want to do it anymore."

"With anyone else, yeah. But not Rese. It's what she lives for."

Lance swallowed. "Not anymore."

Brad looked toward the house. "She thinks she can let it go. But it's all she's got of him, and he's all she ever had. She should sell this and come back."

Sell it? "She's happy with this place. She'll do a good job." Why was he defending her?

Brad shrugged. "I don't see it happening."

Who asked him anyway? So what if it was the same things he'd thought. Rese wasn't a natural innkeeper, and she probably would go crazy without something to hammer. But it was her business. Lance raised the shovel.

Brad said, "Remind her she's got options, okay?"

Lance nodded. If she took that option and sold the villa, could he buy it? He flashed to Sybil saying her family owned the bank. Impossible; he'd never qualify. But if it was truly Nonna's property as he'd begun to suspect, could he contest the deal, prove an unlawful sale? And where did that leave Rese?

He understood now why she had almost passed out that day on the scaffolding. How could she go back to renovation with such horrific memories? But he was not allowed to think of her in sympathetic terms. That became personal. Personal was taboo.

He could only work for her. No more chats, no sharing thoughts or fears or hopes. It was business. And now that he'd found the cellar, he was glad for it. She would have no reason to enter his place once they had it done. His purpose was once again clear.

It was more than an hour before Rese came out and headed for the carriage house. Lance had worked where he could see her coming. He had agreed to let her trim it, but now he had to be part of the process. As much as he would like to avoid sharing the same space, he needed to guard the floor device.

She looked up as he joined her. "I'm going to trim it out now."

"If you cut and fit, I'll tack it on."

"I can do it, Lance."

"I know. But I'd like to work on it." She hadn't actually ordered him off. It was not insubordinate to assist her. In fact, it showed good faith. He might have avoided her completely.

She started to say something, but stopped herself. She was tight as a cat, crouched and ready to spring, as she set up her workspace and gathered her tools. She measured the lengths and marked them on trim boards. He let her do it all herself, not lending a hand where he would have before, but becoming as unobtrusive as the spider that climbed the wall. If she wanted blind obedience, he could give her that.

She put on her safety goggles and made sure everything was right, then fitted the first stained board into the miter box. Her tension was tangible. Maybe she'd wanted to work alone so he wouldn't see her struggle.

She gripped the saw. The noise filled the space, and he wondered how she could stand it. A moment's hesitation before she cut, a ragged breath at the end of it. She was fragile—probably more so after Brad's visit. He'd churned things up.

And, of course, their own dealings had been stressful. Lance wished he could undo that part. He should never have made it personal. It could have been simple. Do what Rese said; find what he came for. Trying to befriend her had mucked things up.

They worked efficiently together, but it went slower than if he'd done the job himself. She was meticulous to a painful degree. Every cut, every fit perfect. The sun climbed the sky, but she didn't mention lunch. Stretched taut, she worked hard to look relaxed.

Star brought them lemonade but didn't stay. "This friction makes my hair stand up." She forked her fingertips to her skull and walked out.

Rese looked over. "Brad told you why he came?"

She must have seen them talking. "He wants you to go back to work."

"Dad's reputation was stellar. While you were building homes for the poor, we were doing million-dollar remodels on weekend houses, renovations on historic Nob Hill." She sounded bitter.

"There's a place for everything."

"Brad wants my name so he can take the market back from the upstarts I sold to."

Why was she telling him this? She'd been ready to fire him that morning for wanting to get to know her. She would have too.

Rese shook her head. "Rosita told him. I guess that's how Star knew also." She sighed. "She probably thinks it could be like it was. She doesn't understand it can never . . ." Her voice caught.

Lance would have reached out. Did she realize the position she kept putting him in? Another woman, sure. Rese? Probably not. He looked away.

She drained her lemonade and set the glass by the door out of their way. He did the same with his, and they went back to work. A minute later she said, "Lance . . ." Her brow creased as she fought for words.

"We've reached an understanding, Rese." She couldn't have it both ways.

She nodded, swallowing, then used the saw. Her hand shook, no doubt a new phenomenon for steady, self-controlled Rese Barrett. She'd have to find her way, make up her own mind. If this place mattered to her, as it should, she would not let it go. But if it mattered to her, his actions would be that much worse. He couldn't worry about that. If he was in God's will, things would happen the way they had to.

Her neighbor, the nurse, stood outside her door, as he often did before heading to his night shift at the hospital. "Anything you need, Evvy?" His smile was soft as the rest of him, the sort of body type that smoothed out muscle as though he was made of dough and baked to a golden brown with fine blond hairs on his forearms and a thin covering of the same atop his head. His eyes were green candied cherries pressed into his face, with a caring in their depths that would be comforting beside your bed.

He had tried to persuade her into the hospital, especially when Dr. Beldham had ordered it. But they both knew she was not leaving her home for the sterile comfort of a hospital room. Her own might be simple and bare, but it was hers.

His wife, Patsy, who worked the shift with him, rarely came over. Pretty and petite with her blunt hair and pert features, she had more important things to do than worry over an old lady neighbor. Dennis did, too, but he couldn't help himself.

"Not a thing, Dennis, thank you."

"How's the cough?"

"Lingering."

"Are you eating? Sleeping well?"

She smiled. "All my bodily functions are in order."

He glanced over his shoulder as Patsy opened the garage door and climbed into the car. "Well, if you need anything, you know where to find us."

She nodded. That would be it, his check-in complete.

But he paused, then turned back. "Have you met the new neighbor?"

"Both of them."

He raised his brows. "I thought it was just Rese Barrett."

"She's hired a cook. He's making over the carriage house."

"Oh. Well, I hope it's not disturbing to you when they start bringing in guests."

Her house being the nearest, she was the likeliest to be disturbed she supposed, but she just shrugged. "Why should it?"

"This little enclave has been residential since Ralph had the place. It's diffcrent having a business there now."

"It's hardly a tattoo parlor."

Dennis laughed. "Right. Well, I'll see you then. Take care."

Evvy watched him cross the street. He really was a kind man. And Patsy must have compassion of her own, working nights with ailing patients. She supposed it took a special person to minister healing in the still quiet halls after dark and retain any sort of good humor at all.

Evvy started to close the door when she saw Michelle from the church drive up. It would take three minutes at least to clear everything off the passenger seat to make room for her. Evvy stepped inside to grab her sweater. Dennis had thrown her off her preparation or she'd have had it on in readiness for Michelle.

Michelle bustled to the door. "Are you sure you're up to this, Evvy?" Her long brown hair was swept into a ponytail that accentuated her broad, plain face. But such honest joy showed there, it was hard to notice even the sacks under her eyes and the mottling of the skin. The Lord had disguised an angel.

She must look as worn out as she felt, but she said, "The day I'm too weak to break open God's word with the women of my church, you can bury me." Evvy started down the walk, then paused.

"What is it? Forget something?" Michelle looked ready to bound back for whatever it was.

Evvy glanced at Ralph's house. "I was wondering if we shouldn't invite the woman next door."

"I can clear another place."

Evvy chuckled. Michelle's car was like Mary Poppins's carpetbag. Staples like soap and toilet paper someone might need, bags of clothing and canned goods, coloring books and crayons, and boxes of Bibles in the trunk.

"Maybe next time." She wasn't sure why the Lord had warned her off. A little more hoeing or mulching required? She was always wanting to plant the seeds before their time.

She climbed into Michelle's passenger seat and nudged up against an enormous package of throw-away diapers. Never having used either sort, she was not without the imagination to know which kind she'd choose given the chance. Michelle squeezed in on the other side of the diapers and started the car.

As they passed Ralph's house—she really had to stop calling it that—she wondered about Dennis's comment. It hadn't occurred to her to be bothered by the enterprise next door. Sonoma was no longer the farming community it had once been. It was the understated seat of viticulture. And that drew people in, people who needed lodging. What did she care if they slept next door? She'd lived too long to be petty.

But it reminded her again that she was surrounded by youth, with all their issues and all their gripes. The drama next door had been hard to miss—not that she had tried. It brought flavor to her day to watch them spar, but this last had been especially edgy. Whatever Lance had done, he'd almost lost his place.

And for some reason that didn't feel right. Maybe it was an old woman's foolishness, but she felt he was supposed to be there. For Theresa's sake, or his own, or some other reason altogether, she couldn't say. It was something in the way he walked through the garden, that pensive expression he sometimes wore. There was purpose in his presence there. No coincidence at all.

CHAPTER TWENTY

What careful strength in Nonno's hands.
Pale half-moon nails waning into flesh as warm and tender
as the dawn.
Binding quickened vines, life clinging like a breath.
Gathering the dead with gentle care for the bounty they
once bore.

In a way the work was good. Two days in the spring air, expending his stress with a shovel and hatchet. With Rese detailing the carriage house, he'd rather be outside. Her oblivion to the hatch the first day had eased his concerns, and it was better now to keep his distance—as he should have from the start.

As detail-oriented as Rese tended to be, he'd been sure she would see the metal strip. But, recessed and disguised by the dirt he'd pressed back into the crack, it blended invisibly, as it was no doubt intended. Knowing it was there played on his mind, but he couldn't make excuses for being in there without looking obvious. She would imagine interpersonal motives, and that was the last thing he intended.

Lance dug out the overgrowth of another leggy bed, more zealous in the discarding than he might be otherwise. There were a lot of timbers to put to use as he recalled, having resisted another look. He forced himself to wait until he could use them discreetly before opening it up again and attempting to pull them out.

The garden actually needed the work he was doing, and his seven months in landscaping qualified his overall approach. Building up and outlining the beds would keep them from overflowing the paths. Creating different levels added interest and drew some of the decorative plants nearer the eye—and nose. A big part of his replanting would be herbs.

"Cleaning up the garden?"

He looked up, but could not see the source of the voice at first. Then he spotted Evvy parting the hedge like a curious monkey peeking through jungle growth.

"Yes, ma'am." He rested his hand on the shovel.

"Good soil there. Ralph mulched it."

"I noticed." That particular patch of ground had been wildly overgrown with weeds, but when he'd cleared most of it out, he'd seen why.

"That was his vegetable patch. Grew tomatoes like you never tasted."

He didn't argue, though he'd tasted some pretty fine tomatoes.

"Did she like the lasagna?"

He had to think back to when Rese liked the things he did. "She loved it."

"Smart girl. This hedge could use some work. Know anything about trimming?"

He nodded. "I've done some."

"I've a few others you could look at too."

"I'll do that." He brushed a drop of sweat from his forehead.

"Sooner would be better." Evvy snapped the hedge shut.

He watched to see if she'd reappear, then punched the shovel into the earth, bringing the rich loamy aroma to the air. It was great soil, and maybe he'd put some vegetables in as well. Then he shook his head. He wouldn't be there for harvest, and somehow he didn't see Rese doing it.

What would she do when he was gone? That depended on what he found, didn't it? He sighed, left the shovel standing and took the shears from the garden shed. "Sooner would be better" sounded like an order, and Rese shouldn't complain if he helped Evvy out. He was on the clock, but he wouldn't record the time this took.

Evvy didn't look at all surprised when he pressed through the break in the hedge to her side of the yard. He suspected the opening was intentional. Evvy must have read his thoughts. "Ralph cut it so I could come through. Wanted to take the whole hedge down, but I told him 'good fences make good neighbors.'"

"Is that what it takes?" No wonder he'd messed up with Rese. He didn't set good boundaries.

"She'll come around, you know."

Having spent years with Nonna, he was not surprised by Evvy's intuition. Nor did he feel inclined to evade. "It's better this way. We know our places."

Evvy scrutinized him. "We are never allowed to give up, young man. You must fight the good fight to the end."

Was there something physical that betrayed his tendency to quit and run? He hadn't come there for the long haul. The trouble came when he mixed his motives, lost sight of his purpose. He slapped the handles of the shears together. An electric trimmer would have been nice, but in the plethora of power tools in Rese's collection, he'd seen no trimmer. These shears might have been Ralph's and could use sharpening.

"What's the state of your soul?"

He glanced over his shoulder. "I beg your pardon?"

"You heard me."

He tucked his tongue into his cheek to keep from grinning. This one was a match for Nonna and Conchessa combined. Was it his fate to be chastised by every woman over seventy? "My soul is God's. It's the rest of me He wrestles with."

She pointed one crescent finger. "Then your charge is clear."

"What charge is that?"

"To win the world. One piece at a time."

He snipped at the hedge. It badly needed trimming, but he suspected she'd brought him there more for the lecture than the work. "I do my part, Evvy, but it doesn't always work out the way I intended."

"That's the Lord's problem. He shouldn't have made you so lumpy."

"Lumpy?" He had to grin.

"Some pots are nice and smooth. Others are cracked and worthless. Most of us hold water but aren't much to look at. It's his job to smooth out the bumps. He's the potter, after all."

That might be, but he'd never been one to sit still for the process. Momma had pinched his ear more than once when he'd squirmed away from her washcloth. He wanted those lumps removed, but he tended to let the Lord know which ones and when.

After two hours trimming Evvy's yard, he went back to digging out the beds. As he filled the wheelbarrow and rolled it around to the back of the carriage house, Baxter danced beside the wheel. "What—you think it's a bike?" Lance dumped the dirt and grinned. "Fine. Jump in."

Baxter leaped into the wheelbarrow and sat like a king all the way back to the bed. Lance tipped the barrow. "Now out." Baxter jumped out barking. A new joy. If only it was so simple.

***

Rese ached in a way no heavy labor could cause. The grief she had stifled for months was breaking through. Brad's visit four days ago had churned guilt and remorse for selling Dad's company and now damaging his reputation. He had also undermined her confidence. Could she do this when everyone automatically doubted it?

Lance no longer teased, but she knew his opinion. And since he'd also stopped offering input and advice, her tension multiplied. What did she know about running an inn? What did she know about anything? She felt like a bad wire, surging and sparking, ready to short out.

Was this how it started with Mom? An overwhelming weight she needed to escape? Why not invent a friend or two? Especially since she kept pushing her true friends away. Rese didn't like that thought. It resonated in what had happened with Brad and the others, with every friend but Star, even with Lance. He'd been scrupulously aloof in the days since their agreement.

The tiles had come for the carriage house roof. Lance would have settled for asphalt, but she wanted to match the villa. So for the last two days he'd fitted tiles, working for nothing more than the completion of his quarters. It was hard to consider that fair anymore. As strictly an employee, he should be compensated for his work, even if the offer had been his. It was her property and she would—

"I already cleaned it." Star's voice caught her by surprise.

Rese looked up from where she knelt wiping down the immaculate bathroom floor in the Redwood, reserved by a couple for the weekend.

Star crossed her arms and sat on the edge of the sleigh bed. "You're making me paranoid, doing everything over. Like Maury obsessing on his paintbrushes." She tipped her head back and threaded her fingers through her hair. "Did you put my brush in turpentine? Déjà vu. Did you put my brush in turpentine? Buh, buh, buh." She shook her mouth.

Rese pulled her thoughts in and focused on Star.

"What did he think, I'm a child? I'm a moron? I'm a brain-deficient drug baby?"

"No one thinks that."

"So he gets this ferret, right? And somehow it gets out of the cage. Somehow it's out of the studio. And it's, 'Where's my ferret, Star? Where is it?' Like I'm the ferret godmother." She sucked in a laugh that might have been a sob. "Like I turned it into a footman. Maybe I need a pedicure, so one ferret footman coming up."

Rese went and sat on the bed beside her. "It's all right, Star. Let it go."

Star bunched her hair up. "I already cleaned the bathroom."

"I know. And it looks really good."

"No one's even used it."

"It's great; I'm just . . . nervous."

"Nervous?" Star collapsed on the bed. "You can't be. You're my rock."

Rese swallowed the irony. A rock? When she felt anything but solid.

"You never move; you never wash away. You're invincible, but I . . ." Silent tears slipped from Star's lashes, down her temples, catching in her curls. "I can't do this life thing."

"Of course you can."

Star shook with the tears coming harder. "Why couldn't he see?"

"He missed something beautiful." Rese took Star's hand.

Star looked at her through pain-washed eyes. "Am I?"

"You're radiant."

Star closed her eyes and drew a ragged breath, then let it slowly out. "I am sun; I am rainbow. I am Star; see me shine."

Rese swallowed. A rock. Never moving, never washing away. Unthinking, unfeeling; just there, existing. She didn't want to be a rock.

—————

Lance followed the voices to the Redwood and paused in the doorway. Star lay across the bed and Rese sat beside her. He couldn't see Star's face, but Rese looked troubled. Not his problem, in spite of Evvy's lecture. She thought he was there for Rese, but he was there for Nonna, and these last days had strengthened that conviction. "This a private party?"

Rese looked up. "What do you need, Lance?"

"What's the plan for furnishing the carriage house?" He hung his hands on his hips. "I could move out there tonight if I had something to sleep on." And have undisturbed access to the hatch and whatever it hid.

Rese let go of Star's hand. "I didn't budget furniture for that."

Star sat up and dragged strands of hair from her damp face. He must be interrupting some catharsis.

"You okay, Star?"

She smiled. "I'm radiant."

Amazingly she was. Her smile had a poignancy he couldn't help responding to with his own. He turned back to Rese. "I could use the hammock for a night or two."

Rese frowned. "I have a sofa in my office and maybe a table."

"Got a lamp?"

She nodded. "Probably."

"Then all we need is a bed." She would need that much for the next person, and he was not springing for furniture after all the work he'd done *gratis.*

"That won't be cheap."

Were they back to that again? He tried to penetrate her wall, see what she was thinking. She had wanted him out there, not in the house. She would need his room soon. Wasn't it in her best interest to facilitate his move? "Order a mattress and make the frame."

"Make it?"

"You can slap together something, can't you?" How hard would that be for Rese Barrett, carpenter emeritus?

Her face brightened. He'd turned her switch back on, and some of the shadows fled. "I've never built that kind of furniture." But he could see her wheels turning. A new challenge, a focus she needed and understood. And less opportunity to notice his landscaping.

She stood up. "The sofa's small, just a love seat, actually." She started out of the room. "It was left in my suite with a bunch of old stuff. I moved it all aside to set up the office."

Aha. Lance hadn't searched Rese's suite, of course. But any mention of old stuff was important. He followed her downstairs with Star trailing along. Lance stopped at the door. Was he actually being permitted through?

"It's in here." Rese headed for the office. A quick glimpse showed him her bedroom was perfect, nothing out of place. The office, neat as well, though to the side, as she'd said, were pushed some extra things. The love seat was at least two decades old, quilted, with wooden arms and legs, definitely not the kind to curl up in. But it would work for something to sit on in his main room, good enough for him if not the guests she planned to house there eventually.

Rese took one end without asking his opinion. "Open the doors, Star. We may as well move it now."

After placing it in the bare space, they went back, and while Rese grabbed a pillow and blanket, he searched through the other things she had. A side table and a dangerous looking lamp, and two pictures for the wall. One was a portrait of a man with an oval mat and ornate frame. Heart hammering, he slid it back with the other. The glimpse he'd gotten was promising indeed.

Star leaned over his shoulder. "That looked like you."

He tipped his face up toward her. "Bad light, I hope. But maybe I'll hang these. Have something on the walls at least." He took the two frames and stood up. Like members of a parade, they marched the lamp, table, and pictures to his space. He set the pictures against the wall and said, "Help me with the hammock?"

The thing weighed a ton and, even with the new sling, would be no picnic to sleep on for long. They moved it into his bedroom where it looked strange. No breeze to sway it or branches overhead to dapple it with shade. But he could move out there now, and that was what mattered.

Rese stood a moment measuring the space with her eyes. "I ought to build a queen size."

Thinking in terms of renting it, no doubt. He certainly didn't need that size. "Whatever you want."

She walked the room. "I have maple left from the shelves. I could frame in a closet."

"Great. I'll move my skeletons."

She smiled. That had to be a first these last few days. They'd had very little interaction, with him tiling his roof and her doing whatever she had been up to in the house. He hadn't made meals, and she hadn't asked. He would resume when their guests came, but not before. Strictly business. But planning the woodworking seemed to have lifted her spirits. Maybe Brad was right. She couldn't leave it behind.

Star was crouched at the pictures and looked from the portrait to Lance. It was dim with the single lamp, but her artist's eye was not missing what he'd caught as well. A definite family resemblance. She stood up. "Too bad it's so drab. You need color in here. I'll paint you something."

Beside him, Rese caught her breath. He said, "Sure," thankful her thoughts had gone that way instead of making the portrait an issue.

"What would you like?"

"Anything." There he was sounding like Rese. He amended it. "Nature. A landscape or still life." Not that he could see Star painting a bowl of apples. But it didn't matter. He'd offered an opinion at least. Shown an interest.

He ushered them out before more could be made of the portrait. But as soon as they were gone, he took it out and studied the face that had caught both his and Star's attention. He couldn't say it was an exact likeness. But he was definitely looking into the eyes of his past.

It was what she had wanted, what she'd stipulated from the start. But moving Lance out only widened the gap between them. He'd become a model employee. He did his work and showed respect: cooperative and appropriate, no more simmering hurt, but no exuberance either. It was as though his excitement for the project had evaporated.

She had fed on his ideas, drawn strength from his encouragement. Now that was gone, and the closer they came to opening, the more she dreaded it. To be honest it wasn't only his professional excitement she missed. It was all the interaction.

She wanted him to ask for equipment, to hand her frothy chai tea and smile at her grumpiness. She wanted him to try out a dish on her and get frustrated when she didn't praise it. She wanted him to sing and play and soak her with his gaze. But she had stopped all that to be in charge. Her throat squeezed.

Star circled an arm around her waist as they walked to the house. "Poor Rese."

She stiffened automatically. "I'm fine."

"Of course, you are. Nothing daunts the dauntless; no shaking the unshakable."

Rese laughed, but it felt bitter. They went into the kitchen. She could have asked Lance to fix her a steamer. But he was in the carriage house now, not upstairs between her and the ghosts in the attic. Now he stood watch over the tomb. Only he didn't believe the dead threatened them. They went to spend eternity with Jesus or without.

Maybe if she had someone invisible telling her what to do, she would do better. Her temples ached. She was not going to sleep.

Star yawned hugely. "The frogs are singing." She blew a kiss and went up to her room.

Rese stood in the empty kitchen, listening to the creaks of Star moving about, then the silence of the huge old place. She almost wished for creepy moans, so she wouldn't feel so alone. What was she doing?

Nothing. And it would drive her crazy. Clenching her hands, she went into her room. Instead of climbing into her bed, she measured it and recorded the dimensions, then went out to the shed and set up a workspace. She had leftover cherry from the banister that she could use for posts, and boards from the stairs for the headboard. It was good wood, and she had no intention of slapping something together, as Lance had put it. His bed would be her first piece of freestanding furniture, and she didn't want to look at it with regret.

By the time morning light was creeping through the shed window and dimming the overhead bulbs, she had the posts turned and shaped on the lathe, grooved to insert the headboard and side frames that were measured and cut. The headboard would include a crowning piece she intended to carve. Nothing fancy, just a scalloped crest. She would pick up the hardware later. She pulled her goggles down over her eyes and sawed the footboard.

The shed door opened, and Lance leaned against it.

She raised the goggles and met his stare. "I hope you like cherry."

He took in the boards and posts and sawdust, lost for words. At last he said, "You're lucky no one called the police."

"The police?"

"Do you have any idea how loud saws and lathes are?"

She looked over what she'd done. "Did I keep you up?"

His eyes trailed her head to toe. "Nah. Nothing like power tools screaming all night. Good thing Evvy's ninety years old."

Evvy was the nearest neighbor, and even if she had heard the noise, Rese could hardly see her calling in a complaint. The one to their left was an airline pilot, rarely home, who had come over once to suggest she keep the construction Dumpster out of sight. The couple across the street were night shift nurses at the hospital. They'd brought wine and asked that she not allow her guests to park in front of their house.

No one else was close enough to have been affected. But Lance probably did get an earful. She hadn't thought of that. She brushed sawdust from her arm. "I'm sorry. I started working on your bed and just kept going."

"Why don't you sleep, anyway?"

She shrugged. "I don't know."

"Bad dreams?"

"No. Once I get to sleep I'm fine." And talking about it was making her wish she had.

His eyes narrowed. "So it's surrender you don't like. Losing control."

"I haven't analyzed it, Lance." But his words struck a chord. She could sleep once she was past the falling part. Maybe it was being out of control, the thoughts and fears of what might happen if she wasn't ready. She sighed. She had dealt with it so long, she'd stopped wondering why. "I didn't mean to keep you up."

"Not like the last time?" One corner of his mouth jerked.

She brought up her chin. "Last time you deserved it."

He poked his tongue into his cheek. "But now I behave."

A pang seared her. Yes, he behaved. She lowered her face before he could catch her grief. What was wrong with her? It had to be delayed strain from Dad's death, the huge changes she'd made during a point of stress, giving up all she knew to begin something she was unsuited for. Great plan.

"You ought to get some sleep. I can stand the hammock another night or two."

Her eyelids gritted. Her limbs hung like wet plaster. What little energy she had left drained from her. She pulled the goggles from her head and laid them down, then walked woodenly to the house.

CHAPTER TWENTY-ONE

Doubt billows in like fog.
Whispered suspicions bleed into my mind.
I cling to what I know.
With slippery fingers I cling.

Lance headed for church, trying not to think about Rese. He hadn't realized how bad it had gotten for her. He'd focused so hard on not noticing, that her pain this morning caught him by surprise. She probably thought she was hiding it. But he understood, now, the concern Brad had voiced. Rese wasn't dealing with things in a healthy way.

Not his problem. Not his place. His job was to do what he was told, and to find what he had come for. He was weary after the noisy and uncomfortable night, and he had a long day ahead. Now that he was in the carriage house, the need to clear the hole gripped him, but Evvy had asked that he dig her flower beds. Was she in cahoots with God to rub off his impatient lumps?

He knelt and rested his forehead on his folded hands. He was supposed to focus on the words of the Lord at the Last Supper, but instead he pondered the situation with Rese. It was wrong to hide his actions from her, but he could hardly tell her what he intended. For a while he had hoped their purposes could mesh, but he'd been fooling himself, avoiding the truth. If he found what he hoped for, he'd be pitted against her.

He received communion with a distraction he almost never experienced. There was a sense of impending storm. Was he losing his way again? *Lord.* The desire was there as always. And the commission. There was no doubt the Lord's will meant more to him than anything. He just didn't get it.

How can I do this without hurting her? How can I take back what was wrongfully lost without leaving Rese with nothing? How could he undo the wrong done to Nonna and her family, when Rese would be caught in the middle? *Show me, Lord. I can't see it.*

When he returned to the villa, he focused on digging Evvy's flower beds and put his concerns aside. Rese was smart, determined, capable. She'd be okay. She knew how she wanted things. His concern this morning was way overblown, the shadows in her face probably exhaustion. He hadn't meant to get her so excited that she worked all night. But that was just another example of her resilience. Rese Barrett was anything but frail.

"Have you told her yet?"

He jumped. For an old woman, Evvy could maneuver with stealth. Or else his thoughts had been more consuming than he'd realized. "Told her what?"

"That she needs Jesus."

Oh sure. Rese didn't want or need his advice in any area of her life. He sat back on his heels. "Not my place, Evvy. I'm just the hired help."

"Working for whom? The King or the counterfeit?"

"I don't really . . ."

"Because if you've got the truth and you don't share it, you've buried your talents in the sand."

But some truths had to stay buried. At least for now. "She might take it better from you." He'd be a hypocrite to spout faith when he might become her adversary.

"You'd let a feeble old woman do your job?"

He rested the spade against his knee. "Feeble! I haven't been bullied like this since . . ." *Nonna's stroke rendered her incapable.*

"Well, I didn't take you for a coward."

That stung. He'd been overshadowed by a hero and still never thought himself that.

She hooked a hand his way. "The trouble is you won't let yourself be what you're supposed to be."

"And how exactly would you know that?" Disrespectful maybe, but she could be sharp enough to draw blood . . . while he was on his knees at her flower beds no less.

"I know wasted promise when I see it."

He swallowed. "Then why do you think I'm the one for the job?"

"Because she trusts you."

He started to protest, but she held up her hand. "I have it from the Lord, young man. He put a finger to my lips until you've done your part. But in case you haven't noticed, I don't have all the time in the world."

He sighed. "Evvy, I'm telling the truth. Rese does not want anything but cooking and digging from me."

"Since when does anyone know what they want?"

"Since God made Rese."

Evvy leaned on her cane. "You miss your chance, and you'll regret it. God can choose another vessel, but who wants to sit on the shelf?" She turned and headed for the house.

His head ached. He had put the storm aside until Evvy blew it into a tempest. What did she think he could do? Just sit her down and say, "Rese, what you need is Jesus. Why don't you commit your life to this invisible being, so I can stop wasting my promise?" He shook his head with a jerk, then grabbed the spade.

His concern was Nonna, and that was the Lord's business just now. But it was as though Evvy's claw had a grip on his brain. Maybe he'd been wrong to shut Rese out after their altercation. She wasn't the enemy, just the obstacle.

When he went back over to the villa, he threw together an antipasti and a creamy spinach soup, ate his at the counter with no sign of Rese. The phone rang, and he snagged it in the kitchen before the extension in the office woke her. "Wayfaring Inn."

"Rese Barrett, please."

Lance glanced toward the door to her hallway. No sound. "She's not available right now. Can I take a message?"

"I need to speak with her directly. It's very important."

"Let me take your number. She'll get back to you."

The woman on the line gave her name and repeated the message of urgency. She sounded very official. Lance jotted down the number. "I'll tell her." Maybe he should have gotten Rese up. But this way he could feed her first . . . in case it wasn't good news.

———

Hair still damp, Rese went into the kitchen. She had heard activity and wasn't completely surprised to see a plate of meats and cheeses, peppers and olives, and a bowl of creamy soup on the table. She was surprised by the poignant stab to her heart.

The soup in the bowl was hot, but Lance wasn't around. She realized with a jolt it might not be for her. "Lance?"

Then she noticed the note, a phone message with *Eat first* jotted beneath.

She looked out and saw him crossing the garden with Baxter at his side. He'd left her food but had not stayed to share it with her. He must think she wanted that. She'd made him think it. Sharing a meal was personal to him. *"The breaking of bread signifies connection, acceptance, relationship."* She sat down, feeling heavy again.

The soup was hot, but not scorching. He must have timed it by her shower, then ducked out just before she emerged. She lifted the spoon, then paused. *"Bless us, O Lord, and these thy gifts?"* Lance's prayer impressed on her mind. What if it was a gift from some unseen entity, someone like Lance who gave and went away, not even waiting to see her try it?

He had burned at her ingratitude before; now he didn't care. She could eat it or not, for all he knew. She took a spoonful of the creamy soup with a taste of spinach and buttery garlic. Not too heavy and strong, but not bland and boring either. The sliced salami and cheese with slightly biting peppers was great beside it. A perfect balance. Exactly what he didn't have in his nature. But then, neither did she.

As she ate, she wondered briefly where Star was, but since they'd staved off a plunge last night, she was probably out somewhere being sun and rainbow. Lance might know. Or not. They had stopped communicating as a threesome. Her eyes went back to the message. Peggy Blodgett. Not a name she recognized. Lance would have taken a reservation himself. Wouldn't he? She picked up the phone, unsure of even that much. It wasn't really his responsibility, and she'd made his position all too clear.

He'd given her enough time to eat and call, and the sense of impending storm had not eased. Lance headed for the house. Rese had just hung up as he stepped in.

He waited for her to turn, but she didn't. "Rese?"

"They found my mother." Her voice was a rusty gate swinging grudgingly over the words.

"You mean her death certificate?"

"I mean my mother." She turned, her eyes a desert. Even though he'd suspected the possibility, it still caught him off guard. Rese must be shattered, but she stood there trying to look whole. He moved closer, drawn to her trouble like a wolf's tongue to its wound.

Her anger ignited. "How could he?"

He? Her dad?

"He locked her up in a psycho ward and left her."

Even with space between them Lance felt the explosion building. If what she said was true, he understood her horror, but there had to be more to it. People didn't treat mental illness like a crime anymore. "You don't have all the facts."

"Facts? No wonder he said there was nothing after death." Her clenched knuckles turned white. The air felt as though they'd used up all the oxygen. "No reason to visit a grave, is there, when there's no grave to visit!" She drew a sharp breath, then let out a sound, half wail and half shriek.

Lance caught her upper arms as she exploded.

"I should have known! She said he'd do it. She told me he would."

He held on as though he could stop the meltdown. "You don't have the whole story, Rese. Wait until you know . . ."

Sobs burst from her. "I should have known."

He understood that anger and guilt. He'd gone through it all with Tony's death. No words would help. He'd pay for it later, but he pulled her to his chest. She didn't succumb gracefully. She pinched the sides of his shirt—and a good part of his skin—in her fists and sucked shrieking breaths between her teeth.

"He lied. Why would he lie?"

"Probably to protect you." It was all he could think of. Lance should have considered the possibilities and prepared for this, had something better to offer than speculation.

"Protect me?" she ranted, clenching his sides with a death grip. "Telling me she died would protect me? How could he think . . ? Why would it. . . ?" She looked into his face, pain deep in her eyes. "Help me."

A sliver through his soul. How many women had said that to him, how many tearful pleas? Yet none had stabbed so deeply. He wanted to help, needed to, a need that sprang from his core and triggered a reaction too powerful to resist. He caught her face in his palms and took her mouth with his, absorbing her pain, drawing the hurt out like venom from a bite.

She clung to his waist, and he responded more ardently, training and claiming her mouth until there was nothing hard, no steel left in her. He kissed her until the sobs stilled in her chest. "It'll be all right." He clutched her to him, pressing his lips to her temple. "It'll be all right."

Rage and anguish gave way to a pain equally damaging. Lance's arms around her, his lips on hers. She wanted . . . and the want hurt as much as the shock of her news. Her mother was alive.

How was it possible? All these years believing her dead. Lance's pulse beat beneath her ear pressed to his neck, comfort and confusion. What was she doing? She'd made a fool of herself.

"Don't." He rubbed the nape of her neck.

"Don't what?"

"Your spine is stiff, your neck is tight, you're about to tell me to quit kissing the boss."

A smile caught her unawares and she covered it with her hand.

"Ah. Reinforcements." He stroked the fingers guarding her lips.

What was she doing? Everything was collapsing, everything she'd believed, the mother she'd lost, the dad she'd trusted. Was everything a lie? She dropped her hand and expelled her breath. "I can't think."

He massaged her shoulders. "Now isn't a good time to try."

"I have to. My mother's in a mental health facility in San Francisco. Lance, she's been there since I was nine. She didn't die." The shock of it rose up again. "The hospital's been looking for me since Dad's death. I need to talk to them. I need to see her."

He stroked her arms. "Not today."

"Why not?"

"You're in shock."

He was right. Her whole system felt stunned, scorched, as though something had blown up inside and burned its way out through her skin. She gripped her hair. "I don't know what to do."

"Give yourself time to catch up."

He was right. Her thoughts and emotions were ragged. She had to get it under control. She needed a plan, but she couldn't plan until she had the shock behind her. She had acted irrationally after Dad's death, and . . . Fury surged again. He had lied to her!

"Hey." Lance brought her back. "You can't do anything this weekend."

This weekend. She'd been in a stew over the opening, the arrival of her first paying guests. Now . . . She clenched her hands, grasping for something familiar. The weekend would be interminable. "I can't do *nothing*."

He considered that a moment, then nodded. "Okay." Catching her wrist, he started for the door.

She resisted his tug. "What are you doing? Last time I went with you—"

"I'll behave."

She did not believe that for a moment. The question was whether her common sense was demolished enough to succumb. He pulled her outside and headed for his bike.

"No way." She dug in her heels.

He turned and clasped her elbows. "Just to town, slow and easy."

"No, Lance." She didn't want to ride with him again. Not just because he'd been reckless. She could excuse kissing him in her hysteria, but holding him now? That was premeditated torture.

"Come on." He drew her with him.

Adrenaline surged when he pressed the helmet onto her head. She wasn't scared; she just preferred to be shielded on four sides, not dangling behind a capricious daredevil on a screaming machine with a mind of its own. But she climbed on and gripped his shoulders.

"It's better if you hold my waist."

Better how? A sensation seized her like a too hot shower that you bear until it feels too good to get out. She did as he requested, just hands to his sides. He pulled out and down the lane, then rested his left arm over her thigh and cupped her knee in his palm, a comforting pose that made her heart scamper worse than the drive.

He was exceptionally careful, not slow exactly, but so smooth and aware that she had no worry at all. And she realized now the other drive had been equally masterful in execution . . . intended to terrify. Yet she'd been safe. Could she trust him now?

They parked at the plaza and he strapped her helmet to the seat, then took her hand and walked her into the park that formed the center of the square. She had obviously undone every professional barrier. One didn't blubber all over the cook and recover easily. How could she hope to regain control? But with his hand solid and warm around hers, did she want to?

Her life was imploding, her entire reality. Waves of angry confusion. Mom alive! In a mental hospital, and they had never once gone to visit. Sorrow. Anger. Fear. She seethed. Wincing, Lance freed his hand and circled her shoulders instead.

Warmth and strength. Compassion. Even after she'd almost fired him. She didn't know how to take that. They passed beneath a stand of massive eucalyptus. As they came out of the shade, she glanced sidelong. The sun glinted off the diamond in his ear, and she tried to recall the scorn she'd felt at their first meeting. A man with an earring. Total emotion. Trouble. She couldn't find any of it.

He met her eyes. She had never been so out of control in her life. But he released her gaze and squinted up through the branches of an old majestic oak. "Tell me about your mom."

A rush of gratitude. The subject had been studiously avoided for so long, no one asking, no one mentioning her mother except for Star's dark comments. It might help to talk now, to tell him what she remembered. To try to understand. But where to start? Once again the memories clashed, good with bad. "She was wonderful and terrifying."

Lance's thumb stroked her shoulder. It shouldn't feel so comforting. Wasn't she the rock? If anything else dashed against her now, she would dissolve like sand. But she wouldn't show it. She had to pull it together and somehow make sense of it all.

A green-throated mallard waddled near, tipped its head to ogle them, then jabbed a fallen bud with its beak, shook it, and passed on. Children scampered about the small playground, laughing, pretending. *Pretending.*

She sank into her memories. "She was always waiting when I got home, ready to play, to dance. One time we danced on the roof. Well, it was the flat part between two peaks, but someone told Dad and he told me not to do it again." Funny he hadn't told Mom.

"Sometimes we drew pictures. She taught me to draw." Rese could see Mom's face taking stock of her picture, then proclaiming it a Picasso or Cézanne or Kandinsky. She didn't realize until later that those artists didn't tend to get the shapes right. But it didn't matter, because she believed she could draw, and that developed into the sketches that became her carvings.

"Some days I didn't even go to school." Mostly the days when Mom was sad and Rese was afraid to leave her. She was the strong one these days, most days. "We didn't tell Dad. There were a lot of secrets." Some darker than others.

Dad's stern face. "Did Mommy burn Mrs. Walden's rosebush?"

"No, Daddy. She wouldn't do that."

But why had Mom come in giggling as with the greatest joke after Mrs. Walden left the house angry? Rese hadn't seen her burn it, but she didn't tell about the giggling or the smell of smoke in Mom's hair and shirt.

Her throat squeezed. Had the dishonesty begun with her? No. She remembered Mom's finger held to her lips. *"Don't tell Dad. It's our secret."*

Had he known? All the things they hadn't told—had he known anyway and used them to justify his lie? Pain. How could he? She missed him so much, but now rage and betrayal grew inside her like redwoods stiffening her spine.

Lance squeezed the nape of her neck—sensing her tension? She wished he wasn't so intuitive, but would she be here with him if he wasn't? His hand communicated comfort, support. Dad had hugged her when she was little, when she'd impressed him, a kind of sideways hug with a pat to her arm. Lance's touch drove every thought away, made her want it to last forever.

She went on, "Mom could play, really play. We invented all sorts of games. Fairies one day, giants the next. One time we pretended to be earthworms."

That got raised brows from Lance.

"Her imagination was incredible." Imagination? "But sometimes the pretending got scary."

"When the invisible friend came?"

She nodded. "Walter was mean."

He didn't contradict that, just asked, "Do you know what's wrong with her?"

"Some disorder, I guess."

He stopped and eyed her. "Your dad didn't tell you?"

She expelled her breath. "Why would he tell me that, if he couldn't tell me she was alive?" She clenched her teeth as the betrayal slapped her again.

His eyes softened. "I know you're hurt."

"I'm mad."

"Yeah, well, mad is a secondary emotion." His brow pinched. "Mad is what happens when you don't process sad well. What gets you handcuffed in the back of a squad car for crashing an anti-war demonstration, carrying your brother's picture from the 9/11 victims' wall."

She stared at him. "Your brother?"

The tendons in his throat tightened. He looked away. "Tony."

NYPD. The brother in the station who set him straight? "Lance, I'm so sorry."

His jaw clenched. "No blood for oil? It wasn't oil in Tony's veins. And they hadn't seen my mother, my sisters, his wife and kids, and the whole city lighting candles, crying . . . or maybe they just didn't care."

She felt pain rising from him like heat waves on blacktop. For a moment it overwhelmed hers. No one would tell him his brother was alive. Ground Zero had yielded no survivors.

He turned back with a grim smile. "That's mad."

She could picture him provoking the protestors, doing what he thought was right, but ending up in handcuffs. "Exactly how many times have you been arrested?"

"Never actually booked."

She cocked her head. An evasive answer if she ever heard one.

"Since I spoke for most of the force that time, they let me go with a *'Keep it cool, little brother.'*"

As if he could. As if Lance Michelli ever cooled the fires that drove him. He drew her close. "You know what I think?"

"I'm not sure I want to."

"You need to do something daring, something really outrageous."

She snorted. "Right, Lance. Like what?"

"Let's get your ears pierced."

"What?"

"Twice."

"No way." She pulled back.

"Okay, once."

She shook her head. "I'm not getting my ears pierced."

"Ever put a staple through your finger?"

"Yes."

"It's nowhere near that bad." He pulled her down the path.

"Pain isn't the issue."

He checked the street then jogged across with her in tow.

"Lance . . ." They headed down Napa Street a couple blocks to a shop that advertised piercing. The poster in the window could have been Sybil from ribs to hips. "You're not listening."

"I'm not saying it's pain free." He pulled open the door. "But I survived it."

She bristled at the challenge. He could take something she couldn't?

With a hand to her elbow he brought her to the counter where a girl who looked all of twelve sported more metal than flesh in her ears. Not to mention the ring in one nostril and who knew what other body parts.

"I'd go with gold over surgical steel." Lance pointed to a display.

"I'm not going with either. What is it with you and earrings?"

But he was already choosing from the velvet board the girl had set on the counter.

She snapped her gum. "It doesn't hurt. I just did, like, a three-year-old a minute ago."

Lance turned to her. "A three-year-old, Rese."

She glared. "That is not the point."

"What's your birth month?"

"July."

He pulled off a card with two red stones encircled in gold. "You'll have to wait for real rubies until after you can take out the starter studs."

She took the card and stared at the sparkly red earrings. No way they were going in her ears.

The girl swung a gate open. "Sit on the stool there, and I'll get the gun."

Gun? Rese pictured the compressed air gun she used to drive nails, but the girl came back with a handheld thing more like a stapler. That was still not the point. She had no intention—

Three-year-old, Lance mouthed, and held the gate open. It was Bobby Frank all over. He thought she was afraid. He'd done it, but she couldn't. Her blood surged. She didn't have to prove anything, but she stalked through the gate and took the stool.

The girl made a mark on each earlobe, then loaded the first post and held it to her ear. Rese raised her chin. *Pop.* Not as bad as a staple through a fingernail, but she winced in spite of herself. It was nowhere near the shock the phone call had given her. She almost welcomed this pain. It was the physical kind she knew how to deal with.

Lance grinned, and she glared as the girl set up for the other ear. She jumped at the sting and the noise of it. She had just put metal through her body. Years of caution with every kind of tool, an accident or two, but never intentional. . . .

Lance took out his wallet and paid the girl. Rese felt suddenly branded, as though he'd bought and marked her. But when the girl held up the mirror, she stared at the red stones glittering in her earlobes, looking feminine and . . . pretty.

Lance's face joined hers in the mirror. "Looks nice."

She couldn't argue but was thankful that Brad hadn't seen them.

Lance thanked the clerk and took the little card with care instructions and a bottle of ear-care antiseptic. "They'll be tender for a while."

She reached up to one burning lobe and felt metal. "I don't believe I just did that."

"You can't resist a dare."

She stopped and faced him. "You intentionally baited me."

He smiled. "Now, you have guests coming tomorrow. You don't want to greet them in painter's pants and a T-shirt."

She drew herself up. "Why not?"

"You have a beautiful historic villa. People are paying hundreds of dollars to stay there. You have to look the part."

Look the part? Like playing a role, like . . . She stiffened.

His eyes narrowed. "What's the matter?"

"I can't do that. I can't pretend to be someone I'm not."

His smile pulled gently. "How do you know you're not, until you try?"

Her chest tightened.

"Just a skirt, Rese. A skirt and blouse." But he was studying her with a pucker in his brow. He didn't understand. How could he?

"I didn't tell you about Alanna."

He cocked his head. "Another friend?"

Rese shook her head. Why was she baring all this? "Alanna wasn't someone who came. Mom actually became her . . . for Walter." She watched his comprehension dawn.

He said, "I didn't mean anything like that. Just dressing appropriately. Something softer to greet your guests in." He didn't say *our* guests, didn't say *we*. And she missed it.

He walked her back to the plaza, took one of the side alleys through a mural-painted tunnel and stopped outside a shop with racks of gauzy cotton skirts and sleeveless embroidered blouses.

"This has possibilities." He walked her in and turned her over to the sales clerk.

A fluffy dog on the counter watched her with bulging eyes and two lower fangs protruding. Rese went to the dressing room with a multi-hued red skirt and a cream-colored blouse embroidered with green trailing vines and tiny red flowers.

Putting it on scared her more than walking a ridgepole, but she was not going to show it. She buttoned the blouse and turned to the mirror, seeing . . . her mother. Chest constricting, she pressed her hands to her face. It was more than a likeness of features; it was . . .

Lance spoke outside the curtain. "Come out, Rese."

Her throat cleaved. "I can't."

"Is it on?"

She groaned. "It's on, but . . ."

Lance pulled the curtain. She jerked around. He drank her in like a hummingbird at a hibiscus, then swallowed. "That'll do."

She snatched her pants and T-shirt. "I need to change back."

"You look great." He caught her elbow and led her firmly from the cubicle.

He did not understand. Of course, he'd never seen her mother, had no point of comparison, couldn't fathom the disturbance inside her. He took out his wallet and paid, bagging her jeans and T-shirt. She should protest, but only held up her arm for the clerk to clip the tags. She was disintegrating, losing the self she'd created to avoid any semblance to her mother. At this rate, she'd be dragging herself across the floor every time Lance looked at her.

Outside he glanced down at her sturdy work shoes clunking under the skirt. "One more thing."

A store right on the plaza had sandals along the back wall. He looked from her to the choices, picked a pair that was little more than a few criss-crossed straps. The clerk brought her size and Rese slid her foot in like a stepsister to the glass slipper.

Lance stood her up. "How's it feel?"

"Barefoot." She walked to the low slanted mirror and looked at her feet in the flimsy sandals. She'd never worn anything so unprotective, but in them the transformation was complete. She was soft and pretty and terrified.

Lance told the clerk, "We'll take them," then put her shoes into the bag with her other clothes. Something was wrong with this picture. Very wrong. Control. She had lost it.

Outside the store, he stood and looked her over. "Wow."

Why had Dad's praise never meant so much as that one word?

He touched her earlobe. "Sore?"

She raised her chin. "Nothing I can't handle." Nowhere near the piercing of her heart and mind.

He grinned. "They look great."

"Now I can forever say on the day I learned my mother was alive I got my ears pierced." Could he hear the desperation in her voice?

He drew her close. "I like kissing a woman with earrings." But he didn't do it. Because he knew she'd let him. And when she came to her senses and realized her ears were pierced and she'd worn a skirt and laid her head on his shoulder, she'd be hot enough to peel paint. He didn't want his kiss adding to it.

Technically, he shouldn't have kissed her at all. He could have comforted her without it. But the word "help" from Rese Barrett's lips had put him a little past sanity. He was thinking clearly enough now to resist. But the kiss hung between them, and in a way that was better still.

"Let's window-shop. Maybe you'll see some dishes you like." Although he didn't expect her to make any decisions about something so mundane, they cruised the plaza and other shops along the side streets. Rese got the hang of walking in her sandals and skirt, but he wasn't sure she noticed.

He might be distracting her, but the tension in her spine betrayed her strain. At least she didn't slip into the previous shrieking fury. Women needed to cry often enough to learn how to do it without damaging themselves and others. His sides still stung from the pinch of her fists. But he was glad he'd been there when she broke. Had Evvy seen it coming?

The sun lowered in the sky, and his stomach signaled dinnertime. He could take her home and cook, but he chose a bistro instead. Maybe Star would be at the inn, but she didn't seem to comfort Rese. And Rese was not in a position to be strong for anyone else. She had let down her guard, and he did not take that lightly.

For once, he hardly noticed what they ate since he kept a running monologue through the whole meal. He was telling her about Tony teaching him to ride his bike, making him learn all the hand signals and street rules before he knew how to pedal, when Sybil came to the table. He hadn't seen her come in, but the moment she was there, the air was charged with some feminine malice he could almost taste. He didn't think it was coming from Rese.

"Hi there." Sybil included them both in her greeting, actually looking longer at Rese than him. She rested one hand on her lower back, but for once her navel was covered. It was higher up that things got skimpy.

Her message was hard to miss, but he could ignore it. "How are you, Sybil?" He stood up.

"Manners too." She smiled, then turned to Rese. "He's too good to be true. Makes you wonder what he's hiding."

Lance took his seat, reminding himself not to do that again. Her remark sent a shiver of disquiet through him, fallout of a guilty conscience.

She said, "I came by to see you, but you didn't call. You must not be interested in what else I have."

Bait and spear in one shot. He'd forgotten about her visit. "I meant to. And I am interested." Though he didn't want to talk about it now in front of Rese. The last thing she needed was more concerns about gunshots and executions. Or him.

"I'll hold on to it. For a little while." With a fan of her fingers, she left them.

Rese followed Sybil with her eyes, then turned back to him. "She must WD–40 her hips."

He laughed. "I think it comes naturally. That particular motion is inborn."

"She walks like a woman?"

He leaned back in his chair and eyed Rese—earrings, blouse, no makeup or nail polish, but without her edge, downright pretty. "A certain type of woman."

"What type?"

"The kind who knows she's attractive."

Rese ran her hand down her water glass. "She reminds me of Alanna."

"Your mother?"

She gave him her hard stare. "Alanna was not my mother."

He studied her a long moment. "You're talking about some serious stuff here."

"I know."

He hadn't wanted to get back to her mother until they were out of there, but Rese didn't seem as overwhelmed as before.

She released the water glass. "I'm not pretending it wasn't bad. I just can't excuse . . ." Her voice broke.

Still at risk. He did not want to see her lose it in front of Sybil, who was no doubt watching, journalist that she was. Lance stood up, but didn't take Rese's hand. No sense complicating things further. "Come on."

They walked out past the table where Sybil sat with the tall brunette and another blonde, a table that probably had the waiter thinking he'd found paradise. Lance gave Sybil a smile as they passed. He couldn't afford to alienate her, and she couldn't help it if she had all the seductiveness Rese lacked, even if her siren song was wasted on him.

The evening had cooled substantially, and he gave Rese the lady's leather jacket, an interesting combination with her skirt. The earrings looked good, but the tender lobes wouldn't feel good in the helmet. "It's just a few miles. Want to ride without?"

"No, I do not." She took the helmet and eased it over her head, wincing when it pressed against her ears.

"Tough as nails." He smiled. "Galvanized."

"How am I supposed to ride in this?" She pinched the skirt.

He stooped and swung her onto the bike. The skirt hiked up to her knees, but nothing indecent. He tucked it under her thighs so it wouldn't fly up.

"You did that with experience."

"I've had the bike a long time."

"And have taken plenty of women along."

He didn't answer that. Rese would form her own opinion, especially after Sybil's attention. Everything he'd done today could get him into trouble, considering she'd almost fired him for taking her on a picnic—for the reck-lessness that followed. All he was trying to do was help her over the shock of her news. Talking about his past experience was not necessary.

He climbed on and felt her hands on his waist. She could hold his shoulders, but it was nicer this way. The helmet really would be hurting her newly pierced ears, so he took her home expeditiously. She swung off the bike with a far different motion than Sybil's, but for some reason, it grabbed him as Sybil's had not. What was he doing?

What he always did. Trying to be somebody's hero, and falling for her in the process. If anyone had told him Rese needed someone, he'd have scoffed. He still didn't believe it. She'd been knocked down, but not out. He walked her inside and stopped at her door. "Are you all right?"

"I'm fine." Somewhere between the restaurant and home, she had climbed into herself again. Her chin was up, her gaze direct, forcing a confidence she wanted him to believe.

"Want a steamer to help you sleep?"

She reached for her doorknob. "I'll be fine."

He stepped back. "Okay." He'd give her the courtesy of belief, even though he doubted she'd sleep at all. He started for the back door, trying to grasp the day in all its strangeness.

"Lance."

He turned.

"Thank you."

He nodded. "Antiseptic on your ears."

She reached up as though rediscovering the earrings there. He went out before she blamed him. The thought of piercing her ears really had come out of nowhere. But he couldn't help smiling.

CHAPTER TWENTY-TWO

Rese stood at the door after Lance went out. Maybe the damage wasn't done. He had not pressed his advantage. Both times that he'd kissed her, she had been distraught, vulnerable. If she didn't show that need again, he might not press it.

She went into her room, frustrated and confused, but not furious. *"Anger is a secondary emotion."* Possible. Mom had only gotten mad after Walter hurt her. Rese didn't want to think of that. She wanted to recall the good things about her mom, but the memories were all entangled.

Lance had been right about waiting, but now she had to wait through the whole weekend. With guests coming tomorrow, she couldn't be falling apart. But how could she pretend everything was fine when it was all so wrong?

Rubbing the back of her neck, she started to undress, then turned and looked at herself in the mirror. Mom had loved anything soft and flowing. She'd been so pretty in the dresses she wore, even in jeans and silk blouses. She didn't need Alanna to make her attractive. Dad couldn't keep his eyes off her.

Rese looked into the mirror. The peak of her eyebrows, the tilt of her lips. What else had she inherited? Shudders ran down her spine and knotted at its base. *What if . . .* She swallowed. She was already older than Mom had been when she married and had her. No one had yet appeared that others couldn't see. But how would she know? She closed her eyes and gripped the dresser. If what she thought was true turned out to be a lie, how would she ever know?

Odds were against Rese sleeping. Lance looked through the French doors to the villa. Her light was on, but he doubted she would come out. She'd been decisive in her dismissal. Although, after their first kiss she had come barreling up to his room to confront him, so it was a possibility. She had more reason now to believe it sympathy—it was.

As he stood there, Star's yellow Volkswagen Beetle pulled up to the side of the shed by his bike. Good. Star would keep her company, and he had a hole to clear.

He wished he had a way to cover the glass-paned doors. If he'd known about the hatch when he framed the carriage house, he'd have done things differently. Maximizing light and airiness had put him in a fishbowl.

With only the flashlight lit, he opened the hatch. Propping the light so it illuminated the space beneath the floor, he examined the timbers below. The first timber would be the worst. Once he dislodged it, the others would not be as tight.

If Nonna had done this, he should be able to undo it. But time and gravity would have worked on it too. He crouched down and wedged the crowbar in between two boards, hardly budging them at first, then managing a small amount of motion. He levered it again, this time throwing his weight into it. A small shift.

He lay down and gripped one of the boards, but it was still too tight. Again he worked the crowbar in, then took hold with his hands, scooching farther in to get a better grip. The smell that had caught him in whiffs now became a presence.

There was mystery in it, age and sorrow. Gripping the edge of the timber, he wondered. *Lord?* Purpose stirred, but it seemed muddled. Lance closed his eyes and waited, but no sound came, no sense of direction. He grabbed hold of the timber and nudged it back and forth.

Something shifted, and he jerked the timber up a little more than an inch. If he could just get at it better. He focused the pressure on upward motion now, and little by little the board slid free. He had it. One final jerk pulled it loose, and he hand-over-handed it onto the floor. One down, and a forest of them to go.

He could only do a few tonight and use them tomorrow. But as he reached for the next board his excitement awakened. There might be nothing down there but rubble. But why then go to all the trouble to block it? He reached in and took hold of another timber. *Lord, show me what's here. Let me do what I came for.* His sense of history, of family, kicked in. This wasn't his decision, he was certain. It had been made before him.

Rese had no idea what to tell Star. Pouring it out to Lance was one thing. He'd never known her mother, or her father for that matter. But Star had. There was all kinds of history connected to that. And frankly she didn't have the strength to delve into it yet.

So she opened the door to Star's soft query with a smile that would have impressed even Lance. Playing the part? Maybe she could after all. Maybe she had been all her life. Because when everyone else looked for something to be wrong with her, Star saw what she wanted to be. Star saw her strong.

Star stood in the doorway, chest heaving. "I did it."

Rese raised her brows. "Did what?"

"Took my things and left." Star passed into the room, opened her arms wide and leaned her head back. "I'm free."

"What are you free from, Star?"

"Maury."

She thought Star had left him already. Wasn't that what they'd mourned the first time? She searched Star's face for signs of damage. Sometimes it was a delayed reaction, but she actually looked fine.

"I took my paints, my canvases, my brushes. There is no part of my art left in his studio."

Now she understood. Star had left part of herself behind, her least resilient part. This was a huge step. Rese smiled. "That's great." She had been afraid Star wouldn't paint again, that the part of her she expressed through art would be lost because some inconsiderate bum shafted her. Now it seemed she really was going to paint something for Lance. Why else retrieve her supplies?

"You know what he did?" Star turned. "He cried."

Rese didn't know who this Maury was, or even if Star's version was accurate. But it had to be healthier to have it over if there was any semblance of truth to the pieces of the situation she'd glimpsed. Star was drawn to compulsive controllers, not beefy beat-her-up sorts, but psychological abusers. His tears had probably been just that—an attempt to draw her back in.

"What did you do when he cried?"

"Well . . ." Star sat on the bed and drew her knees up, looking sheepish. "It was the last time. I told him that."

"I hate when you let them do that to you." Manipulating Star's emotions was no different than shoving her against the wall. "He doesn't respect you."

Star laughed. "Why would anyone respect me?"

"Because you deserve it."

"'I shall th'effect of this good lesson keep as watchman to my heart.'" Star clasped her hands beneath her chin. "But I don't want respect. I want love."

Were the two mutually exclusive? Star found "love" with every person who took advantage of her, while Rese had fought so hard for respect people despised her. Neither seemed a worthwhile trade-off. The grudging admiration she'd gotten from the crew had not really been worth it, but then Star hardly seemed happy either. Whichever side the coin landed on left half the wager lost.

Star grabbed her shoulders. "You're wearing earrings. You have your ears pierced!"

Rese frowned. "It's no big deal."

"No big deal?" Star caught her hands.

Rese scowled. "Lance . . . dared me."

Star burst into laughter. "That *is* the only way you'd do it. Does it hurt?"

"No." Only an insistent throb. She still needed to soak them in antiseptic and turn the posts.

"Red is nice with your hair and eyes."

"Lance picked them." At least she had changed out of the skirt into her nightshirt before Star came in. She didn't want to answer for all the craziness she'd allowed.

Star cocked her head. "So . . . you're talking again?"

Blood burned up her neck. "We've been talking, Star." But not as they had today. He'd shared so much of himself, his family, his hurt. And he knew about Mom. How could things ever be as they were? She couldn't think of him as an employee. He'd won that battle, after all.

———

Lance woke to an eerie, breathless wailing. Heart pounding, he sat up so suddenly he tipped off the hammock and landed on Quillan's stone floor. Had someone, some*thing,* come up from below? What had he disturbed? He had told Rese the dead didn't bother the living, but he had a sudden desire to pray with all his might.

Jesus, name above all names; before you every knee must bow, every tongue confess you Lord. He'd always stood on that promise when fighting forces of darkness, and the noise seeping into his room sounded like no living being.

He got to his feet and peeked out to the other room.

The darkness was only faintly illuminated by heaven through the sky-lights, and he kept the name of Jesus on his lips as he searched the space with his eyes. The wailing came again, but this time he could tell it was coming from outside. Was the whole place haunted?

He ducked into his room, felt through a stack of clothes, and pulled a sweatshirt over his head. Then he went out into the yard and turned toward the keening. A white shape at the base of the oak almost drove his heart to his throat, but the being was affixed to the ground and a little more substantial than smoke.

Head cocked, he started toward it. The whine subsided to agonized sighs.

Jesus, he murmured just in case. But he made out her hair in the dim light. "Star?"

She pressed her hands to her face and wailed again. It wasn't like Rese's ferocious shrieks. This noise could be from another world, soft and plaintive as pain itself. Rese's distress had a concrete cause; this seemed the voice of undefined agony. *Jesus.* He might as well be dealing with the supernatural.

"What's the matter, Star?" He cupped her shoulder.

She took her hands from her face and found him in the darkness. "Hold me."

Her skin felt like death as she sank into him, boneless, cold flesh absorbing the night and mist. The string-strapped fragment she wore offered neither warmth nor concealment. He hadn't hesitated to pull Rese to his chest—at personal risk. But he hesitated now. *Lord.*

With a swift motion, he pulled his sweatshirt off, then tugged it down over her, engulfing her little limbs and adolescent frame.

She sniffled. "I just need you to hold me."

The tug was almost irresistible. Between Star and Sybil and Rese, he had more people needing something from him than even he could stand. The villa was dark, and he hoped that meant Rese slept. She needed it, or he'd send Star to her. Rese would know how to handle this.

He said, "What's wrong?"

She pressed into him, crying again. "'It is a tale told by an idiot, full of sound and fury, signifying nothing.'"

He eased her back. "I'd understand better if you said it straight."

"'Oh, call back yesterday, bid time return.'"

Okay, she regretted something, maybe wished she could change it. Something he understood too well. But he was not the one to counsel her there, or now. "You need to go in, Star. Try to sleep."

"'Thou art all ice. Thy kindness freezes.'"

He was chilled, shirtless in the night, but that wasn't what she meant. Maybe he did seem hard and cold. But she wanted something from him he couldn't give, not after the day with Rese. Strange, when Star seemed by far the more needy.

"Come on. It's the middle of the night. You're going to worry people." He walked her slowly to the house.

"'She receives comfort like cold porridge.'"

"I can't help that, Star."

"Because of Rese?"

Her snap into reality caught him unprepared. He could give her lots of reasons. But he said, "Yes." He didn't want to think how Rese would react if anything happened between him and Star. That would be wrong when Rese had finally let down her guard.

He walked Star to the door. "Get some sleep. You'll feel better in the morning."

She sniffed. "'O, it is excellent to have a giant's strength, but it is tyrannous to use it like a giant.'"

"Well, tyranny or not, you'll be better off inside." And no one had ever mistaken him for a giant.

Lance hadn't cooked breakfast for a while, but when Rese got up, he was there in the kitchen. She'd slept only three grudging hours in the middle of the night, and when she met his eyes, she was sure he could tell. Thankfully he didn't comment. She did not want to repeat yesterday's meltdown. She'd wrestled enough with that humiliation.

She had two days to get through, open her business, play her part. Doubt gnawed. Last night's thoughts and memories had left her weak, but she couldn't show it. If she knew how to play any part, that was it. Tough, secure, dauntless. She should see herself through Star's eyes.

Lance's baked eggs with salami and *parmigiano* went down like silk. Not something she would ever have chosen, but it tasted better than she'd expected. "What are you making for our guests tomorrow?" She had actually said that without sounding terrified.

"Almond focaccia and sausage frittata."

She nodded. "Sounds good. Not that this isn't good. It's delicious, Lance."

He sat down and took her hands between his. "You can stop pretending."

"I'm not. I like it. It's a little weird, but . . ."

He stroked her thumbs with his, sending shock waves up her arms. "That's not what I meant."

She couldn't acknowledge what he meant. She seriously regretted yesterday's collapse. If she let down again, she'd never get through today.

"How much sleep did you get?"

"A few hours."

His gaze was so soft she could wrap up in it.

"Lance, I . . ."

"How are your ears?"

"Fine." She'd had to lie on her back all night.

He shook his head with a smile. "Nails."

She frowned. "I need to talk to you."

He leaned back and cocked his head. "Am I fired?"

A flush burned her cheeks. "It wasn't your fault." Even now she wanted him to hold her.

"Well, you'll have to, if you want things to go back the way they were."

She met his eyes staunchly. "I don't. I just don't know what else to do."

"I like the sound of partners."

"Partners?" As she and Dad had been? The thought soured. Partners trusted each other. Partners didn't keep secrets, dark terrible secrets.

He stood up, walked around and massaged her shoulders. After a long night of lying stiff as a corpse and blaming herself for everything from her mother's situation to the day with Lance, his fingers were heaven. But she could not give in to it.

"Rese, your heart's not in running this place."

"Well, I . . ." But he was right. She dreaded the guests coming that afternoon. Renovating the villa had been painfully cathartic, a chance to face the trauma and regain her confidence. Doing it for Dad. Now it just magnified the betrayal.

Lance's thumbs pressed and circled. She closed her eyes. "I can't think when you do that."

"Then listen." His fingers working into the knots. "You did a great job bringing the house back. Now let me run it."

She huffed. "And what would I do?"

"Well, I'm no expert, but that carving you did for the dining room is great."

Why did every praise he spoke warm like down? "So?"

"So why not focus on that?"

"Just carve?"

He came around in front of her. "You could incorporate it into decorative pieces or even furnishings. Market them on a spiffy Web site."

She had no idea if there was a market for that, but to focus on the parts she loved best—carpentry and her signature carving. *In your face, Brad.* She chewed her lip. "You'd take care of reservations and everything else in addition to food and entertainment?"

"For a split, once the money's there."

"*If* the money's there." She could not expect the insurance anymore. They might not make enough to support two of them.

"You wouldn't have to greet the guests or make small talk."

She frowned. "So I pierced my ears for nothing?"

He tucked her chin up with his finger. "Not nothing."

An electrical charge started at the base of her spine and crawled up her back, a sensation she'd battled all night. "Lance."

"I've got it under control."

"Right. Mr. Emotional." She rolled her eyes to the ceiling.

"You have a lot on your mind. I'm offering to ease the load."

She pinched her brows. "Why? What is it to you?"

He squatted down beside her. "Well, for one thing you asked for my help. Or did you block that completely?"

"I wish I could."

He laughed softly. "I'm sure you do."

"I know what I'm doing. At least I did. Before. When my crew listened and followed instructions." She had seen the rebellion in Lance at the first glimpse. It was there still, disguised by the warmth of his touch, the playful glow in his eyes.

"So make me your managing partner, and we'll forget all that hierarchy malarkey." He took hold of her hand.

"I knew you'd be trouble."

"I'm the best thing that's happened to you."

She huffed. But it was so true it hurt. "I'll think about it." She would not be swayed by emotion. She knew better. And it was time she acted like it. She pushed up from the table. "I have a bed to finish."

Star came in, yawning and stretching in an oversized NYPD sweatshirt and nothing else that Rese could tell. *NYPD?* She looked from Star to Lance.

He held her gaze. "It would be great to have that bed soon. The hammock's pretty bad."

He hadn't missed a beat. She swallowed. What was the thing suddenly eating her from the inside out?

Lance turned to Star after Rese went out. In the dark he hadn't realized the sweatshirt was the one Tony had given him. Had she worn it intentionally to provoke Rese? That didn't seem like her, or the relationship he'd viewed so far. More likely she'd slept in it without realizing it might have significance to anyone else.

"Some fair aroma doth call forth hunger—"

"I'd appreciate the sweatshirt back."

Star looked down as though she hadn't remembered she wore it. "Oh." She reached down to pull it off.

He caught the edge and tugged it back down, frustration surging. "What are you trying to do?"

She looked up at him, blue eyes filled with concern. "Give you your sweatshirt."

"Do you mind getting dressed first?"

"What difference does it make? You're in love with Rese."

He stared at her. Where had that come from? He'd fostered friendship, and, yeah, there was chemistry. But attraction wasn't love. He'd learned that long ago. He turned and nudged Star toward the hall. "Go get dressed and bring me my shirt."

He didn't want anything else upsetting Rese. He was making headway on tenuous ground, especially with what he'd suggested moments ago. After Star woke him, he'd spent the remaining hours of the night rethinking his position. He hadn't come there with the intention of staying any longer than it took to get Nonna's answers. But upon arrival everything had shifted as though he'd sensed his roots there. Maybe this was the break he needed, no band, no living with Chaz and Rico and the rest of the family, no living under Tony's shadow. If he ran the inn, and Rese had something she loved— not him, her wood—maybe they could both come out of it happy.

There was still his promise to Nonna, and he would honor that. He just needed a way to make things right for everyone.

Star brought the shirt back with the look of a child unsure why she'd been scolded. With it tucked under his arm, Lance muttered his thanks and headed out the back door. Did Star even realize how awkward this morning's scene had been? Rese's look had been a power drill right through him, and it was all he could do not to blurt excuses. But that would have looked guilty for sure. Star's "Hold me" could have meant nothing more than that, or much more.

Rese's body language when she entered the kitchen earlier had not been as stony as he'd expected, but he wouldn't call it welcoming. He hadn't been fired. That was a good thing. And she had loosened up when he rubbed her neck, listened to his proposal even if she hadn't agreed. But Star was way off with her assessment.

His behavior toward Rese yesterday was philanthropic; she'd asked his help. That he was attracted to her, that he cared, were side effects. He could deal with that. As he'd told Rese, he had it under control. Inside the carriage house, Lance took the boards he had removed last night and began building the flower beds. Then he opened the hatch for more.

It still looked like giant pickup sticks down there, but soon he'd be able to descend. To what? An underground storehouse with access from the stable? He tried to make sense of that, and every scenario came up looking shady. A wine or root cellar would be accessed from the house, wouldn't it?

But it would have been on whatever plans Rese had used for the renovation. She would have known about a tunnel or cellar. No, the access was from the carriage house for a reason. And it was no accident that he'd ended up in there. He'd been grasping when he caught sight of the old stone structure and suggested his own renovation, but he knew now he'd been led.

He rose to his knees and gathered the rough boards he had removed, carried them out to the garden and continued building the beds. The sound of Rese's tools rang out from the shed, where she worked on his bed, he supposed.

Star wandered out, climbed the tree and watched him, but didn't speak. He hoped it had not been personal last night, that he'd just been the available shoulder. But he wasn't sure.

Maybe Tony was right. *You give out signals, Lance. Sucker signals.*

All right, so he hadn't always read people well. He didn't want to be suspicious like his brother. He wanted to trust, to take people as they seemed.

Rub a little deeper next time.

But he didn't want to, because he didn't want them rubbing deeper either. He was fine on the surface, but inside? He was still trying to find himself, inside his brother's footsteps.

CHAPTER TWENTY-THREE

Papa is restless in the field.
He cannot find the rhythm. He doesn't know the step.
His eye upon the horizon; his mind is in the world.
His heart has left us already. His feet will follow.

Rese checked her watch. After three, and the Taylors had not arrived. As Lance said, just because check-in began at three didn't mean they'd be there on the dot. Unwilling to relinquish control, she had showered and put on her skirt and blouse. Now she was wishing she'd stayed in the shed with her tools. At least there a sort of frantic activity had possessed her mind and occupied her limbs, the sort of activity that had filled her life ever since Mom's . . . she could no longer say death. Incarceration? Hospitalization.

If she could stay physically and mentally busy enough, forcing her concentration, finding that place with the wood . . . but she couldn't greet her guests all sweaty and dressed for work. According to Lance, she had to look the gracious proprietor.

She arranged the small easel with Lance's entertainment poster in the entry of the parlor and walked the length of the room to the filled bookshelf at the end. A book in hand would look natural. But not for her. A saw, a drill, a sledge hammer. . . . She expelled her breath.

Lance came up behind her. "You're going to wear yourself out worrying."

"Good. Maybe I'll sleep tonight." But she didn't think so with strangers in the house. Why hadn't she thought about how awkward that would be? Then again it hadn't been with Lance. Maybe it would be fine. Sleep didn't have to be her enemy.

She had chased away the ghosts and—She glanced up at the bookshelf where she'd heard the noise in the wall. Stupid to think of that now, but . . .

the room seemed to hold a sudden chill. "Lance, was everything all right out there last night?"

"Well, that hammock is no picnic."

"But nothing . . . disturbed you?"

His expression was enigmatic. "Of a supernatural sort?"

She nodded.

"We discussed that."

"No bumps in the night, no gunshots?"

He eyed her quizzically. "Did you hear it again?"

"No. I was just wondering." And sounding silly.

"You don't want the Taylors seeing ghosts?"

She squeezed her hands together. "I just want it to be right."

He smiled. "It'll be better than right. It'll be great."

He said it with complete authority. And why not? In the weeks he'd been there, he'd become the place. Actually, he'd seemed to belong the first moment she saw him. Again she felt herself the one who didn't fit.

What did she know about welcoming guests? She should have worked harder at public relations. She had learned to get control and keep it, but that didn't leave much practice in the finer arts of conversation and humble service. She nodded. "Of course it will."

Lance started out of the room.

"You're leaving?"

He turned. "I need to make a call." He slid his cell phone from his khakis.

"Who are you calling?" None of her business, but it had come out automatically.

He tipped his head. "Who do you think I'm calling?"

Now she felt really stupid. Of course he had people in his life. Friends and family. Maybe even . . . "A girlfriend?"

"Rese." His look scolded her. "I'm calling my nephew. It's his birthday, and I'm missing the party. I'll probably talk to my parents and a sister or two, whoever's there."

"Oh." She pictured it like a Hallmark commercial, zooming in through the window from the cold outside.

"Let them know I'm not in jail."

"You are a hothead." Rese eyed him directly.

He came over and took hold of her hand. "I'm learning to behave."

"Good." Definite misbehavior inside her chest cavity. Yesterday there had been anguish. What was it now? "Why was Star wearing your sweatshirt?"

His gaze was direct. No evasion, no discomfort, just frank assurance. "She was distraught in the yard last night. I covered her up."

"Star was upset?"

"Crying and quoting Shakespeare, or something like it."

"From her Renaissance festivals. She has whole scores memorized." Star fell into that mode when she couldn't bear to be real. Were they all just playing parts? Maybe Mom hadn't been crazy at all. Or maybe they all were.

Rese frowned. "Two weeping women in one day?"

His mouth quirked. "One wailing; one assaulting."

"Assaulting?"

"My sides are bruised."

His sides? "What are you talking about?"

He pulled up one side of his shirt, and she could see grip marks in his flesh, but she could not remember doing it. "I don't . . . I didn't mean to . . ."

He drew her close. "You needed to get it out."

"I didn't mean to hurt you."

"Nothing I can't take." Closer still.

"Lance . . ."

"I'm not going to kiss you."

"You're not?"

He shook his head.

Roaring disappointment.

Again that twist of his lips. "You'd think it was sympathy."

True.

"Or payback for bruising me."

Definitely true.

"You'd make up all sorts of excuses."

She jutted her chin. "I don't make excuses."

He laughed. "Then you kiss me."

Waves of shock. How could he totally disarm her with a thought? She took up the only weapon she could find. "I don't kiss the cook."

His gaze on her mouth might as well have been a kiss. "But now we're partners."

"I said I'd think about it."

A car pulled into the drive. Rese jerked a glance over her shoulder. A charcoal Mercedes, man and woman, just the sort to be making the wine country tour and staying at her bed-and-breakfast. They sat while he closed the sunroof, then climbed out and eyed the villa.

How different could this be from directing her crew or making a bid?

Lance clamped his palm to her lower back. "Want me to handle it?"

No way. She had let him take over yesterday—and had the pierced ears to prove it. She pulled herself up stiffly. "I can do it."

A gentle knock sounded and the couple came inside. The slight man said, "Hello. Mike and Roberta Taylor. We have a reservation."

Lance turned her with his hand still planted in her back. His easy smile. "Hi." Their feet crossed the room, two couples coming together. Lance held out his hand. "Lance Michelli. And this is Rese Barrett."

She held out her hand and shook twice.

Lance released her lower back. "Nice drive in?"

"Lovely," Roberta said. "We can't wait to get up into the vineyards."

"Do you have a plan?" He was warm and engaging, the perfect host.

Roberta took a guidebook from her purse.

Lance told her, "You can call ahead for tours and tastings," then motioned toward the small table with the guest book. "If you'll just sign in." He explained the setup and took their credit card.

Rese could have done all that. Roberta sent her a smile, then looked up and around the front room. "This is lovely."

She could tell her everything that had gone into it, but doubted the petite redhead wanted to know.

Lance said, "Rese will show you to your room," and handed her the key from the thin cabinet above the guest book.

She took it from him. "This way." Her voice was flat but audible. She led the Taylors up the stairs to the Redwood, unlocked the door and waited while they did a quick inspection. Then she surrendered the key to Roberta. "If you need anything, Lance or I will be around."

They thanked her, but she was already heading down the hall, down the stairs to the parlor and through the dining room to the kitchen where Lance had taken out his phone. He must not have dialed yet, because he lowered it when she stopped beside him. "I had it under control."

"Oh. Those moments of dead silence were for effect?"

She frowned. "What moments?"

"The ones before I stepped in and greeted them for you?"

Had it been that way? The dull lump in her stomach suggested it had. She gripped her hands together.

He pulled her close. "We make a great team."

He kissed her mouth with businesslike precision—what someone might call soundly, the period at the end of the sentence. He'd made his point and punctuated it?

"I thought you weren't going to do that."

"You wanted me to."

"I did not."

"Better run a check on your body language." His mouth pulled at the corners as he leaned in close again. "You all but begged."

"Oh! You . . ." Unable to come up with a word fierce enough to fit the choler, she stomped his instep, and he jerked back, wincing.

She clenched her hands. "I never beg."

With a limp forward, he pressed her to the counter. "You are so tough, aren't you?" The amusement was gone from his eyes, replaced by a fiery intensity. "It would be so humiliating to actually need someone."

"I don't—"

"Well, here's a flash for you. You were created to know and serve God. Beyond that, you came from *my* rib."

A fierce huff escaped her lips. Of all the arrogant . . . His rib? She had a sudden flash of a storybook with two people in a garden and a snake whispering with Alanna's voice. She swallowed tightly. "That garden of Eden myth is a children's story. Your God is no more real than Mom's fantasies."

The tension seeped from him. His grip softened. "You're wrong. God is real."

"You've seen him?"

His glance gentled. "In every firefighter's face. In every volunteer who sifted rubble for body parts. In the tear streaks of people who hadn't lost anyone. There is a God, Rese. And there is evil. And nobody stands alone before either."

Lance could not put out of his mind Rese's face as he'd laid the truth on her. It was an uneasy, humbling thing to put your trust outside yourself. To know that another ordered your days—and numbered them. As C. S. Lewis put it, *"We are not necessarily doubting that God will do the best for us; we are wondering how painful the best will turn out to be."*

Lance knew how painful it could be. He had to trust it would all be for the best, and try like anything to make it so. In their phone conversation, his sister had told him Nonna was fighting. She could not talk yet. After nearly six weeks, she could still form little more than rudimentary sounds that only made her angrier. Momma thought if she didn't try so hard it would come easier, but Lance understood Nonna's panic. If he was trapped inside himself, he'd fight every second of it.

Talking to his nephew had been bittersweet. The boy had grown up too fast with Tony's death, and Lance could feel the hole left in the party. He should have been there in his brother's place. He'd been teaching Jake to play guitar before he left, and he told him about the plan to play tonight for their guests and anyone else who showed up. Jake feigned interest, but it was clear he'd have rather had him at his party.

The boy's disappointment lingered as Lance tuned up in the empty room, surprised by the good acoustics. He shouldn't have to strain too much unless people packed in. Not likely. It wasn't as though he had a name or a following. He'd left that behind, no matter how many new agents Ricardo found. Tonight was just a lark. He might attract a few curious people from the flyers Rese had posted around town, but he didn't expect much. And he didn't want much either.

He warmed up with a song he'd written in Italian, back when he needed to convince Conchessa he wasn't the imposter she suspected. Not even Nonna's letter in his possession had convinced her at first. It was only after he'd helped her in the kitchen, and she'd seen his fingers in the dough, that she'd relented.

Then they had spoken long and in depth about Antonia and the letters written between them since they were girls, letters that had stopped after the one Conchessa put into his keeping, the one that spoke of fear and danger. Then he understood why she had doubted him. She was convinced Antonia had perished. To have someone who claimed to be her grandson appear, wanting answers . . .

Lance smiled faintly. He'd certainly had to prove himself lately. But he'd left the convent with Conchessa's blessing and her prayers lifted in humble and expectant simplicity. Thoughts of her still brought the peace that had leavened him like yeast at the convent, and his song became a prayer sung in her language to a Father who knew every tongue.

> *Into your heart, into your hand,*
> *All that I am, naked I stand.*
> *Should I depart, searching in blindness*
> *When I have known the kiss of your kindness?*
> *Selah, O Lord, Selah. In the silence You find me.*
> *Selah, my Lord, Selah. In the stillness refine me.*

Not at all the song to open a set, unless he needed to remember tonight wasn't about him and recall the reasons he'd left performing behind. He wasn't even sure why he'd agreed to do it now, except that Rese had asked instead of ordering him. As he practiced, Evvy hobbled in. He looked up, surprised, but she said, "You don't think we'd miss opening night, do you?"

We? "Great to see you, Evvy."

By the time he finished the next song, her gang had gathered at the various tables. Three gentlemen in shirt-sleeves and sweater vests, and seven women who smelled like a Wal-Mart fragrance department. He hoped he could sing with the cloying scent in his throat. But he was glad they'd come.

In her Renaissance festival barmaid costume, Star flitted between the tables, serving wine and coffee lattés and the chocolate-dipped *biscotti* he'd made earlier. There was no sign of last night's tears, replaced by her alternate effervescence. If she was faking it, she was superb in her role.

The Taylors came in, followed by a few others—a young couple and three guys who seemed to recognize Star. The diverse crowd allowed him to mix in some contemporary tunes along with some of his own newer songs. It rushed in on him, what he'd loved about performing: the energy that charged a room, that buoyant feeling that lifted him out of himself.

He could almost imagine Chaz and Ricardo beside him, their voices blending in harmony with his, Rico's drums and any of the instruments Chaz threw into the mix. Even solo, it was good to sing and play again. He didn't care who filled the seats, what sort of music they wanted. He had so many songs in his head, and if he missed a verse or two, they filled it in for him. It was easy.

He glanced at Evvy swaying and clapping her tiny fingers. What secrets had she and Ralph shared inside these walls? Maybe they could visit the old guy. That idea caught hold. He had discovered the underground vault, but he wanted to know what happened and why. Maybe Ralph could tell him, and Evvy might know as well. He looked into her face and sang an old Sinatra tune, complete with croon. If she were the swooning sort, she'd be at his feet.

Over the older folks' conversations, he had to sing louder than he'd intended. He hadn't seen Rese yet, but he was sure she could hear it all from the kitchen. She probably had her hands full making their steamers and lattés. But he wished she'd come out and see the energy in the room. It wasn't the crowd he'd expected, but they were fun, counting the coins out of their purses for Star and placing their song requests.

The crowd roared and sang along when he started "That's Amoré," and then Rese was in the doorway. He found her with his smile. They had talked about this, laughed and imagined. Now it was real. Their eyes found a common wavelength, sharing humor and excitement and more. A sharp pain somewhere near that missing rib. *Partners,* he thought, and forgot everyone else.

———————

Dressed in the snuggly comfort of her pajamas, in the sanctum of her suite, Rese bathed her pierced ears in capfuls of antiseptic, then painfully turned the studs in her ears. That's what came from giving up control. Watching Lance sing to the room had almost put her over the edge. Near the end, when he sang to her, she toppled.

He had won. Just like Brad and the others, he had fought her every step. But unlike every other man, he had won. Terror like nothing she'd known seized her. How had she given in? Where had he found the unguarded spot to sink his spear?

She couldn't let him see it. If he didn't know, it might not be too late. Her only armor was control. But the thought exhausted her. Was there never an end to it?

"There is a God, and there is evil." His words had locked in her mind like a deadbolt. Was there some striving of opposite forces, some primal conflict she was caught between? She shuddered, recalling the aching dread sucking at her the night that "presence" had striven for her. Good versus evil? Or a natural facet of her mind resisting the danger her lungs inhaled—as she now resisted the peril to her heart?

Lance talked of God and sang of love: two mysteries she could not explore. She needed Dad's arms around her, legs pumping, rushing her out and away. Prudent. Pragmatic. Confident. He had made her what she was. *But he had lied.*

CHAPTER TWENTY-FOUR

What little I know in my innocence.
Ideals like pebbles in the creek.
Wash away, wash away.
There is no logic in life.

Lance rocked the turns home from church the next morning to get breakfast prepared. He had baked the almond focaccia and kept it warming in the oven with a pan of water to keep it moist. Now he sliced the delicate strawberry and honeydew fans to garnish the plates. Beautiful and edible.

Last he cooked the sausage frittata and served it steaming when the Taylors came down to the dining room. There was no sign of Rese, so he greeted them and asked if they'd slept comfortably.

"Oh, yes." Mrs. Taylor beamed. "Like a dream in that down bedding."

His neck ached worse than ever.

"Enjoyed the music last night," Mr. Taylor said.

"Thanks."

They chatted about where they were from and where they'd been. Lance had gotten around with the Peace Corps and Habitat, but the Taylors liked fancier getaways. They lived in Ohio, but escaped whenever they could.

"Well, I'll let you enjoy your breakfast."

"You are a wonderful chef." Mrs. Taylor dabbed her mouth. "It was the food pictures on the Web site that made us choose this place."

"Thank you." He went back to the kitchen as Rese dragged herself through the door, no doubt intending to greet her guests.

He headed her off with a hand to her elbow. "Huh-uh."

She sent him a glare. "Huh-uh, what?"

"Don't go out there. Not like that."

"Like what?"

He eased her into a chair. "Like you spent the better part of the night wrestling." A surge of concern caught him square in the chest.

She dropped her chin and pressed her elbows to the table. "I didn't sleep until seven."

Since it was now ten after eight, that made for a very short night. "Go back to bed. I have it under control."

She shook her head. "I have to take care of the Taylors."

"I already did. They're doing just fine. Slept wonderfully."

She dropped her face to her hands. "Something smells good."

"I'll serve yours fresh when you wake up for real." He raised her to her feet and led her to the door off the kitchen. "Sleep, Rese." Her fatigue was painful. He watched her into her room. The door closed softly, and he hoped she would drop right off. That was the worst he'd seen her yet. What was with that insomnia?

He checked to see if the Taylors needed anything, refreshed their coffee and inquired as to their plans for the day. Full, as he'd hoped. With them gone and Rese sleeping, he'd have time to work. Even if Star came out and watched as she had the day before, he was simply landscaping.

It was almost titillating to use the wood as he removed it, slowing his descent to a ritual pace. It imparted a ceremonial quality that eased his doubts. He was accounting to Nonna, but keeping his word to Rese as well, bringing back the garden and doing anything and everything else she needed.

The vines he had trimmed back to get at the carriage house were leafing. He hadn't been sure if they were even alive when he decided to keep some of them. Rese had assumed he knew a lot more about landscaping than he did. He knew a little gardening from Nonna and a little herb lore from Conchessa. He could box a flower bed, and Evvy had instructed him on hedge trimming. But mostly he was working with what was there—a lot more than he'd ever had to work with before in his Belmont neighborhood in the Bronx. This small garden in Sonoma was practically Eden compared to that.

Dogwood and forsythia had already bloomed, but their scent seemed to linger with the honeysuckle hanging heavy now and the whole garden bursting with life and vitality. But as he opened the carriage house door, that smell of age wafted over him. It had to be the cellar. It was stronger than ever since he'd opened the hatch. He glanced up at the portrait he'd hung on the wall separating the bedroom from the sitting room. His ancestor's dark eyes scrutinized him.

There was no nameplate on the portrait, but by the clothing and expression, he guessed Vittorio Shepard had sat for the artist. "Were you a gangster, old man?" But the man in the portrait wasn't old, had never grown old, if the story was right. Only old enough, Lance thought, to produce Antonia and through her his father and him. "Who did you torque off?"

He shook his head. "You haven't left me much to go on. Any of you." Maybe there were things he shouldn't learn. Vittorio had died for whatever might be down there. But these were his people, his secrets. Who had a better right to pursue it than he?

He opened the hatch and took a step down, pulling out a board as long as himself. He laid it beside the opening and went down three steep stone steps, anticipation building. He pulled another board free and the rest tumbled to a pile at the bottom.

The space was dim, even with the sun shining through the skylight, so he climbed back up and got the flashlight from his bedroom. When he reached the bottom, he was grateful to see only the neck of the passage had been blocked.

Shining the flashlight into the narrow tunnel, he sensed the lives that had passed that way before. He was about to follow when he heard knocking upstairs. His heart hammered. Rese? He had promised her breakfast, but he hadn't expected her to wake up so soon.

He switched off the light and clambered up the stairs and through the hatch. It now seemed so evident that it was there. How could anyone miss it? The boards he'd removed lay there as well. He had taped a couple sheets up over the French doors and through the gap he saw Star, not Rese. He closed the hatch and opened the door.

"Morning, Star."

She spread her arms wide. "I am Morning Star."

She wore a turquoise shift that hung to her ankles but split at the bottom into broad ribbons. Her feet were bare.

He smiled. Whatever her issues, she was original. "Hungry?"

"I helped myself."

He glanced at the villa. "Is Rese up?"

Star shook her tangerine mane, then caught his hand and pulled him out the door. "Choose your scene."

"My scene?"

She swung her arm across the garden, and he noticed an easel and canvas ready. She was going to paint, as she'd said. He studied the areas not plundered by his spade and chose the most colorful patch.

She clapped her hands. "The elf grove."

She must be seeing something besides the yellow buttercups and California poppies, the feathery plumes and purple lupine. But then, maybe not. She turned her canvas and prepared her pallet.

Since he was out now, Lance headed for the villa. The sound of running water came from Rese's suite, so he cut her some focaccia and started her frittata. She looked better than she had before, but he wouldn't call her serene now.

She took the latté he offered but didn't sit down. "The Taylors?"

"Off and running."

Her face was tight. "I should have handled it."

"Everything was fine."

She frowned. "Nonetheless—"

"I'm seeing 'managing partner.'" He arced his hands like a marquee.

She frowned.

Undaunted, he caught hold of her waist. "Repeat after me. Lance, you're just what I need to run this place."

She pulled away from his grasp and sat down. Where was last night's rapport? He had sung her the most personal song he'd written, the one about losing Tony. He'd done it late after Evvy's group was gone and only a handful of listeners remained. He could have sworn she understood.

He moved behind her and rubbed the knots from her shoulders. This would become a morning ritual if they didn't solve her insomnia. "Why didn't you sleep?"

"I don't know." She bit into her focaccia.

"Have you seen a doctor?"

She shook her head. "It's not every night."

"It's often enough. What are you, twenty . . ."

"Four."

"That's way too young to have sleep issues. Are you afraid?"

"No."

But he felt her tense. Interesting. He worked the shoulders again, then moved up her neck.

She took a bite. "I slept like the dead the last two hours."

He cocked his head. "Maybe daylight helps. Are you afraid of the dark?"

She twisted to look up. "I'm not afraid, Lance; I just can't sleep."

"Hmm."

"You don't believe me."

He pressed his thumbs between her shoulder blades with a rolling motion. "It's not what I feel."

She huffed. "You think you know what I feel and what I need and what I want. But you don't."

He stopped massaging. "What's the matter, Rese?"

"You're the matter." She turned on him. "I told you I didn't want to get involved." She pushed up from her seat, leveling the field.

"I only said partners."

"That's what you said, but it isn't what you meant. I saw it all last night." He slacked a hip. "Saw what?" What had he done?

"The way you drew everyone in and held them right here." She raised and clenched her hand. "Everyone under control, everyone—"

He caught her hand in his. "This isn't about everyone, is it?"

Her glance shifted sideways. Tendons twitched beneath the skin of her face, its contours reminding him of the stone virgin in the convent courtyard. A sweeping tenderness seized him as he tucked a finger under her chin. "I'm not trying to take control. I care about you."

Her eyes jerked back. "What?"

He was wondering the same thing. Caring was different from attraction, more hazardous than chemistry. With all the secrets between them, all their differences and animosity, it was the last thing he'd intended. "It's as much a shock to me."

She stiffened. "Lance Michelli . . ."

"Oh, Rese, give it a rest." He pulled her into his arms. With the words out he may as well finish the job. Kissing her plumbed depths he had doubted he possessed. He'd fallen in love a dozen times before he realized feelings weren't what made you cleave to one person, become one body. That was some mysterious element he had skirted every time.

He felt Rese go soft and realized the power he held. Some balance between them had shifted, and with it he felt responsibility. He cupped her face. "I won't hurt you. I promise." He would be her shield, her guard—even from himself.

Distance was definitely in order. With Rese working in the shed, Lance headed for Evvy's front door. He had leads to follow up. He'd half expected Sybil to come hear him play last night, but it seemed that if he wanted what she had for him, he'd have to take the next step. That would be tricky though. He'd start with Evvy.

She answered the door in a blue print pant suit and Oriental slippers. Her hair was swept up in a twist that framed her face in a soft cloud. And he noticed now that her eyes were a china blue with graying rims. It was a face you had to love, or at least straighten up and pay attention to.

She leaned on her cane. "Lance Michelli."

"Good morning, Evvy."

"Morning? It's almost noon."

It could be. He wouldn't be surprised if she told him it was midnight, even with the sun shining down. He'd maxed out his surprise function moments ago with Rese.

"Come in." She motioned with her free hand.

He stepped into her home and breathed the aroma she carried around with her. It was hard to put a word to it, not a bad odor, just noticeable, like fading mums.

"I was having cheese and crackers."

"I'm sorry I interrupted."

"There's enough for two." She hobbled on her cane. "I have a whole box of Saltines."

Lance smiled. "I didn't expect you to feed me."

"Well, it's not lasagna or any of those fancy drinks your girlfriend serves."

"She's my partner." He was still trying to grasp the rest. He followed Evvy into the spacious but cluttered kitchen, the only room, of those he'd seen, with more than it could hold.

"I can't keep up with the lingo. Partner, girlfriend, whatever you like."

"My business partner, Evvy." Though Rese hadn't exactly agreed to that yet.

"Well, you're certainly working up to more." She took out a square of cheddar and pulled a paring knife from the sink, then smiled, innocent as a dove. Wily as a serpent?

He cleared his throat. "I wanted to thank you for coming last night."

"We had a lovely time. I'll let you cut."

He took the knife and cut himself a few squares of cheese. "You have a great group."

"Oh yes." She slid the package of crackers his way. "We keep each other hopping. Except poor Ralph."

A better segue he couldn't have found himself. "Would you like to visit him?"

"Visit Ralph?" She actually blushed. "Why, I haven't seen him in months. What if he doesn't remember me?"

Lance sat back and eyed her. "Evvy, you are unforgettable."

She reached over and patted his hand. "I know why that girl's smitten."

"What girl?"

"Your Rese."

He opened his mouth to explain again, but Evvy raised a hand. "I saw her when you sang."

Then he hadn't imagined the current. Maybe that was why Rese hadn't slept. If she was as scared as she seemed, she'd have beaten herself up all night with it. But he hadn't come to talk about Rese. "I could take you to see Ralph. We could hear his stories."

"Oh." Evvy's eyes turned misty. "He'd like that."

"Do you have a car?"

"I haven't driven in years."

"No problem." Lance munched a cracker with cheese, looked around until he saw the cabinet that held glasses. The door hung partway open; something he could fix for her. He got up and poured them both a drink from the sink. "What do you say?"

"Well." She touched her hair. "We could, I suppose. I'm not doing much else today." She dabbed a few cracker crumbs with her finger and put them into her mouth.

"Okay, then." Lance helped her to stand.

She reached for her cane.

"You can use my arm."

She looked up into his face. "I didn't know they made men like you anymore."

He smiled and walked her carefully to the door. "Do you have a jacket?"

She took a waterproof zip-up from the closet. He helped her put it on, then walked her from her house to the front of Rese's. Baxter jumped up when he saw them approach the bike. Lance fondled his head. "Not this time, boy." He took the helmet and turned to Evvy.

"We're driving this?" She eyed the bike, askance.

He tipped his head. "You'll have something to tell Ralph." He could ask Rese if they could borrow her truck . . . but that might lead to questions he didn't want to answer. Evvy would be fine; she might even enjoy the ride.

She paused, lips pursed, looked from him to the bike, then shrugged. "Why not?"

He'd read her well, spunky little bird. Lance slid the helmet on. A little loose, but not bad. He strapped it under her chin. "That'll help with the noise."

"What?"

He leaned close. "I said, that'll help with the noise." He helped her climb onto the seat, then he joined her. She was hardly bigger than a ten-year-old girl, but she hung on with a vengeance.

He started the bike. "Ready?" he hollered.

"Ready," she hollered back.

They cruised out of the drive and onto the street. He had looked up the facility where Ralph lived when Evvy mentioned it the first time, but she hollered directions anyway. It was in a newer part of town, some ten minutes' drive, and they parked without incident in the small lot at the west side.

She looked a little like a hatchling when he removed her helmet, but he didn't tell her so. "Well?"

She touched her hair, aware of her dishevelment. But her cheeks were flushed and her eyes shone. "I wish they could have seen that."

He laughed. "You'd have them all begging for rides."

Evvy snorted. "You wouldn't get a half of them astride that machine. Not for a banker's pension."

"Then you have one on them." Lance supported her slowly to the doors.

"More than one, my boy. More than one."

They stopped at the desk to check in, then Lance helped Evvy down the hall.

"Sure does stiffen up the legs."

"I'm sorry." He offered more support.

She waved her free hand. "Sitting in my kitchen stiffens up these legs." She pointed. "This is it, Ralph's room."

Lance knocked softly, then pushed the half-open door. His nose stung from odors far worse than Evvy's house. Evvy didn't seem to notice. They walked in and spied the man sitting by the window in a wheelchair. His hair was wisps of white, and he trembled with palsy.

"Hello, Ralph." Evvy's voice was softer than he'd ever heard it.

His parchment face folded into a smile. "Evvy, my love."

So he did remember her. Lance warmed. Maybe he wasn't as forgetful as she thought.

"I want you to meet the new man next door. He drove me here on a motorcycle."

Ralph shifted his gaze. "A motorcycle. My Evvy on a motorcycle."

Lance took the gentleman's hand. "My name is Lance."

"Lance. Have a seat. I just need to look awhile at this beautiful lady."

Evvy blushed. "There you go again."

"I don't know what day it is, or who's president of the United States, but I know your face in my dreams."

Lance felt the sweetness washing over him. He helped Evvy into a chair he pulled close to Ralph's, then sat on the edge of the bed a short distance away. While they murmured together, he looked at the pictures on the walls, then folded his hands and simply waited.

Too soon Evvy said, "Lance wants to hear your stories. About the villa."

Ralph's eyes stared across the room and his mouth hung slack. "No, no. I don't know any stories."

Evvy sent Lance a glance. "About the murder."

Ralph folded his hands in his lap and rested his gaze there. "Oh, they murdered him all right. At least that's what Papa said. Or did I . . . was it on the television?"

"No, it wasn't on TV. You found it in that book."

"That's right. The diary. In the carriage house."

Lance leaned forward. "There was a diary in the carriage house?"

Ralph looked at him. "What did you say your name was?"

"Lance. Lance Michelli."

Evvy touched Ralph's arm. "He's living in the carriage house. He made it up real nice." She winked at Lance. "I peeked in your window."

That was news to him, and a caution. He hadn't covered that back window. "Whose diary was it?"

Ralph answered with a hint of whimsy, "Antonia's."

An electrical thrill. "Do you have it?"

"No." Ralph shook his head. "No, I don't have any of that stuff. I . . . don't know what became of it."

"Your family cleared it out. It's probably in a dump somewhere."

Lance silently moaned. His grandmother's diary in a dump. "Did you read it? What was in it?"

Ralph smiled. "A good many of the lines I used on Evvy."

Evvy jolted straight. "You old fake."

He laughed. "That gal wrote all the things her beau said. Mark, Marcus . . ."

"Marco?" Lance offered.

Ralph nodded. "That was it. Marco." Ralph squeezed his brow. "A salesman, I think, or was he a . . ." He shook his head.

Nonno Marco. Lance forced himself to breathe. "What did she say about the murder?"

"She?"

"In the diary. Did she tell about the murder?"

Ralph sat back in the wheelchair. Again the pucker in his brow.

Evvy touched his knee. "Just tell the story, Ralph, the way you used to."

Ralph stared at the wall a long time. "I don't remember."

"It was Prohibition," Evvy prompted.

Ralph spread his shaking hands. "It's all in the soup. I . . . I . . ." A tear glistened in the corner of his eye.

She rested her hands on his knee. "Are they treating you well in here?"

He shrugged. "They keep me fed and diapered."

"Ralph!" She gave him a little smack.

He took her hand. "But I miss my girl."

She leaned in and kissed his cheek. "I miss you too."

Lance deflated. He'd heard nothing he didn't already know, except that there had been a diary and now it was lost. He couldn't bring himself to force Ralph's memory, as Evvy had obviously decided as well. It was bittersweet to see their devotion. It reminded him of Nonna and Nonno, before Nonno Marco's heart gave out.

"It's time for your nap." She patted his hand.

He nodded. "Are you going home on the motorcycle?"

Evvy looked at Lance. "Well, I suppose we are."

Ralph waved a finger. "You be careful with my fiancée."

Lance helped Evvy to stand. "I promise."

They walked out together, Evvy leaning heavily on his arm, more heavily than before.

"He's not what he was." Her voice grated.

Lance helped her past a man with a mop and bucket. "He certainly remembers you."

She sighed. "This was a good day."

He drove them home and helped Evvy inside. "Anything you need?"

"I'll just lie down awhile."

Lance lowered her onto the sofa. It seemed to take a lot out of her, that one small connection. Love was life's big risk. No guarantee of happiness, and the possibility of loss and pain. Worth it? The pain in Gina's voice when they'd talked the other day had been evident even over the phone. Would she rather not have loved Tony? Would he?

Lance couldn't approach relationships lightly. Not when the restlessness inside and his tendency to mess up would bring pain to someone else. He'd promised not to hurt Rese, but all his steps had been driven by something beyond him since the day he came. Now thoughts of her made a sweet hollow inside him like a honeycomb he couldn't help filling, even if it might get plundered.

He went to the shed and found her looking fierce in her protective eye gear as the sander spewed sawdust. The smell of wood filled the shed, and he eyed her progress. The bed pieces seemed ready to assemble, but maybe not to Rese's standards. She might worry the thing down to nothing while he developed a permanent crick in his neck.

She shut off the sander and held it against her waist. "Where'd you go?"

"I took Evvy to visit her beau."

"You took Evvy on the motorcycle?"

He shrugged. "Sure."

Rese shook her head. "I wonder about you."

He laughed. "She liked it. Enjoyed telling Ralph about it." He motioned toward her pieces. "My bed?"

She pointed to a flat piece lying on a separate surface. "I'm almost done with it. Just the carving and final finish."

He walked over and saw the crowning piece shaped like a scallop. "That's nice, Rese. I didn't expect anything that special."

She set down the sander and joined him, running her fingers over the carving. "I know it's obsessive, but I can't do things halfway."

He touched her arm. "That's a good thing."

She looked up in her silly goggles. Miss Safety Conscious. Or was she warding him off?

"I'll let you work."

She rubbed sawdust from her cheek with the back of her hand. "Are you making dinner?"

The Taylors had not placed a reservation, but if Rese wanted a meal, she'd have one. "Sure."

He went to the kitchen and prepared a marinated vegetable salad. He would broil chicken for it later, but now he covered and put it in the refrigerator to let the flavors blend. Then he baked some Kalamata-olive rolls and prepared caramelized oranges for dessert. In the midst of that, a middle-aged couple arrived without reservations, and since only one room was in use, not counting Star's, he checked them into the Rose Terrace.

He probably should have consulted Rese, but they were functioning within their primary capacities and it would only panic her. He'd tell her when she came in—so she didn't meet them in the hall and think she'd seen a ghost.

Thoughts of Nonna's diary plagued him while he worked. How could anyone toss something so obviously worth holding onto? Of course, he didn't know its condition. And it might be of no interest to anyone but himself. Still, to think that it had been there, in the carriage house! If only he'd come sooner. He sighed. He couldn't change that now. All he could do was see what was under his room.

CHAPTER TWENTY-FIVE

Dread breeds like larvae in a pond.
Things I have heard; things I have seen,
without understanding.
Only clouds gathering in my mind,
brooding over when it might storm.

Lance shined the flashlight beam into the tunnel. His stomach was full from the meal he'd shared with Rese and Star, and it was late enough that nothing should interfere with his exploring the tunnel. The weekend had passed without a clear opportunity presenting itself, but tonight he would take a chance. He descended the stone steps to the bottom and scanned the narrow walls and ceiling with the beam of his light. If it wasn't a tomb, the place could become one. Still, it had stood this long.

He drew a breath and started forward, skin tingling with anticipation and that vague sense of reverence. The smell was pervasive, musty with a slightly sour undertone. After about twenty steps, he came to an iron gate that reached from ceiling to floor. He pushed, then pulled, but it held fast. Locked. It would take a major tool to cut through, or a locksmith. Unless . . . He bent and studied the lock. *Lord?*

He turned and made his way back to the stairs and up. In his bedroom, he rummaged through Antonia's box for the key he'd found in the corner of the floor. A slight chance only, but maybe it had been hidden in that corner—not lost, but concealed. He lifted the key and studied its shape, then jumped at the knock on his door.

"Lance?"

Baxter scampered up from his spot beside the hammock and went to the door, his nails clicking on the stone, tail wagging his whole hind end. Lance dropped the key back in, slid the box under a pile of clothes and went out to the main room. He could not see Rese in the darkness outside the French doors, but he guessed she could see at least his silhouette. The tunnel gaped open, and he suddenly recalled all the sayings about living in a glass house.

Should he just let her in? Tell her everything? But he didn't know anything for sure. As soon as he knew, he'd tell her. He hurried over and closed the hatch. Then he went to the door.

Rese looked awkward standing there, but not upset. "Your light was on."

"I'm still awake." And he should have turned out the lamp if he didn't want to be interrupted.

"Parcheesi?" She held up the box from her parlor.

He looked into her face. "Can't sleep?"

"It's quieter than power tools."

"No doubt."

She reached down and petted Baxter. "I'd have asked Star, but she goes berserk with anything that has rules. And you said people should play games and talk and read to each other." She straightened up as lost and stiff as she'd been on their first walk together.

He caught her elbow and brought her inside.

She pulled the box up to her chest. "I didn't know how you'd feel about—"

"Parcheesi?"

She glared. "About me coming here and . . ."

He drew her close. "I like you coming here." And that was the truth, even though he burned to try that key. "That's why I subdivided. So I could entertain mysterious brown-eyed visitors who appear in the night."

She snorted. "Mysterious. Right."

"Believe me, Rese, you are a mystery." He would never have guessed she'd show up with a board game—or without, for that matter—even if he had put the idea into her head.

She raised her chin. "I thought you had it all figured out."

"Not by a long shot." He cupped her face and tasted her lips. How could anything to do with Rese Barrett be so sweet? "Can we lose the box?"

"We can set it up."

He got the point. "Okay." He carried the game to the table, nudging the lamp to its corner.

"You need more furniture."

"Bed first. Then you can build anything else you want." He settled onto the love seat and opened the box. "Benny Steiner taught me this game and wiped me out every time. I still think he left out a strategy or two."

Rese sat cross-legged beside him on the love seat. "If you know any strategy you're ahead of me."

"Yeah. Maybe he just moved pieces when I wasn't looking." He hadn't expected her visit, was fully intending to go right back down and, God willing, open the gate. But he had to admit it felt good that she'd come. It was probably a huge step for her to make the overture.

"Guests all tucked in?"

"A long time ago." She set up her pieces. "No doubt sleeping soundly."

But she was wide awake. And she'd come to him. He put his pieces in his starting circle, then motioned toward her. "Ladies first."

She stared flatly. "We'll flip a coin."

"Got one?"

She shook her head.

"Then toss your dice."

"High roll goes first."

He'd meant for her to toss the dice and move, but if it was an issue, they'd roll for that honor. She rolled high, then shook them in her little cup again, got a five and a three. One man out and three paces forward. She obviously didn't mind going first if she won the right. Just don't do her any favors. What had he gotten into?

They played two full games, which was his limit. He was not at all surprised Rese played to win. Parcheesi was truly soporific, but she showed no sign of flagging. "Getting sleepy?"

She sighed. "Are you?"

He had enough in him to search the tunnel once more. Unfortunately, she looked anything but ready to curl up and snooze. He set the game board aside and adjusted his position on the love seat. "Come here."

She looked surprised, but scooted over and leaned against him.

He curled her into his arm. "Favorite ice cream?"

She shrugged. "Dad brought home vanilla in a tub that lasted for weeks." She narrowed her eyes. "But I have a vague recollection of pink and green peppermint-candy sugar cones."

"Your mom?"

"Maybe." She turned slightly. "Favorite movie?"

"*Braveheart.*"

She drew her knees up. "The battle scenes?"

He shook his head. "The archetypal sacrifice of the Christ figure."

"Christ figure?"

"Patterned after Jesus giving his life for the world. An innocent one who dies for others."

She grew still. "Like Tony."

His stomach clenched. "Yeah. Like Tony." He hadn't expected that assessment from her. Tony would have had no thought that day but to help and serve; Tony, so set and determined. Death would have surprised him like someone jumping out from behind, but he'd know its face. And that day it was as calculating and without conscience as Satan himself.

She raised her knees and rested her chin. "Does it still hurt?"

"Yeah."

"I wish the pain went away."

He rubbed her back along her spine. "It helps to remember the good times." Because there were too many others that drowned him in regret.

The silence stretched. Then she sighed. "I'm going to see Mom tomorrow."

So that was it. He tried to imagine learning someone you believed dead was alive. He knew the dread of hoping against all odds that a loved one was still alive. It had taken weeks to admit that Tony was not coming out of Ground Zero, longer by far to fend off the rage of his loss.

But Rese had the chance he would never have. She could find her mother, see her, talk to her, tell her things everyone would say given one more chance. Death was overturned for her. A rush of bittersweet joy filled him. What wouldn't he give to learn Tony was alive? To grip his brother's hand, to grab him close, to thank him for being there, for always being there.

It could be different for Rese. There were things she didn't understand yet. It wouldn't be easy getting the answers. And he sensed she knew that. "Are you ready?"

"I have to be. I guess it was good to wait through the weekend, but now there are all the questions and decisions." She looked into his face.

"It doesn't all have to be done at once."

She didn't answer, just leaned her knees across his lap in a girlish position he found endearing and tender, two words he struggled to attach to Rese.

"Do you ever lie, Lance?"

His heart hit his ribs with a thump as his hand rested uneasily on her side. "To you?"

"To anyone."

He wrenched his thoughts off the tunnel and the key and the box. He hadn't lied about any of it. *Or his purpose there?* He was doing his job, and more. He swallowed. "When I was, oh, seven or eight, I went through a phase of lying to my mother. Sometimes I lied just to see if I could make her believe me." He'd been too deft and convincing for his own good. "But she caught on and said she couldn't trust me anymore."

He sent her a glance, hoping that wouldn't put the thought into her mind. "I didn't realize what a big deal that was until it started playing out. In every imbroglio with Tony or my sisters, she'd take their word over mine, even though they never told the whole story. She'd look at me sadly and say, *I'm sorry, Lance. I can't believe you.*'"

He expelled his breath. "I saw real fast how badly I'd messed up, swore I'd never lie again and begged her to trust me." He still remembered the warmth of her hand on his head. *"All right, Lance. We'll start over."* "And she did."

"Did you still lie to her?"

"Not in any way that mattered. I'm sure I only told my side of the story, but I never intentionally lied again." Even when he'd had cause, as he had too many times.

"I lied to my dad." Rese rested her head against his collarbone. "I didn't see it as lying, but as keeping the secrets."

Keeping secrets. A cold weight settled inside.

"It was all part of the pretending, the ever-changing shades of reality."

He cupped her knee with his palm. "What secrets did you keep?"

She sighed. "All kinds of things. Once, Mom set fire to a neighbor's rosebush."

Whoa. "Really?"

"I didn't see her do it, but I'm pretty sure. After the cruel things Mrs. Walden said about Mom, I thought she deserved it."

"Then why lie?"

Her brow puckered. "I don't know. It was like we lived on two levels. It was shades of gray for Mom, but black-and-white with Dad. That's why I expected the truth from him."

"Sometimes it's hard to see the truth. Or know what to do with it."

"But he wasn't just my dad, he was my hero."

And heroes sometimes fell.

"After Mom was gone, he became everything I needed. Not always what I wanted. There's a difference. It wasn't warm and cuddly. But it was solid."

Interesting choice of word.

She glanced sideways. "You're not anything like him."

No, nobody would call him solid.

"He's the one I would never have doubted."

As she doubted *him*?

"What if everything I thought about him is wrong?"

Lance stroked her knee with his thumb. " 'Everything' is pretty broad."

"But it's like your mom told you. If you can't trust someone, how would you ever know what's true and what's not?"

He frowned, not liking where this was going. "Maybe it's all shades of gray, choosing what to tell and what to hold back."

"My keeping Mom's secrets was not the same as what he did." Her face pinched.

He squeezed her knee. "Maybe he was keeping them too."

The thought found an uneasy resonance that she fought with everything in her. She'd rather be indignant. How could you tell a child her mother had died? Live as though that person no longer existed? Anywhere. He didn't even give her the myth of heaven.

"You're tied in knots again." Lance rubbed her neck.

Rese closed her eyes and sank into his fingers. No one had ever touched her that way. After days of backaching work, the most she could hope for was a hot soak in a tub. Lance's fingers found the ropes and smoothed them into jelly, but the thoughts weren't as easily conquered. "It wasn't right."

He didn't argue, just kept rubbing until the warmth coursed down her neck to her spine and sank inside. He cared about her. Working in the shop, with his words inflaming one emotion after another, she had grappled with the thought.

She had believed Dad cared. He took care of her, but was that the same? "How can you trust anyone if lies like that can be so real?" Lies and other things.

"I don't know, Rese."

She'd expected something else, some assurance that there was a way.

"I know there is truth. But it takes faith."

Faith. Believing the invisible. Trusting the unseen. She recoiled at the thought, but what if he was right? "Explain it to me."

He turned her by the chin and studied her face. "Okay. But let's do this." He eased her down across his lap, cradling her head in his arm against the end of the love seat. "Now I can see if you're falling asleep."

"Not likely." Her position was way too vulnerable, like Baxter rolling over at Lance's every glance. Her first instinct was to shove herself up and establish equal ground, but she resisted. With her head in the crook of

Lance's arm, and a clear view of his face, perhaps she'd grasp something that until now had eluded her.

After a moment, he said, "It starts with love. With an all-sufficient being creating humankind, people to govern and guide, to help and sustain, but most of all to know and love."

She'd heard the story of creation and the "fall" from her mother. She remembered the book now, a glossy hardback with brightly colored pictures, fruit and fig leaves and fairytales. She had heard that story and others one summer at vacation Bible school, but even then she'd had reservations. Lance didn't try to convince her of the details; he gave her the essence instead.

"Once people rebelled, it broke the bond. There was no way they could fix it, bring back what was lost. Sin is in the world. Bad things happen. That's reality."

She stirred. "Good things happen too."

"Good things happen. But only because God didn't give up on it. He looked at this thing He'd started and the pitiful beings who'd lost the perfection He'd wanted for them and had mercy." He touched her chin. "As you had mercy on me."

"What?"

"I broke your rules. You could have canned me, but you didn't."

"I didn't want to."

His smile showed everything he felt, right there to see. She loved that transparency. She could trust it.

He brought his finger to her lips, the softness of his touch mesmerizing her. "And God didn't want to can us either. So He made a way to come back into relationship. He took all the guilt onto himself."

"I thought that was Jesus."

"Jesus is God, and don't expect me to explain the Blessed Trinity. Jesus became man and died for us. The Christ, taking onto himself the sin of the world."

"Like William Wallace in *Braveheart*, dying to make the Scots free."

"In a big way." Lance smiled. "Real big."

She closed her eyes and thought about it. "So if he did it, why isn't everything back the way it was?"

"Nothing broken can be unbroken." Lance traced the line of her jaw. "It's renovation. He made a new way, despite the death and suffering we brought on ourselves."

Renovation. Keeping the heart of it, but making it new. Bringing them through the death and suffering . . . as the presence had brought her through the near death and terror of that horrible night? She jolted awake. "Lance."

"It's okay. You can sleep."

She shook her head. "I think I'm afraid to because . . . because I almost died." It came to her now with a new clarity.

"When?"

"The night my mother . . . went away."

"When the furnace malfunctioned?"

She nodded. "I was in my room. Mom had made me go to bed early, and I was afraid."

"Why?"

"Because Walter was there. And she'd been crying and promising him she loved him. He was dragging her around."

"Dragging?"

She searched her memory. "It's how it looked." Though Walter's part was invisible, of course.

"So you went to bed scared."

"And somewhere in the night, I knew I was dying. But there was something there, some*one*. A presence telling me not to give in, to fight it, to resist."

"Your dad?"

"No." Rese looked into his face. He'd think her crazy like Mom. "Nothing I could see, but I knew it was there. It made me hold on until Dad rushed in and grabbed me up and ran outside." And now she had a flash of memory she hadn't recalled before. Her mother standing outside. How could she be if . . .

Rese shook her head. "Do you think I'm crazy?"

"No."

"People always looked as though I might be. They called Star and me the Looney Toons."

"You're not loony." His eyes were warm and certain. "But you are blessed."

"Blessed?"

"Who do you think was there with you?"

She couldn't say it. "But why? We never prayed, never went to church." Mom's storybook was one of many, and there were others she'd liked more. "One session of vacation Bible school doesn't count for much." Even if she had said the little prayer they gave her to let Jesus into her heart.

"He loves you, Rese."

What did that mean? She wanted to see it, know it was real. "I don't know what to do with that."

"Believe it."

"That's the hard part."

"You already did the hard part. Admitting your need."

"I was a child; I was scared." Would she do it now? Even then she had tried to be what everyone else needed: Dad's sensible girl, Mom's sensitive daughter, her own best friend.

"You trusted. You just didn't know who."

She had trusted the presence. In the dark silence of her room she had begged someone to help her, though she only guessed her danger. Inside she'd sensed her utter helplessness and cried out. She closed her eyes and pondered that. Had Jesus saved her?

Like the guy inside the whale, she'd been carried to safety. It was Dad's arms, but what had brought him there in time? Someone bigger. A heavenly father? It wasn't just physical safety she'd felt. Had her soul recognized the Lord and clung?

And hadn't that stirred inside her every time Lance prayed, part of her hoping there was someone listening, some powerful, benevolent being, someone to give purpose to the empty reality? Again she sensed the presence. Jesus? But why would he bother with her? Why spare her in that unbelievable way?

A thought came like mist. To save her mother? Waves of confusion. Why, how, what was she supposed to do? Was her father, her hero, mentor, and idol, the heartless liar he now seemed? Tomorrow she would know. Tomorrow . . .

CHAPTER TWENTY-SIX

Rese woke in the hammock with a blanket over her and Baxter's nose in her palm. She lifted her head and discovered a crick in her neck. Poor Lance. *Lance.* She jolted up. Where was he, if she was in his bed? She looked around the room, strained to see into the other. She was alone.

She got up and used his bathroom. It smelled like his musky aftershave, and moisture lingered in the air. She must have slept deeply. Her toothbrush and everything were in her own bathroom, so she started for the house with Baxter prancing at her side.

Lance must have left him there to keep her company. She loved-him-up at the door, then went into the kitchen. Something pungent and buttery scented the air. Lance's voice came from the dining room with others. Her guests! She had deserted them again. She sighed. How had she thought she could do the hospitality thing?

She went into her room and showered, dressed in jeans and a knit shirt, but not her usual oversized style. She was going to see her mother and the people involved with her, and she didn't want to look sloppy. Back in the kitchen, she paused as Lance openly appraised her. *Admit it.* She'd wanted him to notice.

"Hungry?"

Her stomach squeezed. "What do you think?"

"Have a seat. I'll make your omelet."

"Aren't you going to ask how I slept?"

His mouth pulled sideways. "I don't need to. You never stirred when I tucked you in, and you hadn't moved when I looked in this morning." He took down the pan, looking thoroughly pleased with himself. "I was afraid you'd wake up if I carried you farther, so you got the privilege of the hammock."

She had no memory of him carrying her. "Where did you sleep?"

"The love seat is definitely worse." He broke and whisked two eggs in a bowl.

She joined him by the stove. "You could have used a room."

"I didn't want you to wake up disoriented."

He'd slept on the awful love seat in case she woke up scared? "Your mattress set comes today. If I don't get the bed done—"

"I'll use the mattress anyway." He poured the eggs into the greased pan and sprinkled on spinach, diced artichokes and cheese. Then he turned and took her hand. "Don't worry about the bed. You have enough to think about."

"It's a miracle I slept."

He smiled. "Whatever it takes."

"Lance . . ."

Star came in, and Rese started to pull away, but he drew her to his side and circled her waist with his arm.

Star took them in. "Convergence at last."

Rese glowered. "More like collision."

Lance released her to fold and remove her omelet. He set her plate onto the table, the golden eggs still steaming next to a sliced grape and raspberry garnish on a dollop of yogurt. "Let me refresh our guests' coffee, then I'll get your omelet going, Star."

She picked up the pot. "I'll do the coffee."

Rese caught her slanted look, but she was not going to pick up where they'd left off. She'd been about to tell him . . .

"You were saying?"

How did he do that? He took her hand again and drew her close.

She swallowed. "I wanted to thank you."

"For what?"

Too much. Her throat thickened. "It could have been really bad last night. I doubt I would have slept at all. But the things you told me . . ." She shook her head. "It really helped."

He raised her chin and studied her face. "Good."

"Lance, I . . ." Rese fought herself. Star's voice carried from the dining room, laughing with their guests. She had the moment, but she couldn't say how much he mattered to her. "Appreciate it."

The corners of his smile deepened. Amusement found his eyes. He would kiss her and she'd be more confused than ever. But he said, "Your food's getting cold."

She sat down and ate an omelet as wonderful as everything else. He was way too good for her little operation. Star came back and Lance served her, then made one for himself and joined them at the table. Sitting there with Lance and Star, she felt bolstered to face the day.

Where was the panic? The rage? Trepidation, yes. Uncertainty. Questions. But it didn't seem overwhelming anymore. Because God was in control?

"I'm off to paint." Star gathered her supplies from the counter by the door.

Rese watched her. "What are you painting, Star?"

"Lance's garden." Star slipped through the door.

Lance's garden. It was his garden. His inn. Rese carried her plate to the sink, and he met her there. Taking the plate from her hands, he lowered his mouth to kiss her. She drew back only far enough to whisper, "Lance, I meant to say . . ."

"I know what you meant." He kissed her again.

A profound need settled inside him, so raw and perilous it rivaled his faith, something tender and real between them. She couldn't say so, but he knew she cared. He was going to screw it up; he knew that too. Somehow he would take this chance and blow it. But not even that could make him run away now.

Lance closed his eyes against her hair. Until she'd fallen asleep in his arms last night, he'd had a pretty good handle on things. He'd been midsentence when she had drifted off, peace settling over her features like a soft blanket. Recalling it still left him nearly breathless with yearning. He stroked her back, caressed her face, found her mouth again and lost himself. He groaned. This was not in the plan.

Rese drew back. "I have to go. My appointment is at eleven."

"I know." But he couldn't let go. She had to get to San Francisco, find the mental health facility and deal with her own crisis. And there he was clinging to her like a lost boy to Wendy's nightgown.

She smiled, a devious one she'd birthed at this moment. Where had that feminine trait hidden? She knew exactly where she had him, and she liked it.

That thought started a fire he could not afford to stoke. "Want me to go with you?"

She shook her head. "I have to do it alone."

He'd suspected that. She wasn't used to thinking in pairs. Neither was he. "Then you should go." He slid his hands to her waist and held on a moment more.

A flicker of apprehension found her face.

"It will be all right. The Lord's got his hand on you."

"I hope so."

He kissed her softly. "Get out of here." At least her reluctance matched his. "I'll check out the guests. And give me your password so I can look at reservations."

He hadn't expected her to argue, and she didn't. Her mind was elsewhere, obviously. She wrote the information down, then fetched her purse and joined him once again. "I'm going."

He stayed where he was and nodded. "Be careful." He meant that in more ways than one. He did believe she was in God's hands, but that didn't make things easy. And she'd be facing a lot in the next few hours.

The roar of her big truck engine calmed him, and he was suddenly glad she drove a tank. If only the rest of her was really so tough. He drew a slow breath and released it.

Two things he had to do while she was gone: talk to Sybil and try the key. The second burned most desperately, but he made himself call Sybil first. It was only fair he let her know where things stood. He didn't need any more complication than he'd caused himself.

Her silky voice came on, and he asked when they could meet. Lunch didn't surprise him, but he wished she hadn't suggested it. Well, he owed her.

"Where?"

"Your place. You're cooking."

He silently groaned. "It will have to be early. Elevenish." He didn't want to think how it would look to Rese, his cooking for Sybil. They had to be done before she got back. But there was still Star. That was it. He'd include Star. But not for the discussion. He'd have to manage that separately.

He kicked himself for not getting what he needed from Sybil before things had gotten personal with Rese. He'd forget it altogether if not for Nonna and the promise he'd made. Something, though, was not right with the whole picture. But what else was new?

He planned the meal, checked out the guests, stripped their beds, started the laundry, then found Star in the garden. She'd forbidden him to see the work in progress, so he stepped to the back of her easel, blocking her view of the elf grove. Whatever she painted he would hang, but he hoped it was something halfway decent.

"Star, can you plan on lunch today?"

"Getting it?"

"Having it." He stuck his fingers in his pockets. "Sybil's coming by, and I'd rather not eat alone with her."

Star pressed the handle of her brush to her lower lip. "Where's Rese?"

He started to answer, then caught it back. How much did Star know? "She had a meeting in San Francisco."

Star's smile teased her lips, then spread. "You need Star power."

"Right. We might visit awhile first. Then I'd appreciate your presence."

"I'll shine."

Lance grinned. "I'm sure you will."

He went into the carriage house and met Vito's eyes. The man had lived precariously, and now that seemed a little too close to home. Lance might not get shot, but he certainly had a lot to lose.

He went to the hatch and opened it. Rese had been in the room last night for hours and not noticed. Of course, she wasn't looking. When Parcheesi was over he'd kept her occupied. It wasn't intentional distraction, just effective.

And then she'd fallen asleep, and slept more soundly than anyone he'd ever seen. He supposed once her mind succumbed, her body took over with due diligence. It warmed him that he'd helped, even if all he did was trigger the memory of a faith she'd long ago embraced.

Her childhood encounter didn't surprise him. He was too well acquainted with Scripture to doubt supernatural intervention. And Rese was just the kind of unsuspecting person the Lord would choose.

He climbed down. The smell had grown familiar, and he wondered if he would carry it on himself as Evvy carried hers. A valid consideration that only heightened his feelings of deception. He intended to tell Rese. He would. He just needed the right time.

The air was cool and still. In the glow of the flashlight, he made his way through the narrow passage to the gate, then stood there and fingered the key. If it didn't work, what then? He breathed a prayer and tried it in the lock. It turned. His breath escaped in a rush. *Grazie Dio.* It must have been hidden in the carriage house corner for this purpose. To let him inside to find what he was meant to.

The iron creaked badly, but there was no one to hear. He must be half-way between the carriage house and the villa with nothing but stone and earth above and around. He left it open behind him, though it would be no big deal if it closed. As long as he held the key he could reach through and unlock it again.

He flashed his light on the space before him. The tunnel continued without branching, a single passage as wide as a big man's shoulders. He caught a noise and jerked the light up. A mouse skittered along a tiny ledge of uneven blocks near the ceiling.

Lance returned the beam to his path and pressed forward several steps, then stopped still. Bones and white hair and teeth. Indisputably human. Their position of repose, intentional. His heart hammered. The tunnel *was* a tomb.

He approached slowly, his mouth suddenly dry. It was not Vito, since he was buried in the graveyard. Who then? By the length of the bones, the tatters of clothing and the shoes, a man, in spite of the long hair. His arms had been crossed over his waist. Either he'd been left to die in that position or placed that way after death. He hoped the latter.

Reverently, he dropped to his knee beside the skeleton. Why would it be lying there in the passage? Had he fallen? But again the position suggested intent. Fallen, maybe, but then arranged?

Lance touched the hair, long and silvery white, and his mind flashed to the picture of Quillan Shepard, who'd worn his hair long in spite of fashion. Lance felt his chest close in. Was it his great-great-grandfather lying there unmarked, unmourned?

This stalwart man of doughty countenance is the stuff of today's hero. Was this what it came to in the end? Lance sagged. All his hopes of honor and great deeds. His driving need to measure up. This man had done all that and more, yet . . . he lay there in the dark, his bones dried and forgotten.

It must be Nonno Quillan, who else? There was no grave for him in the graveyard. Still, wouldn't it raise questions if a man was simply gone? Unless . . . unless it was assumed he left with whoever had arranged him there.

Could this be what Nonna wanted him to find? His heart rushed. Had she left her grandfather in the tunnel and fled? Had she blocked the tunnel and covered the floor with dirt, the only burial she could give him? A surge of thanks washed over him. Nonno Quillan had at least that much.

Lance sighed. He did not find it morbid to rest his hand on the skeleton's chest. The flesh had been eaten away, and the bones and remnants of clothing were dusty and dry. If this was his great-great-grandfather's skeleton, he felt only sadness and reverence.

He swallowed the sudden thickening in his throat. Quillan Shepard deserved better than this. But if he exposed the skeleton now, he'd have to reveal it all. He wasn't ready yet. He hadn't found what he needed. Surely Nonna sent him for more than this—too many questions surrounded her sudden disappearance from her home, Vito's death, and the other inferences in the article.

Lance shined the flashlight on his watch. No time for more. He had to wash up and prepare lunch. Regretfully, he left the bones as they lay and went back through the tunnel to the opening. Climbing out, he realized he was more shaken than he'd realized. Emotion built inside like a tide.

Quillan Shepard left to die in a dark tunnel. His family deprived of their home, their property. Had Nonna intended to come back? Was she prevented? What ugliness lay as buried and forgotten as Quillan's skeleton? He had to find the truth.

Meeting Sybil suddenly took preeminence. He wished he hadn't alerted Star. But his actions with Rese required integrity. He'd learn what Sybil had and explain his position. He only hoped what she had was enough.

Chapter Twenty-seven

Gunshots through stone and earth.
Papa!
Nonno falling. Falling, falling.
Cannot catch him; cannot hold them.
Useless arms. Useless hands.
Need. Anger. Pounding sorrow.

Rese cruised over the Golden Gate Bridge past the tollbooths into the city. Before buying the property in Sonoma, she had lived in Sausalito with her dad. An easy drive across the bay would have brought them in to see her mother. She didn't understand.

Even if her hospitalization was warranted for a time, why cut her off completely? And why lie? Rese shook her head. That was what she couldn't forgive. The deception of it all.

And then she recalled her mother's fear. At first she had thought the whispered threats were part of the game. *"He'll lock us up if he knows, Theresa. It has to be our secret."* In the same way, she'd built the suspense in her spooky stories when the lights were low and the house still and silent.

Dad didn't know how to play. She knew that at a very young age. He came home serious and suspicious. But she loved the way he smelled of sawdust and varnish, his callused hands and strong muscular arms. She loved the size and breadth of him, the look in his eyes when he approved. She didn't believe he would ever do something to hurt them. The hurting part, that was the game . . . Walter's game.

Rese shuddered. Sometimes she'd begged Mom not to invite Walter. *"Let's play without him, Mommy."* But Walter always came. Sometimes she imagined him in her room, long after he should have gone away, lurking in the shadows of her closet. That fear was unequivocal, but had she missed the other one she should have feared?

She gripped the steering wheel. Dad took her mother away. He locked her up. All these years, she could have known her, seen her, talked to her. All these years she had missed her. And he never said one word.

Even as he lay dying in her arms he had not spoken of it. As his life drained away, could he not have told her? The memory poured in, Dad gripping her arm, his last words, "Be strong." Was that it? Mom had not been strong? No one could ever believe her strong. Just soft and beautiful and tingling with mystery.

Everything Rese was not. She'd become the woman Dad expected her to be. Nothing like her mother. She drew a long painful breath. Day by day, moment by moment, he'd annihilated every aspect of Mom from her. How he must have hated her, hated them both.

Sybil wore a simple suit with a clingy silk shell and heels. Very professional, chic, and savvy. Lance hated that it affected him. It was how she moved inside the wrapping, how she caught him with her smile and that hint of wickedness in the eyes. This was the last time. As soon as he knew what she had found, he'd tell her where he stood.

"Something smells good." She slid him a smile.

"Risotto with shrimp and fresh bay scallops."

As he led her back to the kitchen, she said, "I was hoping to see you in action."

"I didn't want to keep you waiting." He eyed the envelope she held. "Is that for me?"

"Maybe."

"What is it?"

"Something that corroborates the first article."

His chest clenched. So it was true. Vito had been shot down. "From the archives?"

"Not the paper's."

He raised his brows. "The police files?"

Smiling, she stroked the envelope with her perfect oval nails. "I was thorough the first time. The police don't have this; the paper doesn't have it. Only I do." She stepped in close, the shell falling loosely enough to demonstrate her intentions. "You should have told me it was personal."

His heart jumped. "What do you mean?"

"Michelli." Her gray eyes darkened. "Marco Michelli."

He swallowed. *Nonno Marco?* Before he could speak, she reached behind his neck, pulled him forward and kissed him.

Head spinning, Lance pulled back. "What are you doing?"

She smirked. "I know you're an altar boy, but I don't believe for a minute you're as innocent as you pretend."

A purely destructive fire coursed his veins. "I never said I was."

She slid the envelope to the counter. "Then show me." She slipped off her jacket and tossed it atop.

His heart pounded. "What does Marco Michelli have to do with Vittorio Shepard?"

She pressed into him. "It's all in the letter."

"A letter to whom? And who's it from?"

"I blocked out those names."

He searched her face. There was a glimmer on her eyelids, subtle and exotic. Even her freckles added to the allure.

"Let me see it."

"You can do more than look."

She had twisted his words and her thought drew his gaze down. He shuddered. "I thought you wanted lunch."

"Let's start with dessert." She took hold of the waist of his jeans.

He caught her wrists. "Sybil. I didn't mean to give you the idea—"

"My ideas are my own. And I've had some very creative ones about—" she pressed in close and whispered against his neck—"right here where you cook."

The flames torched him like a sinner at the stake. Was this how Rese felt that day with the molesting employees? There was nothing good, nothing right in it. Even as his blood pounded to have her, he felt sickened. He put her back from him. "You misunderstood."

She dropped her hands to her sides with a knowing glint. "Misunderstood?"

"I thought we were friends."

"Friends?"

Conviction swept him. He had let her believe whatever she wanted, to get what he wanted. She'd made herself clear from the start. But he had to salvage this somehow. "Sybil . . ."

"It's very simple, Lance. You give me what I want; you get what you want."

He was in over his head. "Sybil . . . I'm involved with Rese." She would take that for more than it was, he knew. But the heart of it was true.

"You've got to be kidding." Her face was the picture of scorn.

He swallowed. "No." He wished he'd never invited her into the kitchen. It was Rese's place, and Sybil did not belong. He saw it so clearly now he could hardly believe he'd made the mistake.

Her eyes took the appearance of glacier ice, and he was the insect frozen inside. But the corners of her mouth tipped up. "I only want—"

The back door opened and Star breezed in. Sybil might remember her from the jazz festival or not. In her funk, Star had been all but invisible that night. He prayed now she wouldn't make things worse. She fixed Sybil with an utterly guileless smile. "Hello."

Sybil gave her a withering glance. "Who are you?"

"Lance's fairy godmother. You must be the wicked stepsister."

He closed his eyes, then looked again as a noise came from Sybil's throat. Freckles stark in her paling face, she snatched her jacket from the counter, gave him a deadly stare, then swiped the envelope and stalked out.

He had lost it, the letter that mentioned Nonno Marco. A critical piece, he knew, if Sybil had blocked out names and connected his own. His quest was crumbling, but he looked at Star, her face the image of radiance. *Star power.* He couldn't blame her. In a very real sense she'd saved him.

———

Rese entered the facility with dread. Her expectations had made the place more ominous than it was. Attention had obviously been paid to the reception and waiting areas to portray a level of comfort and ease. A privately run facility with quality care at a cost. No wonder she and her father had never gotten ahead.

As she was ushered into the administrator's office, everyone was friendly and professional.

The office smelled of stale coffee and vinyl blinds. The woman offered her a seat in one of the comfortable chairs in muted hues of green and beige. The nameplate on the desk read Dr. Elsa Whittington. Good thing, because Rese had forgotten the name the moment they were introduced. Dr. Whittington offered her coffee.

"No thanks." She presented her birth certificate and picture ID, which had been requested as proof of her relationship to Elaine Barrett.

Dr. Whittington poured herself a cup of coffee and sat down. "I must say I was relieved to receive your call. I hated the idea of turning your mother's care over to the state."

"I didn't know she was here." Didn't know she was alive.

The doctor sprinkled a packet of sugar substitute into her cup. "Elaine's been in our care a long time."

"Fifteen years."

Dr. Whittington nodded. "I naturally assumed you knew."

"That would be the expectation." In a normal scenario where people told the truth. "I thought she had died."

Dr. Whittington raised her brows delicately.

Get it all out on the table. "The person from Health and Human Services told me she was here. I'm still adjusting to it."

"It must have been a shock."

Rese wished she'd taken the coffee. Her mouth was sawdust. "Why is my mother here?"

"Many of the patients here come for rehab or assistance through a difficult time. Others spend their lives under the careful treatments they need." Dr. Whittington opened the file that lay on the desk. "This is a copy of the court order granting your father guardianship. Also the commitment papers. It was considered in her best interest to have the level of care she receives in this facility."

Rese swallowed. "Did the court commit her?"

"Your father, acting in conjunction with the court's recommendation."

A surge of injustice. Couldn't he have defended her? "What did they say is wrong with her?"

"Paranoid schizophrenia."

Rese ran the words through her mind. They made it sound so . . . disturbed. "What does that mean?" She'd never studied psychology.

"In lay terms, she doesn't have a grasp on reality. Her mind creates voices and images that aren't there, and she interacts with them in dangerous ways."

Rese's head whirled. *"I don't want him to come, Mom. Can't we play by ourselves?"*

"We wouldn't want to hurt his feelings. We must never hurt his feelings."

"But he isn't real!"

She pressed her fingertips to her forehead. That was the first time Mom had slapped her face. Rese swallowed. "Is she cured?"

Dr. Whittington slid more papers toward her. "These are some articles and other materials about the disorder. They'll help you understand the work we're doing, the strides made through medication and behavioral counseling."

"Can I see her?"

The doctor folded her hands. "Ms. Barrett, I'd like to know your expectations."

"I want to take care of her." As she had before? She'd been the one protecting, soothing, and comforting as much as Mom did her. They were . . . equals.

"Take care of her, how?"

"Bring her home." She hadn't thought through the details, had simply imagined freeing Mom from the place Dad put her.

Dr. Whittington removed her glasses and let them hang from the fine chains. Her hazel eyes were rimmed in long sparse lashes. "I won't tell you that's impossible. Elaine has made some strides. But because of her profile, she might not acclimate to a less controlled environment. With your father's death, she became a ward of the state. You would have to gain guardianship before any decisions could be made."

Rese nodded. The woman from the human services agency had said the state took temporary guardianship until she could be located. She would do whatever was required.

"If you are appointed guardian, you would have legal responsibility for her care and safety, and for her actions."

Rese considered that. How accurate were her memories? Had Mom been dangerous, or simply mischievous? Or just afraid of Dad?

Dr. Whittington replaced her glasses and sipped her coffee, then she asked softly, "Do you know why she was committed?"

A well of fear opened up, fear that had no grounding. Where was it coming from? She drew herself up against it. "No."

"It's in the file there. The request to seal her records was denied, due to the criminal nature of her actions."

"Criminal?"

The doctor paused, probably assessing her. "She made an attempt on your life."

Rese stared. Waves of shock rolled through her. "It was an accident."

The doctor shook her head. "She disabled the furnace."

Rese started to shake. "She made me go to bed. Walter wanted . . ."

Dr. Whittington raised her eyebrows. "You know about Walter?"

"I know." Her voice rasped.

Dr. Whittington stood and poured a second cup of coffee. This time Rese accepted it. The black bitter taste was nothing like the wonderful coffees Lance made, and she suddenly wished with everything in her that he was there.

"It wasn't Mom. It was Walter."

Dr. Whittington leaned on the desk. "They are one and the same."

Rese clenched the mug and shook her head. Mom wouldn't have hurt her. Mom loved her, held her, rocked her. They laughed and sang and danced. It was the monster in her head that made her mean.

"Maybe it would be good to see her another time, when you've had a chance to absorb some of this." The same advice Lance had given before.

Her whole purpose today had been to see her mother. She had thought the worst shock was over, just learning her mother was alive. This was infinitely worse. Mom had wanted her dead. Rese wanted to see her, but how could she disguise the pain coursing through her?

Now she recalled her mother standing outside on the sidewalk, emergency lights flashing across her face. She hadn't risked herself. Only Rese. Only her child.

It hurt so much she wasn't sure she could bear it. "I guess I'll come back." She gripped the arms of the chair and stood up.

"Call, and we'll make an appointment with Doctor Jonas. He's had charge of her care for the past three years."

Rese nodded.

"Are you all right?"

"Yes." These were facts. She would deal with it. She couldn't change how it felt, but she didn't have to show it.

"Do you have someone to talk to?"

She nodded, but would she? Could she tell Star, tell Lance her own mother wanted her dead? Her eyes stayed dry as she walked out. Tears were not an option. She'd fallen apart on Lance, and how had it helped? She had to deal with the facts, facts she should have been given long ago. How could you do a project without a blueprint?

The wind blew in gusts across the bridge, buffeting her truck as the thoughts buffeted her mind. She had blamed Dad, but as Lance suggested, there was more to the story. She remembered him carrying her to safety, believing it was too late for her mother. But she had never imagined Mom meant for her to be poisoned with each fearful breath.

A car horn blared, and she jerked the truck back into her lane. She had to focus. Tragedy happened when you weren't careful. She glanced at the folder on the passenger seat and shuddered. How could anyone hate her so much?

CHAPTER TWENTY-EIGHT

Alert.

Aware.

Dreams and memories slip away.

Thoughts tumble.

Tangled. Confused.

Sounds from my mouth are primal.

What I want to say, what I need to say stays locked inside.

Lance. Search, find, know. Make it right.

Angry.

Too late. All too late.

Lance heard Rese drive in. Wiping his hands on his jeans, he went to the front window and watched her turn off the engine, then rest her forehead on the wheel. He wanted to rush out there and hold her. The brush with Sybil had left a sick feeling inside he wished he could purge, but it was not the time for confessions or atonement.

Rese climbed out of the truck, lips moving as she talked herself up, drawing back her shoulders in a semblance of control. She took a folder from the seat, closed the door, and started for the house, her demeanor not quite the sledgehammer in full swing that it used to be, but close.

He met her at the door. "How'd it go?"

"I didn't see her."

"They wouldn't let you?"

Stepping inside, she looked as though she wanted to answer, but stopped. Lance cupped her elbow. "Rese?"

She gripped the folder to her chest. "I have to read about it first. Then

I'll go back." Every line in her body was straight and hard. He knew how her neck would feel under his fingers, the ropes resisting. At the same time she looked like she'd blow over with a single breath.

He caught her other elbow and looked her in the face. "Talk to me, Rese."

"I don't want to."

"You don't process well alone."

She snorted. "What are we going to pierce this time—my navel?"

The image was incriminating, as though she sensed Sybil's presence. But that was his problem. "Don't close me out."

She grew brittle in his hands. "Lance, I've known you three weeks."

Typical operating time for him, rushing in where angels feared to tread, then rushing out again. Maybe she was wise. "Then talk to Star."

She shot him a glance. "Have you told her?"

"You haven't?"

Her glance jerked to the side. "It's complicated."

"You need someone, Rese."

She drew herself up. "No, I don't."

Where was she? Had he imagined their connection that morning, her reluctance to let go? Was this some defensive position? Back off, leave me alone. Should he? She had come to him last night. Somewhere inside she trusted him, but it was her call. "Whatever it is, Rese, God has a plan. Remember His presence."

She seemed to crumple, but she didn't give in. She stepped back. "I need to work on your bed."

Work might be what she needed. Or it might be her mode to dig deeper. But again, it was her call. He let go. "Okay."

Rese dropped the folder on the table and went out to the shed. He looked at it lying there as Sybil's had earlier. He could open it and learn what it was she wouldn't tell him. But those were her secrets, and he had his own.

He would not invade her privacy, but he did wonder what she had learned that brought the walls up between them. Three weeks wasn't long, but they'd connected pretty deeply in that time. He had thought there was something between them, enough to sacrifice Sybil's information. If it weren't for Rese . . . would he have traded sex for answers?

No. Even without his feelings for Rese, he would have resisted Sybil. That was all part of the mess he'd left behind. Sybil saw the remnants of his past in him, but that didn't mean he had to act on it anymore. He would have resisted. He had. But that didn't stop him regretting the lost piece, and it ate at him.

While Rese worked in the shed, the mattress set arrived. He took delivery and directed the movers to the carriage house. He thought Rese would come out, but she didn't. He and Star moved the hammock back to the yard where he gratefully bid it *adieu*. Still no sign of Rese. She must be so deep in her zone, nothing penetrated—or upset enough to ignore things she would normally take charge of. Whichever it was, it gave him the freedom to continue his search.

He returned to the tunnel with a sense of foreboding. The darkness neither welcomed nor repulsed; it simply watched for him to make his own mistakes. He knelt once again beside the skeleton. "Why are you here, Nonno Quillan? Why am I?"

After long moments of silence, he left his ancestor's bones and pressed deeper into the tunnel. Within a dozen steps it became a chamber filled with racks. In the racks, bottles and bottles of wine. A slow breath escaped his lips.

Lance walked the rows, running his fingers over the dusty glass. The crisp wavy label read *DiGratia Vineyard, 1930.*

The DiGratias had come from the Piedmont region, according to Conchessa, highly connected aristocrats who left long before the Fascists came to power, while the regions still warred with each other. He understood better now why Nonna sometimes held herself separate from the predominantly Southern Belmontese, why she carried within her a nobility bordering on scorn. He felt his heritage there in the cellar, a proud, unyielding line.

But that still didn't tell him what he was supposed to do. Lance looked around the dark cellar as though it would give up its secrets simply because he wanted it so much.

Along one wall were empty oak barrels. And now he placed the smell: ancient fermentation. The fruit of the vine, the essence of his family's labor. Treasure? To no one but himself, perhaps.

She should have told him. She had intended to. But when it came to it, she couldn't. Looking into his face, she could not say her mother wanted her dead. Not without dissolving altogether. Lance would have held her, kissed her, made her feel whole. But she wasn't whole. Her mother had tried to kill her. Why?

She couldn't expect a reason. What motivation could there be for killing your child? Rese drilled the holes for the hardware and attached the brackets. She had rubbed in the finish yesterday, and the final coats on some of the pieces were still sealing, but Lance would sleep in his bed tonight.

Work, accomplish, do. It was something concrete she could grasp. She knew that mode, but the folder hung in her mind like a noose, and she was afraid it would strangle her as the fear and poisoned air had done.

"Whatever it is, God has a plan. Remember His presence."

They weren't just words. Lance believed it. Did she? Last night it had seemed possible. But she'd been hopeful last night. Now . . . what had changed besides everything? Dad wasn't a monster. He had protected her from the woman who wanted her dead. Mom wasn't a victim . . . or was she?

Rese pressed her hands to her head, images of that night searing her mind. Mom weeping, begging, being dragged, it seemed, by Walter. *"How can I prove it?"* Her grim despair at whatever answer only she heard, and then . . . Mom, standing outside like a damaged twig swaying in a wind no one else could feel. When Dad told her that Mom was dead, she must have blocked that image, placed her tragically inside the house breathing the same poison, to her death.

If her own mind could be so duplicitous . . . Rese closed her eyes. Her temples throbbed. Maybe there was no absolute reality. Maybe everything was filtered through the mind's impressions and conclusions. She'd tried so hard to make life concrete, like the steel and wood and stone she shaped and placed, bolting and gluing, no margin of error, no miscalculation.

What if life was as flimsy and insubstantial as Star's world, and they were all just sun and rainbow?

––––––––

Lance walked the rows of bottled wine, looking for anything more, anything out of place. It wasn't a thorough search by any stretch, only a start. But each time into the tunnel he drew closer. He could feel it.

Maybe Quillan's presence acted like a silent guard. Could heroism linger? Might his strength, his character, count for something still? Lance shook his head. What mattered was for him to do what he needed to. *Lord, let me do this right. Show me.* But in spite of his need, he couldn't focus on the search, not with Rese so upset. She might think it didn't show, but her mute withdrawal and insular focus told him plenty.

That wasn't his mode. His family smothered grief with words, hugs, and tears, kept it right there where you could taste it. And maybe that was what

Rese needed. At least he could try. He went up and met her coming out of the shed.

"Your bed is done." She held two pieces upright. "You can help me carry it."

She must have been on her way over, and he realized he had timed his exit perfectly. The Lord's answer to his prayer? He had not been down there long, but he might have been. He should not risk going down when she might want to find him. Of course, with Rese that was twenty-four hours a day. They hauled the bed pieces from the shed to his room.

Star watched from her easel as they passed with the headboard between them. "Ah, the nuptial couch."

Rese made no sign she'd heard, but he did. He'd been trying hard not to go there in his thoughts, then with a single salient phrase, Star stripped away his illusions. Sybil's forceful offer had not tempted him, but Rese did without trying. Well, thoughts were one thing; he was not about to break what fragile trust they had by acting on them.

He stood the headboard against the wall and eyed the carved decoration. "This is really nice, Rese." He stroked the scallop, unsurprised at its softness, the smooth perfection of the shape, every curve precise. She'd made the bed for him. He didn't give it the significance Star had, but it still sank in and warmed him. With her hands she had created something for him.

She said, "Let's put it together."

Her stony manner contradicted his thoughts. Maybe it didn't mean anything at all to her. Maybe it had been a chore, and he'd misread her diligence and meticulous effort. They bolted the side-frame pieces to the headboard and then to the footboard, then settled in the box spring and mattress. He straightened. "My neck thanks you."

"I have sheets, but no comforter." Rese looked around the room.

He'd hung the other painting from her stash, a vineyard oil dominated by greens and purples, on the side wall. Since there was no window to offer a view, that picture and the skylight kept it from feeling like a cave. She jutted her chin at the picture. "I could work with that. Do a wine country theme."

"Sure." Though his room décor was hardly the relevant subject. Why was she shutting him out?

"I'll see what I can find and order it. Can you use the blanket until then?"

"What do you think?"

"I think after the hammock anything would do."

"Anything but the love seat."

She stiffened . . . annoyed by the reminder of last night? She'd been vulnerable then, but now she meant to tough it out alone. Brad had said she shut down the other time and didn't speak for weeks. She was talking now, but hardly communicating.

"I'll get going on the wardrobe."

"No." He took her hands. She obviously didn't expect an argument. But even formidable as she was, he would not let her cement the wall around her. It wasn't so much that he'd be left out as that she'd be trapped inside.

"Come on." He led her out, Baxter licking their joined hands as he tugged her to his bike and held out her helmet.

"Where are we going?" It was more demand than query, but she hadn't refused.

"Nowhere." He scooped her onto the bike and climbed in front. "Hold on." He took the road north toward the commercial vineyards, some large and glamorous, others family operations. As they passed the various gated and decorated entrances and the rows and rows of grapevines between, Rese's stiffness eased. A few more miles and she moved with him, finding the rhythm, unresisting.

He rested his arm over her thigh, and her hands were on his waist. There were ways to communicate without words. The road had always called and soothed and made him forget. A person could count on that. Space. Distance. Motion.

He picked up speed, and the nubby rows of vines fanned by on either side, bright flashes of flower beds ornamenting their edges. He had no destination in mind, just the rise and sway of the road, but he sensed Rese unwinding, and that was definitely his purpose. The haze had cleared and halcyon sky crowned the fertile hills. He drank it in, the hum and vibration of the bike enhancing the experience.

After a while, Rese's arms came around his waist as they cruised, leaning together, joined in the motion. He could go on forever that way, but if she had softened enough to hold him, she might be able to talk. He looked for a place to stop. They had left the cultivated fields and entered untended landscape, rustic in its natural beauty. He pulled the bike off the road into a narrow dirt track that wove down and away, scented by the pale grasses on each side and culminating at a narrow creek with its own verdant aromas.

He pulled to a stop, secured the bike and stood. As Rese removed her helmet, he captured her gaze. "Talk to me, Rese. Tell me what's wrong."

She stood a long minute, staring at him with eyes of glass, then she said in a flat tone, "My mother tried to kill me."

He absorbed her words, stunned, but not surprised. Not with everything else.

"She disabled the furnace."

No accidental malfunction. "I'm sorry."

She glanced away. "It wasn't really Mom. It was Walter."

"How does that work?" He had no experience to draw from and didn't want to argue from a point of ignorance. Something he'd learned from Tony. *"Try having the facts before you open your mouth, Lance. That way you don't look stupid."*

Rese expelled a breath. "I don't know. I guess the file they gave me will explain it." She headed for a wide flat rock on the creek's bank, her posture still demanding "no trespassing" but no longer "trespassers will be shot."

She removed her shoes, tucked her socks inside them, and rolled the legs of her pants. Then she dipped her feet in up to the pointy protrusions of her ankle bones. He joined her there, reminded of the silly lyrics he and Rico had put together by the fountain at Lincoln Center. *Ratta-patta dip-a-dip doe. Ina watta tip, tip, toe. Splashy, flashy ina da eye. Outta da watta drip, drip dry.* He could see Rico's quick, narrow hands drumming the beat on the concrete edge. He had found a rhythm in everything and drawn more than one glare from the sisters at Saint Martin's for employing his desktop during class.

The water pushed up and over her seemingly disjointed extremities, speckling her ankles and calves in its insistence. "I used to do this with Mom. We'd pretend we were mermaids dipping our tails." Eyes closed, her face softened with the memory as she held her feet against the current. She couldn't stop the hurt any more than her feet stayed the flow of the creek, but she was trying so hard not to let it show.

He circled her with his arm and prayed silently: strength, comfort, grace.

After a moment, she sighed. "You always know what to do."

"Not even close." How could he anticipate the creek providing a good memory to counter the hurt? That might be the Holy Spirit, but he didn't take credit there. "Hitting the road usually helps." He sensed the barrier coming down. She had trusted him with the facts if not the emotions. He squeezed her shoulder. "Thank you for telling me."

She stared into the water. "You'd have forced it out eventually."

"Is that how it feels?"

She slackened against him. "I don't know."

"You just can't handle everything alone."

She pulled her knees up, planting her soggy heels on the rock. "I wish you'd stop that."

"What?"

"Looking inside me like . . . X-ray vision or something."

Her feet had gathered a film around the edge he wanted to wipe off, but the thought of touching them was too intimate.

She said, "I didn't expect it. What they told me."

"How could you?"

She shrugged. "It seems like you should know things, big things like your dad's going to die, or your mother wanted you to. It shouldn't be a surprise."

"Would you really want that?" He gave her a moment to think about it. "How would you go on if you knew in advance what you'd have to go through?"

"I'd rather see it coming." Her face hardened. "You can't block a blow from behind."

He picked a grass stem and tossed it into the creek. "Some blows you can't block at all."

"That isn't fair. Everyone should have a fighting chance."

He thought of Tony and all the others as tons of steel and concrete turned to ash around them. The image had haunted less frequently, but hit now with dizzying force, the whole world a shifting torrent of hatred. His chest squeezed; his throat constricted.

"Lance?"

He drew out of it painfully. He was supposed to be helping her. Giving her the answers. There had to be one somewhere. God's will and free will, the warp and weft of life.

"Are you okay?"

He slid his arm from her shoulders and took her hand. "This isn't about me."

She looked into his face. "It helps."

"What helps?"

"Knowing I'm not alone, that everyone has junk."

He swallowed. "That could be a bumper sticker."

A flicker of a smile found her lips. "I didn't think when I said that. I mean about Tony, about having a chance."

"Yeah." His throat tightened again. "Sometimes it doesn't make sense."

"Then what?"

"Then you get through and try to be better for it."

"Better how?"

He shrugged. "Life peels us like onions and each layer is softer and sweeter."

She snorted. "You're hoping."

He hadn't meant it as a personal critique. He raised her chin. "I like you just the way you are."

"That's why my ears are pierced, and I've worn a skirt for the first—"

"That's just trappings. It doesn't change the real you. And the more I see, the more I—" He'd almost said love. There it was, his Achilles' heel.

"The more you what? Want to peel the onion?"

Sybil would do something with that line for sure. "The more I like. Inside that hands-off façade is a special woman."

"You wouldn't understand *hands-off* if it was plastered on my forehead and wrapped with barbed wire."

A masterful deflection. She might have received more compliments if she didn't fend them off with a bat. His gaze sank to her lips.

"You have that look again."

"What look?"

"Like I'm a nice fat chicken."

He huffed a laugh. "Chicken?"

"Soften her up with a little marinade, season her just right, then into the frying pan she goes."

"Rese."

"Admit it."

"I have never thought of you as a chicken."

She raised her chin. "Tough and stringy maybe, but you have a cure for that. You have a cure for everything. 'Let me make you a steamer.' 'Cry on my shoulder.' 'Don't handle anything without me.'"

"Now, Rese."

"You are smooth, Lance. So smooth I didn't see it coming."

"See what?"

"That I would feel—" She expelled her breath. "No man I've known has let me see him struggle."

"You'd have taken their heads off with a sledgehammer."

"What about you?"

"I have no self-protection mechanism. Rico destroyed it."

"Rico?"

"My buddy. He was the littlest kid, but he picked the biggest fights."

"That you fought for him?"

"Usually with. He wouldn't be left out."

She searched his face. "Is that what you're doing now, fighting my fight?"

"I'd rather fight with you than against you."

"Why?"

"Your irresistible charm."

She snorted. "Right."

He spread his hands. "You can't argue with results, Rese. You've hooked me in somehow."

"Me?" She huffed. "I said business."

"It's just that, what comes out here—"he touched her mouth—"isn't what's in here." He pressed his palm to her heart, felt its rhythm.

She drew a ragged breath. "Lance . . ."

He took his hand away. "The thing is, I'm falling in love with you."

She expelled a breath as though he'd punched her. He hadn't meant to. Maybe he shouldn't have said it aloud, but his feelings for her were superceding his cause. He wasn't sure what to do about that, but at the moment he didn't care.

"I don't expect anything."

Her face pinched. "You've expected something from the moment you walked in."

She had it more right than she knew. But it wasn't what she thought. *Tell her the truth.* "Rese, I did not intend to feel this way. I came here . . ." The words stuck in his throat. "You've taken me by surprise."

Her hands clenched and unclenched. "It's a little shocking on my end too. Like grabbing a frayed power cord."

"Yowser." He caught her hand and kissed it.

She laughed. "You really are impossible."

He drew her close. "So I'm told."

CHAPTER TWENTY-NINE

Face hanging like a sack.
Tongue a lump of wool.
Too many things to say. Too many things unsaid.
Words trapped in flesh.
Wah, wah—worthless sounds. Worthless thoughts.
Wah, wah, wah.

As the Harley came to a stop in the driveway, Rese took off the snug helmet and wished she could remove everything else that easily. The hurt still pressed in on her, but she couldn't show it. Lance had gained too much ground already. If they were playing capture the flag, she might as well hand the flag over, but they were playing with her heart, and right now it felt a little battered.

She'd been downright philosophical with her one previous crush. Of course, that had been on Brad, and she would rather have died than let him see it. Thankfully she'd grown out of that before they'd vied for the second crew. But if she'd hidden it once . . .

Who was she fooling? Lance was not Brad. He saw inside her, knew her thoughts and feelings before she did. He knew things she'd told no one else. It was as though he'd climbed inside her mind and taken over, his thoughts replacing hers. Her life flipped before him like the pages of a book blown open in the wind. Everything he wanted to know and more.

She'd never felt so transparent, mainly because no one had ever wanted to see. They'd believed the front she put on, taken her at face value, but not Lance. He demanded honesty, even if it meant baring her deepest hurts. And she didn't seem to have any resistance, because when he took her in his arms . . .

Star joined them at the bike, her gaze penetrating. Rese's chin was raw from Lance's, her face warm, and she had hoped to slip inside and recover. Star must see it all. But as Lance climbed off the bike, she turned to him, a fragile pride lighting her face. "It's done."

"Your painting?"

Star nodded. And just like that the focus shifted.

"Can I see it?" Lance's enthusiasm didn't sound feigned, but did he realize how important this was for Star, the risk she had taken to create again, and to show it?

Star desperately feared failure. Instead of pursuing her gift, she had lost herself in her roles at the Renaissance festivals and hidden her paintings away, those she ever finished. The recent fiasco with Maury hadn't helped. Rese frowned. This was the quickest she'd ever finished something, and the shortest recovery, but it would take very little to destroy her confidence.

Rese tried to catch Lance's eye, but Star had his full attention. They started toward the garden together. *Make him like it.* A prayer? Fine. *If you're as real as Lance says, don't let him hurt Star.* Not that he would intend to, just . . . he might not understand.

In the slanting evening light, the garden had a magic of its own. Lance's doing. He'd cleaned it out and built new beds that were coming to life with pungent scents that vied with the sweet florals. He must have planted herbs. She hadn't paid much attention, but she saw it now with Star's eyes and agreed. It was Lance's garden.

He stepped around to view the painting in the easel. Star stayed on the other side and studied his face. She would read every nuance, and any disapproval, even something as slight as incomprehension, would spear her. Lance's eyes moved over the canvas. Rese saw surprise, intrigue, and pleasure. He liked it. Or at least he appeared to.

Rese stepped around and looked at the painting. In Star's flamboyant style was a cacophony of color suggesting the flowers, leaves, and ferns, and worked into the green recesses was the profile of a face. Incredible that she could tell that with the image formed only of leafy shadows and stems.

"The elf grove," he said, and it meant more to Star than any praise. He got it; he saw what she intended. "It's amazing, Star."

She threw up her arms and came to a stop beside him. "It's you. The elf lord."

Lance nodded. "I see that." He turned to her. "Is it ready to hang?"

"It can dry on the wall. You'll smell the paint though."

"That's okay." He lifted the canvas and studied it again, then carried it into the carriage house as Star opened the door. He circled the main room, studying the walls. "Got a hammer and nails, Rese?"

She went to the shed, a warmth of gratitude filling her. She had come home from the mental health center numb and resistant, but Lance had broken through with tenderness. Now he'd shown Star more kindness than he might even realize. Was he real?

He was more like the being in her room that night than any real person she'd known. Could that being have taken form and—Good grief, she was crazy! Could someone invisible kiss and hold her? A cold dread washed over. Wasn't that exactly what Mom had thought? Was Walter as real to her as Lance?

The realization struck again that Mom had tried to kill her. She gripped the hammer. How could Mom love someone, real or imagined, enough to do something so terrible? And what about the love for her daughter? Rese gritted her teeth against the pain. The raw edge of it staggered her. Had she imagined that love, projected her own?

She scattered the assortment of extra nails with her palm and chose two that matched. She had told Lance, but she hadn't let him see how it hurt. Because she didn't trust him? How could she?

With hammer and nails, she headed back to the carriage house. Lance had leaned the painting against the wall beneath the place he'd chosen for it. He reached for the tools, but she said, "I can do it."

She had brought concrete nails, and with firm blows, she drove them into the wall. "For now you'll have to hang it by the frame of the canvas. I might be able to rig a wire onto it later, but we'd have to lay it face down. Not a good idea wet." She breathed in the potent smell of the oil paint and hoped for Lance's sake it dried quickly.

Star stepped back as he hung the painting on the nails. "You'll have to frame it yourself if you want one. I'm broke."

"That's the least I can do." He seemed as pleased and impressed as he'd been with the bed, and for the first time, Rese considered how little he owned. What was he doing with hardly more than his bike and guitar? With his varied and competent skills he could be well established somewhere, not cooking in a bed-and-breakfast for room and board.

She stepped back beside Star. The painting added color and energy to the room, and showed how badly he needed furniture. The thought of building it for him warmed her. That was a normal sort of pleasing, of giving, though the furniture would in fact belong to the inn, she supposed. Star's painting too? Why was she even thinking about that? Lance wasn't going anywhere.

Star's stomach growled. "Are you cooking?"

He cocked his head. "Let's order Chinese."

"Takeout?" Rese hadn't imagined he knew the concept.

"With fortune cookies!" Star draped both their necks with her arms.

Lance laughed. "Why not?"

With Star half dangling between them and Baxter barking alongside, they headed for the house. She could feel Star's excitement in the trembling of her arms. She was almost dangerously exuberant. But she had a right to be. She'd accomplished something wonderful. That should matter; it should somehow balance the bad. She could be happy for Star. Truly.

Lance batted Baxter's head in a playful tussle before motioning Rese into the kitchen before him. As she passed, he caught her gaze and washed her with warmth and reassurance. She'd received the cruelest news of her life, and he'd taken away the sting.

Star called the restaurant, ordering enough for a week. "I'm buying," she said.

With what, Rese wondered, but Lance took out his wallet. "No way. I owe you big time for that painting."

"I'm not selling it. Money is worthless. What matters is karma. The more joy you give, the more you get—a great circle of generous thoughts."

Lance studied her gently. "Then I'm providing the celebration. Just a little joy back at you." He smiled. "For the pleasure I'll have from the painting."

Rese's heart clutched up inside her.

"You really like it?" Star pressed her hands to her chest.

"I really do."

She fairly quivered, the praise working in her like a drug. "It's my own technique." She explained how she layered the paint to give the hidden image depth and make it appear to emerge from the surface. Whether Lance understood it or not, he gave her his full attention.

Rese washed up at the sink, refusing to begrudge Star her moment. She deserved Lance's appreciation. But did he realize what he was setting into motion?

He leaned on the counter. "It's effective. Mind-grabbing."

Star's breath escaped in a rush. "Mind-grabbing."

"I mean . . ."

"No, don't explain." Star closed her eyes and mouthed the phrase. When she opened her eyes, they sparkled with tears. "That's what Maury couldn't see. He said it was a cheap trick. Poster art."

Lance frowned. "Who's Maury?"

"My persecutor." Star crossed her wrists as though bound. "'It is an heretic that makes the fire, not she which burns in't.'"

"And no one needs a heretic." Rese tried to catch Lance's eye, to ward him off that subject, but he kept the conversation there, drawing out details that Star had not shared before, and amazingly she responded without disintegrating.

Rese looked from one to the other. It was the same thing he'd done with her, making her voice the pain, sharing the burden of it. The twinge grew to a cynical pang. He turned and met her eyes before she could hide it. She hated that. His transparency was one thing; hers, another altogether.

Star sat down at the table, shoving a wad of spirals behind her ear, but her hair had survived the talk of Maury, and except for the red rims of her eyes, she'd survived it too. There'd been no hysterics, no talk of not making it, though her hands still shook. She reached for the folder. "What's this?"

Jarred from her concern, Rese thrust her hand out. "It's nothing."

But Star had already opened it and read the facility letterhead. Her brow puckered. "Mental Health Center? Elaine Barrett?"

Rese dropped her hand. Her throat squeezed tight. She didn't want to discuss Mom with Star, not now, not at all. Star's mother had been irresponsible and oblivious, but she had not tried to kill her. The impact of that hit her again, but at the same time she felt fiercely protective.

Star stared up at her. "Elaine's alive?"

Rese took the folder and clutched it to her chest. "I just found out."

Star let out a mournful sigh. "'Too much of water hast thou, poor Ophelia, and therefore I forbid my tears.'"

"Star." Lance chided softly. He didn't understand the impact this would have; how, to Star, Mom's miraculous death was now lessened by her resurrection. She understood Star's shock and the thoughts behind it. If one mother could come back from the dead, how could she hope to be free of her own?

But Rese hadn't wanted to be free of hers. She'd mourned her. "She's been in the hospital since the night . . . of the accident. I don't know much more than that." Only that Mom wanted her dead. "I guess I'm responsible for her now."

Star jammed her fingers to her head. "'Thus hath the candle singed the moth. O, these deliberate fools!'"

The doorbell rang, and Lance went to pay for their food. Star stared at her, then sprang up and trailed after him, already putting it out of her mind. Rese set the folder aside, thankful for the interruption. They came back, laden, and set the wire-handled white boxes on the table. Star pulled napkins, chopsticks, packets of soy sauce, and fortune cookies from the bag.

As hungry as she had been minutes ago, Rese wasn't sure she wanted to eat.

Lance took both their hands and blessed the food. Then he added, "And give us wisdom to know your heart and purpose, Lord."

Chopsticks raised, Star appraised him. "Oh, for such faith, I would sell my soul."

"That's all it takes." Lance smiled.

"My ill and tattered soul would buy me but a moment's audience wherein to earn me everlasting flames."

"That's not how it works, Star. The more ill and tattered, the greater the grace."

For a moment Star looked hungrier for that grace than the meal before her. But her issues were deep, and the thought of mercy incomprehensible. Rese could hardly find an instance of it in Star's entire life. Or her own, it seemed. And suddenly she wanted there to be something more; she wanted it painfully.

A cloud of aromatic steam rose up from the first box Star opened. She plunged in with her chopsticks and pinched a wad of long brown noodles like a wig from the carton. She heaped more food onto her plate than Lance, and she'd eat it all too. Whether she'd keep it down, Rese wouldn't hazard a guess. Her agitation was evident, but she'd always had the knack of ignoring whatever she didn't want to face.

When they had made their dent in the tangy-hot and sweetly piquant food, Lance closed up the rest and hauled it to the refrigerator. Star watched him as she had throughout the meal, then stood with a dramatic flourish of her arms. "The night beckons. I must away." Which meant she was going out to find comfort in whatever form it took, and there was no telling when she'd come back.

Lance watched her head for the door in swift, spirited steps, then returned to the table. "She's really leaving?"

"Why wouldn't she?"

He sat down. "I thought she would support you."

"It doesn't work that way."

He took her hand. "Seems a little one-sided."

Rese shrugged. "The day Star sees me as anything but her anchor, I'll faint."

"Strong, tough Rese." He squeezed her hand. "Even your meltdown was momentous."

Something she'd rather forget. "How are your sides?"

"Fine. It's *in*side where I'm in trouble."

"So you say." She still didn't buy it. Not when people she trusted had lied and tried to kill her. She was better off expecting the mouse to jump out, the whispered taunts and rough laughter. Better off keeping her face and heart hidden, especially with the way Star had looked at him.

He leaned close and kissed her, scattering her resolve like a flock of butterflies. "You taste like teriyaki." He made even that sound endearing, but she was not giving in.

She looked into his face. "I know what you're doing."

"What?"

"Just what you did with Star."

He tipped his head. "I've never kissed Star."

He may as well have. "You took her pain and gave her strength." He'd actually taken on her own role and played it better.

He caressed her knuckles with his thumb. "Have I upset you?"

"Of course not." She reached for the folder. "I guess I should get it over with."

He touched her earlobe. "You survived these."

She glared. "Directly provoked by your baiting."

He laughed. "Can I help it if you're compulsively competitive?"

Rese couldn't argue with that. She looked down at the folder and drew a hard breath, wishing the pain was as tangible as the stud piercing her ear. "I knew something was wrong. I heard the whispers. But I denied it. Seeing it here—"she pressed her palm to the folder—"makes it real."

"It's better to know, Rese. Facing the fact that Tony was gone was easier than the awful wondering."

Maybe. But ignorance had worked for a long time. She opened the folder, took out the contents, and laid the sheets before them. Lance sat as close as their chairs would go. He rested his arm across the back of hers, and they read the first informational page together. At the second paragraph, a giant fist caught her solar plexus.

Lance sensed it and cupped her nape. "What's the matter?"

It was the genetic connection that had socked her in the stomach. She touched the section with her finger. "I wondered. But I didn't know I might really . . ."

"Thirteen percent isn't very high."

Rese swallowed. "To your non-related one percent." Lots of factors contributed, including viruses which struck indiscriminately, but genetic predisposition raised the stakes considerably.

"That's still eighty-seven-percent chance you won't have it at all. I'd bet on those odds."

Rese stared into his face. How could he be so nonchalant? But she knew how. They weren't his statistics. She suddenly recalled something Brad had said when she was unresponsive after Dad's death. He'd leaned close to Jake and murmured, "Hope she isn't schizo."

He'd known? Had Dad told him? Rese pressed her hands to her head. "Lance, what did Brad say to you when he came here?"

"He wondered how you were."

"Because?" His hesitation was enough. "He thought I was psychotic?"

"He thought your reaction was extreme, but the circumstances were too."

She clenched her hands. "Did he mention Mom?"

Lance nodded. "He told me she was schizophrenic."

"You knew she was alive?"

"Would I keep that from you?"

"I don't know." Fury was building inside that threatened another explosion. "Why would Brad know about her?"

"Your dad told him."

Of course. Brad was the bosom buddy. Who else knew? The rest of the crew? No wonder they'd kept trying to put her over the edge.

Lance leaned back. "Brad said your dad asked him to look out for you if something happened to him."

"I couldn't look out for myself if I was psychotic, could I?"

"I think it was more generic."

"He knew about Mom."

Lance rubbed his face. "Just her diagnosis, Rese. He said nothing about her being alive."

"They all probably thought—"

"You have no idea what anyone thought, or what they knew." He clasped her arm. "Would Brad have come looking if he thought you were crazy? He wants you back on the job, Rese."

That was true. But it didn't excuse it. For any of them. How many more times would Dad stab her from the grave? She rubbed her eyes.

He slid his hold to her hand. "Maybe we should wait until tomorrow." His voice was gentle, offering her an out.

She shook her head and gripped the paper, but the next section was just as bad, describing the symptoms. Lack of emotional response. Lance's words—*"Got a concept of emotion?"* Was her self-control a "negative" symptom of the disease? Onset for women was typically between age twenty-five and thirty. She'd be twenty-five next month. She started to shake.

Lance took her in his arms. "You're reading too much into this."

"You said it, Lance. No concept of emotion."

"You were grieving, Rese. You've had serious stress. And you've had to guard yourself. I know what all that looks like. You're not psychotic."

He couldn't know that. She had shut down at Dad's death. They called it shock, but catatonia was more like it, and that, too, was a symptom. "You might want to cut your losses now and run."

"Is that who you think I am?"

"You have no idea what Dad went through. Look how he reacted."

He sighed. "Let that go for now. This is about your mom. Read it for her." He clasped her hand tighter. "Let's see what we're up against."

We? How could he say we? Because he didn't know. He didn't really understand. He hadn't lived with it.

Walls came up inside, and even as they built they terrified her. How could she know what was normal self-protection and what was schizophrenic non-reaction? She took in the rest of the information on the introduction sheet, the drugs that were used to treat it, the positive recovery or control rate when caught early and medicated with dopamine blockers, the drugs that had been in use since the '50s. Why had Mom not been medicated? If Dad knew, and he must have if he told Brad . . . then why?

She took up the court order that had made her father the legal guardian.

State of California, Superior Court
City and County of San Francisco
Case No. 1982-CV–12875
In the matter of Elaine Barrett, by her Next Friend Vernon Barrett,
Petitioner.
ORDER GRANTING MOTION TO APPOINT GUARDIAN AND
APPOINT CONSERVATOR OF ASSETS.

Rese shook her head, skimming through the legal jargon that noted Dad would heretofore be known as Petitioner and Mom as Barrett, getting the gist that Dad was given control of Mom's destiny based on testimony from the examining doctors and other witnesses. *Mrs. Walden, a neighbor of Petitioner and Barrett . . . Georgette Douglas, sister of Petitioner . . .* Aunt Georgie? Rese had stayed with her through the "funeral" after leaving the hospital. Aunt Georgie had testified against Mom?

There were also emergency reports of two different suicide attempts and an occasion of violence toward a person Rese didn't know. She had no memory of any of that. She closed her eyes and tried, but nothing came. Maybe she'd blocked it. She half expected them to surface as the other one had. Her mother standing outside, swaying, but no look of grief or fear or any other emotion.

Mom cried, but only in the wake of Walter. And the laughter had sometimes been so inappropriate. As with the kitten she and Star had found dead. That was a memory she hadn't recalled, but it blazed to life now. There were more. But she didn't want them.

> *Because of the medical condition and symptomology evidenced in the record, and based on the weight of the testimony of the witnesses, the Court concludes that Barrett lacks sufficient competency to manage the ordinary affairs of daily life, such that a Guardian should be appointed to take charge of her welfare until such time as she may regain such competency.*

So the Court had allowed for improvement in her condition, for a cure? The other information made that sound unlikely. But not impossible. Rese pinched the bridge of her nose, afraid to hope for what might never be, and more afraid of what might.

She'd thought Mom trying to kill her was the worst of it. At least then she'd only be dead. This . . . the specter of actually being like Mom, seeing things that weren't there, doing things that no one in her right mind would do, being a burden and a danger . . . She felt too battered even to think.

Was it happening already? Her thoughts jolted. If the records were true, her mother had changed, blocked, rationalized, and perceived things differently than they were. A cold chill passed through her.

"What's the matter?"

Rese couldn't admit her doubts, her insecurity that even Lance existed. Hadn't he simply shown up at her door? In her grief and stress, she could have conjured him. From her loneliness, created him. What real person would care about her as he did?

"Hey." He stroked her arm.

Goose bumps raised up under his fingers.

"Rese . . ."

She couldn't even ask him. No figment of her imagination would admit it. But it made more sense than a real man showing up to be everything she needed. How could he love her in so short a time? If he was real, he'd see all her flaws. Waves of horror coursed through her, and she shook her head, vainly denying what grew more apparent by the second.

But Star saw him too. She talked to him, she . . . Was Star another? A friend conjured from the isolation of her childhood? Someone even crazier than herself to ease the stigma? The chill made her teeth chatter.

Lance chafed her hands. "Talk to me, Rese. What are you thinking?"

"Don't you know?" No wonder he could read her mind. He was part of it. Her whole body shook. She was crazy. Just like Mom.

CHAPTER THIRTY

He had seen signs of stress in his sisters, his mother in the shock of grief. But this was different. Rese looked as though she'd disintegrate. Her lips were tinged blue, and she didn't seem to be drawing enough air. Her limbs had stiffened, and there was some primal terror in her eyes.

"Talk to me, Rese."

She shook her head, pressing her eyes closed, then looking again as though she expected him to disappear.

"I can't help if you won't tell me what's wrong." He imagined Brad in his position, trying to get her to talk as she'd sat covered in her father's blood. He started to rise.

She clutched his wrist. "What are you doing?"

"Calling an ambulance."

"No! They'll lock me up."

Lord! Was she having a breakdown? "They won't lock you up, Rese. They'll treat you for shock."

She clung to him. "They'll make you disappear."

Disappear? He stared into her face, trying to fathom the twisted paths she'd taken from the information on the page. *Jesus, give me a clue.* "Tell me what's going on, or I'm making that call." He didn't want to sound harsh, but she was scaring the daylights out of him.

"I don't care if you're not real. I can't go through this without you."

Not real. Disappear. He swallowed as the realization dawned. She had jumped to a crazy conclusion, scaring herself senseless and losing touch with reality. He closed both her hands in his. "Stop it."

His tone jarred her. She looked into his face.

"I'm not some figment of your imagination."

Her breath came in sharp gasps.

"You might be having a panic attack, but that's pretty understandable with the number of blows you've received in too short a time without letting yourself grieve. Geez, Rese, if you'd just cry like a normal woman . . ." Bad choice of words. "You're not crazy."

"How do you know?" Her voice was flat. "Can you prove you're real?"

He expelled a short laugh. "Well, I've had to prove myself a lot, but never in quite that way." He searched her face, trying to see things from her side. Then he pushed up from his chair, taking her with him. "Come on." He tugged her out the kitchen door, through the garden to the hedge. In the deepening twilight it was difficult to find the gap, but he did and pressed through into Evvy's yard.

"What are you. . . ?"

He rapped on Evvy's back door, circling Rese in his arm and pressing her tight to his side. Her shaking had subsided, but that wasn't enough. He wanted to purge her doubts completely.

Evvy opened the door, leaning heavily on her cane. "What in blazes . . ."

"Sorry to bother you, Evvy. But do you see me?"

"As clear as the end of my nose. What's this all about?"

Rese sagged against him.

"Just a little concern Rese was having."

"Well, if she thinks you're going to disappear, she ought to take a closer look." Evvy jabbed a finger at Lance, then fixed her gaze on Rese. "That man's in love, sweetie. I know what it looks like."

Not exactly what he'd intended, but he'd admitted as much already. "Thank you, Evvy. Have a wonderful night."

"I'll laugh myself to sleep. You two are better than a sitcom."

Rese would strangle him if she wasn't so relieved. A sitcom? All she needed was to be the new neighborhood attraction. She'd been there already, thank you. But how else could he have convinced her? Warmth was infusing her limbs even in the evening's cool air as she followed him back through the hedge.

"Wanna try the neighbors on the other side?"

"No."

"Anyone down the street?"

"No!" At least Evvy had drawn a different conclusion, thought it a love spat, not a case of altered reality. He'd made his point, and she didn't need to be paraded around like a freak.

They went inside, and he sat her down at the table. "I think it's time you experienced the Bronx egg cream."

"I'm not hungry."

"It's not food."

She blinked. "You said egg—"

"I did. But it doesn't have eggs or cream." He went to the pantry and took out a bottle. "Genuine Fox's U-bet chocolate syrup."

He thought chocolate syrup would help when she was reeling from imagining Mom's world? Waves of sorrow coursed over her as she watched him make her drink.

"Two parts milk, one part chocolate, and seltzer poured over the back of a spoon. That's essential to form the head. Don't let anyone tell you different. People have other ways to do it, but this is the only way to make a perfect egg cream."

What was he rattling on about? How could he think she cared when her own mind could be . . .

He brought the thing and placed it between her hands. "Drink up."

She took a sip, coating her upper lip with froth. "Chocolate soda?"

"Made any other way with other ingredients, sure. But this is an egg cream."

"Why is it called that?"

"I have no idea."

Maybe she wasn't the only one losing her mind. She pressed her fingers and thumb to her eye sockets.

Lance pulled her hand away. "Rese, do you really think if you made me up you'd have put a diamond in my ear?"

She licked the milk from her lip. "If I was crazy enough."

"Well, you're not. You'd have come up with some truck-driving, cigarette-smoking, hammer-wielding hotshot."

The description materialized into the person she probably would have conjured, and a blush burned her cheeks. *Don't let him notice.* Fat chance.

He tipped her chin up. "Too true?"

She glared. "Maybe. A long time ago."

"Brad?"

How did he do that? If he wasn't a figment of her mind, how did he get inside and know her thoughts? She tried to break his gaze, but he wouldn't let her go.

"Does he know?"

"No!"

"How old were you? Twelve? Thirteen?"

"None of your business."

He let go of her chin and nudged the glass toward her. "Drink your egg cream. It's a masterpiece." He got up and went out the back door. She followed him with her eyes. When had it grown dark? The scent of frothy chocolate rose up, and she sipped the drink. It was tasty, even if she didn't understand the fuss. But that was Lance, all worked up over things she didn't get. Were men so different?

She sighed. Halfway between her age and Dad's, Brad had been her primary competition and number one annoyance. She could well imagine Dad telling him the things he'd kept from her. If not the son he never had, Brad was at least the friend and partner Dad wanted. She worked her tail off just to measure up, to prove that she could do anything better than Brad. And somewhere in that effort, she'd worked up a school-girl crush.

As she was now? Didn't Lance annoy her every bit as much? More. But that was where the similarities ended. She could never have imagined him—if it worked that way. But would Mom have come up with Walter if she had a choice? Rese pressed her fingers to her temple. How was she ever going to figure this out?

Lance returned, guitar in hand. He glanced into her glass, set the guitar against the wall and waited. She drank it dutifully, then carried the empty glass to the sink, soaped and rinsed it, and overturned it to dry.

Lance nodded toward her door. "Go get ready for bed."

"I won't sleep."

"Yes, you will."

She didn't argue. Arguing with Lance was like telling the sky not to rain. She left him in the kitchen, dressed in her jersey pajamas, brushed her teeth automatically, and washed her face. As she started down the narrow hall, Lance poked his head through the doorway. "Can I pass?"

She glared. "Like you need permission." He'd used the computer in her office, even had her password. That door had never been a barrier, in his mind anyway.

He came through. "Well, I haven't gone into your bedroom, but I promise I'll be appropriate."

She sighed. "I'm not even sure what is appropriate." And in her current mood, she didn't care. She was overwhelmed and too shaken to even cry like a "normal" woman.

He motioned her into the bedroom and pointed to her bed. "In you go."

Exactly when had he appointed himself her keeper? But she climbed under the comforter as he took the overstuffed chair and placed his guitar across his knee. "You're singing me to sleep?"

"That's right. And the sooner you drop off the better—no reflection on my talent."

She settled into the down. "It'll be talent, all right, if you can put me to sleep after . . . everything."

"No thinking. Close your eyes."

"I'd rather watch you." But she obeyed.

He started a melodious picking and Rese rocked her head into the pillow. "Sing me your songs."

"Any one in particular?"

"All of them." Then she would pretend to sleep so he would go.

But whether it was the power of suggestion, or the memory of their last success, or just the comfort of Lance, she grew drowsy. One song ran into another, and the timbre of his voice and the tones of his guitar captured her thoughts and held them mute. She sighed as he kissed her softly, but the click of her door barely registered.

Lance set the guitar down and sat at the table with the papers before him. He'd been more focused on Rese than the information before. Now he read in closer detail, taking in the magnitude of her predicament. It was daunting. But she didn't understand his nature if she thought he'd leave now.

The greater her need, the stronger his desire to stand with her. He had no experience with this particular scenario, but the thought of leaving her to deal with it alone was inconceivable. He'd fallen for her in his typical head-long fashion, but there was more this time, that sense of connection that had gripped him from the start. He might just see this one through to the end. The thought was sobering. It would be a first.

Rese was not a woman he'd have picked out in a crowd. Not that she wasn't attractive; she was. Attractive, amusing, annoying, engaging . . . but she was daunting too. In the past, he'd avoided anyone who might ensnare him. Rese had seemed the safest thing yet. But she compelled, provoked, invigorated. And she'd managed a grip he wasn't sure he could break. Wasn't sure he wanted to.

Lord? He bowed his head in prayer. Nonno Quillan lay unmarked in the cellar, and Nonna's secrets were still undiscovered. But Rese's fear had so filled the kitchen he'd tasted it. Her whole future had been overshadowed, and she needed him. At least for now, he would give her whatever he had.

A sense of peace came with that decision. He would walk her through this, no matter what. Nonna would understand. He could not be double-minded right now. Whatever he found, whatever he learned he would hold until he'd done what he could for Rese. He had to make a choice, and this one seemed best.

Star was no help to her, and who else did Rese have? He gathered the papers and put them back into the folder. She might be Star's anchor, but this current was too strong for her to stand against alone. He glanced toward her room, heard only silence. Then he went to the carriage house. The smell of the oil paint overcame the usual scent of the cellar and confirmed his decision to let that go for now.

CHAPTER THIRTY-ONE

Heavy.
Hands like dough. Useless.
Squeeze the ball.
Squeeze.
Useless. Useless. Useless.

Somehow she slept like a baby and woke up early, both refreshed and strengthened. Exactly what Lance had intended no doubt. And there was a plate of fruit tarts and deviled eggs with a note folded beneath the edge at her place on the kitchen table. Rese opened the note.

Back soon, like it or not. Love, Lance. She closed her eyes. *Love, Lance.* This was way out of hand. Rese looked down at the food and for once couldn't think of eating it. The folder lay on the table, and she took it and sat down, then pored over the contents again.

She had decisions to make and hardly knew where to start. At some point she would probably need legal counsel. But for now she had to understand her mother's reality. What she had experienced last night had been terrifying. Her mother had been living it for years. Rese pressed her fingers into her eyes and rubbed.

There were two business cards clipped to the pocket of the folder: the facility administrator and Dr. Wilbur A. Jonas. She should make the appointment to speak with him and learn whatever he could tell her about Mom. Then . . . she'd see her.

Rese released a slow breath. After reading about the differences in the brain that caused symptoms of schizophrenia, she could not blame her mother for what happened. How could she blame someone who had no gauge on reality? To Mom, Walter was as real as her child. But she'd still made a choice, hadn't she? And that hurt; *it hurt so bad.*

Rese rode the whirlwind of anger, grief, and betrayal. She had to know it all. She couldn't bear any more surprises. She dug out her address book and found the number, keyed it in and, when the woman answered, said, "Aunt Georgie, it's Rese."

"Rese. I . . . how are you?"

How long had it been since she heard that voice? Maybe her aunt had come to her dad's funeral. She wasn't sure. There hadn't been much contact over the years, just two different lives running their course. But Aunt Georgie had been part of her life before. "I know about Mom."

The silence spoke of secrets and lies taken to the grave. "Oh."

"Dad's death left her without a guardian." Not that her aunt would have thought of that; a crazy sister-in-law was hardly her first concern after all these years.

"It broke Vernon's heart to put her away. But after—when it wasn't safe for you anymore, he had no choice."

Rese hadn't thought about it that way, and it hurt to do so. Dad's death was still too fresh. She didn't want to think of something being painful for him. He had done what he thought was best for her. Once he'd carried her to safety, he never stopped protecting her. Even if it was by lies.

She closed her eyes. *Oh, Dad.* Maybe that was why he worked so hard and stayed away with Brad when she was old enough to be alone. Did he blame her for losing Mom? Whatever the case, he'd found his solution and stood by it, as he had with every decision of his life.

She thanked her aunt and hung up. Her chest squeezed with sobs that would leave her empty and weak. But getting them out now when Lance wasn't there would be better, wouldn't it? Cry like a normal woman? If only she could.

She scraped her chair back, clenched her fists, and paced. It hurt. That had to be good. She felt pain from something that should hurt. And anger, too, secondary emotion or not. She had the feelings; she just hated to cry. Couldn't that be normal?

She stomped her foot. Why wasn't there a clear line, a clean cut between normal and not? She'd spent fifteen years training herself not to cry, not to show any weakness attributable to being a girl. Why should she expect to act like one now? She would drive herself crazy trying to be something she wasn't.

Not crying didn't mean it didn't hurt. She missed them both. Maybe her love for Mom was irrational, but it was there. And Dad? She'd loved him fiercely. Then a senseless accident had taken him away.

Where had the presence been then? Why had the Lord saved her life, then let Dad bleed to death in her arms? Or had the Lord been there, and Dad hadn't seen, hadn't looked. *"There's nothing after death."* He'd been so sure.

But Lance was just as sure there was. *"He'll find an open heart."* Could God be there, waiting for a heart that never turned His way?

An ache more terrible than any before. *Oh, Dad.* But no one could tell Vernon Barrett anything he didn't want to hear. He was fully in control down to the last detail of his work and of his life. Everything she had tried to imitate, demanding the same respect he received, the same mute obedience. Even his last words, *"Be strong,"* indicated self-sufficiency, determination.

He would never listen to voices, never obey an unseen entity. Yet she had drawn a desperate strength from the presence. She caught hold of the table edge, breathing the scent of fruit tarts, maybe, or just a sweetness in the air, like the sweetness that had blocked the poison filling her lungs. *Fight. Don't give in.*

She remembered so clearly. Nothing else from that night was so impressed on her mind. Not that her mind was any great judge, it seemed. All this had shown her how blurred and confused perceptions could be. Just because she saw or heard or felt something didn't make it real. Her mind could twist and change or leave her altogether. But if there was something outside what her senses perceived, wouldn't that remain?

The sound of Lance's Harley in the driveway sent her pulse racing. He had put her to bed like a child, and she'd let him. Amazing, if she thought about it. She should have been more resistant than ever, now that she knew what had happened the last time someone urged her to sleep. The fact that she had succumbed surprised and scared her.

He came inside, hair tousled by the wind, leather jacket open to the waist, brash and confident. He'd started his day with God, which made him better in some way he hadn't explained. He'd grown up immersed in faith. He didn't have to wonder if it was real.

She raised her chin. "Well?"

He slowed his approach. "Well, what?"

"What did he say?"

"Who?"

"God."

Lance took in the set of her jaw, the line of her mouth. He'd expected a couple possible scenarios this morning, that she'd regret telling him about her mom, that she'd try to shut him out, avoid it all. But Rese was obviously going to take this thing head on.

Having just spent intimate time with the Lord, he should have the answer right there in his hand. He should be able to open her palm and place it there like a treasure, a response so keen it cleared away the doubt in her eyes with a great "aha."

But if God had ever spoken to him that way, he hadn't heard it. He knew the Scriptures, his catechism, hymns and songs, but he was no Moses with a burning bush. He took off his jacket and slung it over the chair. "Were you looking for something in particular?"

"Weren't you at church?"

"Yes."

"So didn't God talk to you, tell you how to be better?"

He thought about the Scripture readings that morning. Had there been something implicit he was supposed to pass on? He hung his thumbs in his jeans and said, "He raised Lazarus from the dead."

"What?"

"That was two thousand years ago, but people are still talking about it."

She scowled. "I want to know about now, what we're . . . you're supposed to do."

He studied her face, getting the drift, but still not sure how to answer. "God isn't Walter, Rese. He doesn't drag me around barking orders. So if that's what you're looking for, it's not my God."

"Then what is He?"

Lance stared at her. In twenty words or less, for the big money . . . what is God? "He's truth; He's meaning. He's my purpose and yours. With terrorists wiping people out, dealers hooking kids on meth and ecstasy, violence and cruelty; there's still love, comfort, joy, and hope. That's God. Without him, none of it makes sense."

"Then He intends everything that happens, all the things you said."

"He intends freedom." Lance wasn't sure where that had come from. How did freedom work with God's will? Freedom was why he kept screwing up, missing it, running away. "He didn't make us prisoners to His will. He gave us our own, and freedom to choose."

Rese snatched up the folder from the table. "Mom had no freedom. If she could choose . . ." Pain flashed over her face before she could hide it.

He didn't know how to answer that. Freedom assumed understanding.

Had Rese's mom known what she chose? "I don't know how that works, where responsibility and conscience lie for someone like your mom."

"So it changes. There isn't one way for everyone."

Baxter whined at the door, and Lance let him in. Rese hadn't forbidden him the kitchen specifically, and she said nothing now. "Some things are set and can't be altered, Rese. What is good and what is evil." What her mother did was evil, but did she know that? "Things either offend or glorify God. I don't think He's neutral about much."

She shook her head. "What if you don't know?"

Was she trying to excuse her mom, or was she speaking personally? He took her hands and sat her at the table. Baxter flopped down at her feet. The dog might have a purer sense of all this if he could just say it. "I used to think life was a maze that everyone had to find the same way through. Lots of trick walls to run into, pits and traps to punish a wrong turn." He rubbed Baxter's ears. "But everyone has different challenges, different needs and strengths. Choices have consequences, but I now think that, even in the pits and traps, the Lord can make a way through."

"Spoken from experience?"

"I've caught my ankle in the trap—thinking I knew better, I had all the answers, I was justified in bending this rule or that."

She chewed her lower lip. "So if someone does wrong, but doesn't know it . . ."

"Mercy covers a lot."

She closed her eyes. "I just don't see it, Lance. Where was the mercy for Star?"

He squeezed her hands. "Right here. God gave her you."

She looked up and searched his face, absorbing that thought, then tripping on the next. "And Mom?"

Very thin ice. "I need more information there."

She half smiled. "Then you'll have the answer?"

"Maybe."

"I thought you knew everything."

"So did I." He stroked her thumbs. "Conchessa pretty much wiped that idea out."

"Conchessa?"

"My second cousin twice removed. I spent a few weeks at her convent in Rome."

"Testing her vows?"

He chucked her chin. "Twice removed, Rese. She's ninety-one." He sat back. "She blasted my maze theory. Said it's all about possibilities, and God meets us in them."

She had challenged his whole life plan—to find God's will and do it—said he was fixated on finding the one thing God intended for him, when every moment was an opportunity. What if she was right? Could one choice be God's will, and another as well? It might not be about finding the one right answer as much as knowing the heart of God and choosing from the possibilities. He saw her point now as he pondered his own situation; helping Rese or helping Nonna or somehow finding a way to help them both.

He didn't know what he would find in the cellar, didn't know what he had missed from Sybil. He didn't know where things would go with Rese, or even what he wanted there. But he knew that the core of it all was Christ. "If there's anyone worth trusting, it's Jesus."

Rese sighed. "I don't do invisible well. Not after Walter."

"But Walter wasn't invisible. Not to your mom."

Her brow squeezed as she pondered that.

"What you experienced in your room that night was more real than any hallucination your mom ever had." He waited for her to recall, to tap into the experience. "There's a whole reality outside our finite understanding. A spiritual battle of good and evil. You could have died, but God intervened."

"Why?" It was hardly more than a breath.

She had asked him that before, and the answer seemed so obvious, but she couldn't see it. "Because you're His, and He isn't done with you yet."

———

You're His. Dad had carried her out and become her hero. But the truth was, he wouldn't have come in time. Something had created a cushion of air that smelled like fruit and blossoms, not the sickening scent of the gas. Something had urged her to fight, to hold on.

Lance had said all she had to do was believe, but he didn't know how hard that was. Everyone had lied to her. Mom and Dad, Aunt Georgie, Brad, everyone else who kept the secret. . . .

But Lance hadn't lied to her. He believed what he said. She saw it in his face when he blessed the food, told his stories, when he held her and prayed silently, when he spoke to her of God.

"You knew He was there, Rese. You listened and lived."

Maybe that was true. Maybe it was all true. But she didn't know enough to say for sure. Too many things had seemed true and had not been. In the end, Dad's arms had carried her out, not the invisible being, no matter how comforting.

———

The look on Rese's face proved he had not convinced her, but she said, "So God made the world and Jesus saved it. What else?"

He laughed. "That was the abbreviated version. The rest takes pretty much all your life."

"Then you'd better start talking."

"You can read it in my Bible. Oh, I forgot you don't read."

She leaned forward. "I want to hear it from you, why you believe it, or is it just what you grew up with?"

Before Tony died he might have said it was. Growing up in a milieu where every thought, every move was measured and weighed according to the already understood standard and culture of faith made it easy to live that faith without necessarily internalizing it.

But when their world got rocked it wasn't easy anymore. Either it was real and he could cling to it, or he'd been lost that morning as well. "I do believe it, Rese. It doesn't mean I understand it, but I'll tell you what I know, and you can decide."

No one would ever make up her mind for her, and if Evvy thought he had some magic key to turn on the truth for Rese Barrett, she was mistaken. They'd get down and dirty before it was over, he could tell. But if that was what it took . . .

Lance got his Bible so he could show her some of it in black-and-white. He couldn't resist teasing her with things like, "If your right eye causes you to sin, gouge it out and throw it away. It is better for you to lose one part of your body than for your whole body to be thrown into hell." A Scripture he had taken to heart, tearing out one thing that had mattered so much but consistently got him in trouble. He tried to make her see that sin had consequences.

Then they battled over the contradiction of hell and a loving God. Her experience of the Savior had been so comforting, she couldn't fathom the judgment side. Or maybe she didn't want to.

They walked out to the end of the street where Baxter patrolled the empty fields with lolloping strides, an eager nose, and the firm intention of marking every inch his territory.

"So you're saying Dad is burning in a pit of fire?" Rese's eyes were sharp with pain.

He'd pierced through a vulnerable place he hadn't meant to go. "I don't know, Rese. God judges the heart."

"And if Dad's heart was closed?"

Lance took both her hands and looked into her face. "Would I be standing here with you if you hadn't opened up and let me in?" Not that he was God, or anything close, but the analogy stood. "The Lord gives us a lifetime to accept His love."

"But if it's cut short—"

"Every day is a gift. Did you earn today?"

She stared at him, annoyed. She didn't want to be boxed in, but central to faith was realizing how utterly helpless they were.

"There's no guarantee either one of us will be here tomorrow. Look at Tony. And your dad." Both strong men, if his guess was right, but one surrendered to grace and ready to meet death when it came and the other unwilling to give up control.

"Wouldn't Jesus try. . . ?"

"Did I break down your door?"

She ignited. "You pushed every limit, ignored every boundary, refused to hear 'no'."

He smiled. "You stopped saying it."

"But . . ."

He drew her close and kissed her forehead. "The Lord is what He is. We accept that or not."

"It's not fair." She meant to fight this all the way. He couldn't blame her. Things hadn't shaken out in her favor.

"It might not seem fair to you, but look at it from God's side. Jesus made the way, but we have to choose it. The Father's willing to let us reject Him."

She shook her head. "I don't understand that."

"I know what you mean. I've been trying for twenty-eight years."

She straightened. "You're twenty-eight?"

"Last October."

"Why didn't I know that? It's like you tell me all these things, and then I realize I don't know you at all."

Where did that come from? Was she deflecting away from the sticking point of faith? They could stop the topic any time she wanted to. "What do you want to know?"

"Everything."

He spread his hands. "I'm the youngest of five, born and raised in The Bronx, half a B.A. in music performance, one year in the Peace Corps digging wells in Zimbabwe, two years with Habitat in Jamaica and Nicaragua, fourteen years off and on with a band, and a sackful of other jobs that paid the rent. You saw my résumé, talked with my employers. If you'd read the birth date on your own forms you'd have known my age."

She blinked. "Oh."

"I've shown you who I am, Rese."

"It just seems . . ." She looked away. "I don't know what to think or believe."

No surprise with the twists her life had taken these last days. And he'd come to her under false pretenses that had yet to be explained. Now? How could he when the trust she had in him supported the faith she needed? As good as it would feel to come clean, he couldn't risk it.

"That's understandable." He should have told her before this. The longer it went, the more complicated it got. "But you're on the right track."

She sighed. "I guess I want new construction, and it's only renovation."

"Renovation is an art. And you're in the hands of the Master." He tipped up her chin. "Do you know what Jesus was before He started His ministry?"

She shook her head.

He ran one finger down her cheek. "A carpenter."

CHAPTER THIRTY-TWO

As they turned into the driveway, Baxter lurched forward, baying at the burgundy conversion van parked in front of the shed. Rese frowned. "Did we have a reservation?" She shouldn't feel such disappointment at the thought. It was the point, after all.

But Lance said, "No." He had a strange look on his face as he started for the van. Two men got out, and the three of them converged, hooking fingers and slapping backs in a male ritual of recognition. Baxter thrust himself into the melee with doggy delight.

These were people he knew. She observed the tussle with mixed emotions, the joy of their reunion stinging in a way it shouldn't, worse than last night with Star. As though Lance had no right to other relationships. Pathetic. He motioned her over.

"Rese, this is Rico Mirez and Chaz Fortier."

She shook hands with Rico, who wore two small hoops in both ears, his hair layered to his shoulders with a strand on the side wrapped in colorful thread. His face was narrow, and his slight, compact frame made Lance seem tall. Then she looked up to the elegant features of the one he called Chaz, who clasped her hands in long dark fingers and spoke with an accent. Lance rested his hand on the small of her back in a gesture she recognized as proprietary, though no one had laid claim to her before.

"Whatchu doin' here?" New York stood out in Lance's speech with that one phrase, though she hadn't noticed it before.

Rico tapped a rhythm on the side of the van. "You got a gig, man. Jake told us."

"I played one night in a dining room." Lance cupped his hand around her side. "As an experiment."

Rico took a folded paper from his pocket, opened it and displayed one of the flyers she'd hung. Lance and his guitar looked out from the page. "It says Saturdays."

He frowned. "We're still figuring it out."

Rese glanced at Lance. Why was he denying it? His first night had been a roaring success. She fully intended him to play again, and he'd never been reluctant where his music was concerned.

Rico pinned her in his gaze. "He was hot, wasn't he?"

"Sure, put her on the spot, Rico." Lance shoved his friend's shoulder. "And that's not the point. I'm not—"

"You're playing."

"I'm not getting paid."

"You're performing."

Lance rubbed his face and glanced at her sidelong.

She wasn't sure what was going on, but she said, "We only opened last weekend. Nothing's settled yet."

"We'll settle it." Rico was as wiry and intense as a terrier. He opened the back of the van. "We brought the equipment. I told Mr. Samuels we'd send a CD. He's hungry, Lance. We need to feed him."

Rese eyed the sound equipment, instrument cases, and drum set in the van. Was this the band Lance had played with?

"This is a bed-and-breakfast, Rico. Not the Village."

Chaz had stood grinning through all of it. His smile broadened now, forming two long creases in his cheeks. But he said nothing, letting the two smaller men argue.

Rico tugged a case free and opened it on the edge of the van's floor. "Just look at her."

The guitar was reddish-hued, detailed with mother of pearl, and Rese could swear even the outlining was inlaid wood. She didn't know much about instruments, but the craftsmanship was incredible.

Lance shouldered Rico aside. "If you've banged that up . . ."

"I wrapped her like a baby."

"I know how you drive."

"I drove like a grandmother." Rico's fingers tapped his thigh. "Tell him, Chaz."

Chaz leaned on the van. "Like your Nonna Antonia."

"Yeah, she could have won the Indy." Lance's hands were on the guitar.

He didn't take it out of the case, but Rese saw his desire to. The other guitar was his travel companion . . . and this one?

"She was lonely." Rico's voice grew velvety. "You can't leave her so long without stroking her."

Lance glared at him and closed the case. "Cheap shot, Rico."

Rico tugged a tightly packed sleeping bag from the van. "So where do we camp?"

Lance looked from Rico to Chaz. "Got a couple hundred for a room?"

Chaz's smile shrank. "I told you we should call, mon." He shook his head at Ricardo.

Rese stepped forward. "If they're your friends, Lance—"

"They can have the attic. For tonight."

She shot him a glance. The attic?

"Great." Rico shouldered his bag and pulled a navy duffle free. He flashed Lance a grin as incorrigible as any she'd seen.

Rese hid her own behind her fist. It was satisfying to see Lance steam-rolled for a change.

Chaz bowed his head her way. "Is that all right with you?"

Turn away his friends? She would not have offered the attic; maybe the carriage house with Lance, but he'd spoken first. She shrugged. "No one's using that space."

"Except the ghosts." Lance sent Rico an incorrigible smile of his own. "Was it moans you heard, Rese?"

"It's been quiet lately." And she'd been way too stressed to even think of ghosts. She looked up at the attic window.

Lance took his guitar from the van, but he didn't offer to help with anything else. A contradiction of emotions emanated from him. Excitement and affection, irritation and strain. When he started for the carriage house, she told the others, "I'll show you the attic."

She hadn't been up there since Lance finished cleaning it out, and it spread before her now with surprising size and emptiness. The others walked in and eyed it.

"Wow. We could set up at the end and have tables and a dance floor—our own private club." Rico did a quick shuffle and spin that, even laden with his luggage, displayed a fluid motion. She could almost see the wheels turning in his head as he considered the possibilities.

Chaz looked down on them both, his shaved head the most perfectly shaped she'd ever seen. Hair would spoil it, just as hair gave Rico his rakish look, and Lance his style. All of them so different from those she'd worked

SECRETS

with. Or maybe she hadn't noticed the defining characteristics before.

But these were Lance's friends, people who mattered to him—who proved he was real? "Have you known Lance long?"

"A while." Chaz set his things against the wall. "Ricardo grew up with him."

Rico shrugged. "We didn't nurse at the same breast, but most everything else."

They had behaved like siblings, like people with history and familiarity. "So I guess you know about Tony."

Rico fixed her with a stare that confirmed Lance had not made that up. Had she doubted it? The pain he'd shared was too real.

But Rico was reassessing her now. He shot a glance at Chaz. "Gotta be a record." He thumped his bags down by the window and looked out.

"What record?" She asked Chaz.

He spread his hands. "Rico says crazy things. Don't listen to him."

At the window Rico just laughed.

———

Lance took the top three stairs at a jog, stopped and eyed the sound equipment and instruments set up at the far wall. Not *déjà vu* exactly, but something close. Rico tapped an air brush on the cymbal he'd just tightened into place. "Great jammin' room."

Lance hadn't thought of that when he'd proposed the attic, only a place they wouldn't find too comfortable. As good as it was to see them, he couldn't encourage Rico. One note of eagerness, and the man would pounce. "You're wasting your time."

Rico laughed. If he was getting ideas, this would not be pretty. Only Rico would think he could drive out there with the setup and lure him back in.

Chaz leaned against the wall. "You look better."

Compared to when they'd last been together? Seeing Nonna incapacitated, knowing she needed something from him, had caused a strain he hadn't bothered to hide. They'd have seen through his attempts anyway.

"He ought to." Rico did a roll on the snare with his fingers and ended with the brush on the cymbal. "He's got a hot mama."

"It's not like that." Lance frowned. He'd put his arm around Rese to warn Rico off, not give the impression he'd obviously gotten.

"Man, you had me searching my conscience in sackcloth and ashes with all that 'finding the meaning of life' talk."

"I meant it. And there's nothing happening with Rese."

"She's eating out of your hand."

"I'm the cook."

Three inches shorter than Lance and weighing the same as he had at fifteen, Rico still faced off like a pugnacious Chihuahua. "You told her about Tony."

"So?" But Rico knew he would never have shared that with someone who didn't matter. He was pressing an advantage. With their fiery natures and Rico's quick trigger, they had ended up in a clench too many times because Rico baited him as he was now.

"I care about her. But there's nothing happening."

Rico snorted, reminding him of Rese.

"I meant everything I said before. I still do. You're wasting your time."

Chaz opened his bag and took out a water bottle. "The Lord has called him out of darkness." He took a long drink.

Rico scowled. "I'm not talking darkness, Chaz, just fame and success. Not listed in the seven deadly sins."

"They should be," Lance said softly. "They sure lead to them."

"Only if you let them." Chaz had said that before, but Chaz didn't have the same temptations. The oldest son of a minister in Kingston, Jamaica, he'd seen degradation, violence, and iniquity—and had been chiseled into a pillar of integrity Lance both envied and admired. No lifestyle, no surroundings, no temptations shook him from his course. At least that Lance could see.

They had met on a coordinated effort with Chaz's father's church, and in the evenings, after days of sweat-soaked labor, there had been music for the soul. How many guys played Mozart on a steel drum? Chaz's talent and Lance's sponsorship had brought him to New York, and the money he sent home kept his family and most of their church alive.

The three of them shared an apartment in the building his family had owned for years. They contributed enough rent to cover the property taxes and they provided all the maintenance. What the three of them couldn't do themselves, they paid for. It was a good arrangement for everyone. But the guys had come to Sonoma now, and Lance knew why.

"You can find another guitar, Rico."

Rico shook his head. "It's not the same." He held up two fingers stuck together.

Yes, they were close, closer than he'd been to Tony. From the time they could walk, he and Rico were inseparable—which was the main reason

Lance had found so much trouble. The sisters had learned quickly that alphabetical order sat them next to each other and scrapped that method of seating. But nothing could really separate them, except for the life-changing impact of Tony's death.

Lance rubbed his face. "Have you guys eaten?"

His friends shared a look, and Rico grinned. "And spoil your fun?"

"Yeah, yeah." Lance shook his head. Having grown up on Nonna's fare, Rico said nothing derogatory when Lance took up where she left off. He knew a good thing when he saw it. Lance didn't miss the irony of their coming to Nonna's old house just as he'd switched focus back to Rese. But it was one more complication in a situation already spinning out of control.

Evvy had not thought of Ralph's stories in a long time. But waking from her nap with the name Quillan Shepard on her lips put her in mind of the man Ralph had said his family revered like a saint. She didn't go in for any of that, but she understood a debt. According to Ralph, his father, Joseph, owed Quillan Shepard his life, and that was somehow connected to the villa next door.

He never did tell her the nature of the debt or how exactly it came about. She suspected Ralph didn't know, or he would have enjoyed the recounting. But when she teased him about leaving the old place since it was too big for him, he'd say there was only one thing that could get him out of there. One thing. . . .

Evvy shook her head. In the end, it was something else, something he hadn't wanted but couldn't stop. His own son's plans. There should be a lesson in that, but never having children of her own left her without insight into that particular aspect of life.

She had thought once that she was missing something, but she'd obviously not missed motherhood too much, or she'd have made it happen. Childbearing might be a noble cause, but there were other ways to fill up God's kingdom—like reaching out to the offspring of other wombs. She didn't have to bear them to be burdened by the souls around her, so when she stepped outside and saw Rese and the dog near the end of the driveway she started toward them.

She'd been bitten by a nasty bulldog as a girl and never cared for dogs since. But this one didn't bark or bite that she could tell. It did push its snout into her hand. No manners at all in the entire species. But she'd bear with that to have her say.

Evvy opened her mouth to inquire about the condition of Rese's soul when a coughing spasm seized her such that even the dog backed off. Rese reached out a hand to steady her. "Are you all right, Evvy?"

There the girl goes stealing her line. She wanted to know if Rese was all right with the Lord yet, if that doubting Thomas of a cook had spoken his peace, but she guessed he must have more to say, because once again the Lord had shut her up. "Fine," she gasped between coughs.

Rese called the dog away from her hydrangeas and made him sit. Kind of a pleasant animal in a loppy-eared sort of way. "What is he?"

"Golden retriever and cocker spaniel, according to Lance." Rese rubbed the dog's head. "Smaller than a pure retriever, and you can see the spaniel in the eyes."

"I suppose." Evvy wouldn't know a spaniel eye from a retriever eye, but she'd take her word for it. "You like dogs?"

"I love them. I always wanted one." Rese squatted down and hugged the dog like a child. "Of course, Baxter is Lance's dog."

"You wouldn't know it by the look on his face."

Rese smiled. "He's just a big pushover."

"Like his master?"

Rese quirked her gaze up. "Hardly. Lance is more trouble than anyone I've known. Well . . ." She glanced toward the villa. "I guess that's not really true. I've known some real jerks, and Lance isn't. It's just . . ." She shrugged. "I don't know."

Evvy laughed softly. "Sort of gets under your skin, doesn't he?" She wasn't sure if it was his boyish respect or his brazen disrespect that attracted her more. Someone had done a good job on that young man, Evvy decided, though Lance himself couldn't see it. "You could do worse than that."

"That's what makes me wonder." Rese stood up.

Evvy almost asked what she wondered, but she supposed she knew. Rese was insecure in her own worth. She didn't know who she was and couldn't see what Lance saw, what the good Lord saw.

With the dog wagging at her side, Rese turned. "I'd better get back. Lance's friends are here from New York."

"Don't let that worry you."

Rese looked puzzled, but didn't ask. If she had, Evvy would have told her Lance was not the sort to be swayed by others, but Rese needed to see that for herself. A little of the edge was coming off, but she had so much to learn. Evvy didn't know her story, but she saw a fierce determination and fortitude. The Lord could use that, if the girl would let Him. But would she?

Rese said, "It was nice talking to you."

The dog slurped Evvy's hand as she turned back to her house. She'd need a thorough washing, and she didn't even have anything to show for it. Sometimes she thought God was a great big jokester, giving her a hunger for souls, then making her nibble at the edges.

When she'd seen Evvy coming Rese had expected her to complain about the dog or something. Maybe she was paranoid, but where neighbors were concerned, she expected the worst. If they minded their business, she'd mind hers. But Evvy . . . well, Evvy was different. Why had she said that about not letting Lance's friends worry her?

Did it show when she mentioned them? Did she sound possessive or insecure? Two things she despised and flatly rejected. Frowning, she left Baxter at the door and joined the men inside.

After a long evening of Bronx-style conversation—fast, overlapping, and punctuated with hand gestures—Rese sat in the small armchair they had brought up to the attic from the parlor. Strains of music coursed over her.

She did not have a very musical ear, but she could tell they were good. Lance and Rico's harmony resonated. He had griped about Rico bringing the red guitar, but he played it now with loving fingers, and the energy between the three was mesmerizing.

She would let them live there free if they played Saturday nights, but she suspected that was not Rico's plan. As close as they obviously were, there was tension between him and Lance, and it made her uneasy. What was that Mr. Samuels hungry for? Lance?

She dropped her head back against the chair and closed her eyes. He had been overqualified before she even saw this side of him. Multi-talented. What if Chaz and Rico had come to lure him back? Last night she had suggested he cut his losses and go, and he'd refused. But now?

Rese opened her eyes when the song ended. Rico looked ready to start another with the click of his drumsticks, but Lance slipped the strap over his head and set the guitar in its case. She had no idea how late it was, but she was tired. "All done?"

"You are." Lance extended his hand.

She stood up. "I'm enjoying it."

"You're tired."

She didn't want him to exclude her. She had the feeling that, if she left them alone together, they might all be gone by morning.

They walked down and stopped outside her door. She groped for something to say. "You guys sounded great."

"Yeah, well, Rico and I've sung together since fifth grade. Chaz joined us four years ago. Another couple guys fill in as needed, but this is the core."

And he loved it. She'd seen that the night he played alone, but it was magnified now. "Why did you break up?" She'd gathered that much from the comments over dinner.

"It's not a lifestyle I want." His brow pinched slightly.

There was more to it, she could tell, but she didn't ask. Mostly because he was kissing her. Her heart rushed as she gripped his shirt. "I thought I would hate this. After Charlie, I thought I'd hate to be kissed."

"Do you want me to stop?"

She laughed. "As if you would."

"If it bothered you, I would. If it made you think of that. I want to erase it, wipe it out of your memory." And he was doing a good job of it because, even though her chin was still tender, she did not want him to stop.

He drew back. "Will you sleep?"

She shrugged.

He glanced behind him at the kitchen table, reached down and snagged the Bible they'd left there. "How about a little light reading?"

If it had mattered enough for him to bring it on his bike when he had so little else, it might be worth a look. "All right."

He studied her a moment. "Are you okay?"

He was reading her again like the open book she'd become. She nodded toward the attic. "What do they want?"

"Something that's not going to happen."

"You?"

He held her waist and considered his answer. But before he could say anything, she asked, "What are you doing here, Lance?" Showing up on her doorstep like a stray dog with nothing to show for all his talent.

For just a second his gaze wavered, then he said, "Looking for answers."

Days ago she would not have understood that. Now she had so many questions she didn't even want the answers. She looked into his face. "I hope you find them."

Rese had asked, and he'd answered. But he'd told her nothing. Why was he there? To prove her property belonged to his grandmother? To claim a cellar full of vintage wine and whatever else might be down there? To vindicate a murdered man he'd never known?

Or maybe two. There was Quillan's skeleton as well. Had he been shot in the tunnel? But he discounted that immediately. No assassin would arrange him so carefully, and why hide his body and leave Vittorio's? As he'd told Rese, he did need answers. But when he found them, what would he do?

Lance sat down on the floor under the eaves in the attic. Rico had used most of dinner to complain about Steinbrenner losing half his starting rotation and, that in spite of a lineup that compared to the '27 Murderers' Row, they'd probably lose the Series again. Lance just believed that every time his team put on the pinstripes they would take it all. He'd been there opening day almost every season he'd been alive. The memory brought a pang now that added to the unease created by Rese's questions. Who would he be if Antonia had not been run off her land, chased to the other side of the country?

He rested his forearms on his knees and watched Chaz and Rico roll out their beds. "So how's the family?" His people were as much family to these two men as their own. Rico's dad had spent more time in jail than out, and his mom had more than she could handle with her brood. She hadn't known or cared where Rico was most of the time. Chaz's parents were solid, but economic reality forced a geographical separation and loneliness that Lance's family had eased.

Rico shook out the foot of his bag. "Your pop's doctor says he works too hard; he should slow down."

Lance smiled. "Fa-get-about-it." The day Pop slowed down they'd be holding his visitation.

"Momma's worried about you, says you took Nonna's stroke too hard. She don't know what's going on, but she's not happy her mother-in-law sent you all over the world on some secret quest." His mother had worried every day of his life, and she'd always been a little resentful of his relationship with Nonna. But Rico was expressing his own frustration as well. Lance hadn't told him his business, and Rico wasn't used to being shut out.

Lance swallowed. "And Nonna Antonia?"

Rico held his gaze, trying to break through the barrier between them. "She sent a message."

Lance straightened. "She's talking?" That had to be a recent breakthrough. He'd called regularly, but no one had said she could manage more than a word or two.

Rico rocked his hand to mean so-so.

"What's the message?"

"Jack's son."

Lance frowned. Someone she wanted him to contact? "Who's Jack?"

Rico shrugged. "She tried to say more. Something about a quill, but I must'a got that wrong."

"Quillan? Quillan Shepard? Or maybe Nonno Quillan?"

Rico sat back on his haunches. "It's hard, man."

Lance knew it. He could picture her twisted-up face, her mouth trying to form the words, tears trickling from her eyes.

"She got all worked up when she heard we were going to see you. She does better when she's not upset. Especially now that she's home."

Lance brightened. With all the help she had at home, she'd rebound for sure. His family was a throwback, mostly due to their owning a four-story building. With rents off Arthur Avenue what they were, most of them were glad to make use of the property. And Nonna thrived on her family.

But all of that seemed far away. He'd started to think of the inn as home, started looking ahead, making plans. Rese needed him now, and it felt right to be there for her. It felt better than right a few minutes ago downstairs. She was trying so hard to deal with everything. He admired her fortitude, even if he suspected there was tenderness inside that would be equally compelling if she ever let it show. He wanted to be there to see it.

But somewhere, entwined in all of that was what he was supposed to do for Nonna. He needed a clear path, and all he was getting were conflicting possibilities. He pressed his fingers to his brow and prayed.

Lance had said to start with the New Testament unless she wanted to boggle her mind. He didn't realize it was already boggled. But she took the book and settled down in her bed.

She opened at the ribbon and her eyes went to the bold *Chapter 5* on the second column. Lance had underlined parts of it. *"Therefore, since we have been justified through faith, we have peace with God through our Lord Jesus Christ, through whom we have gained access by faith into this grace in which we now stand."*

She felt anything but peaceful with God. She'd rather stand Him up and demand some answers. And depending on that, she'd decide whether to retain or can Him. Ironic that she envisioned Him more like the guys of her crew playing mean tricks than like Lance, when He was the one instructing her.

" . . . *And we rejoice in the hope of the glory of God. Not only so, but we also rejoice in our sufferings. . . .*"

Rejoice in our sufferings? How did that work? Should she be glad her mother tried to kill her, that her Dad made her into the opposite of the woman he loved, then bled to death in her arms before they could have a true relationship? Rese frowned at the page.

This was why she didn't read. Even in school she'd struggled to understand how the teacher pulled the supposed meaning from what the words actually said. When students piped up with their own brilliant deductions, she'd wanted to throw something.

But this section must have meaning to Lance if he'd underlined it. She returned to the sentence. " . . . *because we know that suffering produces perseverance; perseverance, character.*" That part she could see. It wasn't suffering that built character, but the persevering through it. Not the pranks that had made her strong, but her withstanding them, the cruelty driving her to find focus and excellence. She could see that. Lance had endured his own grief, and wasn't his character what she had sensed beneath his troublemaker looks?

So perseverance produced character, "*and character, hope. . . .*"

Hope. After what she'd learned about her own chances to lose her mind? To become the outcast her mother was, to never know what was real or what her twisted brain had created? And yet . . . the fear had lessened, as though there really was the possibility of hope.

" . . . *And hope does not disappoint us, because God has poured out his love into our hearts by the Holy Spirit, whom he has given us.*"

Like cool creek water running over her bare feet, the words took hold in her, washing away her resistance. "*God has poured out his love into our hearts.*" She had felt that love when the Lord—if that was the being in her room—had sustained her. She couldn't even compare it to any human love she had known up until then. Mom's love had been frightening and inconsistent; Dad's solid but conditional. The love she had felt in her room that night had not required anything from her but trust.

Rese swallowed a fierce tightening in her throat. Tears filled her eyes, but the surprise of their coming was far outweighed by the awesome comfort of their falling.

CHAPTER THIRTY-THREE

Time.
Past and present run together.
A watercolor wash of moments.
Nonna Carina's hand on my head.
No, it is my daughter's hand.
"It's Dori, Momma."
She thinks I don't know my own daughter-in-law?
Who knows what I mumbled with my stubborn mouth?
It does what it likes.

So what's the plan, Rico?" Lance had fed them breakfast, and Rese was out in the shed working on his wardrobe, he supposed. They hadn't had much chance to talk alone, and he wanted to get her on his bike and find the connection they had when the rest of the world didn't get in the way. Chaz was taking a shower in the carriage house, and it was as good a time as any to let Rico have his say.

"You know the plan." Rico launched into the attributes of Saul Samuels, agent above all agents with connections all the way to God, to hear Rico tell it. Their big break was only the nod of his head away, and playing with them last night had awakened a thirst he'd thought quenched by all his firm intentions to leave that life behind.

Just what he needed—another possibility. *Lord! Haven't you tried me enough?* If he took the path to uncover Nonna's secrets, he risked alienating Rese. If he pursued their relationship, he would let Nonna down. If he chose Rico's dream, he would fail both of the others. Where was the simplicity Conchessa seemed to find in her theory of possibilities?

Lance toweled the last dish dry and put it on the shelf. "I can't do anything with that right now. I've got other responsibilities."

Rico's hands gripped his hips. "Cooking?"

"That's part of it. I took the job."

"I can't count the jobs you've left."

"This is different."

Rico snagged a lime from the bowl on the counter, tossed and caught it. "Take her with you. Won't be the first time a woman's followed your gig."

"Rese is no groupie. And this is her place."

"So she's got a house. We can base out of here if you want. Pop'll get good rent for our apartment. Or your sister Monica can spread out."

Lance turned a chair and straddled it. "You know that's not all, Rico."

"I been thinkin' about the rest." Rico took a stool to face him. "So it went to our heads. So we made some mistakes."

"And we'd make them again, and you know it."

Rico shook his head. "What happened to Tony changed things. Not just for you."

"What, you found religion?" Rico had been the devil on his shoulder too long to believe that. They'd attended Mass every day, but the grace Lance found there rolled off Rico like oil on a hot skillet. His heart was true, but his head didn't follow.

"With you and Chaz on the straight and narrow, I can't go wrong." Rico beamed a roguish smile.

"You can. And when you do, it's me you're dragging down, and somehow it's me taking the fall, and Tony's not here to pull me out, Rico." The pain hit him squarely in the chest. "I have to get it right myself."

Rico grew serious. "I know that. But you've got it closer than you think."

"Close isn't enough."

Rico hunched forward. "You're not perfect. You're never going to be. And neither was Tony."

Lance stared at him. If anyone had reason to revere Tony, it was Rico, whose tail had been dragged from the fire more often than even his own. He was not going to listen to this. He pushed up from the chair.

"You think he's a saint. But he had faults, just like the rest of us."

Lance's throat squeezed. "Name one."

Rico looked away. "I just don't think you should—"

"One fault, Ricardo."

Rico's hands tightened on the chair in front of him. He had something, or thought he did.

"Say it. What do think Tony ever—"

"He had a thing for Gabbi."

Lance stared at his friend. His breath shot out of his lungs with the force of a fist to his gut. "You're saying he cheated on Gina?"

"I'm not saying he cheated, man." Rico spread his hands. "But I saw him with my sister."

"Saw him how?"

Rico made a fist. "With her heart in his hand."

Lance fumed. He knew Rico well enough that he wasn't making it up. But he'd misinterpreted something.

Rico didn't back down. "It wasn't just Gabriella. He liked the attention he got."

That was pushing it. "He couldn't help that." Tony's magnetism had been as unintentional as his skin. He was born with it. "What proof do you have he ever used it?"

"No proof." But Rico held his gaze like a dog on point. He believed Tony might have, and that was too much.

Lance grabbed him by the shirt. "You don't know what you're saying." His voice was tight with fury.

"It's dangerous to see too much in anyone. And worse to think you have to match it."

"This isn't about Tony."

"It's always about him."

Lance let go as Chaz walked in, fresh from his shower and smiling. But he took in the situation and sobered.

He spread his hands. "I leave you two alone for ten minutes . . ."

Neither one of them smiled.

"I don't know which is Cain and which is Abel, but if you were thinking of knocking each other's heads, mon. . . ."

Lance scowled. He felt like knocking him. Rico couldn't accept that things were different; he was different. Or did he only want to believe that? He forced back the fury. Rico was wrong. Tony only wanted to help. Lance knew how that was. If Gabbi took it wrong . . .

But he was haunted by too many faces himself. Something in the way Rico had closed his hand like a figurative fist around his sister's heart. . . . Gabriella had her own problems, just like the girls he'd tried to help. Like Rese? Lance swallowed, pulled his gaze from Rico to Chaz. "No one's knocking heads."

"Someone ought to," Rico said. "Before yours is the size of Tony's."

Lance lunged, jerking Rico to his feet and knocking the chair to the floor before Chaz got between them.

"This is not the way. Violence is never the way." Chaz stared him down until Lance stepped back.

His conscience stabbed. What was he doing attacking Rico? Proving he hadn't changed at all. He caught his forehead with his fingertips. They wouldn't be having this conflict if Rico wasn't trying to force the band thing again. Lance knew how much he wanted it. But to drag Tony down to make his point. . . .

Rese came in smelling of sawdust and stain, rubbing her cheek with the back of her hand. "Can you help me with something?"

He had to smile at her oblivion. With wood on her mind, the tension in the room was lost on her. "Sure." He left Rico to Chaz and followed her out. As soon as they'd cleared the window, he pulled her close and kissed her.

"What was that for?"

"So now I need a reason?"

She cocked her head. "It felt like it."

He was still adrenalized. But he tipped his head back and tried to fake a nonchalance he didn't feel. "The sun's shining, the birds are singing, you smell like wood and . . ." He found her lips with his gaze. ". . . looked like you needed kissing."

Her brown eyes narrowed as she glanced back toward the kitchen. "Did I interrupt something?"

"Yeah. And just in time. I was about to knock Rico in the head."

She frowned. "Why?"

"It doesn't matter." He hooked her elbow. "Let's go for a drive." He had a serious need for the road.

"I'm working." But she didn't resist his tug. As he handed her the helmet she added, "Hiring you has diminished my productivity."

"Stop whining."

She drew herself up stiffly. "I never whine."

Now he was picking a fight with Rese? "So get on already."

She stared into his face, her ire rising.

"Please." He did not need another argument. Baxter looked hopeful, but Lance wanted her. "Please."

She climbed onto the bike, and he took the road faster than he might have without Rico's words burning inside him. He never pretended Tony was perfect. But he and Rico together didn't come close. He pictured Gina at the memorial. It was all she could do to stand. That was not a woman who'd been cheated on.

Rese's arms tightened, and he eased back on the gas. Rico was jealous. He'd always envied Tony. They both had. Sure women noticed him. Everyone did. He was that kind of man. The kind who stood firm and did things right. But memories of his own were eating at the edges of his conviction.

He would not believe for a minute that Tony had betrayed Gina, but had Tony known how Gabbi felt? Had he allowed a sort of hero worship, sought it even? Not just with her, but others as well? Lance unleashed the bike. He was projecting his own issues. Or had he learned it from his big brother?

"It's dangerous to see too much in anyone. And worse to think you have to match it." Lance couldn't begin to match it. So why was he trying to be everything Rese needed? Why had he made her need him at all?

Lord? It was hazardous to search too deeply. Motives and intentions never looked as pure as he thought. Was it God's will he wanted, or a little of the power, the adoration? He'd taken a hard, determined woman, a woman filled with confidence and direction, and had her—as Rico said—eating out of his hand. Maybe there was more of Tony in him than he thought.

The road wasn't calming his mood. He pulled over abruptly, turned into the Chateau St. Jean vineyard. The long drive was shaded and blooming, elegant and stately, as he imagined Nonna's property had been once. It wound into a visitors' parking lot, and he parked the bike and climbed off. He strapped the helmet down and took Rese by the hand, striding along the walk toward the chateau.

The gardens were carefully planted to delight the senses, and tables awaited picnickers. He wasn't hungry or particularly interested in wine at the moment. He led Rese around the outside of the chateau to an area he supposed was not intended for visitors, and she started to point that out.

"Don't talk. Kiss me." He'd issued the order, but followed it himself, decidedly.

She pushed him away, scowling. "I don't know what happened with you and Rico, but I'm not the cure."

Her words penetrated the haze. What was he doing, accosting her like that? His whole system was charged with destructive energy. He'd been thrown into some macho role, some need to prove . . . what? He dropped his chin. "I'm sorry."

She softened. "What happened, Lance?"

He clenched his fists. "Rico." He couldn't tell her more than that, couldn't voice the things he'd said about Tony.

"Do you want them to leave?"

He imagined Rese giving Rico the boot with the same cold steel he'd seen when she'd almost fired him. But there was too much between him and Rico to let her solve it. "I just want him to lay off."

"'Suffering produces perseverance; perseverance, character.'"

He raised his brows. "Where'd you get that?"

"Chapter five of a Roman letter."

His heart rushed inside him. Here she was handing him his faith, when she didn't even believe it. Or did she? He wasn't getting a clear picture. She still argued vehemently, yet she'd memorized part of the book of Romans and applied it now to him.

He took her hands. "'And character, hope . . . because God has poured out his love into our hearts through the Holy Spirit. . . .'" Was his character godly? Did he persevere and rejoice in the hope of the glory of God? He wanted that more than any revenge on Rico, more than anything. He wasn't trying to be perfect, just to get it right.

He drew her close and kissed her forehead. "Thank you."

She raised her mouth and met his with all the tenderness he'd hoped for. It sank right to his heart, exposing all that stood between them, the secrets, the things unsaid. He sighed. "Rese, I need to tell you . . ."

She put a finger to his lips. "Don't say it."

He searched her face, wondering what she'd thought he was going to say. It couldn't be what he had intended to say.

"If you're leaving, just—"

"I'm not leaving."

She released a slow breath. "You're not?"

"Not unless you want me to." And she might, once she learned the truth.

———

She hadn't seen him this worked up since she'd almost fired him, and it reminded her that he was not just the comforting person he'd been lately. From the start, he'd been intense and volatile. But not like this, not even when he talked about Tony's death. He'd been emotional, but now he seemed shaken. Because he wanted what Rico offered?

He might be denying it, even to himself, but making music with Chaz and Rico had brought him to life like nothing else, not even his cooking. She couldn't compete with that. There was only one thing he seemed to want as much. She said, "Lance, I'm making you the managing partner of the Wayfaring Inn."

He didn't exult as she'd expected, just stared at her and said, "Why?"

Why? When he'd been the one imagining his name in lights?

"Because you're as much a part of the place as I am. I made it strong and beautiful, but you give it life." She didn't know what she'd expected, but not the pained look that came into his eyes. Did he want to leave so badly? She said, "Don't you want that anymore?"

He frowned. "Of course I do."

Relief rushed in. "We can make it official, draw up an agreement."

"Don't worry about it."

"No, I want to." She wanted it concrete and settled. She might own the property, but the business itself was more Lance's than she'd wanted to admit, until his friends made his leaving a distinct possibility.

He didn't speak, just sent his gaze across the vineyard spreading out beyond the chateau.

"Do you need to think about it?"

"No."

"Then you'll take the job?"

He put a hand to her waist, but didn't answer.

Why was he being so unemotive. "I thought you'd be happy."

He cocked an eyebrow. "Wha-a-t, I don't look happy?" There was his Bronx talk again. Rico had infected him.

"I thought you'd show it. I thought you'd back me into the wall and kiss me."

"Maybe I don't kiss my partner."

She put her hands on her hips. "Right."

He released a slow breath. "I'm just trying to see it."

"I'll put it on paper. And I won't interfere. You can do everything your way."

"That's hardly a partnership."

She huffed. Wasn't that what he'd wanted? She straightened.

"Don't do that." He reached out and took her hand.

"Do what?"

"Get all stiff and rigid."

"Well, I'm a little perplexed."

"More like exasperated." He smiled.

"Torqued." She glared.

"Scary."

She gave him a shove.

He caught her wrists. "You wanna mix it up, woman? Cuz I am more than a match for anything you can throw my way."

She scoffed. "Until I give you what you want. Then you stand there like a mime all lost and confused."

"Well, I am lost and confused. But it's never stopped me before."

"So we have a deal?" She all but hollered it.

"Oh, baby, do we have a deal." He pressed her back against the wall.

"You must have been a serious discipline problem."

"Still am."

"Are you going to kiss me?"

"No."

"Why not?" Because he was incorrigibly obstinate.

"Because there's a limit to my control."

"Hah. You'd control the world if someone gave it to you."

"Not that control."

It hit her like a hammer, almost taking out her legs.

He groaned. "Don't look at me like that."

"Like what?"

"Like you'll do whatever I say."

But she would.

They stood there long enough for her legs to solidify, then he let go of her. "Can you walk?"

She glared. "Of course."

His mouth pulled up slowly. "Nails." Then he released a slow breath. "Hope I can."

Well, he could hardly have made his situation worse. Partners in the Wayfaring Inn? Managing partner, she'd said. Everything his way. He hadn't believed she would do it. What was she thinking, handing over the business? But she wasn't thinking. That had been perfectly clear.

He squeezed the Harley's grips. She might have given her crew man a black eye, but she'd been sweet invitation for him against that wall. Surrender in the least likely woman. And she didn't even see it. *What am I supposed to do with that, Lord?* Rese had gone from a sneering, domineering termagant to an appealing woman he respected and desired. And he had her in the palm of his hand.

Did Rico have it right? He'd watched Tony operate, helping, comforting, becoming indispensable. What woman wouldn't want that? And what man wouldn't realize . . . and use it? As he was with Rese? Lance leaned the bike around a curve; Rese leaning too, with none of her early stiffness, no resistance; she flowed in tandem with him. Exactly what he'd wanted?

He'd almost said no to her offer, told her she should think about it. She might have experience with a crew in her field, but she was awfully naïve in this. So why had he said yes? Because he wanted it. For her, and for himself.

He slowed to enter the driveway and nearly hit Evvy waving her cane with a look of urgency that jerked his heart. He put the bike into a skid, wheeling around behind her. "What's wrong, Evvy?"

"It's Ralph. His heart." Hers looked none too steady. "I need to get there." Her eyes glassed with tears.

Rese climbed off. "Use the truck. I'll get the keys." She hurried for the house as he helped Evvy to the truck. She probably didn't have the strength for the bike today, and Rese was thinking clearly. With Evvy between them, she drove to the care facility as he directed her and sustained Evvy.

Ralph had seemed tremulous when they visited him—warm and loving, but not altogether connected to this world anymore. Lance knew the helplessness Evvy must feel, as though the air had been sucked from her lungs and left her in a vacuum. Was it only weeks ago he'd been in a similar hospital room with Nonna, hoping and praying it wasn't the end? He knew her time was coming, but it didn't make it any easier saying good-bye.

The room held several brusque staff members who moved for Evvy to approach on his arm. Though she weighed next to nothing, it seemed Lance held her up by that arm alone. Ralph was awake in the bed, but didn't seem to know her or anyone else. His face was a picture of pain, physical maybe, but psychological for sure. He didn't know what was happening, and he was scared.

Lance seated Evvy up next to the bed, and the staff quietly dispersed. The smell this time was heavily medicinal, and he noted the IV and other monitors. As Evvy took Ralph's hand, Lance slipped out past Rese in the doorway to gauge the situation. Since he wasn't family, they gave him no details, but they did say Ralph's son was on his way, if he could get a flight, and it was good that Evvy had come directly.

Taking Rese by the hand, Lance went back in and stood a short distance from the bed. Evvy spoke in low tones, explaining who she was and asking whether Ralph understood or not, and he clung to her hand. Lance had images of Nonna, pleading to be understood, to understand. He ached. *Lord, have mercy.*

Evvy murmured, "If you have the fight left in you, use it now, my darling man. If not, the Lord has a place prepared for you. And I'll be there soon to share it."

Ralph met her eyes and held them. "Evvy." His voice was so weak, Lance was surprised to hear him at all. What he uttered next stopped the breath in Lance's chest. It was the intimate phrase Nonno Marco had saved for Antonia, *La mia vita ed il mio amore.*

Lance closed his eyes as Ralph's gaze dulled and his hand slipped from Evvy's. This was how it ought to be: a long life, a peaceful death. But he stood, fighting tears for a man he hadn't known, unsure why he felt the loss except that Ralph had been somehow connected and now that thread was gone. More than that, Lance tasted the bitter ash of Evvy's grief. That was always the hardest for him, seeing someone suffer.

The monitors signaled Ralph's departure, and someone came and turned them off. Evvy murmured, "'Give thanks to the Lord for he is good; his love endures forever.' My hope is in the Lord." Then the room was silent a long time.

Rese had not spoken a word, and he wondered if this was churning her recent loss. According to Brad, she'd checked out for a while at her dad's traumatic death. He wasn't sure how much she remembered even now. Maybe she shouldn't have come, but if she was upset, it didn't show.

He understood that better now. She wasn't stone; she was strong. Not uncaring, guarded. Her concerns about her lack of emotions were unfounded. He saw them now that he knew what to look for. Leaning together at an angle of repose, they found a balance neither had alone.

But Ralph's death kindled a fear that Nonna could be gone before he had the chance to bring her peace. He had to do that, but without hurting Rese. How could he bring it all together? He was trying to do God's will, but he was still giving away that Mickey Mantle card.

––––––––––

It was all she could do to stand there with Lance as Ralph died. There was no blood, no panic, no struggle, but it was still death. And Evvy's words had speared her.

It was like that part in Lance's Bible, boasting in affliction—but thanking God for love and goodness even when He'd taken someone away? There was something radical in their faith, something unnatural. You didn't thank someone who hurt you. You might not strike back. You sure didn't show it. But thank?

When Jake let the air out of the truck's tires she rescheduled her bid; when Sam poured syrup in her toolbox she did not retaliate or even complain. She'd heard them calling her the Stone Goddess because she'd cleaned it up without a tirade. She endured it all, but she did not appreciate it. There was no gratitude! That would have invited scorn and humiliation, when at least she had grudging respect.

She wanted to tell Lance and Evvy how wrong they had it, but she kept going back to the moment Ralph left and sensing a difference. Maybe it was no more than the obvious; she didn't know, didn't love him. His death wasn't violent and premature. But she couldn't shake the thought that the manner of death was not the point.

Leaning into Lance's shoulder, she closed her eyes and saw herself running, Dad falling, all the awful details. But what haunted her now was the moment he slipped away. *"Be strong."*

There had been a determined look on his face, not the surrender she'd seen minutes ago. She didn't want an eternity with Jesus or without, not when some could make a choice that others refused. . . . Why should death be different from one person to the next? *Why should it be up to us to choose or reject what Jesus did—if He did it, if any of it was real at all.*

But the room was filled with an awful peace, a finality that left her groping. If Lance was not holding her up, she'd collapse as she had that time on the scaffolding, all her strength sapped. Dad had charged her to be strong, to withstand everything life threw her way. Maybe he'd known more than she'd thought about the crew's pranks, ignored or . . . encouraged it. If he thought it for her own good, had he toughened her up intentionally?

For the second time that day her legs almost went out. The day Sam and Charlie "fought," did he see her scraped face and swollen lips? He did not want her hurt; she knew that. And he'd taken those two on his crew when they split. But he wanted her tough. Had he thought he could make her strong enough to resist Mom's condition? Did he think strength of will honed by harassment could help her withstand disease?

Lance curled his hand around her waist, no doubt sensing her distress. The complete and total opposite of Dad. Lance let her express hurt and showed her his own. Tears filled her throat. She had made him her partner, but was that fair? He didn't know how much she was coming to need him. Or how much she might.

CHAPTER THIRTY-FOUR

I t took more strength than she had to get a cup of tea, but Lance brought her one, then crouched beside her sofa, wrists resting on his knees. Evvy glanced at Rese standing in the doorway, a little stiff and uncomfortable. Death did that. Left people without words.

But not Lance. Once he had gotten her home, he had repeated Ralph's final phrase with reverence, told her about his grandparents and their great love and the meaning those words had for them. Some people might have hesitated to tell her a love story when she'd just lost her leading man, but he understood the temporal nature of their separation, and she appreciated that.

Evvy swallowed the lump that seemed to fill her throat. She would think of Ralph; she would cry. But it wouldn't be much different from other days since he'd moved into the home. She'd been bedfellows with loneliness too long for any surprises there. Unfortunately, her body still went through the process. Her legs would not hold her, and the two young people had helped her to the bathroom where Rese had seen her inside.

They didn't realize that even if she fell and broke a hip, it was only one more step toward the inevitable. She was the oldest of her gang and tired of waiting in line while others entered before her. *I don't mean to complain, Lord, but haven't I done my time?*

She often thought James had the best of it, to leave this world with all his dreams intact. But then, they'd probably been shattered by the war in a way she couldn't begin to imagine. Hers had simply faded, just as she had faded. But there she was, giving in to melancholy. *"This is the day the Lord has made, let us rejoice and be glad in it."*

She reached over and patted Lance's arm. "You'll get a crick in your knees, my boy, and they don't last forever." Her voice hitched with tears.

He covered her hand with his. "What else can I get you?"

She shook her head. "Not a thing. Just take your girl home and cherish her. That house needs some joy." The tenderness in his squeeze transferred comfort that climbed from her hand to her heart and remained. "You're a good man, Lance Michelli. Don't let anyone tell you otherwise."

"Do I look like they might?"

She laughed. "Frankly, yes. A bit of the buccaneer about you."

He shook his head. "I keep getting that."

She couldn't sustain the humor. She might know in her head that a reunion was in store, but her heart had still been hollowed like a harvest pumpkin. Her lips trembled. "Go on, now. I'll be—" The thought halted. Now? When she had so little energy for it?

But she turned to Rese. "There is but one thing that stands. Put your trust in the Lord. When all others fail, He will never fail you."

She couldn't tell if the words sank in. That girl could rival the sphinx. "Of course, you have to admit your need." Something had made Rese Barrett too self-sufficient by far. Evvy sank back. She might be looking in the mirror.

Lance set a paper on the side table. "That's my cell phone number and the inn's. If you need anything . . ."

She nodded. "Michelle and others from the church will be by to check on me. Never fear. I'll be running them off with my cane."

Lance rose to his feet, and Rese straightened in the doorway. Did she realize what she had, that girl? But then, did anyone? As they walked out the door, she turned her thoughts heavenward. "Whatever it is you intend for me, you'd best be about it. Or I just might show up unexpectedly."

Not that anything could surprise the author and finisher of not only her faith, but every detail of her existence. As the tears came, she hungered for the joy Ralph knew, the vigor with which he would embrace heaven, and the awe he would find before the throne.

———

Lance pressed the trowel into the dirt, thankful for a few moments alone. He'd smoothed things over with Rico yesterday, not accepting his suspicions about Tony, but admitting his own attempts to measure up. They had needed to explode, maybe, to find a fresh balance, just as he needed to square up all the rest.

He had planned to go down and search the cellar last night to find whatever there was once and for all, but Rese was sleepless again, and they had talked long into the morning hours. She was serious about him managing the inn, but she had good instincts about advertising and community awareness.

She was used to word-of-mouth promoting, and her previous profession had been almost exclusively referrals. He liked her belief in doing something so well people couldn't help but talk about it. His being her key to doing the inn well had him a little concerned. Sure, he had the ability, but was that his purpose?

Lance shook his head. God had directed him more clearly to this point than ever before. If it was muddled now, he'd done it. But what could he have done differently? He couldn't let Rese face her crisis alone. Jesus wouldn't have abandoned her to pursue His own agenda. The caring that came was out of his control. He could no more stop feeling than breathing.

But he hadn't had to act on it. He hadn't needed to show her how he felt; he'd wanted to. He'd wanted her to need him, wanted her to want him. She'd been the biggest challenge yet, hard and sufficient, caustic and dominating. But he'd won her over.

He'd been willing to take advantage of the situation, to get what he needed for Nonna. He would even have left Rese without help, if he'd found his answers right away. But something in her had called to him, something he couldn't ignore. And the more he let her into his heart, the less certain his purpose became.

He had wondered if he'd find someone who could still the restlessness. Tony had married Gina at twenty-two. Monica and Lucy were younger than that. Sophie—well things hadn't worked out too well for Sophie in the marriage department. Not that he was looking to marry Rese—his hand slipped from the trowel into the dirt.

Partners, sure. He had control of the inn, the property that had been Nonna's. They had drafted their agreement last night, and Rese had faxed it to her attorney. But marriage? He was not sure he could ever pull that off. It took someone like Tony, who always got things right. Someone who knew his place in the world, not a wandering gypsy looking for meaning in every face he helped.

The gravel ground on the driveway under the wheels of Star's yellow Volkswagen, back from wherever she'd been since their Chinese dinner. He stood the trowel in the front bed he was planting with verbena and sat back on his heels as she climbed out. "Hey, Star."

She was not the same girl who had presented his painting the other night. Her eyes were too bright, her fingers trembling as she closed her car door and approached, wearing a white, gauzy dress falling in layers that ended at her knees. The bruise on the side of her neck could mean a lot of things, but he wasn't naïve enough to assume most of them. As she squatted next to him and breathed in the scent of the flowers, he noted the fine blue veining through the brown and reddened skin and the finger marks on the other side.

"What happened?"

"Does it show?" She had to know it did, and she could have hidden it with a scarf if she didn't want him to notice. "Rese'll kill me."

"She's less homicidal than she used to be." And whoever had bruised Star seemed the more likely candidate. Her hair smelled musty and hadn't been brushed in a while. "Who hurt you?"

"It doesn't matter."

He pressed a line of white through the bruise as a slow anger grew inside. "Are there more?"

The breeze caught her flimsy dress and flattened it to her body—hiding signs of battering?

"Was it Maury?"

She blinked slowly and her brow pinched. "It hurt him more than me."

Lance swore. Star shot him a glance, surprised by his vehemence. But how many times would he hear that lie and be expected to swallow it?

"I shouldn't have told you." She wilted.

"Kind of hard to miss choke marks."

"He didn't mean to."

Lance stared at her. If he didn't gravitate to women in need, he wouldn't see all the ugliness. There were good, strong relationships out there, built on love and respect, women who were cherished. Did Star even know that?

"Don't tell Rese. She'll lecture me on respect."

"She'll see it herself."

Star shook her head. "I'm just getting my clothes."

He caught her wrist before she could stand. "Stay here, Star. Don't go back." The thought of her returning to that guy burned. He slid his grip to her hand and softened it. "Look at me." She did, and there was a pathos in her that clenched his insides. "You've been assaulted. You should press charges." But he knew in that sick, tight place that she would not do it.

"He just couldn't let me go." A corrosive brilliance illuminated her eyes. She needed to believe that. In those words was a want so deep no amount of pain would compare, the want of a love that couldn't let go. And she thought she'd found it in an abusive man.

Lance fought the building rage and the helplessness that came with it. What could he say? "This guy is not what you need, Star."

"Yeah, well . . ." She glanced sidelong. "Is that an offer?"

She knew the answer, but this was exactly how Tony must have felt with Gabbi and countless others. Too much need for any one man. *Lord, help me help her without compromising.* He stood up, drawing her with him. "Stay here and heal."

The expression on her face speared him. "'Tis healthy to be sick sometimes.'"

He was losing her; he could see it. "Not like this. You don't—"

The burgundy van pulling in broke his thought. Chaz and Rico. Great. He let go of Star, half-expecting her to bolt, but she stood there as they parked and got out, and he realized with silent amusement that they had blocked her in.

Chaz was driving. He would have been aware of Star's car and was courteous to a fault, yet he'd maneuvered in behind her. He came around the van, now, with a broad smile and a slow wave. But it was Rico who had caught Star's attention. Not unusual, and not unusual that Rico had likewise fixated. But it was definitely unusual to have it all on the heels of a prayer.

Rese slid the chisel deeper, breathing in the scent of cut wood like perfume. Was it working with the wood she loved, or avoiding everything else? In her zone she could pretend no one wanted to hurt her, no one wanted her dead. In her zone every detail was controlled. She had power over what occurred; even a mistake could be modified. But a mistake in life could be final. That was why she'd worked so hard to maintain order, discipline, respect.

The wood did not resist. It allowed her to express herself, lent itself to her talent. But she could not have relationship with wood. She had thought it didn't matter. She could live alone, run the inn for strangers who would pay the bills but not interfere, not expect something she couldn't give or reject what she had. But Lance had exposed her inadequacy there.

She dreaded the small talk he handled with ease. He said it wasn't small talk; it was little connections, a touching of lives that might never cross again but had come together for that moment. He saw every minute as part of the pattern of life, and he wanted that pattern as full and intricate as he could make it.

Watching him reconcile with Rico had almost brought tears when she realized Rico had slandered Tony. She knew how that must have hurt, but Lance reestablished their tie, took Rico back to his heart as he'd taken her every time she hurt and offended him. She'd never had that before.

Not even with Star. At the beginning, their differences had caused clashes like Lance and Rico's, but instead of talking it out as Lance had, she just learned not to expect anything from Star, to let her handle things her own way, then be there when they came crashing down. It didn't allow for much honesty, or any real intimacy, but it didn't require much either.

Lance was the first person who had made her lose her temper. Not even Bobby Frank with all his dares had accomplished that. And Lance was the first to make her question her self-sufficiency. He didn't make her need him, but he made her want to.

They had talked late last night, Lance reading to her, just as he'd described before when she couldn't imagine it. But it hadn't been strange. As he'd read, she had pictured Jesus forgiving the woman they wanted to stone, arguing with the know-it-alls, working miracles for the crowds.

It all came alive much more powerfully than any story Mom had read, because Lance described it as though they were there. He couldn't just read the words; he'd break away and say, "Just think, Rese," or "Can you see it," and whatever followed would sink in with added fervor.

As she'd listened, she had felt a part of her open up, a part she had locked away where it couldn't be hurt, a part the presence had sustained through her dark fearful night. She could well imagine Jesus reaching out to her, giving her breath as He'd given it to Jairus's daughter.

She didn't see God as a recalcitrant employee anymore. Instead, as she used her plane or her chisel, she pictured Jesus' hands doing the same. Jesus the carpenter. That made Him real, as Lance had known it would. But what made Him more real was Lance himself. His care for Evvy in her grief had been achingly tender. He had the capacity to connect beneath the surface as she imagined Jesus had done, touching and healing and loving people—as he loved her?

No one in his right mind would fall in love with her, especially knowing what Lance knew. But his words had sunk in and nested. Rese gripped the chisel. She still had to contend with everything: Mom's situation and all the fears that went with that, the inn and the guests coming. Lance would—

The door opened and he came in. She knew the light that flooded the shed was sunlight from the open door, but . . .

"Star's back."

It was not what she'd expected him to say, and a rush of irritation surprised her. It was one thing to lose a room if Star was going to use it, another altogether if it sat empty while she was off who knows where. All the housekeeping had fallen to her and Lance since Star went out the other night, and when she thought about having to wait the tables herself tomorrow night, she'd been ready to bag Star's stuff and throw it out the window. But Lance approached now with a troubled look.

"What's the matter?"

He released a slow breath. "She's been roughed up."

Rese took that in. It wasn't the first time, but it hadn't happened since Star left home and her mother's boyfriends behind.

"She thinks you'll be angry."

"Was it Maury?"

He shrugged. "That's my guess."

"Then I am angry. She knew—"

He removed the goggles from her face. "It's not that simple. She's not solid like you."

With his eyes on her like that, she felt anything but solid. But there it was again; the rock. And she would let Star crash upon her like a frothy wave drawn back and tossed in an endless pattern forever at the mercy of forces beyond her. Or would she? "There's no getting through to her. If I thought she'd listen to anything—"

"I'm not sure it's a problem." He spoke softly.

"Well, you haven't known her seventeen years. At any moment she'll fly off again, back to Maury as likely as not, and—"

Lance caught her shoulders. "I think the Lord is working here."

"I'm sure He is. But as you've pointed out, it takes two to tango, and Star's a little stubborn about things that cramp her style."

He smiled. "What would you know about stubborn?"

She raised her chin. "We're not talking about me. I never should have counted on her. I knew better."

"Rese." He cupped her face. "I don't think Star's going anywhere."

She folded her arms. "And why would you think that?"

"You know that high-voltage activity we've experienced?"

A jolt of it seized her at that moment. "So?"

"Star and Rico just lit up the yard."

Rese stared at him. Sure Rico looked colorful enough to catch Star's attention, and what man wouldn't notice what she flaunted? But the last thing they needed was her bed-and-breakfast becoming the onsite shoot of some seamy flick. "Great. It'll take Star all of three seconds to find Rico's sleeping bag, and it's anyone's guess where it will go from there."

Lance slid his hands down to rest on her shoulders. "I've got leverage. As long as he thinks I might say yes, Rico will behave."

She dropped her head back with a huff. "Great. I lose my partner to the road, but Star's virtue is saved."

Lance leaned in and kissed her lips. "You're not losing me to the road. We're just buying her a little time."

She didn't want him to care as much about Star's problems as hers, to have that tender look when he mentioned her condition, to find a solution that kept Star where he could watch over her. How callous was that to resent Star's having exactly what she, herself, appreciated most about him?

"We can help her, Rese. And Rico's not a bad guy." He said that with just a hint of doubt. But then he readily admitted his own faults too.

She released her breath. "Well, you're the managing partner. If you want to keep her on, go ahead. I'm not waiting tables tomorrow night."

He smiled. "Nope. Got a sink reserved for you."

"Very funny."

But he obviously found it so.

"Would you leave so I can finish?"

The look he gave her was anything but Christlike. "Say please."

She met his glare. "Stand there if you want. I can be perfectly oblivious." But she couldn't, and by the time her goggles were back in place, the "please" had burst from her lips. Thumbs in his jeans, he turned on one heel and swaggered out. She heaved a chunk of wood after him, but he'd cleared the door already.

Jamming with Chaz and Rico that afternoon built an energy that crackled. Several of the guests had come up and stood around or sat on the floor, clapping and nodding. It was like playing back home, with friends, and friends of friends—and people off the street, he sometimes suspected—and Momma applying the broom handle to her ceiling more times than not. Rese threatened to soundproof the attic, but with the house set back from the street, and with the distance between all but Evvy's place, Lance hoped it wasn't really a problem.

Star danced, showing none of the angst he'd seen earlier. In the gauzy dress, with a shimmery scarf around her neck, she skimmed like a nymph across the floor, Rico's eyes following as he drummed the rhythm that moved her. The strangers there seemed alternately amused and enthralled, and Lance felt some of that himself. But when she asked for his microphone, he turned it over with no clue what she'd say or do.

"Play 'Memory.' From *Cats*," she told them. Chaz played an introduction on the sax, then Lance and Rico came in and Star sang, her voice clear and rich, strong from stage projection and full of emotion. She was no old cat with most of her life behind her, but she'd had enough in her twenty-four years to capture all the pathos of the song. She finished with a deep, spectacular bow, and then held the mic out to Rese who looked like she'd rather stone her than take it.

"I'll do it." The young woman staying in the Seaside room stood up. She named her tune, tossed back her big brown hairdo and drawled "New York, New York" to death. Rico looked like he wanted to pull the plug, but the rest applauded her, and she held the mic out for any takers, tried once again to give it to Rese, then put it back in its stand.

Lance could almost imagine the attic made into a Sonoma hot spot. They'd have to advertise the inn that way so they didn't get folks who wanted the place quiet, but maybe two or three nights a week, they could play and even open up the mic for a set or two. He shook his head. What was he thinking? Rico wanted the big time, not some attic venture—though you wouldn't know it to look at him.

If he'd just opened his eyes to the sunshine for the very first time, he could hardly be more enthralled. Lance drew in a slow breath. He'd never had much success as Rico's conscience, but he'd made himself crystal clear— Star did not need a rebound. Amazingly, Rico seemed to get it.

Lance looked at Rese as they started the next song. Of all the people there, she was enjoying this the least. Something had her bugged, and he didn't think it was being handed the mic. She'd probably deny it, but it was there, under the surface of her sober expression.

After the song, he took the guitar from his neck and bowed out. He needed to prepare dinner, since most of their guests had reserved for it. Rese walked down with him but said nothing. Was she regretting her decision to put him in charge? She'd seemed more than okay with it last night.

He reached up to the shelf for a mixing bowl. "Want to help?"

"Cook?" She said it with disdain closer to her old waspishness than he'd heard in a while.

"What's the matter, Rese?"

"I don't want to cook, all right? That's what I hired you for."

"Yeah, sure. That and the toilets."

She glared.

"Now why don't you tell me what's really wrong."

She expelled her breath. "I'm just not used to . . ."

"Loud, raucous, good times?"

"So many people. I liked it better when it was just . . ."

"The two of us snapping at each other?"

She eyed him. "Yes, actually. Now there's always someone around, demanding your venerable self. I know there are more fun people, even Star, as I saw by your expression when she sang. And I know—"

"No, you don't." His irritation grew. "You're putting all kinds of things on me that don't belong there. If I was interested in Star you'd have known it before now. Just because I don't want her going back to someone who chokes her, doesn't mean I want to sleep with her."

Rese glared. "You didn't mind singing with her."

"I'd sing with you too."

"I can't hold a tune."

"I'd sing with you anyway." He caught her hand and pulled her to him. "Haven't I shown you how I feel?"

"I just . . ."

He closed her into his arms and made it clear. He hadn't expected jealousy in Rese; she probably hadn't either. But if he'd brought it on, then it was his responsibility to assuage it. When he was through, most of the starch had left her and she was breathing with difficulty. "Get it?"

"Okay, so I like your kissing better than Charlie's."

"You must." He smiled. "You haven't rendered me mute."

"That would be a feat even for God."

He chucked her chin. "Watch it."

She gave him a smug smile and walked out, but her stride was nowhere near as stiff as it had been. If he tried to plant her now, she'd blossom.

CHAPTER THIRTY-FIVE

Progress.
They clap over a few stumbling steps.
Am I an infant that they make so much of so little?
One step, two steps.
What I'd really like is to kick . . . all of them.

Steam from Rico's shower billowed into the carriage house as he stuck his head out the door. "Toss me my kit, will you?"

Chaz reached over and gave him his toiletries. Lance shook his head, grinning. That was so like Rico to be halfway through his grooming before he missed the items in the kit he'd left on the table. Lance didn't care that he must have used his soap and shampoo. He'd been lending, sharing, and giving to Rico as long as he could remember, though he drew the line at his toothbrush. Even friendship had its limits.

But he had to admit that playing with the guys Saturday evening and again on Sunday had been pretty close to heaven. If Rico made it up there, they'd do a thing or two with the angel chorus.

Perched on the sofa, Chaz threaded his fingers around his knee, one long leg crossed over the other. "So when are you going to tell me?"

"Tell you what?" Lance leaned against the wall.

"What you're doing for Antonia."

He had tried not to think about that. He'd expected Chaz and Rico would be gone by now, leaving him to handle Antonia's quest as he had been—with no one the wiser. Then Rico got Cupid's arrow between the eyes, changing his immediate priorities and there was no departure in sight. But Chaz had seen Nonna's urgency, and would not take it lightly.

The question was what and how much to tell. Lance crossed his arms as a sudden desire to lay it all out gripped him. He'd never been the type to handle things alone. He thought best through tossing words around with people who mattered.

But this was a delicate business, people depending on him in too many ways. For a moment he wondered why he'd wanted that. He didn't feel powerful or important, just inadequate. He slid down the wall until he sat on his heels. "It can't go any farther."

Chaz nodded. That was his code even if you didn't stipulate secrecy. The hum of a blow dryer came from the bathroom. What about Rico? If he told Chaz, he could hardly keep Rico out of the loop. But maybe that was why they'd come. Maybe it was God directing his course. It could use some directing right now.

Lance drew a breath and said, "This was Nonna's home when she was a girl."

Chaz raised his brows.

"She couldn't tell me what she wants me to find or learn or do. But she sent me to Conchessa, a relative in an Italian convent who told me about this part of the family, their vineyard and villa. So I came here to find it and whatever else Nonna has kept secret all these years."

Chaz rocked slightly, still holding to his knee. "Does Rese know this?"

Not "what have you found" or "what have you learned." Chaz always went to the heart of it. Lance shook his head. "I need answers first. I took the job she had open so I could search the property."

Chaz released his knee and leaned forward. "It looks like more than a job."

Lance rubbed his face. "Yeah, well, it is, now." He knew how weak that sounded.

Chaz shook his head. "And what have you found?"

"Pieces." Lance glanced at the hatch involuntarily. "But everything's gotten so complicated I haven't put them together." His gaze went to the portrait behind Chaz. "That's Vittorio Shepard, my great-grandfather."

Chaz turned.

"He was murdered in the villa, and I think Antonia disappeared at the same time. I guess she went to New York, but I need to know why. I need to know who forced her out. I think she wants the truth to be known."

Chaz turned back. "Truth is a good thing." The words stung as Chaz knew they would—he wasn't talking about Antonia.

"I intend to tell Rese, but I need all the pieces first." Lance forked his fingers into his hair. "And everything I get just leaves me with more questions. The message Nonna sent—*Jack's son*. What's that supposed to mean?"

Chaz tipped his head. "I think maybe Rico didn't hear it right."

Lance lowered his hand and met Chaz's eyes with a quickening in his spirit. "What did you hear?"

"'Jack son.'"

Lance sat still as the subtle difference transformed in his mind. *Jack son. Jackson.* A cold chill passed through him. Sybil? That couldn't be right. How would she know about Sybil? Another Jackson, a previous generation? What was it Sybil had said? *"The police don't have this; the paper doesn't have it. Only I do."* Because it was a personal matter? A family matter? A letter, she told him, that corroborated Vito's murder—and included Nonno Marco's name.

Lance sagged to the floor. Had Marco Michelli killed Nonna's father? He shook his head, dazed.

"You don't look too good."

Lance stared at the hatch to the stairs leading down, the tunnel where Quillan lay, racks of wine bottled in a year that forbade its sale. He thought of Marco, a cop, the grandfather who'd inspired Tony to join the force. Had he taken out a gangster?

Maybe the letter spelled it out. Was it the proof he needed? Who else besides Sybil might know? Ralph, but he was gone, and his knowledge had been muddled already. Evvy? There had to be someone. Because if there was only Sybil . . .

Rico came out of the bathroom looking like a rock star, wearing Lance's cologne. He beat a rhythm on the wooden edge of the sofa. "So, what's happenin'?"

Lance rested his head back against the wall. "Too much."

Rico stopped tapping. "What'd I miss?"

Lance looked from one to the other. Rese had an appointment with her mother's doctor and had left a short while ago. He had tried hard to go with her, but she wasn't willing to let him in, not where it mattered, not where it hurt. And maybe that was right. Maybe now was the time to deal with the rest. He wasn't going to sleep with Sybil to get the letter, so there had to be another way. Possibilities. He needed to think in possibilities.

He got up from the floor, crossed the room and opened the hatch, raising the quadrant of tiles to reveal the stairs.

"Whoa." Rico stared. "What's that?"

"One of the pieces." Lance recapped what he'd told Chaz and swore Rico to secrecy. That didn't go without saying. "Not a word to Star." Spelling it out was also required. He gave Rico a pointed look.

Rico cocked his head. "Now how can I use this?"

"You can't. If you want to be part of it, you'll keep your mouth shut. My situation is precarious enough."

"It doesn't have to be." Chaz spoke softly, as he always did when illuminating the truth.

Lance went to the bedroom for the flashlight. Baxter whined, but Lance ordered him to stay, then led the way down the steep wooden stairs to the tunnel where Quillan lay. They squeezed through the metal gate, and Rico jolted to a halt and crossed himself as the light's beam touched the skeleton.

"Watch your step," Lance said as he passed his great-great-grandfather.

Chaz muttered something, and both men stayed close, passing between the wine racks with hushed exclamations. Rico dusted a label with his fingers. "Wonder what you'd get for one of these at auction."

"I won't get anything if it belongs to Rese."

Chaz raised his brows. "If?"

Lance shrugged. "If my great-grandfather was killed and Antonia forced off, there might be interesting property issues."

Rico caught his drift. "You'd sue her?"

Lance shook his head. "I'm trying to see how to put it all together."

His friends shared a look.

"Listen, I didn't mean to get personal with Rese."

Rico cocked a brow.

Lance raised his hands. "I know. But this time I intend to do it right."

Chaz shook his head. "You're not off to a very good start, mon."

"I thought I could work for her until I found what Nonna needed, then . . ." Then what? The next part had never been clear. "This thing with Rese snuck up on me." But there was no undoing it. She meant too much to him.

"You can't be double-minded." Chaz spread his hand. "You'll love the one and hate the other."

Lance hated how Chaz applied Scripture sometimes. "Well, I love Nonna, and I love Rese." His friends would know he didn't say it lightly. "I have to find a way to make them both happy."

"Let's take the show on the road." Rico grinned.

Lance gave that a short laugh. "The answer to everything."

"You stay here, you got trouble, any way you cut it."

Rico was right. But he was tied to the inn for more reasons than one. Lance looked around the ghostly shelves, shadows crowding in. "I have to do this. There's something here, something that's stayed too long in dark-ness."

Rico looked over his shoulder to where the skeleton lay invisible now. "You're creepin' me out."

"You have to tell her," Chaz said.

"I will. I just need the right time."

"Who's the stiff?" Rico jerked a thumb over his shoulder.

"My great-great-grandfather Quillan."

"Gee. Nice burial."

Lance gripped the edge of the rack. "That's all part of it. Maybe the most important part, I don't know. But I can't do anything about that until I know the rest."

"You think there's something down here? More than bones." Rico shud-dered dramatically.

"Maybe now's the time to find out." Lance swung the flashlight over the walls. A mouse scuttled along an edge.

"I got a light on my keys." Rico tugged a mini flashlight from his pocket. "What are we looking for?"

"I have no idea." Chaz walked one way with Rico, Lance went the other, starting down the racks one by one. They were as orderly as a modern ware-house, but something felt wrong in their quiet repose. Something more than a Prohibition vintage and a skeleton in the tunnel.

Rico had reached the end of one row and was pushing on the wall.

"What are you doing?"

Rico shrugged. "Loose stones, secret passages, more skeletons. I keep an open mind."

Lance smiled, pushing on the wall at his end. Solid. He moved on to the next row and the next. There was probably nothing there but wine waiting to be sold. If Marco had busted Vito . . . then there'd be police files. Unless it went bad and got hushed up. Lance shook his head, unwilling to believe that. Nonno Marco would take responsibility. There had to be another expla-nation for his connection to Vito's death. And where did Antonia fit? He chafed at the aggravation of too many questions too late.

"Shake, rattle and roll," Rico sang as he rapped and pressed the wall. "Knockin', knockin' knockin' on death's kitchen door."

Chaz shook his head. "You shouldn't mock the dead."

Lance frowned. That was too true. At any rate the wall had proved solid all the way to the end of the racks. But as he turned around the last corner, he stopped. Another staircase. They must be at the house.

Pulse pounding, he climbed the stairs and found a wall instead of a trapdoor. A metal bar was wedged into the mechanism and braced into the corner. It didn't budge when he tugged. Lance ran the light's beam around the edge, trying to guess where he was. The beam caught a piece of something sticking out near the bottom.

He leaned close and recognized the chunk of wood he'd wedged into the hole in the pantry. So that explained Rese's mouse. The mice weren't in the wall; they were in the wine cellar. A scraping noise behind brought him around.

"Hello." Rico whistled.

"What is it?" Lance hurried down the stairs to where Chaz and Rico stood.

His flashlight beam shown on the floor where Rico had pushed aside the end of a rack. Lance's breath stopped. A gap in the floor was filled with bundled bills. He dropped to a squat, feeling weak. Who had that kind of money during the Great Depression?

Rico raised a wine bottle and tossed it lightly. "Thought the empties might mean something."

Lance looked from that bottle to the ones in the next section. He could see the wine in them. The ones at this end were labeled and dated as well, but held no vintage. As this rack held white wine, only someone looking would have noticed. Lance reached into the hole and dug through the bundles. The cache was almost as deep as his forearm, but that wasn't what mattered. There had to be an explanation, something other than the one that came to mind.

Rico picked up a packet and flipped the bills. "Would this be ill-gotten gains?"

"Not necessarily." Lance straightened. "People distrusted banks during the Depression. They buried stuff all the time."

"Right." Rico nodded.

Lance dug down through the money once more. Cash was one thing; what he hoped for was a ledger or some other records. His fingers felt something rough and cracked. The bottom?

Grabbing stacks of bills, he tossed them aside onto the floor. "Shine the light down here." It looked like wood, and he could just make out a handle crammed against the side. He reached in and worked it loose, then dragged a briefcase out of the hole.

His heart hammered. Whatever lay inside might explain everything. So why did he hesitate to open it? From a distance, he heard Baxter bark and jerked his head around. Was someone upstairs? He shot his friends a look, then swept the money back into the hole.

Chaz and Rico put a shoulder to the rack and slid it into place just as Star's shriek echoed in the tunnel.

———————

Rese studied the man before her. Dr. Jonas had spaces between each of his four front teeth, and his silver mustache stood out like a bottle cleaner ready to spin over his lip and scour the brown stains between them. His eyes were green orbs imbedded in flaps of crinkled flesh beneath two more bottlebrush eyebrows. In spite of his terrifying appearance, he exuded tranquility.

"Very pleased to meet you." He pressed her hand in a warm, spongy clasp. "Elaine is one of my favorites." He leaned close. "Don't tell."

His breath smelled of butter mints, and the smile sprang from her with no intention at all. She had not expected her mother's doctor to be this bristly little Santa Claus. But he sat her down and glanced at the folder she had brought back for this meeting.

"Entertaining reading?"

How was she supposed to answer that? The distress and anxiety, the horror of looking into her mother's reality and her own possible future had hit her afresh as she faced the appointment today. She had thought it would be different, but when Lance had asked to come with her, she realized all the panic and shame was still there. She was supposed to be responsible for the woman who wanted her dead, and she felt hardly capable of caring for herself.

"At least now I know what schizophrenia is."

"I wish you did. I wish I did."

Okay. She had to stop being stunned by everything that came out of his mouth.

"The truth is we look at a mind like your mother's with wonder." Again that wave of perfect calm. He was telling her he had no idea what was wrong with Mom, and it didn't matter at all. She didn't know how to respond.

"We can see anomalies, assume causative or at least connective factors, but the brain is truly an uncharted terrain. I don't understand my own. Do you?"

Rese shook her head, uncertain whether he meant understanding hers or his. This was not at all what she'd expected—a cold, thorough individual who had collaborated with Dad to keep Mom incarcerated.

"We talk about normal, and for legal and practical reasons set a bar for expected societal norms. But can any of us really claim normality?"

Rese had never thought of herself as anything but normal. She had fought for that right, then had it demolished by the paperwork in the file. But as Dr. Jonas expounded on the shadowy landscape of the mind and admitted the limitations in the theories of its science, her tension diminished. At least if he told her she was crazy, she'd fall in with his opinion of the rest of humanity.

He finally came back to Elaine Barrett and the particulars of her condition that had earned her lodging at the mental health hospital. "With the new family of drugs recently developed, we've had greater success in her case than before. She was showing marked improvement until Vernon stopped visiting."

Rese jolted. "Dad visited her?"

"Every week. She looked forward to it. But then he stopped coming. We learned from his office that he had passed away. My condolences."

Her head spun. From his office? And then the tsunami struck—Dad had visited Mom all through the years. And she had never known. How narrow and blind she'd been, like a turtle in its cage. It might be glass through which to view the whole wide world, but only what was inside had mattered.

"Who told you Dad had died?"

Her question seemed to take him by surprise. He shrugged. "I can check, if you want."

She nodded. He opened a file cabinet, withdrew an expanding folder and fingered through the pages. "Death confirmed online with Social Security, that's when we turned her case over to the state. . . . Oh, here it is. We tried unsuccessfully to contact Mr. Barrett by mail—"

"I never got anything."

He read off a post office box she had known nothing about, obviously used to keep her in the dark. "Then we called the work number he'd listed for emergencies and spoke with Brad Plockmen."

"Plocken," she corrected. Brad must have informed them while she was incommunicado. "Did you tell him about my mother?"

Dr. Jonas shook his head. "That's private information. The secretary would have asked to speak with Mr. Barrett and been informed of his death."

But they might have identified the hospital. Had Brad put it together? Or maybe he'd known already. Dad had told Brad things he kept hidden from her, Brad whose deepest moments were spent with a beer and David Letterman.

That was unfair. He had his good points; for a while they'd captured more than her interest. He had probably been a comfort to Dad. Rese chewed her lip, seeing the emptiness of her own relationship outside their work. It was the only thing they'd shared. But if he was keeping something like weekly visits with Mom from her, that might limit conversation. And if he loved Mom enough to see her every week after putting her away, it might cause a sorrow too deep to share with a daughter whose fault it was.

Rese swallowed. "So Mom noticed when he stopped coming?"

"Of course. She has perfectly lucid moments. In fact, the new drugs have provided sustained periods without psychotic episodes. We're very excited."

"Was she on medication before? I mean before she was hospitalized?"

"Dopamine blockers were prescribed, but with little effect. They don't work for everyone. That's why we're constantly seeking new treatments, new understandings."

So they had tried to medicate Mom without success. Dad must have known the danger in leaving his daughter with someone so unstable, but maybe he didn't want to see it any more than Rese had. Maybe that was why the times with Alanna upset him so much. And she had contributed to his blindness by covering for Mom, by denying the things he asked her. They had both tried to love Mom by denying the truth instead of facing the reality before them. But it was time to face it now.

"May I see her?"

"Yes. But you have to realize it's been a number of years, and . . ."

"My memories are faded at best. I just want to see my mother."

He nodded. "We can discuss guardianship and make decisions later. I've told Elaine that you were asking about her. I didn't want this visit to be a complete surprise. Surprises aren't good for her."

"Me neither."

He laughed. "This way."

Just outside the double doors he paused. "She may be thrown by this. Don't expect too much."

The visiting room was warm and comfortable, pale ochre walls with woven yarn hangings and sage corduroy chairs. Rese was not sure what period or effect they were trying for, but it was pleasant anyway. A woman sat at a table, hands folded, watching a bird at the feeder outside the window. An electrical jolt coursed Rese's limbs as she realized it was her mother.

"Here she is, Elaine. See who I've brought you? Your daughter, Theresa."

Mom turned and there was no mistaking her eyes, though her hair was mostly white and her skin pale and slack. She was thin, but not emaciated, yet her skin hung as though it had been draped over her face and neck as an afterthought. Rese wondered if she'd lost weight or if the tissue had simply tired of holding itself firm.

"I'll leave you two to visit." He motioned to another woman sitting by the wall, dressed in a floral scrub. "Bonnie's here if you need anything."

Mom made a noise, and Rese realized she was laughing, but the emotion would have been more appropriately expressed by tears. In spite of the shaking inside, she went to her mother and sat in a chair at the table. "Hi, Mom," she managed before her voice turned traitor.

"What have you done with my little girl?"

"I grew up." She fought the swelling in her throat. "I didn't know you were here. I came as soon as I knew."

Mom tipped her head and studied her. "It's a very good try. You look like her."

Rese searched her mother's eyes. She didn't believe her? Didn't know her own child? But would she have recognized her mom on the street? Yes, a thousand times yes. "It's me, really."

Her mother started to rock. "She's gone, she's gone, she's gone . . ."

"Who's gone?"

"Gone, gone, gone, gone . . ." It kept on like a pulse, then, "I met the president and he was very nice. But I know. Inside his teeth are little bombs, little gas bombs, poison gas. Breathe in, breathe in . . ."

Panic seized her. Horrible gasping breaths. How could her mother say something so cruel?

"Gone, gone, gone . . ."

Had Dad told her Mom was dead so she'd never have to face this? So she'd remember a Mother who played and danced and told stories? He was protecting them both: Mom, from the rage and hatred Rese might have felt knowing the truth, and her from a truth that hurt so much. But he was gone and now all they had was each other.

She fought back her tears and took her mother's hand. "Mom."

"Yes, Theresa?"

She knew her? Soaking gratitude. "I want to help you. I'm going to do everything I can."

Her eyes sharpened. "It'll be our secret. Don't tell Dad."

Waves of pain. Hadn't they told her? "I won't."

"Why doesn't he come? He's gone, gone, gone." Again her mother laughed—at Dad's death?

Mom couldn't help it, but chills slid down Rese's spine, and she had to get away. "I need to talk to Doctor Jonas now."

"Wilbur is a pig's name. A little baby pig."

They'd read *Charlotte's Web* together, but she didn't make the connection until she saw Dr. Jonas's nameplate again. *Dr. Wilbur A. Jonas.* He welcomed her back into his space with a gentle hand. "So you're wondering where to go with it?"

Rese nodded. No comment on what she'd just experienced, no word of comfort or explanation. Did he know she was shaking inside? Her mind was whirling, but she listened as he described the procedures already in place that had given the state temporary guardianship after Dad's death. Since she'd sold the company and moved, they'd been unable to find her, and Elaine required a guardian. She would have to appeal for a change and there would be a personal study conducted to determine her ability to function in that role.

"Will they try to prevent me?"

Dr. Jonas looked surprised. "Believe me, the Department of Mental Health wishes everyone had someone to step forward for them. If you qualify, your petition will be expedited."

"If I qualify?"

He shrugged. "There is the genetic nature of the disorder. Your medical history will be examined and your capacity to act in Elaine's best interest. Have you had any psychotic episodes?"

He might have said, "Sore throat, headache?"

"Would I know?"

He smiled. "Maybe not. But it would be in your record if it has had a diagnosis."

"I was treated for shock after Dad's death. I was with him when he had the accident."

Dr. Jonas nodded. "The state will determine the extent of the study and process your petition."

No comment on her disclosure? "I was kind of out of it for three weeks. I didn't speak much."

He nodded. "I didn't speak much for years after my son died." He met her eyes. "Then I switched from internal medicine to psychiatry."

Rese said, "I went from renovation to hospitality."

They laughed. Then he sobered. "You've read the statistics. You know your risk. The best you can do is face it with appropriate attention and resist obsessing. If you're granted guardianship, we'll work together to determine the best avenue of care for Elaine."

Rese nodded. She'd received another call and forms in the mail from the

California Department of Mental Health. She would begin that process, but processing the rest would be much more difficult. It wasn't Mom as she remembered her. They hadn't embraced in tearful ecstasy, sharing words of love and heartache. Mom had laughed. She'd looked at her daughter and laughed.

Rese walked out to her truck. She had to let go of every expectation, all hope for the relationship she'd lost. It couldn't be that way; maybe it never had.

Before she fell apart, there was something she had to do. She picked up the cell phone she kept connected in the truck and dialed Brad's number. He'd be on a job, but she didn't care. He picked up and she said, "Brad, it's Rese. I need to see you."

"Hey, great. You in town?" He gave her his location, a street she recognized.

"I'll be there in twenty minutes." She hung up. It took her only fifteen, and she parked on the steep incline behind Brad's truck and got out. He was outside the tall, narrow house painted a pale blue that he would hate, discussing something with an architect they had used on occasion.

She waited near the truck, but he'd seen her and started her way as soon as they finished. He probably thought she had come to accept his offer. She didn't even want to go there. She raised her chin. "Why didn't you tell me my mother was alive?"

His greeting died on his lips. He closed his mouth and eyed her with a guilty expression that said all she needed to know. "Vern asked me not to. He was worried what it might do to you."

"Put me over the edge? Make me start seeing people?"

Brad hung his thumbs in his tattered jeans. "I guess you're angry."

Was she? Mostly incredulous. "What about after the accident, when the hospital called you, and you told them Dad was dead? They were looking for me."

"Rese, I wasn't sure what to do. You weren't . . . very stable."

"Someone bleeding to death in your arms tends to have that effect."

He nodded. "I know. It was awful." He patted his T-shirt pocket, but for once it was empty.

"Out of cigarettes?"

"I quit. At least, I'm trying to." He cocked his head. "Look, your Dad did what he thought he had to. I just did what he asked."

Everyone had done what Vernon Barrett asked. He was that kind of man. She looked away.

"Are you okay?"

"Except for all the voices and little green men."

Brad gave a short laugh. "Man, Rese. You're hard as nails."

Lance had told her that too. She turned back. "Any other surprises I should know about? Are you really my brother or something?"

"I sure hope not. I had a terrible crush on you."

She stared at him.

"Hide it good, don't I?" He grinned. "Have you given any thought to my offer?"

"The inn is doing well. I even have a band."

He dropped his chin and shook his head. "It's just not you."

Her throat squeezed her voice tight. "How would you know? To you I'm just Vernon Barrett's crazy daughter."

He cocked his glance up. "Not hardly."

She stepped back. "Good-bye, Brad." She opened the door of her truck and glanced back once to see him bumming a cigarette from the man on the porch.

CHAPTER THIRTY-SIX

Rico reached Star first, but Lance was right behind. Her flashlight illuminated Quillan's admittedly gruesome remains, and she had frozen with a look of horror. This would require major damage repair—to her psyche and his goal.

What was she doing there? She must have seen the open cellar hatch, gone for a light and come back to see what they were up to. He hadn't checked the door, but the guys must have left it unlocked when they came in to clean up. Star wouldn't normally barge in, but she could have just ducked her head inside and seen the open hatch. Who wouldn't be curious? A skeleton was obviously more than she'd anticipated. Rico had an arm around her shoulders, but Lance had her gaze.

"What . . . who. . . ?"

"Let's go upstairs." He couldn't bear his great-great-grandfather being scrutinized like some attraction at a freak fair.

Star glanced back repeatedly until they climbed the stairs to the hatch where Baxter met them in an excited frenzy. Some watchdog. He hadn't barked until Star went down and was only complaining about being left out. But Lance calmed him with his hands. He couldn't expect the dog to consider Star an intruder, and once she'd seen the open hatch, the damage was done.

Rico seated her on the sofa while Chaz closed the hatch.

Lance crouched in front of her. "You okay?"

"What wretched being. . . ? What is that place?"

Lance rubbed her hands. "Just a cellar."

"That skeleton was real." She shuddered.

He nodded. Rico sat down beside her, but neither he nor Chaz tried to explain. It wasn't their problem.

Lance let go of Star's hands and rested his forearms on his knees. "Listen, Star. I don't want Rese to know about this. She has enough to deal with right now."

Star searched his face. "She'll want to know. You can't just leave it there."

Lance held her firmly in his gaze. "She will know. Just not now. Not until I figure it out."

She looked at Rico. "What's happening?"

He said, "Lance has it under control."

Right. He tried to look as confident as Rico made him sound.

"Is this about the painting?"

He frowned. What could her picture. . . ?

But she turned and stared at the portrait instead. "Who is he?"

Lance felt a slow sinking in his belly. "Vittorio Shepard."

She turned back and fixed him with her gaze. "Who is he to you?"

Her eye was too good. He should have known. Star with all her sighs and Shakespeare had nailed him. He sat back on his heels. "My great-grandfather."

"That's him in the cellar?"

Lance shook his head. "One more generation back. Quillan Shepard."

"Why won't you tell Rese?"

"I'm going to tell her everything. I just have to do what I came for first."

Star gripped her hair. "So you don't really love her?"

That must be how it seemed, that he would fake a love affair to get what he wanted. "I love her. That's why I have to do this right."

Star shook her head. "She will not be happy."

An understatement for sure. "I'll make it right." For everyone. God only knew how.

Star seemed to accept that, or maybe he'd done enough for her that she owed him.

"Just don't say anything, Star. Give me a few days to learn what I can." Even if it meant going to Sybil? With things unraveling so badly it might come to that. He couldn't hope to hold Rese off forever. But she'd been shaky earlier, and he didn't imagine seeing her mom would improve things. The last thing she needed now was to doubt him.

Lance stood up and met Chaz's eye. Unspoken was his misgiving. He would have done it all up front. He would have gone to the door and explained everything to Rese from the start. Maybe it should have been that way. But she'd been so hostile. What if she had said no and gave him no chance to help Nonna?

He'd done what he thought was right. But when had it ever worked that way?

———

Lance was there as she drove in, looking as though nothing mattered more than her and that, even though she had refused his company that morning, he was not deserting her. Rese parked the truck, wondering what she would say. If their roles were reversed, he would tell her everything. He kept nothing back, even the things that hurt. Everyone else in her life had hidden things, but Lance gave her truth. Could she do the same?

Looking into his face as she climbed out, she said, "Her hair is white. She's only forty-six and her hair is white." What a stupid way to begin, as though that was what mattered. Rese swallowed hard. "She didn't know it was me."

Lance closed the door behind her. "It's been fifteen years."

And she had changed. They both had. "Brad knew it all. I asked him."

Lance frowned. "I'm sorry."

"It's like some macabre joke." If it didn't hurt so much. Her mother's words, *"Poison gas. Breathe in, breathe in . . ."* Pain tore through like the flame from an acetylene torch. And Dad and Brad thinking she'd turn out the same? Would she be sitting like that in twenty years, laughing at death and seeing the president with gas bombs in his teeth?

Lance took her in his arms. "You don't have to handle it well."

She snorted. "I'm Vernon Barrett's daughter. I only do well."

"Not here in my arms. Here you do whatever you want. You can holler and scream and call me names. You can even pinch and bite and bruise my sides."

He meant it too. If she totally lost it, he'd be there taking the bruises without a word. But she didn't want to hurt him. She was tired of hurting people. What had she ever done but mess things up for everyone in her life? Dad could have kept Mom home; Mom wouldn't have needed to be rid of her. Brad could have had his crew, and the crew the boss they wanted. She had tried to be what everyone wanted, but no one had wanted her—until Lance.

The thought was both bleak and overwhelming, and with it something fractured inside. She took hold of his face and kissed him, nothing held back, no barriers. She sensed his surprise and his response. For once in her life she was wanted. It might not be much, but whatever she had she would give him. He kissed her back until the shock of her mother's laughter, the dread of her possible future, the ache of loneliness and grief vanished in the need of him.

But he drew back. "Rese . . ."

"Don't stop. We can—"

"Don't." He pressed her shoulders hard into the truck, a fierce expression contorting his face. A blood vessel pulsed in his neck, and he seemed to fight for words, something Lance Michelli rarely struggled with. And then it hit her—he didn't want her either. Before she could react, he pulled her abruptly away from the truck and dug for his keys.

She knew what he intended. "No, Lance." If he didn't want her, he should say so, not take off on the bike using miles and motion to say it for him. "Forget it." She tugged free, but he scooped her up and sat her down hard on the bike. She tried to get off, but the engine roared to life. She clutched onto him, hollering, "No!" until they hit the open road and accelerated so fast the wind caught her hair and trapped her breath in her throat. No helmet. No jacket. Only Lance and the road and the rage.

It was a long time before he sensed the anger leaving her. The Petaluma highway wound and dipped and flew beneath his tires, a two lane road forcing him to concentrate, to take the focus outside himself. What did she think she was doing?

He had expected to comfort her, to drag the words out if he had to. He had even expected anger, an explosion of hurt. He had not expected ardor, but he should have. He was the one who first comforted her with a kiss. She couldn't help it if this hurt required a passion he could barely restrain.

Lord! He would keep driving until he hit the coast, lose himself in Muir Woods and the rocky cliffs, take a sailboat into open water, into the heart of the Pacific Ocean and dissolve into the rhythm of the waves. But Rese was with him, and as far as he went, the desire for her would come too.

After Tony's death, he vowed chastity, poverty, humility, whatever it took to be what Tony would have been. He'd left the band and that lifestyle, thrown himself into serving wherever he found need, and he'd found plenty of it. Nonna's need had brought him to Sonoma. Now there was Rese.

Don't think about it. How could he think of anything else? It wasn't like

Sybil plotting to use him. Rese was artless, responding to what he'd started that night in her kitchen, trying to take away a bad experience. Now she thought he would do it again, only she didn't know what he knew, that once they went there, there was no going back.

It hurt to think of it. It hurt not to. He wanted her so bad, but not like that. Yes, like that. Any way at all, and how was he going to stop it? Too much access; too much chemistry. Didn't she realize the restraint he exercised every time he kissed her?

He wasn't steel; he was flesh and blood, and right now his blood was running hot. *Lord, help me.* There were two ways around this that he could see, and she would have to choose. He ran onto the shoulder of the road, skidded to a stop, and got off.

Rese swung her leg over and erupted from the bike like a wildcat ready to spring. Well, he had some adrenaline of his own. He'd misgauged the dulling of her anger.

"Do you want to marry me?" he shouted.

"What?"

"You heard me."

Her eyes shot fire. "Are you out of your mind?"

"Answer the question."

"Don't tell me what to do!" Her hands shook as she clenched them into fists.

He gripped his hips. "A fine submissive wife you'll make."

She grabbed a chunk of pavement and threw it at him.

He ducked. "Yes or no."

She threw another chunk. "No."

"Then new rules."

Her arms stiffened at her sides. "What rules?"

"No kissing."

She huffed her breath. "Right."

"I can stand it if you can."

She glared. "Fine. No hands."

His brows jerked up. "By that you'd mean neck rubs, hugs, walks hand-in-hand?" Because he hadn't touched her in any way he shouldn't, and not for lack of desire.

She drew herself up. "You're Mr. Rules."

He looked at her angry mouth and wished he hadn't started it. But next time he wouldn't be able to stop. "Fine. Get on the bike."

She stood there, arms stiff, glaring as though she could melt him into a pile of lead.

"Yo, Nails. I said get on the bike."

She flounced back on, planting her hands with such force on his shoulders he would have laughed, but she'd take his head off. His energy was dissipating as what he'd done sank in. *"Do you want to marry me?"* He was seriously thankful she hadn't said yes, even if there was a twinge of regret. Okay, more than a twinge. It had been a crazy, impulsive urge, but the only way he could think to handle the situation. With Rese it was all or nothing. But she'd been awfully quick to choose nothing.

―――――――

They stormed off the bike in opposite directions, Rese to the shed, where she would no doubt imagine a piece of wood his head, and Lance into the house, where Rico stood at the foot of the stairs with Star. Neither spoke as he stormed past, but the peripheral glimpse he got suggested symbiosis. Unlike him and Rese. Opposites might attract, but theirs was an energy equaling nuclear reaction.

Chaz was ensconced in the kitchen with a Bible expository the size of a suitcase. His legs were crossed at the ankles and the spicy fragrance of his Good Earth tea rose from the cup. The bag was wadded up on the saucer squeezed by the string, and that was just about how Lance felt. He tossed his keys on the table and barked, "Make yourself at home."

Chaz looked up from the book. "Did you tell her?"

He opened the pantry and began to assemble ingredients for minestrone. "No."

"Then why do you look like a palm tree in a hurricane, mon?"

"I asked her to marry me."

Chaz studied him with a commendable aplomb. Rico would have greeted that announcement with a feigned coronary. Chaz said, "Why?"

Lance expelled his breath. "I don't know. It made sense at the time."

"Not much foundation for a lifetime decision."

"Yeah, well, she said no anyway."

Chaz nodded. "Therefore the hurricane."

"Listen." Lance planted his hands on his hips. "I don't know what Nonna wants, and I don't know what Rese wants, but I'm totally sure they both want something."

"You might try honesty."

"You think I don't want to?" Lance spread his hands. "If I tell her now, she's going to doubt everything else I've said and done since I got here."

Chaz nodded. "A logical assumption, mon."

"Fine. But the truth is I do love her, and I do care how this turns out." He swallowed. "I made a promise to Nonna. She's done so much for me my whole life. Now she's weak and incapacitated. Do you expect me to just drop it?"

"It's not what I expect. What does the Lord say?"

"The Lord's been a little ambiguous."

"His word is not ambiguous. He who speaks the truth from his heart shall never be shaken."

Lance closed his eyes. "Chaz, I know. Just as soon as I've done what Nonna needs, I'll tell Rese everything."

"He will bring to light what is hidden in darkness, mon, and will expose the motives of men's hearts."

"I'm counting on that." Lance planted his hands on the table. "Because my motives are pure."

"Your methods get you in trouble."

Lance met Chaz's eyes, unable to produce a valid argument. He pushed back up and took out a cutting board and knife. Star and Rico came in, looking like Antony and Cleopatra. Did they even talk, or were their eyes just linked in some etheric communication?

Star ran her fingers along the counter to the vegetables he'd laid in readiness. She took a moment to arrange them in a still-life position, tipping her head and adjusting them until they pleased her eye, then scattered them again. "'Striving to better, oft we mar what's well.'"

Lance smiled in spite of himself. "Good thing. Your scene will soon be minestrone."

"Yet art still. The hand of a master renders nothing less."

Hard to tell, sometimes, whether it was Shakespeare or her own poetic words. He handed her a knife. "Would you get me a branch of rosemary?"

She took the knife and went out to the herb bed. He was fairly certain she would get the right one, since they had discussed the different plants at length. He turned. "Earth to Rico."

"No way, man. I like it out here."

What was it with this place? Some aura of benevolence that melted sense and nurtured love's sweet allure? "Star's got issues. You might have noticed by the choke marks on her throat."

"No problem. I put a contract on him."

"That's not funny." Lance grabbed an onion and cut the top, peeling back the crisp layers. "I already have people accusing me of piracy and mob connections."

"I'll take him out myself." Rico's hands tightened.

Lance understood the sentiment. But there would always be more abusers, and women like Star would find them.

Chaz closed his book. "'Vengeance is mine, saith the Lord.'"

Lance glanced over his shoulder. "It's just a little long in coming sometimes."

Rico shook his head. "How could anyone hurt her? She's . . ." His breath seeped out in a sigh.

Rendered speechless? Lance turned back to his onion. He pointed the knife at Rico. "Just remember our agreement. Hands off." Rico could stay, but he was not sleeping with Star. If he could resist, Rico could too. They may as well both suffer.

Only Rico didn't seem to be suffering. "I'm a new man. Transformed by courtly love. No brush of the fingers, no feminine gaze has had such amorous effect."

Lance shared a glance with Chaz.

Rico shrugged. "Sex would spoil it."

Star came back with the spiky branch of rosemary and laid it with care on the counter. Her fingers were elfin in shape and size, the nails cut close to the pink. "Rosemary for remembrance." She looked up into his eyes, held it, then turned to Rico. "The bed sheets in the dryer need folding."

Rico motioned her ahead of him, and they went out together to make the plain domestic chore a courting ritual. Lance could just imagine them bringing the edges together and joining them like steps in a dance. He could court Rese like that . . . if he wanted. He didn't have to touch her. He had more self-control than Rico by far.

Some guests had returned, and he heard them in the parlor where he had set out the afternoon appetizer before waiting outside for Rese. He would ordinarily go converse with them, but he was in no mood for it now. Thankfully the swinging doors Rese had installed at both entrances to the kitchen kept her suite and his workspace private. It had created a sense of unity that now seemed implausible.

The first time he'd ever managed the word marry, and she'd turned him down flat. Of course, he'd shouted it, and they hadn't built much foundation, as Chaz kindly pointed out. Crisis did not a perfect union build, and their whole relationship had been one continuous calamity.

He couldn't even say long calamity, but its brief duration had not limited the intensity. Time had never been a factor for his heart. Not at the front end anyway. It was more believable that he'd propose after less than a month than that he'd be around a year later to do the same.

Out on the road, the desire to keep going had been potent, but for the first time he'd imagined someone planted permanently on the bike with him. Unfortunately Rese hadn't felt the same.

CHAPTER THIRTY-SEVEN

"I ... wan-t ..."

"Good! Better. Now together. I want."

"I ... wa-nt."

"Water. I want water."

"I ... want ..." A sly sparkle. "Wi ... ine."

E vvy took the box from her shelf. She hadn't looked through it for a long time, but the ache of Ralph's passing made her nostalgic. She eased herself down into the chair and rested the box on her lap. He'd been like the littlest angel in the children's story, presenting her with the things that meant the most to him, his worldly treasure. This box was the most precious thing she owned.

Tears dampened her eyes as she reached in for the ring box and snapped it open. A gold band with a vine and grapes coiled into its surface. *"For the day you say yes."*

But she hadn't. Marriage wasn't in the plan for her life. It would have spoiled what they had, made her complacent. At least that's what she'd told herself. Too independent to give up her autonomy, too set in her ways. Too afraid to let go and love again.

She set the ring aside and reached for the next thing. A letter. She'd read it before, but she took it out and read it again.

Dear Evvy,

This deed has been held for two generations in trust for Antonia DiGratia Shepard. My father received it from the hand of Quillan Shepard to safeguard for his granddaughter Antonia in the event of his death. She is the rightful owner of the DiGratia vineyard and the heir to all the estate. I have been a steward only, and claim no ownership for myself. For this reason I could not sell this house, even when it became too much for me.

Your house also lies on the property deeded herein. I don't know how it came to be built and the property divided, the fields developed into the neighborhood where we live. But I have kept the portion entrusted to me for Antonia. It is a sacred family trust for a debt owed.

Yet my mind is failing, though you are too kind to point it out. Therefore I am placing the deed into your care against the day my decisions are no longer my own. I would leave it to my son, but he sees only the value of this property and I fear he would wrongfully sell it. Keep it for the day Antonia returns, or entrust it to someone who will do the same.

Your loving friend,
Ralph Martino

To Evvy's knowledge, Antonia had never returned. She must be too old, or dead herself. At least Ralph had faded enough by the end that he didn't know what happened to the house, that it was sold as he'd feared, and that now the young people next door were giving it life. Maybe she should give them the deed.

She laid the letter down and reached for the book. Antonia's diary. She had forgotten it was in there, and who was it who'd asked about it? She was growing as forgetful as Ralph. No matter; it would come to her. She laid the book back in the box and sighed.

She had coughed all night, the burning in her chest suggesting a fresh grip of pneumonia. She'd kept it to herself this time. God could work a miracle if He meant to keep her ticking. Otherwise, she'd be joining the party.

The last things in the box were the wooden birds Ralph had carved. He knew how she liked to watch the little creatures hop and bob about her feeder. She ran her finger over the wood. That girl Rese had a gift for it herself. She might enjoy the birds. Evvy set them on the table for the next time she saw her. Then she closed her eyes and dozed. *Soon, my Lord. Soon.*

Abrasion could be thoroughly satisfying. The repetitive motion of stroking the sandpaper over the wood until it was softer than her own fingers relieved the tension that had bound her up as tightly as a noose. Seeing Mom had triggered all sorts of memories that crept up like shadows behind the doors and threatened to strangle her. And Lance certainly hadn't helped.

Rese set down the sandpaper and checked the back of the drawer where the tongues fit the grooves and the glue had sealed. Inserted, it slid effortlessly along the glides. She had gotten the wardrobe plans from the Internet, then modified the crest to accommodate the carved scallop to match the bed. She had already given the wardrobe three coats of stain and a hand-rubbed finish. This final sanding was with the finest-grained paper to smooth imperfections only she would notice.

Lance would have considered it done, and maybe she was obsessing. She had made cabinets and banisters and built-in desks, but they'd always been part of the whole. This freestanding piece was like an orphan wondering where it should go, and she was reluctant to be done with it. Rese frowned, refusing to see herself standing there. She was not an orphan.

Her mother might not know her from the president, but she was still her mother, and Rese felt the caretaker role settling over her as though it had never ceased. Put a little girl with a needy, unpredictable mother and a myopic dad and what do you get? An emotionally abandoned super-controller.

So why had she lost control with Lance? Blood rushed up her neck as she tore open the hinge packaging. Didn't everyone have the right to go a little crazy sometimes? Expecially when people thought it already? She'd played Alanna . . . only she hadn't been acting.

And Lance . . . Lance was utterly unpredictable, a knot in the wood, a short in the wire. When she thought she knew what he wanted, he changed it. She didn't like surprises, and he was born erratic. *"Do you want to marry me?"* She could almost think he'd mocked her. A prank. Or else he'd been so confident she would say no . . .

New rules? She hadn't made the old. She had said business. He was the one changing things, making her want, making her think he did too. She wished she'd hit him with the pavement. New rules? Fine with her.

Star pushed open the door. "Dinner is served." That meant the guests had been served and the rest of them could gather in the kitchen for whatever marvelous thing Lance had prepared, before he and the guys played music, even though it was not Saturday and had not been advertised. So far the guests had been all too pleased with the impromptu sessions. Of course, they'd been plied all day at the wineries and came back inclined to extol everything.

"I'm not hungry."

Star twirled a spiral of hair. "He said if you said that, he'd come out here himself."

So if she didn't go in, he'd think she wanted him to come out. She had a padlock and was tempted to use it. But her stomach growled, and Star bit her lip and giggled. She was all lightness and air today. Wasn't that nice.

Rese threw down the hinges. "Fine. If he doesn't want doors on his closet, his skeletons can just fall out."

Star gave her a piercing look.

"It's just an expression, Star." She pressed past her to eat before Lance came after her.

———————

"Aren't you playing?" Those were the first words out of her mouth. It had been like old times, serving her a meal and watching her clam up. Rico, Chaz, and Star had conversed between serving and clearing, but until she filled the sink with steamy suds, Rese had said nothing.

Lance shook his head. "Not tonight." They could, of course, for themselves or whatever guests were interested, even if the posters in town only advertised Saturdays. "Star's showing the guys the Sonoma night life."

"What Sonoma night life?"

"Whatever there is."

Rese slid the plates into the water, but he didn't leave. Her jaw tensed. "Don't you have something to do?"

He took down the dish towel.

She glared. "I can do that."

"I have never questioned your abilities." He had half expected to drag her out of the shed and been a little disappointed when she came in with Star. But this exchange was showing him all he needed to see. They'd taken about twenty steps back; she was stiff and uncomfortable again, and the new rules kept him from changing that.

It had been the right decision, hadn't it? His only other option would have been to sweep her into the carriage house and make history. And the carriage house had enough history already. "Rese, about before . . ."

"Don't."

"What?"

"Remind me." She shoved a plate at him.

"You mean you forgot?" He toweled the plate.

"I'm trying to."

He smiled. "Any luck?"

She sloshed the water. "I'm good at putting things out of my mind. Runs in the family."

There she was. He'd thought for a minute he'd lost her altogether.

"Any chance you can put it out of mine?"

"Lance, your mind has a mind of its own."

"Say that ten times fast."

She almost smiled. This was reminding him too sharply just why he'd asked her to marry him. Unpremeditated, of course. Just that Achilles' heart leaving his head behind. His hand reached out, but she shoved a plate into it. Man, she was good at rules.

He watched her hand move over the dishes, the line of suds caught halfway up her arm, the plunk and splash of the dishes moving in and out of the water. Rico was right. The brain could go just about anywhere with anything.

He dried the last fork and handed her the towel, sorry to see the suds go and the sheen disappear from her skin. She had beautiful forearms, strong and developed. How many more things would he notice now that he was yearning from afar?

She hung up the towel. "Thanks."

She started to leave, but he grabbed the container of minestrone he'd filled earlier. "I'm going to check on Evvy. Want to come?"

For a moment their gazes held, but she said, "I'll go over tomorrow."

Right. No walking hand in hand.

She turned away. "I'll be in the shed if anyone needs anything."

"No power tools tonight."

"I'm past that." He didn't know if she meant cured or at a different stage on her project. Either way, he would bet she'd find something to do out there all night. By the stiffness of her step, she'd have a very productive eight hours.

He walked over alone and knocked on Evvy's door. It was a very long time before she opened it, looking weary and frail, her eyes underscored with shiny blue shadows, her lips pale.

"Evvy, how are you?" He couldn't hide the concern in his voice.

She waved a hand. "Been better; been worse." Her voice sounded hoarse and flimsy.

"May I come in? I won't stay long."

"Why not? It's been a regular circus. People bringing meals, sending cards."

He held up the soup he'd brought. She started to laugh, and it became a cough that sounded like more than a sore throat.

"Have you had that checked?"

She nodded. "I have the nurses across the way nagging at me."

So he wasn't the only one to notice, but if she had medical professionals checking in, it might not be as bad as it seemed.

She stepped back. "I'm glad you came. I have something to give you."

He followed her in.

Evvy sank to her chair, looking exhausted. "Rese might like the little birds on the table."

He reached down and picked up a wooden bird with its head cocked to the side.

Evvy said, "Ralph carved them. Whittled, I guess."

He studied them. "She'll appreciate the workmanship." Or at least the gesture.

"He would have loved what she did for the house. The old place meant a lot to him." She leaned but couldn't reach what she wanted. "Get that envelope, Lance."

He started to hand it over, but she stopped him, saying, "Open it."

He sat back and looked in the envelope. It held two things and one looked much older than the other. "What's this?"

"Read the letter."

He took out the smaller, newer paper, though the sight of the other had charged him for no reason he could tell. But as he unfolded and read, it became clear. He could hardly draw breath, and speech was out of the question. He looked at Evvy.

She murmured, "I'm not sure I have the energy to hold onto that. You and Rese are making the place a home, even if it does house strangers and rock my windows with music." She smiled as she said it. "I don't know who Antonia is, but if she hasn't come yet, I can't see the harm in letting you have that deed."

His heart was pounding so hard he thought it might rock her windows. If he didn't say something, she'd wonder. "Thank you, Evvy. I understand the charge, and I'm sure if Antonia comes, something can be done."

She sank back with a soft smile. "Somehow I knew you'd understand."

Much more than she knew. He was humbled and shaken by her trust, but if this wasn't God's hand, then he'd never seen it in his life. He stood. "Will you be all right?"

"Oh, yes," she murmured.

And he sensed that she would.

———

Strange how peaceful she felt as she watched him leave, as though the weight had left her chest. She knew nothing about Lance Michelli except what he'd told her and what she'd seen. And yet . . .

She closed her eyes. *I hope I did right, Ralph. You can scold me if I didn't. Not that you ever would.* She took the gold ring from the pocket where she'd tucked it, and closed it into her palm. Life was a circle for those who believed, the end only the beginning.

"Open for me the gates of righteousness; I will enter and give thanks to the Lord. This is the gate of the Lord through which the righteous may enter. I will give you thanks, for you answered me; you have become my salvation."

Her chest was too heavy to cough, her eyes too heavy to raise. But inside she felt light as air.

Lance all but staggered to the carriage house, more thankful than he could say that the guys were out with Star. He couldn't face them right now, couldn't face anyone. It might be the Lord's hand, but it had fallen so heavily he couldn't stand. He closed the door behind him and dropped to his knees. *Lord!*

He held Nonna's deed and the letter naming her the heir, and it both thrilled and devastated him. "What am I supposed to do?" He bent over and groaned. If he laid it all out, he'd destroy what Rese had dreamed and accomplished. She might fight him in court, but that would be worse than he could imagine. It couldn't be what Nonna wanted, couldn't be what God wanted.

And yet the house had impacted him from the moment he saw it, calling to him to right the wrongs committed inside. How? He pressed his fists to his face. He could turn it all over to a lawyer, hit the road and put miles between his heart and Rese. He could go back and tell Nonna he'd done it, that without even knowing what she wanted, he had taken back what she'd lost.

His chin sagged to his chest. *Please. Show me your will. I can't do this alone.* What were his motives, the motives God would expose? To score one for the family who lost Tony? To get back what was wrongfully taken long before that? His breath came sharp and tight. To make Rese love and need him enough to give it over without a fight?

He groaned again. It was all so wrong. But Quillan lay unburied, Vito was shot down, Nonna forced out, and two generations of friends had held the property for her in trust. He took it out and stared at the deed that had quickened his heart. His inheritance. His birthright. More precious to him for that reason than the escalated value of the property. The wine, the cash, none of it mattered as much as the lives that had made this place. Yes, he wanted it. But was he willing to hurt Rese for it?

CHAPTER THIRTY-EIGHT

I dream of Papa with holes in him like lace.
Lance tries to put his fingers in the holes.
No use. There is only one thing he can do.
One thing.
Does he know?

Antonia opened her eyes. There was no blood, no bullet holes. That was only in her mind. She'd heard, but not seen it. She swallowed, recalling the fear, the haste, the terrible sound. Nonno's hand in hers. She imagined, but she'd never seen Papa dead.

Only Nonno.

A wave of grief. Why had she left him lying in a tunnel, no headstone, no epitaph, nothing to mark his grave. He would have wanted to lie beside Nonna Carina. His heart had joined her in the graveyard when he laid her there, and his place was with her. Instead he'd lain alone in the dark, secret tunnel. Barricaded, hidden, but not forgotten.

Tears stung. What had she been thinking? Even Papa had been buried. Joseph Martino would have seen to that, she knew. But in her frenzy, all she could think was to hide her Nonno, to keep them from finding him and the cellar and whatever Papa had down there.

She didn't want to remember that night, but the past came now and sat heavily on her mind. The darkness of the night with no moon. The dampness in the air. Car doors closing outside when no one should be there. The glimpse of figures in the yard, then rushing to get Nonno, to hide in the cellar.

Papa had told her to be ready if trouble came. He had shown her the tunnel, the cellar under the carriage house that she had not known was there.

Then he had gone away. Why did he have to sneak off in the middle of the night? What could he be doing at that hour? Something to do with Arthur Tremaine Jackson. How she despised that man. He was cold as the finger of death, and Papa should have seen it.

But he hadn't, and they were all in danger because of it. Rousing Nonno, she took him down, down into the cellar. Was it waking him like that, hurrying him, or the shock of what they heard overhead as they slunk away to save themselves? All of it, maybe, had stopped his heart. She didn't know.

But Arthur Jackson had killed Nonno as surely as he'd killed her Papa. And she had left them there. Her hand trembled, clutched up against her like a broken wing, stiff and useless. She felt the helplessness she'd known that night. Nothing she could do to change what was happening, no way to make it right.

———

The wardrobe had a finish Drexel Heritage would envy. The drawers moved like silk, the doors hung straight and fitted together perfectly. Except that it wasn't in place.

It belonged in Lance's bedroom, and Rese didn't for the life of her want to get it in there. She could ask Chaz and Rico to help move it, but they were in the kitchen with Lance, cleaning up from breakfast. She had snuck in while he did his thing with the guests, grabbed a fruit-filled pastry and escaped back to the shed, but there was nothing left to do. Even the scraps from her project were accounted for, the sawdust vacuumed and surfaces wiped.

Only the wardrobe was out of place, Lance's wardrobe. The closet for his skeletons, as he so humorously put it. He'd been kind over dishes last night, pretending she hadn't made an utter fool of herself, and had left her alone after that. She couldn't avoid him forever, but she might manage a year or two, just to let the hurt and humiliation settle. She had never let Brad see how she felt, but she'd laid it all out with Lance. Here I am; take me. Instead he'd made new rules.

The whole thing had kept her awake all night, producing a wonderful freestanding closet and raccoon circles under her eyes. That wouldn't matter as long as he didn't see her, and he wouldn't see her if she just had something to do. Evvy. She had said she'd visit Evvy and if she did it now, while he was cleaning up, Lance wouldn't try to come along.

Rese left the shed and took the driveway to the street, then headed for Evvy's house, but her steps jammed. The ambulance parked in the driveway made no sound, but the lights . . . Her throat closed up. She couldn't breathe; she couldn't move. Waves of terror; Mom swaying like a branch in the wind. *"Go to sleep, Theresa."*

She started to shake. Her feet had sunk into the concrete, were concrete themselves. Her neighbors stood outside the door, the two night nurses. They must have called for the ambulance. They must have checked on Evvy when they'd come home from their shift. As she watched, the medics came out with the stretcher, the form on it covered completely.

Rese staggered, groped for something, then felt the hand on her back. She turned, and Lance took hold of her. They weren't supposed to touch, but she was not reminding him. *"Everything will be different in the morning."* She closed her eyes as memories surfaced so powerfully she felt herself lifted and borne, the oxygen mask pressed to her face.

She drew hard, shallow breaths, fighting for control, hating the helplessness. Even then she had fought it, swearing she would never be helpless again. She tried to pull back, but inertia had claimed her limbs.

"It's all right," Lance murmured.

It wasn't, and it never would be. She couldn't just put away the experience as though no one had tried to kill her. It was embedded deep inside. *"Poison gas. Breathe in. Breathe in."*

His arms closed tighter. "It's okay, Rese."

She fought to come out of herself. She wasn't the one on the stretcher. It was Evvy. And that brought a sorrow of its own. "She's gone."

"She was ready. I sensed it last night."

"I should have gone with you."

He rubbed her back. "There's no place for should-haves."

Wasn't there? It seemed like that was all she had.

"She gave you something." He eased her away and took a carved bird from his pocket. "There are four of them. Ralph did the carving. She thought you'd appreciate them."

She took the bird and stroked the whittled lines. Not a masterful job, but he'd captured the essence. She looked into Lance's face. "I wish I could have thanked her."

"That's why I tried to catch you. I was going to give them to you before you went over, but you slipped out."

She looked away, sorry for the reminder.

"Can you walk?"

"I don't know. Seeing the ambulance . . ." Panic seized her again, but she fought it down.

"I guessed as much."

He would have. "Will it ever go away?"

"It'll get better. Especially now that you're dealing with it."

Was she? Did freaking out at the sight of an ambulance and accosting him yesterday mean she was dealing with it?

He eased her into motion and she made her legs work. They went in through the gate but not up to the door. Instead he cut over to the side of the house, around the almond tree and behind the sweet bushy honeysuckle. "This'll do."

"For what?"

He didn't answer, just kissed her long and deep.

What was he trying to do, keep her so off-balance she couldn't find her feet? "I thought we weren't doing that."

"That was yesterday." He clamped her head between his palms. "New rules."

She rolled her eyes. What good were rules that changed for every situation?

"Kissing and hugging only. Oh, and neck rubs—you need them."

"Does it do any good to say no?"

"Only if you mean it."

Did she? "How good is your memory?"

"If you're referring to yesterday against the truck . . ."

She grimaced.

"It's stupendous." He tipped her face up. "I'll just consider that your bid."

She frowned. "Will you be taking others?"

"As I recall, you rejected my counter offer."

And there went her legs again. "You weren't serious."

"Wasn't I?"

Rese stiffened as the ambulance drove by from Evvy's, but the paralysis was passing. Maybe she was facing it, taking hold of what happened and dealing with it. Just as she had with the pranks and struggles she'd handled before. Affliction causing endurance causing character causing hope. Maybe, just maybe . . .

Lance had spent the early morning hours in prayer, begging the Lord for answers. He had searched out and denounced every selfish desire connected to the situation: his attachment to the property, his sense of family entitlement, his sense of injustice, his longing for rectitude, his craving for Rese, his fear for Nonna. *Just give me a sign!*

He'd come back from church and made breakfast, still uncertain in his mind. But watching Rese stagger at the sight of the ambulance was sign enough. No wonder she'd panicked when he threatened to call one for her. It wasn't a conveyance of life and hope; it was part of a nightmare. People had hurt her, but he wouldn't be one of them.

Evvy was gone. The thought brought a slow, seeping sadness, even though he had sensed her peace last night, her readiness. It would have been a quiet step from this world to the next, and a pretty good time at the other end. He would miss her wit, her spunk, even her scolding.

She had trusted him with something important to her, and he didn't take that lightly. He couldn't give back the deed, couldn't tell her it compromised Rese, or that he knew Antonia. All he could do was handle it as he saw best. Rese had bought the place on good faith. And Nonna had all those years, while people held the deed, to go back if she'd wanted.

How he'd tell Nonna that, he wasn't sure. And how he'd explain it all to Rese was even less clear. That was the problem with departing from the truth to start with. Chaz would agree. But he'd made a commitment to Rese. They were partners in the business, a responsibility he intended to fulfill. And Rese might not believe it, but he wouldn't have asked her what he did yesterday if it wasn't a possibility taking greater hold of him every day.

He would try to understand what Nonna needed, but she would have to see Rese's side as well. He hadn't expected it to line up that way, and he didn't want to fail Nonna, but the time had come to choose from the possibilities. And the hammer-wielding woman making the best of a traumatic past and a daunting future paled every other choice.

Rese Barrett was brave and determined, frustrating, amusing, and in need of everything he offered. He didn't care how long it took for her to come to the same conclusion. This time he would see it through.

He went into the carriage house and nodded at Vittorio. "I'll introduce you soon." He would have to communicate with Nonna, go there maybe, during a gap in the reservations that seemed to be coming in spurts and bunches so far. He could show Nonna what he had and hope it was enough.

He took out the box that held the things from the attic, the book and letter from Conchessa, and the deed. He laid it all out on the table. It wasn't much to offer, except for the deed, the one thing he'd fight her on if he had to; the property belonged to Rese.

He started to gather it all up, then remembered the briefcase from the cache in the cellar. He had shoved it against a rack as they scrambled to close things up when Star came down. In the panic of it all, he'd left it there. He shook his head, exasperated. It could hold all the answers he hadn't found, and he'd left it lying in the cellar.

Rese was napping after her all-nighter finishing the wardrobe he and Chaz had carried in earlier. It was beautiful, and she had drawn plans for a real table and chairs, but she didn't put up much of a fight when he told her to sleep first. They would lick that insomnia somehow, but right now he was glad she slept. The guys were in the attic teaching Star songs, and once Rico got going he wouldn't stop.

Flashlight in hand, Lance opened the hatch and went down, stopping at Quillan's side, not to explain exactly—it was only bones after all, bones that had lain undisturbed for over seventy years—but to confirm the sense that it was almost over.

The air was cool and still, not chilly or damp, but he felt a shiver up his spine. What did the briefcase hold? Proof of misdeeds? The reason for Vito's murder? Answers, or more questions?

He got through the racks to the one they had pushed aside. The briefcase listed against the next rack over. *Let it be the answer, Lord.* He squatted down and propped the light up. The clasp was the sort that could be locked, but it wasn't. Pulse quickening, he opened the briefcase.

There were brown envelopes inside with little cardboard disks and string to hold them closed. He unfastened one and removed the papers inside. A photograph of a man and a couple of handwritten pages that seemed to be a dossier: name, age, marital status, employer. Then it got more detailed: who he talked to and when, dates, times, and money amounts.

Lance slid the papers back and opened another. Probably more of the same. But the name jumped out at him. *Jackson, Arthur Tremaine.* The name Jackson struck him for obvious reasons, but where had he heard Arthur? It had to be from Sybil, but what had she said?

He racked his brain back to their early conversations. Banking. Her family was in banking and . . . her great-grandfather. Didn't she say Arthur? Or was he just trying to make it fit? He sat back on his heels. This one read like a who's who of American families. A prominent banker would be expected to meet with such people, but at four A.M.?

He pushed the papers back into the envelope. Without a careful study, he couldn't tell what they were or what they'd been intended for, but they'd been hidden in a cache in a cellar for seventy years—a cache with enough bundled bills to raise eyebrows and suspicions, his own included.

He'd made excuses to Rico, but when it got right down to it, he might not like the answers to his questions. Lance dropped the envelope into the briefcase. Should he check the hole one last time? Star's shriek had put the fear of God in them before they finished searching the last time. He stood and put a shoulder to the rack. With so many partial answers, he didn't want to miss anything else.

The bundled bills lay as they'd been scooped back in, and he pressed his arm through to the bottom where his fingers found stone all around. Nothing in there, unless you counted a few hundred grand. He picked up a stack and fanned it. All twenties, and at least twenty bills in each bundle. He could use some money to get back and see Nonna, but he wasn't about to spend it, not without knowing where it came from.

Had Vito robbed the bank? Sybil had not given a sterling impression of her great-grandfather. More likely he and Vittorio were in on something together. Then why did Vito end up dead? Double cross? Had he stashed the money for himself, thinking he'd get away with it? Lance dropped the single packet of bills into the briefcase. He'd show it all to Nonna and maybe get some answers.

He pushed the rack back into place. The scraping echoed on the stone walls, the motion jingling the empty bottles in their curved cradles. He glanced up the stairs toward the pantry entrance. Even if the sound had traveled up to the kitchen, there was no one to hear it. Thank God he'd be done with the secrecy soon. He would tell Rese everything. He just had to communicate with Nonna first, get her blessing.

He picked up the briefcase and headed back through the tunnel, past the moaning metal gate to the stairs. He would present the pieces he'd found, hope she could put them together, and pray it would be enough. His head had justed cleared the hatch when the door opened. Lance froze, but Rese stood there with his cell phone in hand.

Lord!

"It's an emergency." Rese held out the phone.

It hit him in the pit of his stomach as he climbed out and took the phone. "Momma?"

"It's a minor episode. No new damage, but Nonna won't rest until she talks to you."

He swallowed. "Put her on." Rese was staring at the hatch from which he'd emerged. Her confusion mingled with his fear for Nonna and the growing sense that once again he'd blown it.

There was the sound of the phone shifting hands, then, "L-l-ance."

"I'm here, Nonna." She was speaking, not lying unconscious like the first time. A minor episode Momma had said.

"Fin-d Nonn-o. Qu-Qu-Quil-lan."

He closed his eyes. "I found him, Nonna."

"Bury . . . him."

Lance rubbed a hand over his face. That was what she wanted? A proper burial for her nonno? "I will, Nonna."

"Goo-d boy."

His eyes stung. She always thought the best of him. "Nonna, there's other things. I have lots of questions." Not as many as Rese must have right now, but if Nonna could just answer . . .

A long silence in which he pictured her struggling for words, then she ground out, "Bu-ry Nonno."

"Okay." He swallowed. He had way too much to worry about as it was. "I love you."

He hung up and looked at Rese. He must have left the phone on the desk when he had processed reservations.

Her gaze went from the hole in the floor to the things laid out on the table. "What's all this?"

He would have known how to say it when he got back. He'd have found a way to keep from sounding like a liar.

"Lance?"

"My family's things."

"Your family." She looked from him to the hatch in obvious disconnect.

"This property was my grandmother's." He didn't say "is", but she looked back at the deed lying on the table, picked up the letter beside it.

"Rese . . ." He took the letter before she could get too far.

"Evvy? That letter's to Evvy."

"It was from Ralph. He was holding the deed in trust for my grandmother Antonia. He gave it over to Evvy to do the same. She gave it to me last night." And now it sounded like they were all in cahoots.

"The deed to this property?"

He nodded. "I came here looking for answers. These are the pieces I found."

She stared into his face. "You came here . . . you knew this when you took the job?"

"I guessed. Then when I found the first things I knew." He could see the anger rising in her. "I was going to tell you."

Her eyes were shards. "When?"

"When I had it figured out."

She expelled a hard breath. "Oh, you had it figured out. Kiss up to the stupid woman, make her think . . ."

"It's not like that."

"Right from the start." She pressed her palm to her forehead. "All along." She turned and stared at the hatch. "What's down there?"

Numerous answers clogged his throat. At last he said, "My great-great-grandfather."

"I'm supposed to believe that?" She blazed him. "You made up that tomb story to keep me from looking, to scare me away from the stone blocks."

"I did. But it really is a tomb. Don't go down there until I can get him buried."

"You lied to my face." She shook her head. "Just like everyone else."

"Rese, listen."

"Get off my property."

"Please." He reached for her elbow, but she jerked it away.

"Take what you think is yours and get out. You have half an hour before I call the police." She shook with the words, stared one moment into his face, then stalked out.

He closed his eyes, hurt welling up like tar. But it was her hurt. She'd shown anger, but the pain beneath it had all but strangled him.

———

Rese closed herself into her room and locked the door. She felt stiff all over, as though she'd turned to wood. Her arms didn't feel like her own. Her mouth was dry. She went to the bathroom and took a drink without looking in the mirror. She couldn't bear to see herself.

Right from the start. He had come with a purpose that had nothing to do with cooking for her little establishment. He'd convinced her to hire him on, to make him her partner and more. That morning's kiss still warmed her lips, but now they turned to wax.

She stalked from the bathroom to the office. He was on her Web site; he was in her files. He was all over her kitchen and the carriage house. She went into her bedroom. Even there, in the chair in the corner. His music was in her ears, his features behind her eyes. Not even closing them made him disappear. Only one thing could make him go.

"Rese." He knocked on her door, but she didn't answer.

"Rese, let me talk to you." His voice was thick.

She didn't respond.

"Please."

She closed her eyes. In a minute he'd go away. In a minute it would all go away. She knew the place. She'd found it when Dad died. She could do it again. So quiet. So still. She sat on the bed wanting to disappear, to let everything disappear.

But she felt the presence, the Lord, blocking her way. She didn't want to recognize it. That was connected to Lance now, and she wanted no part of it.

Let me go.

But a word came as clear as her own thoughts. *Never.*

It hurts.

I feel it.

She knew that was true, though she didn't know how. *He lied.*

Nothing.

I hate him.

Wells of sorrow. Betrayal. Jesus knew betrayal by the one He loved. Jesus knew the hurt, the despair that coursed through her. He wouldn't let her hide, but He'd be there with her. If she let Him.

"Rose."

She never wanted to hear that voice again, never see those eyes, feel that touch, any touch. It hurt too much. She couldn't hide, couldn't escape it. She had told him everything, and all the time he was using her. A small part of her mind wondered why he hadn't slept with her.

Pain. Betrayal. *Let me hide.*

Peace.

She didn't want peace. Rage was better. Rage was stronger. Strong and hard. Rock. She was rock. Lance could dash himself against her. She wouldn't break. She would never break again.

———

Lance leaned his head against the door. He hadn't imagined it would blow up this badly. He could have lied, told her they were things he found in the cellar. There was nothing identifiably connected to him. But looking into her face, he'd given her the truth, and now look where he was.

He pressed his hand to his face. *Lord.* Silence. He'd convinced himself it would all turn out, that he could make it right. Chaz had urged him to tell her; they all had. And he did tell her—too late. He knew how stubborn she could be. She would not listen, not now, not like this.

But it scared him to think how she'd deal with it. He left her door and found the others in the attic. Star and Rico were harmonizing. Chaz played a flute accompaniment. Lance stood there until they noticed, the notes dwindling to a stop. "She knows."

"Oh, man," Rico breathed.

"I have to leave before she calls the cops, but I'd rather she wasn't alone. If she'll let you, can you stay a few days and give me time to figure things out?"

Star stood up. "She fired you?"

"I guess you'd say that." But it was far more than a job he'd lost. He looked at Rico, surprised he hadn't jumped on this chance to drag him back into the band. But then he realized Star had been singing his lead.

Rico said, "Sure, we'll hang."

Lance turned to Chaz. "You were right."

Chaz nodded. Nothing more to say.

Lance turned and went down the stairs. As he reached the carriage house, Baxter raised his head with a sorrowful mien. How could the dog know their time there was over? Or his at least. . . . No. But Rese loved Baxter.

Lance squatted down and fondled his dog's head. He couldn't leave him. They'd been through too much together. But he thought of all the time Rese spent just sitting with the dog. Lance pressed his forehead to Baxter's. "I've got to go." Alone? He didn't have to decide this minute.

He went inside. Star's painting met his eye. That would have to stay on the wall, and Vito's portrait too. Rese had called the bed and wardrobe his, but he knew better. He could fit his clothes and the briefcase in his pack, the travel guitar in its sleeve, and the things he'd found for Nonna in the bike's compartments.

He could not carry the money or the wine. But he could claim it. *Take what you think is yours and get out.*" Rese could have ordered him off with nothing, but she was giving him what he came for, what he'd thought he wanted. His chest seized up.

Was she crying? Or sitting there like stone. Did she have the strength for one more betrayal? He hadn't meant to, not once he knew her. He'd meant to make it right, but how could he when he had started it all wrong? It hurt to think how wrong.

He wanted to hit the road, put as many miles between them as the continent allowed. Going home would do that. But he had to get Nonno Quillan buried. He'd have to convince Rese to let him. But even if she let him bury Quillan, he could never bury the hurt he'd caused her. She wouldn't forgive him. How could she?

Of all the people who'd hurt her, he ranked right at the top. He hadn't poisoned her, but this would kill her inside. She had opened up and trusted him. He castigated himself. But there was nothing he could do. He closed his eyes. Maybe there was one thing. He could turn her over to the Lord. If she was in God's hands, not even Lance Michelli could mess that up.

He drew a haggard breath, packed all his belongings, then told Baxter to stay and got onto his bike. He drove to the plaza, took a tiny room in the Swiss Hotel, where the ceiling was cracking and needed repair. He worked a deal to do the repairs and stay until he finished his other business. Stooping under the slanted roof, he dumped his pack on the bed and took out his guitar. He sat on the edge and played the song he'd sung for Rese that night in his room. The song of his life.

> *On the brink alone he stands with quick and eager feet.*
> *Jump across and run, boy, don't worry what you'll meet.*
> *For in the days before you, life will intervene*
> *With all the things you yearn to see and all that you have seen. . . .*
> *Don't close your eyes and wonder what lies across the gap;*
> *There is no road before you; you cannot find the map.*
> *For with your heart you forge a way that angels fear to tread,*
> *And gather up your troubles for the day when you are dead,*
> *And gather up your troubles for the day when you are dead. . . .*
> *Run, boy, run. Run with all your might.*
> *The sunrise burns before you, and on your heels the night.*
> *And if the darkness lingers long, you'll lose your soul's own song;*
> *Yes, if the darkness lingers, you'll lose your own soul's song.*

CHAPTER THIRTY-NINE

Star looked from Rico to Chaz. "This is bad, isn't it."

Rico blew a breath between his lips. "It ain't good."

Chaz laid the flute across his knees. "His heart is good. But he doesn't think. Like Peter, putting on his clothes to jump into the water."

Star frowned. "Huh?"

"From the Bible. When the apostles saw Jesus on the shore from their fishing boat, Peter put on his clothes to jump in and swim. Coming from an island, that seems backwards to me. But Peter was passionate. Like Lance."

Lance was passionate. Knockdown attractive, warm, expressive. He'd be wonderful on the stage. She'd play beside him in a heartbeat. She would have done a lot of things beside him if it weren't for Rese. Even that had gotten sticky. For her—not Lance. He cared about Rese.

But she knew Rese, the immovable object. She would use this like a fresh coat of concrete, cement herself in and not look back. Star's breath caught as Rico came over and took her hands. Without Lance, they had no restrictions. She'd give herself to Rico, but . . .

"Lance is worried about Rese. Maybe you should—"

"She doesn't need me. She never has."

Rico's features were sharp and mysterious, his stature perfect. She would lose herself in him, cease to exist altogether. What could be better? No more Star; no more pitiful Star.

"Have you tried?" His voice was velvety soft, but what was he talking about? She'd almost been there, total annihilation.

"Tried what?" She'd do anything for him. The more she did, the less she was.

"To help Rese."

Help Rese? How could she possibly help her? Rese was her rock in the storm. She'd always been the strong one. Help Rese? With what? "'Bid me discourse, I will enchant thine ear; or like a fairy, trip upon the green; or like a nymph, with long disheveled hair, dance on the sands, and yet no footing seen.' But more than that I cannot do. I can't."

She pulled away from his gaze, turned and rushed down the stairs to her room. The thought of reaching out to Rese strangled her more surely than Maury's hands. *Here I am, Rese. Here I am to comfort you. Lay your head in my lap and let me brush your hair.* How the gods would laugh! *Look at her, poor Echo, trying to be seen.*

"I am wind; I am sunshine. I am . . . nothing. Nothing."

She gripped her hair and rocked.

Anger sustaining her, Rese stood up from the bed. She glanced at her clock. Almost an hour since she'd brought him his phone. If he wasn't gone, she'd get the police. He knew what that looked like.

She jerked open the door and stalked to the carriage house, but faltered when Baxter jumped up, whining, and licked her hand. She had thought Lance would be gone, that he wouldn't force her to evict him. She spun, but his bike was gone, her helmet lying beside the shed.

It didn't connect. He'd left Baxter? She dropped down beside the dog, wrapping him in her arms. "What are you doing here, boy?" Baxter whined, and a more plaintive reply she couldn't imagine. Had Lance deserted him?

Maybe it wasn't even his dog; maybe he'd used the animal to get to her. No. She'd seen the love between them. She pressed up and went into the carriage house, Baxter trailing behind. Nothing was gone except his clothes and guitar and the things from the table—including a deed to the property.

Would he fight her in court, try to take it away? Rese sagged. What difference did it make? She couldn't run it without him. But then she stiffened. She would not be lied to and seduced into giving up this place. She didn't need him or anyone else. She turned and stared at the floor. Only when she got down and looked did she find the edge of the hatch.

She had put that tomb business out of her mind, trusted Lance to close it up. She reached down now and pressed the release, then pulled up the hatch to find stairs going down. Lies. All lies. What was down there that he wanted to keep so secret he even lied today?

The flashlight stood on the floor where he'd set it. She turned it on and shined it into the hole. Just a cellar most likely, as she'd guessed before he dissuaded her with his tomb talk. She started down.

The beam from the flashlight illuminated no more than eight feet ahead, and this was just the sort of dark, closed-in space she hated. But she raised her chin. If Lance could do it, she could. Compulsively competitive? You bet.

It wasn't a cellar. She gaped down the tunnel, trying to make out an end, but the light didn't extend far enough. A mouse skittered past and she shrieked. The way it darted out with no warning. . . . She hated things she couldn't see coming.

Pain tried to break through, but she pressed it down. Allowing it had made her weak, blind, stupid. Lance said she couldn't handle things alone, but he was wrong. She could and she would. And now the anger came back to strengthen her. Secondary emotion? Primary defense. She would not forget that again.

She raised the light. A metal gate blocked the tunnel, but it wasn't locked. She pulled it open on creaky hinges and went through into the deepening darkness. There was nothing to fear.

Her light caught something on the floor, and she beamed onto it directly as the breath left her lungs so she couldn't even scream. She groped the wall with one hand and stared. Nothing the guys had ever done compared with this. Lance had told her it was there, told her not to go down. How could she know that part was true?

She shut her eyes and breathed the rank, musty odor. Her stomach clutched. She wanted to go back, but she wouldn't. She had to know what was down there, *all* that was down there. Tight to the wall, she went by the corpse, and shortly after, the tunnel opened into a cellar. Racks and racks of wine covered with dust, but surprisingly few spider webs.

She shined the light around, searching the racks as she walked. Was it worth something? Enough for Lance to seduce her? Fury spouted like a geyser. He could take it all, as long as she never had to think of him again.

She came to the end of the racks. Another set of stairs. A gasp of relief. She wouldn't have to pass the corpse again. She climbed to the top, but a bar jammed the opening mechanism. A shudder crawled her spine, and she spun, shining the light back into the cellar. Nothing. But she did not want to walk back that way. She'd get out right here.

She propped the light and took hold of the bar. Even if she got it free, the mechanism might be stuck. This cellar had not been in any of her structural plans, and obviously it had been a very long time since this end had been opened. She jerked the bar. It didn't budge. She raised the light and studied how it was wedged into place.

It must have been jammed into the toothed gears first, then pressed or hammered into the wall. Putting her hands near the wall end, she yanked again, feeling the smallest amount of give. Or was it desperation?

She could get out the other way if she had to. A skeletal corpse was not going to hurt her. As Lance said, the dead didn't bother the living. It was the living you had to watch out for. Rage filled her, and she ground her teeth and pulled. The bar came free and she stumbled down, knocking the flashlight from its perch just as something popped behind her.

Instinctively she dropped, catching her knees on the edge of a step and sliding to the bottom. She could see nothing. Heart hammering, she groped for the light, straining for any sound, and caught a soft noise. Not someone crawling toward her. No stealthy footsteps.

It sounded like a tiny trickling brook, and she whiffed a sour smell. She pressed up to her knees and breathed it in. Wine? She expelled a breath. Could that loud of a pop have been heard through the walls? She closed her eyes with grim humor. So much for ghosts and gunshots.

Throat tight, she felt again for the flashlight, crawling around the base of the stairs, praying no mice would run over her fingers. She banged her head on a rack, but found the flashlight at its base. Sitting back on her heels, she pressed the switch.

Nothing. "Come on." She pressed it again, shook the light and pressed again, but the bulb must have broken. She dragged herself back to the stairs and sat on the lowest, the useless flashlight across her knee. One thing was certain; she was not crawling back through the tunnel in the dark.

She pulled herself up the stairs, felt the wall until she found the gears she had freed from the bar. One of them had a small handle, and she tried to make it turn, hoping the bar had not broken the mechanism. The metal groaned but didn't budge.

She yanked and shoved, let go and pushed the wall. *Open.* She was not afraid of the dark, but it was in the dark she'd always imagined . . . Walter. And he had told Mom to kill her. Her pulse quickened. He's not real. But she looked over her shoulder as though she could see anything in the perfect blackness of the cellar.

Wouldn't a cellar have a light? She groped the wall at the top of the stairs. A small shelf might have held one once, but it was empty now. She grabbed the gears again and jerked back and forth, but they wouldn't turn. She knew enough about old machinery to guess she was wasting her time. But she couldn't give up. Not yet.

Creeping down the stairs, she searched for the bar that had fallen free. *Please don't grab anything warm.* It was lying against the wall, and she picked it up and went once again to the top. Swinging the bar in the dark, she aimed for the gears and missed. She adjusted her aim and swung again, then tried the gears. At this rate she'd break the handle off before she made them move.

She would not panic. She wasn't trapped. She could get out the other way. She just had to go back through the dark to do it. She tried the gears again. *Just open.* But it didn't. Why would she expect anything good to happen? This was just one more— Pain broadsided her, and she staggered.

There in the pitch-dark hole she could not fight it. Tears came. Tears Lance would neither soothe nor ever know about. Sobs racked her hard enough to hurt her sides, then anger took over again. She slammed the bar into the gears again and again, screaming, "Open up!"

But it didn't. Clutching the bar, she walked down, feeling the stair with each foot before taking it, then found the floor and groped for a wine rack. She could feel from rack to rack to get through the cellar; she just had to concentrate.

There was no one there to jump out at her, no one playing tricks. It was just dark, empty air. The racks would keep her straight. No chance of getting lost. Not some cave with winding passages. Walk. Just walk. But fear crawled her spine.

Lance had read something about darkness and fearing no evil, but she didn't remember the words and there was no evil to fear. No evil. But when she reached the end of the racks, she could not make herself grope for the tunnel. It was stupid. She could hardly get lost. The worst that might happen was a stubbed toe. Or Walter grabbing her.

Stop it! But even knowing he wasn't real could not keep her childhood nightmare away. His evil was real; that morning's memories of the ambulance proof of that. Maybe people only thought Mom imagined him. Maybe she had the ability to see what was really there.

A shudder shook her, and she raised the bar to the darkness. "Stay away from me. I'll crack your head if you have one."

Her voice echoed in the chamber. She had to walk into the tunnel, the narrow walls, the low ceiling, and somewhere a corpse on the floor. She closed her eyes and steeled herself, then let go of the last rack and felt for the wall. Nothing but air. Two steps, then three. She swung the bar to see if she was in the tunnel already. Just air for another step, then metal on stone.

She groped forward and found the entrance of the tunnel. Relief rushed in. She was not going to die, though she was mad enough to kill. Lance knew the cellar was down there. He had laid her down in his lap, with the cellar beneath them, and he never said a word.

All those times when they talked and he sang or read to her. . . . She had to keep it from hurting. If she let it hurt she would lose her mind; she'd be there right beside Mom. Grief was a psychotic trigger. At any moment she might actually see Walter.

She spun around and pressed her back to the tunnel wall, straining in the darkness, not quite as inky as the cellar. Was that movement behind her? A shifting of the shadows. Her heart took off racing. If Walter stepped out of the darkness she would die right there. But he stayed just out of sight, as he always had, working his evil on her mind, on Mom's mind.

"There is a God and there is evil." She didn't know about God, but she could believe in the devil; she'd known him all her life.

Fury surged to her defense. "Come out and get me, you big coward!" She heaved the bar into the smothering darkness and immediately regretted it. As it clanked and rolled on the floor somewhere far behind, her hands felt empty. The metal had given her a sense of safety, and he'd cheated her of it. Just as he'd stolen her safety that night alone in her room.

She stood there shaking, afraid to turn around, to grope past the skeleton with her back to Walter. *He's not there!* But he was. A presence as real and engulfing as Jesus had been. Nothing she could see; she was blind, hardly knowing up from down. But she could feel the hatred that fueled her own, and terror worse than she'd ever known.

Her anger vanished, and she was speechless with fear. She would die, as he'd meant for her to die all those years ago. Her legs jellied; her palms dripped sweat. She could not run. She started to sink. *Just give up.* She would fall, and he would step out of the darkness and drag her into its maw.

Jesus. She could hardly form the thought, but the child inside her remembered.

"Rese?"

She spun and a light shown in her face. She staggered against the wall as Chaz made his way to her. With everything inside, she drew herself up. "I broke the flashlight."

He pressed his into her hand. She grabbed it like a pole in a raging ocean, then turned and shined it behind her. Nothing—at least as far as the beam extended. "How did you know I was here?"

"I heard you banging, but I couldn't get through."

So he'd gone in the other way. She swallowed. "You knew the tunnel was here?"

He nodded. That meant Rico knew too.

"Star?"

"She found it."

So everyone knew but her. She recalled Star's piercing look when she mentioned Lance's skeletons. But Star had said nothing. Sworn to secrecy? Lance sure knew how to sink the spear.

She started past the skeleton lying just feet from where she'd almost collapsed. Her rubber legs hardened as she moved. She sensed Chaz right behind her but didn't check to see. She had looked foolish enough.

Climbing the stairs, her legs actually ached, and not just the knees where she'd fallen. The muscles themselves clutched up. But she was out; she was safe. She was furious. She turned on Chaz. "Where did you hear me banging?"

"In the pantry. I was walking through the kitchen and heard you."

The pantry. She turned off the flashlight and stalked to the house. The pantry required the ceiling light even in the day because of the depth of the space. Chaz stood in the doorway behind her, and she addressed him without turning. "Which wall?" But she'd already guessed by the configuration and the way the stairs had come up to it.

"The end."

Lance had filled the shelves with cans and bottles, but she searched through them for any sort of device, then found a hole plugged with a chunk of wood. She pulled it out and felt the lever inside. She pressed the lever and the metal gears released. No doubt she could have done that from the other side as well, if it wasn't pitch-black and terrifying.

She grabbed a shelf and pushed, and the wall swung out with a ponderous groan. She opened it just far enough to verify the tunnel, then heaved it closed again with a shudder she made sure Chaz didn't see. She left the pantry and shut the door.

Hunger hit her like a blow. She must have burned through Lance's breakfast in the tunnel, and it felt good to imagine it purged, but what was she going to do without him? She had reservations and no cook. No entertainment, no managing partner. . . . She spun when Star came in with Rico, and they were all three staring at her, conspirators with Lance, gaping at her now.

Star had a hollow look, but brightened when their gaze connected. "'Oh it is excellent to have a giant's strength.'" Typical Star, seeing only what she wanted to.

Rese squared her shoulders. "I suppose you'll be leaving now that Lance is gone." She directed it to Chaz and Rico but guessed it might mean Star as well. A wave of panic struck her at the thought of running the inn alone, but she masked her face.

Star said, "They don't have to, do they?"

Rese frowned. They were Lance's friends and had no reason to be there without him. No reason to any of it without him. She slammed the door on that thought.

Star twisted her hair into a wad. "You need help."

"No, I don't." Her Help Wanted sign had caused everything that followed. She'd rather do it all alone than let anyone help her again.

Star wailed, "You can't cast us out. 'The miserable have no medicine, but only hope.'"

Who was Star to think she had the corner on misery? "I'm not telling you to go. I just assumed you would."

"How could we leave you?" Star came and took her hands. "Friends forever."

Rese swallowed. What did that mean? And what possible good was it? "Anyone know how to cook?"

Lance pressed the phone to his ear, relieved Rese had allowed Chaz and Rico to stay. He suspected that if Rico left, Star would go with him, leaving Rese alone with all of it.

"It's only until she hires a cook, mon." Chaz spoke softly. "I thought you'd want to know."

He did. He wanted to know everything: how she was doing, what her neck felt like. But he knew that without being there. He'd taken a crowbar and rammed it in where her tendons should be. "Chaz, I've got to fix this."

"That would take voodoo, and it's not allowed."

Lance squeezed the bridge of his nose. "She's that mad?"

"She's . . . stoic."

Stone. Hard. Guarding herself. He drew a slow breath. "If I could just talk to her. . . ." Hold her, comfort her.

"She said if you set foot on the property she'd shoot you."

"Let's hope she doesn't have a gun." He'd faced some pretty tough neighborhoods, especially Rico's. He'd never been shot, but he'd been knifed, and maybe that was a more accurate description of the pain he felt now, slow and slicing.

"Nonna wants me to bury Quillan."

"Rese would be glad of that."

Lance closed his eyes. "Did she go down?"

"I heard her banging and shouting through the pantry wall. By the time I got down the other way, she had broken the flashlight and was . . . pretty scared."

Lord. He sagged. "What do I do, Chaz?"

"Seek first the kingdom of God, and all things will be added."

Lance sank down on the bed. Wasn't that what he'd been doing? Or was it his own kingdom he'd built, sharing his faith because of who he was, not who God was?

CHAPTER FORTY

Drained, head aching, Lance went into the narrow bar side of the restaurant downstairs instead of the elegant room where he'd dined with Sybil. He chose one of the small tables along the wall, picturing Rese in the kitchen, arms around herself, chin set. *"I don't date my employees."*

"Why not?"

"It's bad policy."

And it was. If he'd kept it business as she had intended, she would not be hurting now. She might be furious; she might be fierce. But he could take that. What he couldn't stand was the visceral knowledge of how much he'd hurt her. Because if what was going on inside him was anywhere close to what he'd made her feel. . . .

He sank into a chair. Behind the bar a panel was carved with the year Prohibition was repealed. The carving reminded him of Rese; the date, of Nonna. There it was in a wooden panel, his dilemma. Just when he thought he had figured it out, it got turned back on him again.

He opened the briefcase of dossiers he had carried down. He had no idea how to make things right with Rese, so he tackled the search that had brought him there in the first place. What had Vito been involved in? Illegal trafficking? Money laundering?

The bartender asked what he wanted. Lance could answer that, given a year or two. But he supposed the man meant in a smaller sense. Food was not tempting, but his head ached from stress and lack of nourishment, so he ordered a burger and fries, then read through the pages on Arthur Jackson.

A period of the man's life was detailed on those pages, but there was nothing overtly damning except the odd times he met with people for what seemed to be transactions. Whoever had recorded it all had gone to a lot of trouble to tell him very little. He knew when and with whom, but not what, as though the what was already assumed and this was just a record of its happening.

Lance narrowed his eyes at the page. Dates, times, payoffs, transactions. Someone watching and recording. But what was the reason for such meticulous scrutiny? Blackmail? The two photos were poor, probably shot from a distance.

He picked up one and then the other, looking closer at Arthur Tremaine Jackson. He didn't see much resemblance to Sybil, and certainly didn't recognize the people with him. But the photos might have meant something to someone.

His burger came and he took a few bites while he perused the other envelopes. Some of the men looked like downright thugs. The muscle of the operation? Their pages also had dates and amounts, but again listed no reason for the payments. No sales of merchandise, no services rendered.

If Vittorio had compiled these, he knew—or was working for someone else who knew—what the entries meant. They were very discreet records, but the fact that they'd been hidden in the cache suggested their incriminating nature. Someone didn't want these found.

And what about the cash? Blackmail? If Vito had something on all the guys represented in the envelopes, that might account for the hefty stash. He chewed a tepid French fry, then pushed the plate aside and uncoiled the string on the last envelope as Sybil slid into the chair beside him. He hadn't seen her come in, and her sudden presence was like a vulture lighting. She must have smelled carrion.

She set down her glass of wine. "You look miserable."

He sighed. "You look great. As always."

"Your flattery will get me nowhere." She flicked her hair back over her shoulder.

He smiled grimly.

"I heard you took a room here."

"You did?" That was quick, even for a smaller town than Sonoma.

She winked at the bartender who blew her a kiss. "Donny listened to me rant after the last time. He thought I'd be interested."

The man had said nothing of Sybil to him. But given their respective allures, that was understandable.

She raised her chin. "All's not well at the inn?"

"I don't want to talk about Rese." Not to Sybil; not to anyone.

She ran her finger around the fastener of one envelope. "Haven't seen one of these before."

Her great-grandfather's dossier was buried, but Lance gathered them all and closed them in the case.

"More research on the inn? Or family history? Or both?"

He didn't answer.

She clasped his thigh. "We're on the same side, you know."

"Sybil . . ." He reached down and removed her hand.

She shook her head with a little laugh. "There you go with all the things you won't do." She took a French fry from his plate. "You didn't eat your dinner."

"I'm not hungry." What he wanted was to be alone. To get a plan, to . . . find his way.

"What if I gave you the letter anyway?"

Meaning no strings attached? He leaned on his elbow. "Why would you do that?"

Her eyes traveled him, enigmatically. "Do you believe in karma?"

"As in past lives?"

She shrugged one shoulder. "As in bad things coming back to haunt."

Oh, yeah. He could write the book. "What bad things?"

She sipped her wine. "What do you think the chances were that we would meet?"

"Had to be pretty good, since we did."

She leaned forward. "Preordained?"

"Sybil . . ."

"I'm not making a pass."

Draped like that, her blouse was making it for her. He adjusted his position to limit the view.

The candle flame glinted on her glossed lips. "There's a reason why you're here, why we met as we did. We have a connection."

He swallowed. "There's no connection, Sybil. I was using you and Rese to find what I wanted. And I made it all some holy quest from God."

Sybil raised an eyebrow. "Well, that's honest."

"Thought I'd try it for a change."

She drained her goblet, and Donny had her replacement before she set it down. She traced the moist path a drop had made with her finger and licked it. "The difference is it bothered you. Of how many people would that be true?"

He shook his head. "I don't know." But before she started thinking more of him than she should, he stood up. "I'm sorry, Sybil. I really am."

She leaned back in her chair. "And I had to fall for the last cavalier." Then she reached into her purse and took out the letter.

Rese clenched her fists. Eyes open and pacing, anger ate at her: a dull rage at Mom for wanting her dead, indignation at Dad's dishonesty and doubts, and a sharp fury with Lance. She couldn't go out to the shop and work, not with guests sleeping upstairs. She couldn't sand floors or build furniture. She was exhausted, but the strain had pulled her neck so tight she could hardly bow her head.

If she tried to lie down it was worse. Every time she closed her eyes she jolted up with a surge of panic. Her heart rushed, her chest compressed. Then she was up again, pacing the hallway of her suite.

Lance had come looking for answers. She didn't know the questions. All she knew was that it hurt. She had removed the entertainment poster, taken his name and pictures from the Web site, but she couldn't delete him from her mind. And as angry as she was with him, she was more furious with herself. Like Mom with Walter, she had seen what wasn't there—a man who loved her.

Pathetic! She was pathetic. Her eyes closed . . . but the moment she lay down, it started again. Waves of panic. *Don't close your eyes. Don't sleep.* Too many things to hurt her—things in the dark and things in the light. She couldn't tell the difference. If Lance could fool her so completely . . . Lance and Dad and Brad. . . .

How would she know? How could she ever know? She hunched her shoulders, gasping for breath. *"So it's surrender you don't like. Losing control."*

"No, Lance. It's betrayal I don't like. And I'll never lose control again."

Lance sat on the bed with the envelope in his hands. He had wanted it, as Sybil knew, wanted whatever he could get, whatever she could find. Answers, information. Pieces to put together. To fix what was wrong. Make it all right.

He slid the envelope back and forth between his thumb and fingers. Sybil had surprised him, giving it up with no return favor. Why had she changed her mind? It didn't matter. He had what he thought he had wanted. Lance turned the letter over. The envelope was new. Like the other things from Sybil it would be a duplicate of the original. Not like the letters from Nonna and Conchessa.

"Use it wisely," Conchessa had said when she gave him the letter expressing Nonna's fears, but he'd been neither wise nor honest. Nonna hadn't talked, just sent him to Conchessa, but he doubted she would approve of his decisions since. With his eyes on his goal, he had excused his means, and hurt Rese. Whatever the letter revealed, it would not undo that.

He tipped his head back, aching. She would not sleep. That would be two nights in a row, and she'd be stressed out in the morning, and there was nothing he could do. Not even Tony could make this one right.

Tony. With his big muscles and his big laugh and his big heart. Tony with his knuckles on Lance's head and his arm around his shoulders. His stories and his lectures, courage and dedication and sacrifice. He'd worn the mantle. He deserved the accolades.

"It's dangerous to see too much in anyone. And worse to think you have to match it." Rico nailing him between the eyes. The problem was translation— Lance trying to be Tony. Maybe Tony did have faults, but the real fault was in him, not his brother. He had made an idol and worshiped it.

Now it was time to fix his eyes on what was real. If he was looking to imitate, where should he turn but to the one who never failed? The one, as he'd told Rese, who made a way even through the failures and mistakes. But man, if he couldn't manage Tony, how would he ever do Christ?

He set the letter on the table and took out his Bible. Starting in Isaiah, he read, *"He was despised and rejected by men . . . and we esteemed him not."* Lance pictured Tony, how hats had literally and figuratively come off in his presence. Not a bad thing, unless one sought after it for personal glory. He didn't know what was in Tony's heart, but it was clear what was in Christ's, and more clear what had been in his own.

"He was oppressed and afflicted, yet he did not open his mouth." Lance saw himself harassing the protestors, venting his hurt, his anger. Not that it was wrong to remind them of the evil that was done, but his own pain and anger had driven him. He wasn't fighting for Tony, but for what he'd lost and could never have again.

And in Paul's letter to the Philippians: *"Who, being in very nature God, did not consider equality with God something to be grasped, but made himself nothing, taking the very nature of a servant."* Lance rubbed his face. He had balked and fumed against Rese's authority, wheedled himself a position of equality—then assumed control.

And John the Baptist's claim: *"He must become greater; I must become less."* There lay the challenge; to *not* prove himself, not fight for recognition and acclaim. To be the mouthpiece of the Messiah, taking no glory to himself.

And finally, Jesus washing the feet of His disciples. Christ as humble servant enabling His people to carry on in His place. Lance sat up with a jolt. That was it.

———

Rico's pancakes were a far sight better than anything she would have put out, but hardly the gourmet breakfast her guests had expected. Rese had dragged herself into the kitchen without having slept at all and started making lattés when Rico offered to give pancakes a try.

Star was in the dining room explaining that the chef was out for an emergency, but she hoped they liked the pancakes. Rese could not bring herself to go out there and make small talk. She would check out the ones who were leaving, thank them for their stay, but she could not go out and be friendly with no sleep and the aching hollow inside her.

Chaz touched her shoulder. "Are you all right?"

"Of course." She finished frothing the milk in the cup and added it to the espresso. She just needed to find a cook. She would call the ad in today, but how long would it take to get someone? It had been immediate with Lance, but then, he wasn't there for the job. It was only a means to an end.

Star came in for the drinks and gave her a silent roll of the eyes. The guests were not happy. She should never have featured Lance and his creations. It was more of a draw than she'd known. It had set her place above pancakes and muffins. People didn't like not getting what they had been promised, and she had a whole summer full of people who'd been promised Lance.

It was looking better and better to cancel reservations and refund the money. But that would be admitting failure. Anger braced her spine. How weak was it to hide in the kitchen while Star made her excuses? *You're nothing but a chicken girl.* Wrong. *You can't handle everything alone.* Wrong.

She drew herself up and stalked into the dining room. "Good morning." She sounded like a CEO starting a board meeting. The guests murmured their responses and looked as though they were expecting something. Well, you can't walk in sounding like you have an announcement, then not make one. "I want to apologize for my cook's absence. I'll be finding a replacement as soon as possible. Until then pancakes will have to do."

The young Hegle couple immediately said, "No problem." Feeling her discomfort no doubt.

Julia Feingold sniffed. "It's not what your Web site promised."

An older pair, the Harrisons, were even less accommodating. "We came here for the gourmet meals."

Rese faced them. "I know there were expectations, but a situation arose that I was required to deal with. There are other good restaurants in town."

Mrs. Harrison wagged the flesh under her chin. "We're paying an exorbitant price for a room with the promise of a chef and entertainment."

Rese was about to offer them a discount when she realized that was backing down. "My price is comparable to any inn in Sonoma. If you want to stay somewhere else, I'll refund your next two days."

"We shouldn't have to move." Mr. Jordan was small, but forceful like a bulldog. "We've arranged vineyard tours for the next two days."

And her rooms were nicer than any he'd find, even without Lance. She was about to tell him that when she caught sight of Star in the doorway, slicing her finger across her neck. Right. "I'm sorry for your inconvenience." She turned and walked out, nearly running into Rico bearing fresh plates of pancakes.

In the kitchen, Star stuck her fingers to her skull and closed her eyes like a crazed ballerina. "Fric-tion . . ."

"Well, what do they expect? I'm doing the best I can." But she had sounded sharp and aggressive. *"You'll have to work on your presentation."* She clenched her teeth. "What's wrong with pancakes anyway?"

Star gave her a probing stare. Chaz wore one of polite concern. Rese didn't want to see Rico's face when he got back from the lions' den. She stomped into her room and shut the door. The Hegles were checking out today, and after her announcement, the others might be leaving as well. She would have to face them, but she was crawling inside her skin.

How had she ever thought running an inn a possibility? She didn't want people demanding things from her, criticizing her efforts . . . as she had criticized the crew? That was different. She pointed out their mistakes so they could correct them. Get it right; make it perfect. She could not make this right or perfect. But she had never delivered less.

Until now. Fine. She was stressed. She was worn out. She . . . never made excuses. She pressed her fingers to her head like Star. Friction? Star should feel the static inside *her* skull. One minute of that would have her thankful for a brain that . . .

Rese slumped onto her bed. She was envying Star's brain? She needed sleep. She looked at her watch. Checkout wasn't until eleven. Maybe no one would want to leave earlier. She put her head down, reliving last night's anxiety, but now fatigue brought sleep.

———————

Why didn't Rese answer? Star knocked again. The guests wanted to check out, and she had no idea what to do. Put her in front of a crowd, give her a mic and a stage—no problem. But business? Forget it. That was Rese's part. Not that Rese was excelling this morning. Her conciliation speech had been dreadful. Didn't she know how to suck up at all?

Rico's pancakes were not Lance's fabulous breakfasts, and she couldn't expect people to be happy about that. The whole place was thick with bad energy. She had to get out. But first she needed to wake Rese. She knocked harder.

"What do you want?" Rese pulled open the door.

"'Fie, fie! unknit that threatening unkind brow, and dart not scornful glances from those eyes.'"

Rese rubbed a hand over her face, but it didn't help. She looked horrible, her eyes red and pinched in. Where was the strong Valkyrie?

"Your guests await your gracious service."

Rese glared. "What time is it?"

"Three quarters past the hour of ten, milady. And thou art still abed." She reached over and smoothed Rese's hair, but Rese pulled back annoyed.

"Stop it."

"Then go check out your guests."

"The Hegles?"

She nodded.

"I wish they'd all go." Her pain was tangible, emanating as she walked away. Rese, the island in a sea of weaker souls. Rese, who had tackled Bobby Frank for calling her friend a psycho. He was right, but Rese had defended her.

Now who was there to defend Rese? And from what? Herself? She'd sent Lance away. A person couldn't sever her heart and not expect to bleed. But what if she required a surgeon? Waves of fear seized her. She couldn't do it. Someone else. . . . but who?

Star went to find Rico, whose energy force she needed. Lance had possessed a benevolent spirit, a warm and watchful aura. Rico's was less certain, a little fractured, maybe. But then so was hers. She found him using nunchucks behind the carriage house. He looked like a pirate, much more pirate than Lance, but the sort who might call you back from the end of the plank, save you at the last moment. But from what?

He stopped working as she approached. His skin had a sheen of moisture, his hair was damp, his eyes a little fey. He hung the nunchucks over his arm, breathing hard from the exercise. Star went up close and made her plea. "What was Lance doing here that was more important than Rese?"

Rico didn't move, and that was significant. He was perpetual motion, one part always playing off another. He said, "You have to ask him."

She raised her arms, crossing them atop her head. "How can I affect a cure unless I know the malady?"

Rico caught one stick and tapped it against the other as they hung by the chain over his wrist. "I can't nark him out."

She understood keeping secrets. But she was scared. "Rese is bleeding."

He jolted. "What?"

"You can't see it, but her life is hemorrhaged."

Rico shook his head. "That's between them."

But it wasn't just them. They'd all come together in a sustaining convergence, each forming a piece of the whole. It was the first time she'd felt essential, dared to hope she could be better than she'd been. But it was disintegrating. And that wasn't the worst of it.

"I'm losing her." Star let her arms drop. Just saying the words sent a tremor through her. Rese was the only person she could trust. She needed her.

Rico reached out and took her hand. "Something's gonna happen."

"How do you know?"

Rico's eyes took a volcanic cast. "Cuz Lance has got a thing for fixin' stuff. And he's pretty tight with God."

Star seized the thought. Hadn't she seen it herself? Maybe it wasn't up to her. Maybe . . .

CHAPTER FORTY-ONE

Rese snagged the mail from the box without looking or caring. The Hegles were gone, but no one had checked out early. Unfortunately. Star had changed the bed, cleaned and aired the Jasmine room. Rese didn't inspect her work. It took more energy than she possessed.

She set the mail on the desk in her little office. If it contained deposit checks, she wanted to send them back and cancel those paid through the Internet. Every payment was a nail in her coffin.

But she looked now at the top envelope, blank with no stamp or postmark. A hand-delivered note? She opened it and took out a folded recipe card. *Crepes, with ricotta filling and berry sauce.* Lance had written the recipe out and added a note at the bottom. *You can do it. Just like before. Lance.* She gripped the edges to tear it to shreds, but paused.

The morning's fiasco was fresh in her mind, and his words had triggered the memory of making the crepes, slowly swirling the batter in the bottom of the pan. It hurt to recall, but could she do it? Herself? He'd laid it out in painstaking step-by-step directions. If she practiced, maybe. She'd mastered everything else she'd put her mind to. And she had a whole day before she needed to serve something. . . .

Lance's name at the bottom brought a surge of anger. She wanted nothing from him. But then she pictured Mrs. Harrison's face. Crepes with ricotta filling and berry sauce were better than pancakes. If she could manage it, they might not mind that every morning.

Rese battled back the anger, then carried the card to the pantry and gathered the ingredients. She had it all set out and was halfway through preparing the batter when Star stopped in the doorway and gaped.

"Lance's recipe." Rese shoved the card her way. "There's some fruit in the refrigerator. Why don't you try designing a garnish?"

Star beamed, reaching for a paring knife and fruit as she might her paints and palette knife. She spent the next hour cutting berries and pears and apples and arranging them on the edges of plates as she'd seen Lance do and then improvised her own. Rese had the three parts of the crepes mixed up; now she had to cook them.

He'd made a special note to cook it over medium-low heat, and she recalled the burnt oatmeal she'd served him. She was not going to burn these crepes after all that work. She had almost scorched the sauce but caught it just in time.

Not too much, he'd written, just a little batter went a long way. She poured, then swirled, let it set a moment, then slipped the spatula underneath and flipped. It was a pretty golden color, and as light and flimsy as his had been. Her heart raced. Taking it from the heat, she slid the crepe onto a plate, filled and rolled it, and spooned the sauce over. Then she handed Star a fork, and they started on opposite ends.

The sauce did have a bit of a burnt taste, but Star stared into her face. "You did it."

Rese nodded, hardly daring to believe it. "One, at least." It would be different with a room full of paying guests, but they had staggered their arrivals this morning within the hour allotted for breakfast. That would help. She got up to make another, and another until all the batter and filling was used. Star went to find Chaz and Rico, and they made a late lunch of crepes and lots and lots of fruit garnishes.

She managed to sleep five hours that night, then prepared to face her doom. Could she repeat it under pressure? It was just a meal. *"A ritual found in every culture on earth. The breaking of bread signifying connection, acceptance, relationship."* She shook her head. Not anymore.

The effort wasn't flawless, especially in the timing, but the guests were pleased and gracious. Chaz and Rico carried out the plates that Rese filled and Star decorated. It irked that it took four of them to replace Lance, but they were doing it.

That day another blank envelope was in the mailbox. She tore it open and took out the card. *Frittata di carciofi*—artichoke omelets. *These are easy, but you have to watch them, Rese, so they don't dry out. You know what they look like. You can do it.* She slammed the card onto the counter. She didn't want his encouragement.

But she did remember how they looked and tasted. Fewer ingredients than the crepes, and clear directions. They had omelets for lunch, a little burnt at the edges and dry as Lance had warned, but she served them nicely golden the next morning. Star added yogurt to her garnishes.

Another morning down. No complaints. Each time she completed a meal, Rese felt as though she were putting pieces back inside herself. She just wished it didn't seem so futile.

———

Lance was not surprised the small church was filled for Evvy's funeral, nor that the tone of the service was so joyous. The testimonies reflected a life filled with wisdom and service, seasoned with humor and spark. Standing at the back, he listened to the stories of Evvy's life from those who knew her best and longest. His few interactions could hardly be compared, but he had still developed a tenderness.

What did surprise him was seeing Rese in the middle of the church. Even surrounded by people, she looked alone, and he ached to be at her side. That wasn't possible, he knew. But it had to be positive that she could come and honor Evvy's passing. In spite of the grief that filled the church, it was a celebration of a life well lived, of someone who'd gotten it right.

Once he'd seen Rese, he had kept to the back so his presence wouldn't distract or irritate her, or worse, make her leave. Even under sad circumstances, this body of believers demonstrated the life-changing power of God's love, and he desperately wanted Rese to experience that, especially after he'd fallen so short. He prayed she wouldn't equate his failing with God's.

When the service ended, he caught a glimpse of her speaking to a woman in a brown ponytail, and that was his cue to slip out. But once outside the doors, it hit him how much he'd lost. Evvy was in heaven, but he and Rese still had to struggle on. He'd made her life worse, and at the moment trying to fix it seemed a monumental task.

He wanted to go to her, talk to her, lay it all out. Make his case, make her see the intentions behind the poor judgment. But even that was selfish. He'd be defending himself by trying to make her understand. He knew what he had to do; he just didn't want to do it. *Lord, I don't want to do it.* And he had no confidence he'd be able to. Why should this time be any different?

He could not begin to think what stories would be told after his death, but he imagined Rese there enumerating his sins. They might be forgiven, but their effects were everlasting. He got on the bike and drove off just as people were emerging from the church. There'd be a banquet in Evvy's honor—besides the one in heaven.

Maybe Rese would go, make some friends, people to help her walk in faith—and he found a new area to relinquish. Did each loss have to hurt so much? He needed the road. He wanted to ride long and far before more wrongs came to light. That was the problem with possibilities. But it was God's way: total freedom, no decision forced upon an unwilling servant. No walls and traps set out to entangle the disobedient, only the sad consequences of their own wrong choices.

———————

Rese left the funeral in Michelle's cramped car. The woman had insisted she join them for the "feast" and claimed driving her to the house was easier than giving directions. Rese had intended to slip into the funeral and out, but they had engulfed her like white blood cells on a germ.

The only one dressed in black—a skirt and top she had bought for the occasion—Rese squeezed into the house, teaming with exuberant people. It was more like a birth than a death, everyone talking about their "sister's" joy. Or maybe it was a wedding because there was a lot about brides and grooms too.

Rese had been sorry she missed seeing Evvy that one last time, but everyone else was looking forward to the next time they met. Michelle handed her a plate. "Just start at one end and eat your way to the other."

The table was spread with meats and cheeses and rolls and salads and casseroles and desserts. Nothing fancy like Lance's fare, but hearty homey food.

"Evvy was so happy to have you next door."

Michelle's comment startled her. Evvy had talked about her? Positively?

"It was hard for her when Ralph went away. Seeing the house empty just made her think how much she missed him." Michelle added olives to Rese's plate. "You have to try these. They're stuffed with jalapenos. Anyway, she just loved watching you work. I think that's what got her over that first bout of pneumonia. She wanted to meet the determined woman and her knavish companion. Evvy's words, not mine."

Michelle scooped up a wad of potato salad, oblivious to the blade she'd just sunk. "Evvy was always looking out, not stuck inside like some old people. To her everyone was an opportunity."

"Opportunity?" Rese's plate could hold no more, but Michelle tucked a strawberry under the lettuce.

"To share the love of Jesus." Michelle led her to the patio where all the chairs were taken, but there was standing room against the lattice. The house wasn't that small, but it stored the food pantry, coat drive, and donations for the crisis pregnancy center in every room and the patio. Like her car, Michelle had said, it was packed ready to meet any need.

"Evvy knew what mattered most. To put her trust in the Lord."

"There is but one thing that stands. When all else fails, He will never fail you." Rese swallowed the tightening in her throat and fought back tears. She was so tired of holding it together. The anger inside had become a lead weight. Everyone had failed her. Mom, Dad, Lance . . . and now she was failing herself.

"Of course, you have to admit your need." If she did that, she would crumble altogether. She'd been proving herself since she was nine. No one would want to kill her if she was good enough, strong enough, more capable, more talented than any other person.

But she wasn't. Evvy had seen it. Like Lance, she'd seen through what Rese pretended to be, right through to the truth. Tears stung, and in small, broken sentences, she admitted her need.

Lance looked up at the villa as he tucked the note into the mailbox. It didn't surprise him that he never saw Rese when he came. She probably heard the bike and stayed out of sight.

Baxter came bounding as usual, but after getting his due, he didn't beg to come along. He knew where he wanted to be. At least one of them had gotten it right. Lance got back on the bike, imagining Rese's hands on his waist as he drove to his hotel room. It could have been so different. So right. He had told her there was no place for should-haves, but he ate, drank, and slept with everything he should have done. And not done.

He got back to his room and picked up Sybil's letter, still unopened. If it was the final piece in his search, he had wanted to do everything he could for Rese before he completed his task. But Nonna was waiting, and maybe it was time.

Given what he'd deduced from the dossiers, the letter might contain answers he didn't like. Misdeeds and mistakes. But who was he to judge? He'd have been the first to walk away when Jesus said, "Let him among you who is without sin cast the first stone."

But he couldn't avoid it forever, and besides, he felt an affinity with Vito, someone else who didn't get it right. He turned the envelope over, slit the seal with his thumb, then unfolded the letter. The greeting was blacked out, but he guessed it was addressed to Arthur Tremaine Jackson. And if this had to do with Vittorio, maybe that was what Sybil meant by a connection, her family and his.

He moved his gaze to the body of the letter and read:

> *Since you are reading this you must have taken me seriously enough to pick it up from the depot. You won't regret it. My information is accurate and valuable. How valuable, I leave to you.*
> *First point, Marco Michelli is a fed.*

Nonno was a fed? Lance stared at the letter, picturing his grandfather in his uniform. NYPD. He had told every story imaginable, but never that he'd been a federal agent.

He read on:

> *Second point, you got a rat. Someone who shall remain unnamed unless we reach an agreement. Since this situation could jeopardize your future, you should consider my services very valuable. To have the problem eliminated, meet me at the depot tomorrow at noon.*

No signature. But the last sentence was telling. A hit man? Hired by Arthur Jackson to murder Marco? Had he killed Vittorio by mistake? Or . . . Lance sat down on the bed. *You got a rat.* Was Vito the inside man? Working with Marco?

Bad things coming back to haunt. Lance squeezed the bridge between his eyes. The letter had to be addressed to Arthur Jackson. Why else would Sybil have it? *"The paper doesn't have this, the police don't have it. Only I do."* Some family archives maybe. Did Sybil think to atone for the past by helping him now? He swallowed. Maybe their meeting was preordained, but there was no karma about it. Once again he felt the Lord's hand.

Maybe he wasn't useless after all. He picked up the phone. When Lucy got Nonna on the line, he said, "Talk to me, Nonna. What was Arthur Jackson into?"

Her silence confirmed his guess.

"I found a briefcase of dossiers." He listed some of the men in the envelopes. "Looks like a racket, and—"

"N-no."

He stopped. "No what?"

"No m-m-more."

Lance picked up the letter. "What do you mean? I'm getting close."

"Bu-ry N-nonno."

"I'm taking care of that. But—"

"L-l-l..."

He pressed his fingers to his temple as she fought for words. "Just let me tell you what I've found."

"L-l-leave it."

Lance took the phone from his ear as though he hadn't heard right, then put it back. "Nonna..."

"No m-more." Her voice caught on a sob.

The last thing he'd wanted was to upset her. "Nonna, listen. Don't worry, all right?"

"Nonno Quil-lan."

"Yeah, I know." He was working on that. But why didn't she want him to get the rest? "You okay?"

"O-o-kay."

Lance turned off the phone and stared at the buttons. What now? Leave it? She had spoken her mind ... adamantly. Anything else would be disobedience. Shaking his head, he tossed the letter on the table and reached for his guitar.

Tears streamed her cheeks. Shame. Anger. Confusion. *Papa?* Why was he going out so late? Why had he said to hide if trouble came? What trouble had he brought on them? Dossiers. Names. People she wanted to forget. *No more!* Antonia rocked, her arm clutched up against her. *Why, Papa? Why?*

The next card she got was for almond focaccia. Lance's note suggested she get Rico's help since he had watched the grandmother who taught him. It was a lot more complicated using yeast, and even with Rico's help, she made three batches before serving the one that turned out. But each time her confidence grew, and Rese realized she didn't hate to cook; she'd only hated the grim ritual it had once been.

She got a call from someone regarding the advertised position, but now she was reluctant to give it up. She couldn't expect Chaz and Rico to stay for long, and Star's plans were as unfathomed as always. Even so, she told the person the position was temporarily filled. She wasn't ready to add a stranger, even if the others left today.

Chaz and Rico set up and played on Saturday night, mostly instrumentals with Chaz on the flute and sax, and Rico on the drums. They were limited without Lance's lead guitar and vocal, but Star sang a few songs with them between serving tables. Rese made the lattés, and she had purchased biscotti.

Since she had gone around town and yanked down all the flyers, they had only their own guests and a few from the previous week. Without Evvy, the old gang had no reason to congregate there. Without Lance, the energy was diminished. Without Chaz and Rico, there would be no music at all.

But she could run the inn without it, at least through the summer and fall. The scarcity of lodging for those seasons assured that much. The off-season would be more of a challenge, but it pleased her that she could think ahead and see herself doing it.

In the week that followed, they added a baked sausage crepe and bowl-shaped popovers to their choices. Each recipe was hand delivered, which meant Lance was still in town, but he'd made no effort to see her, and she was glad. The cleaner the break, the quicker the fix—which didn't exactly excuse her accepting the recipes. She had made an exception there, based on necessity.

But it was no recipe in the envelope Rese opened now, just a note that caused a rush of suspicion. *Rese, I've made arrangements for the burial of my great-great-grandfather. May I have permission tomorrow to see it done? You can give Chaz or Rico your answer, and they'll reach me. Lance.*

She stared at the note. She had forced the carriage house and the cellar and the skeleton out of her mind. She'd been too busy to deal with it, too scared from her last experience, and unwilling to open herself to the hurt of just crossing the threshold. But now, it seemed she had to.

She walked up to the attic where Star and Rico and Chaz hung out. Star had acquired a multitude of colorful beanbags and a decent, quiet fan that made the place more comfortable. Rese handed the note to Rico. "Lance wants to bury the skeleton." She swallowed. "Will you let him know that's fine?"

More than fine. With the corpse out of there, she could close off the cellar and—What about all that wine? Maybe Lance had plans for it too. She just wanted it over. Once he'd gotten what he came for, he'd go home to New York, and the Wayfaring Inn would be as she had first imagined.

Well, she'd never imagined cooking the breakfasts herself, and she'd still need a maid when the others left. There were visits to her mother and the Bible study invitation from Evvy's friend Michelle. Things looked a little different, but essentially she was back on track—unless Lance planned to sue her for the property.

She should talk to her lawyer, especially since she'd made Lance a partner in the business. Written it up and everything. A nice fat ace she'd given him. And it was anyone's bet which deed would stand up in court.

But if he wanted to take it from her, why send the recipes? Why give her success in those first days when it was all coming apart? She left the attic, starkly aware of her separation from the rest of them. When the guys left, she was certain Star would go too. And she'd be alone. But she knew now who stayed by her, and she could be grateful for that. Not grateful enough to be there when Lance came tomorrow, though.

Lance picked up the phone on the first ring. Even though he'd given her the out if she didn't want to talk to him, he was disappointed to hear Rico's voice. "She says it's fine, man. Put the old guy to rest."

He released a slow breath. "Thanks, Rico."

The police and coroner would have gone over anyway, but he had hoped to be present to give his ancestor the dignity and honor he deserved. Identification should be possible with the photograph in Nonna's box that showed the hair and a DNA match to Lance that should be close enough to allow interment. The corpse was skeletonized to such a degree he doubted they'd identify a cause of death, but he suspected Nonna knew already.

And it would stay with her, if she had her way. Why was she being so stubborn? He hadn't called again. He couldn't risk upsetting her, not when any strain could bring on another stroke. But, obedience not being his long suit, he had researched the men in the dossiers through the Internet and the local history section of the library—and had come up with next to nothing. Some of them were connected to San Francisco mobsters, but no mention of Arthur Jackson's involvement. Whatever they'd been up to in Sonoma must have stayed quiet, with the murder of Vittorio Shepard not even recorded in the cold-cases file.

He couldn't change that. Nonna only wanted Quillan buried, so his mission was drawing to a close. He felt hollowed out, as though his bones had been rinsed and hung to dry. But he was no longer consumed with guilt. Regret, yes, and hurt. But even though he'd started with dishonesty and selfish pride, he'd done his best to give Rese what she needed to be free of him.

He knew from the guys that she was making it. He wished he was there to see her all steamy-faced in the kitchen. But soon he'd pick up Baxter and hit the road. He'd head home for a while, make sure Nonna was satisfied, then see where the next road led.

If he thought too hard, the tears would come, but he tried not to go there. He'd lost his soul's song for a while, but he guessed he would sing again . . . sometime. She'd be having a birthday soon, and he wondered if she'd ever get real rubies for her ears. Or had she taken the earrings out altogether?

CHAPTER FORTY-TWO

Maybe it hadn't been a good idea to schedule a visit with Mom when her thoughts were already churning. Once Lance had buried his ancestor, would they all pull up stakes and go? It didn't matter. That was inevitable. Their little group couldn't last forever. She'd heard Rico on the phone with his agent, and maybe now he'd get Lance back in the band.

She brushed her fingers over her hair and walked out of her suite. Star was standing in the front hall, dressed in a simple wraparound skirt and tank. Rese approached, unsure how to read her expression. "Are you okay?"

Star nodded, but it was still there, that tight unease. Was she saying good-bye? Her tongue flicked over the glimmery pink lipstick she wore. "I thought you might . . . want me to come."

Come? Rese searched her face.

"To see Elaine."

It took everything she had not to show her shock. Star wanted to see Mom?

"You know." Her lips trembled. "Be there for you."

A wash of warmth coursed over. Star wanted to support her? She would visit a woman she despised so her friend wouldn't be alone? Rese had no idea how to answer. She'd be vulnerable. The last visit had so undone her she'd shown Lance everything.

But this was so unexpected, so un-Star. She said, "Sure. If you want to."

Star smiled. It was amazing, really, how radiant her smile was. "Good. I think." She laughed.

"Do you have any idea what you're doing?" Rese hooked her arm in Star's.

"Probably not."

They walked arm in arm to the truck, but Rese's eyes still went to the place the bike should be. He would come over while she was gone. She wouldn't see him. Pain coursed her veins. What was wrong with her? Why didn't she stay there watching for him? They didn't have to talk. She could just see him.

But she pulled open the door and unlocked the other side for Star. Mom was waiting, and her friend was coming. That was pretty good stuff.

Star was afraid she might throw up. Her stomach was a tight ball as she rode beside Rese. This was the first sacrificial act she could recall. She was terrified to see Elaine.

Rico had asked her last night to think about going to New York with him. She could crash with one of Lance's sisters in the Michelli hotel, and as soon as they found a guitar player that he and Chaz could tolerate, they'd make a go of it. He hadn't even kissed her yet.

It was a no-brainer. But she wanted to give Rese something before she went. Not an object she could buy with her mother's money, but something Rese would remember. This was all she could think of. They didn't talk much on the long drive in. She was afraid she'd say, "Stop! Let me out!"

Instead she focused on all the things Rese had done for her over the years, the times she had brought her back from the abyss. This hardly compared. They were going to the crazy house to visit, not stay.

The hospital was not a dungeon, and they weren't seeing the cells, only the visiting room. Star hesitated as Rese approached the woman at the table. Her hair was spun silk, her skin soft and loose, but she remembered those eyes. Rese's same umber, with that luxurious excess of tint. She'd been fascinated and repelled by Elaine's eyes, never knowing as a child which nature lay behind—kind or cruel—as opposed to her own mother whose neglect was the one constant in all her life's variables.

"Mom, you remember Star." Rese motioned her over.

Elaine raised her eyes, and Star trembled. She wasn't sure she wanted Elaine to remember her, but as she looked into the woman's face, she felt a melting inside and said, "Hi."

Elaine narrowed her eyes. "Of course, I remember the fairy child. You were always so light, so many fairies around your head."

Star couldn't breathe. She sat down across from her. "You saw fairies?"

"Such beautiful colors." Elaine started to rock. "Beautiful, beautiful colors." She turned to the wall. "Now it's all gray; gray, gray, gray, gray, gray." Her voice rasped. She turned to Rese. "What have you done with your father?"

Star sat mesmerized as Rese gently explained that her dad was dead. She didn't suppose that was new information, but whether Elaine grasped it, she didn't know. The thing she couldn't comprehend was the peace and wonder that had consumed her with Elaine's words. She wanted to touch her, to stroke her hand, her beautiful hair.

After a while Elaine grew agitated, and a woman came to calm her down. "That might be all she can handle today. It's still new." The woman spoke softly, but there was authority behind the words.

Star got up with Rese, having no clue what had set Elaine off. She hadn't heard much of anything after those first statements. They walked to the truck, and then she was inside. Rese was speaking, and Star turned. "What?"

"Are you all right?"

Star nodded, but for a long time she couldn't talk. They were over the bridge and into the farmland before she said, "When it was worst of all . . . when they had me in the bedroom, I'd look up and see only the beautiful colors." She stared out the window, past a low fence that dipped and rose over dun-colored grasses. "I pretended they were fairies."

———————

Lance was as nervous as a teenager at his first prom when he went to the inn. He parked the bike and Baxter greeted him, delirious. Lance loved up the dog a long time before he could stand and face his friends who'd come out at the sound of the Harley. "Hey." He couldn't help looking over at the house. Would she come out?

"She's not here, mon." Chaz put an end to his wondering.

Rico said, "She and Star went to see her mom."

A good safe distance and a long time away. He'd have liked to apologize, but that was obviously not in her plans. He hoped she would be all right, seeing Elaine. And then it registered that she'd . . . taken Star? He was not sure what to make of that.

Star had been anything but supportive, and Rese had refused his offers. But before he could ponder it further, the police arrived, and his focus shifted to Quillan's remains. He oversaw the work in the tunnel, the careful wrapping and removing of the bones from the place they had lain since Nonna left him there.

A sigh of relief escaped his throat. As soon as they'd made an ID, the remains would be buried in the churchyard with the DiGratias and the Shepards. He'd been wrong about the plot—there was a space reserved for Quillan beside his wife, Carina. Ground had shifted and stones had leaned, but his place was there nonetheless.

When the hearse and the police had gone, Lance turned to the others. "How long are you staying?"

Chaz spread his hands. "I need to work, to send money home."

Rico said, "Saul Samuels is champin', Lance. We need your guitar, your songs." He didn't say his voice.

There were no shortage of guitarists in New York. He shook his head. "As soon as this is done with Nonno Quillan, I'll go back for a while. But get yourselves another guitar."

Rico said, "I asked Star to come."

Lance suspected as much. He had worried about her coming off the abusive relationship directly into another, but she and Rico were finding a harmony they just might sustain. "That leaves Rese alone."

"Can't help that."

He didn't suppose they could. They had already stayed longer than he'd expected. "Can you give her a chance to find someone?"

"She won't do it. She cancelled the ad, told the people who called that the job was filled."

Lance frowned. "She wants to run it alone?"

Rico shrugged. "She won't say much."

The hurt inside revived. Was she afraid to hire someone else after what he'd done? And he'd thought he was through with guilt. Baxter's tongue filled his half-closed hand. The animal could always sense it. Lance reassured him with a stroke.

Chaz leaned on the side of the carriage house and crossed his arms. "What about the wine and the money?"

"I'm working on that. I asked a friend of Tony's to look up the numbers on the bundle I have. See if it's hot."

"If it is?"

"The feds'll be down here ASAP."

Chaz cocked his head. "And if it isn't?"

"Rese won't worry about her bills for a while. Those dates are silver certificates. It's worth more than cash value by a long sight, especially in its uncirculated condition."

"What about the wine?" Rico had perked up measurably.

"Depends on the quality. It hasn't been disturbed, and it's a perfect temperature down there. For that vintage, each bottle could auction for two hundred to two thousand dollars."

Rico whistled. "That'd pay some road costs."

Lance half smiled. "I guess it would." He hadn't told them about the deed. No one knew but Rese. Not even Nonna. He might have to tell her when he got back to New York, but maybe not.

———

Rese was not surprised they were leaving. She'd expected it. But Star's gesture had meant so much, going with her to see Mom. It helped, sharing it with someone who cared. She hadn't expected Star to understand, but she had. And Rese was able to look at her mother's situation without the debilitating fear. Yeah, her mom had schizophrenia. It wasn't good, but they would face it. She could trust the Lord for that.

She stood now at a distance, watching them bury the skeleton from the cellar. None of the small group knew she was there. She wasn't sure why she was, except that she thought Lance might get on his bike at the graveyard and drive straight out of town.

So she'd decided to torture herself with one last look. She was too far away to see any details, just the shape of him in his loose-fitting shirt and jeans, his stance, respectful but at the same time with that hint of trouble she'd identified early and should have heeded. What was he thinking as they laid his relative to rest? Or being Lance, what did he feel? The breeze blew his hair and Rico's. Star's was pinned up in a rosy nest of curls and Chaz stood like a compassionate angel watching over it all.

As soon as they bowed their heads for the final prayer, she started for her truck. She was home and in the shed before the van pulled up, but she went to the window and looked. No motorcycle; no Lance. Just the rest of them loading up the sound equipment, instruments, and bags. The stabbing disappointment surprised her. She hadn't thought he would come. He'd accomplished what he'd intended. Or she hoped so. But seeing him at the graveyard had hurt more than she expected.

Star came into the shed, her face alight. Rese couldn't help imagining the fairies circling. "The essential question," Star said, "is do the frogs stay or go?"

Rese smiled. "They're yours. You decide."

Star glided over and squeezed her into a hug. "Come with us."

"And do what?"

"Never ask that if you want to reach the rainbow."

Well, rainbows were a little out of her reach, but she could live with that. Rese set Star back. "This is my place. But you know you're always welcome."

"What if I have to bring Rico?"

"Rico too. He can make pancakes."

Star giggled. "I thought you were going to haul off and deck that wattled woman."

Rese shook her head. "A definite possibility." She still did not handle people with ease. Maybe that would come in time, or not. Whatever the case, it was up to her now.

She was surprised how much it hurt to see them go. She waved when the van pulled out of the yard, at the same time wanting to holler, "Don't leave." But this was her place, her responsibility. And she couldn't do it by herself. She'd have to hire somebody.

The thought did not sit well. She had wrestled it to death, but with reservations full she would never manage it alone. It was hard enough now. Whoever she hired would have to come and go. She would not offer room and board. That was too much like family, and there were only so many times she could lose everyone.

She wandered back to the carriage house and stood without going inside. It had turned out really nice, and once the furniture was finished she'd get a hefty room charge for it. After enough people had slept there, it might stop being Lance's place. Beside her, Baxter perked his ears and raised his head. He made a soft whine, and a moment later she heard the motorcycle.

Of course. He'd be coming for his dog.

———

Lance pulled up beside the shed, surprised to see Rese standing in the yard with Baxter. She must have heard him coming. Why hadn't she run? Or maybe she meant to fight him for the dog. She looked fierce enough.

He climbed off the bike and removed his backpack. He could have just whistled for Baxter, but he might get the chance this time to say . . . something. Rese stood as though she'd been planted in the garden, a beautiful statue, one you'd notice for its compelling form. No whimsical nymph trickling water from a lily bloom.

He stopped a few feet from her, and for a moment no words would come. Then he said, "Thank you for letting me bury Nonno."

She nodded once.

"Rese . . . I wasn't honest with you, and I'm sorry." So sorry it chewed him up just saying it to her. "I worked every angle I could to get what I wanted."

Her jaw pulled tight, and he knew what he'd feel in her neck.

"I know you can't believe me, but I never lied about my feelings for you. I meant every word." Tears stung his eyes, but he refused to play on her sympathies. "I still do, and I just want you to know . . . if you need anything. If it gets too much . . ."

"What? You'll drop by and save me?"

Straight in through the ribs. He swallowed against tears that would not go away. There wasn't much more to say. As much as he'd like it to take forever, any minute now she'd be calling the police. He reached inside his jacket, took out what he'd brought. He held a notepaper out. "This is the name and number of someone who can evaluate that wine. I'd get a second appraisal as well, just to make sure."

She slowly raised her hand and took the note.

"Under the rack with empty bottles, you'll find a cache of silver certificate bills. I'm guessing about two hundred thousand face value." He handed her another note. "This is what each is worth to collectors."

She glanced down and her eyes widened.

"They're from some business my great-grandfather was mixed up in, but they're legal currency, free and clear."

She looked into his face, pain evident in her eyes. He hadn't meant for this to hurt her, but to free her. She probably thought it some ploy, but the last part should convince her.

"And there's this." He held out the deed.

Her fingers shook as she took the envelope and glanced inside. "Your grandmother's deed?"

"She just wanted Nonno buried." At least that was all she'd admit, and he was too weary to pursue it. He wanted so much to take Rese in his arms. He almost reached, but he forced his hands to stay. "I wish you the best of everything. You're going to do just great." And now he couldn't fight it anymore. He turned and started for the bike.

"Lance."

He stopped. She deserved to have her say. He should turn around and face it, but whether it was scorn or gratitude, if he looked at her once more . . .

"I need a maid."

That did not register. He knew she needed help, but why was she telling him? "No cook?"

"I've got five breakfasts down pretty well."

"No dinners?"

"I scrapped the dinner program."

With his back still to her, he jumped when she touched his arm.

"I need a maid, but I'd settle for a partner."

He jerked his head around and stared into her face. She was asking him to stay?

"A *business* partner."

A critical clarification, lest he think it more than a job. "I'm not sure I can do that, Rese." He swallowed. "I don't meet your professional standards." They'd established that right from the start.

"Well, if I can learn to cook . . ."

He shook his head, gripping his jacket edges. "No. I will touch you, and then you'll fire me, and we'll be right back—"

"I can't fire you. You're my partner." Her gaze connected with his as she held up the notes and deed. "With your own assets."

His assets? He stretched his head back. Didn't she see what he was trying to do? He had to be emptied out so she could stand on her own without him.

"And abilities. Star thinks I'll punch out the customers, and I'm not really sure I want to spend day and night in the kitchen."

"Rese . . ." But he knew she needed help. Was it better to leave her with whatever she could find? There she was, trying to look confident and controlled, the lobes of her ears glittering with red stones, and the mouth that could be hard as steel or so, so soft.

She shrugged. "We just need . . . new rules." She crossed her arms and stood there as though saying it would make it possible. But they'd tried that. For one miserable night.

He caught her by the elbows. "Same rules." If she wasn't able to take him on those terms, he understood. He had hurt her, and just having the chance to apologize was more than he'd expected. "I can't pretend I don't love you, and I'm wired to show it." So wired it took everything in him to hold back. "If I stay, you have to know I want a future with you." He watched the disbelief and concern come into her face. So that hadn't been her intention. "I don't expect anything."

And there was her cynical stare.

"I don't expect it, but that doesn't mean I don't want it." Hurt filled her eyes. His own tears stung. "Just a chance. That's all I ask."

Way too long. She would have answered if she could. He dropped his chin. "Yeah, well . . ."

"What were those rules again?"

He cocked his gaze up, unsure what he'd see. "Neck rubs?"

She wasn't showing anything. "I need them."

He swallowed the tears. "Hugs."

"Couldn't hurt."

Oh, but it could. Just the thought of drawing her close was turning his insides out. But he did it anyway. "You remember the rest."

"I'm not sure I do." She raised her chin.

He leaned in, but a woman approached them from the drive and cleared her throat.

Rese pulled back. "Oh . . . Michelle." It was the brown-haired woman from Evvy's funeral.

"Sorry to interrupt." She directed that to him.

"No problem." But the anticipation of that kiss must be almost visible.

"We were packing up Evvy's things and found this." She held up a book with a notepaper stuck to the front. "I'm guessing you're Lance?"

He stared at the book, at his name on the sticky note and *Antonia's diary* written beneath. As the dried leather slid into his palms a peace settled over him. Nonna had refused to tell him more. He wouldn't read her diary without permission, but if he brought it to her, maybe . . .

He closed his eyes and told the woman, "Thank you." And he didn't mean just her. *Grazie Signore.*

Michelle turned with a raising of her brows and walked away. Lance tucked the diary under his arm and drew Rese close with the other. "Where were we?"

She smiled. "You were going to cook a marvelous dinner."

He laughed, letting the anticipation settle deeper. A little restraint might not be a bad thing. "Want to help?"

"Of course."

His heart surged. He was no hero, but it seemed he'd get another chance. If God was for him, and Rese beside him, he just might get it right.

Watch for the sequel to *Secrets*
coming in Summer 2005

Unforgotten returns with Lance and Rese to the Belmont neighborhood of the Bronx where Nonna Antonia hopes to find peace. Instead she learns that what she thought she knew was only a shadow of the truth. Not only has the past not disappeared, but it has affected their future in a real and painful way. Is forgiveness possible, and can it heal the wounds that time has not forgotten?

MORE DRAMA, ROMANCE, *and* SUSPENSE
WITH KRISTEN HEITZMANN

Halos

Trying to start her life anew, Alessi Moore leaves Florida without much idea of where she is headed. Hoping for miracles and happy endings, she thinks the town of Charity, Vermont, will be the perfect place. Soon her car, holding all she owns, is stolen, and she finds that a perfect world is just a dream.

A Rush of Wings

Running from a bleak past and a terrifying present, Noelle St. Claire searches for sanctuary away from those who've betrayed her. On a horse ranch in the shadows of the Rocky Mountains, she begins to discover a new life—until her worst fears are realized and her safe haven is torn apart.